The Tree of Life (2015) "Davis is a very engaging storyteller and Charlotte is a wonderful creation. Fans of magical realism a la Alice Hoffman will feel at home with this story."

4 STAR KIRKUS REVIEW

Falling (2017) "Another carefully crafted, deftly written, reader compelling, unfailingly entertaining novel by a master of narrative storytelling."

MIDWEST BOOK REVIEW

Little by Little (2019) "Davis presents a story that's well written, well researched, and features an intriguing central conflict. An often engaging novel with a touch of magic."

KIRKUS

There's Something I Forgot to Tell You

Dawn Davis

◆ FriesenPress

One Printers Way
Altona, MB R0G 0B0
Canada

www.friesenpress.com

Copyright © 2023 by Dawn Davis
First Edition — 2023

ISBN
978-1-03-919213-3 (Hardcover)
978-1-03-919212-6 (Paperback)
978-1-03-919214-0 (eBook)

1. FICTION, FANTASY

Distributed to the trade by The Ingram Book Company

Table of Contents

To Liz with love
Until we meet again

From the Hilroy of Charlotte
Lisa Hansen

DAY: SATURDAY, AUGUST 28, 1999
TIME: 11:00 AM or thereabouts
PLACE: My house, back porch, wicker chair right beside open kitchen window.
NOTE: 5 new mosquito bites, one on each elbow and three on neck.

Leaving Toronto on Monday night. Tickets have been PURCHASED on a Boeing 747, an airplane that is vastly superior to smaller models which do not cross oceans, and Gwendolyn, Henry, and me will touch down, 7 hours later, in the bustling and altogether magical city of London, England, except it won't be 7 hours later, it will be 12 hours later (which doesn't make any sense).

BUT I will once again see Sarah who visits my dreams with wide smiling red lips and clouds of cigarette smoke mingled with Shalimar perfume.

There are a few small problems which must be solved posthaste.

PROBLEM ONE: Henry has not yet been granted permission by his parents to soar across the ocean in the company of a stranger, even though a ticket now resides on Gwendolyn's dining room table under the name of Henry Jacobs.

PROBLEM TWO: Gwendolyn MacFarlane, the purchaser of the Boeing 747 tickets and our supposed chaperone, is expressing doubts as to the wisdom of visiting relatives she never knew she had. And, facing facts, Gwendolyn hates me, even though for five seconds, she professed to love me for returning to her the magical Tree of Life brooch and giving her

1

the chance to remake the sad, selfish mess she has made of her life during her 71-year forced occupation of time on earth. Also returned, by me, is Celeste (a name Gwendolyn has trouble remembering), the daughter of Charlie's daughter or some such but a relative all the same.

I am a mere 11 years of age and so is Henry, but we both came to know (and despise) the 11-year-old Gwendolyn when we were transported back in time to Toronto 1939 and a world on the brink of war. This transposition, courtesy of the Tower Room, had but one purpose. And that was to find the missing Tree of Life brooch, a family heirloom with a checkered and dangerous past, and return it to Gwendolyn. This was my job, and one might think after locating it, due to my supreme detective skills, I would have given it to the brat Gwendolyn, but I DID NOT. I made certain it went to Charlie, her elder brother, because I felt it was the right thing to do. (For historians who will later be chronicling the adventures of my life for public consumption, I refer to Hilroys #33 to #36, which describe in colourful detail the adventures Henry and I had in a much different Toronto.)

Sadly, and I mean REALLY sadly, Charlie died, way back in 1940, heroically serving the free world as an RAF pilot and the Tree of Life brooch vanished along with him.

Supposedly.

Hilroy, keeper of my greatest secrets and greatest accomplishments, you know that Henry and I found – after 60 years of Gwendolyn's life but only 4 months of our own – what was lost so that the story may continue and complete itself and free me of the thankless job of forcing Gwendolyn to be a nicer person.

As if.

TIME is the central character here. And how to explain it so it will make sense? I can never see time, grab hold of it, stop it, stretch it, or flow inside it, and yet time does all these things to me completely effortlessly and with a large grin on its face.

Crazy!

I have travelled through decades in the flash of a second and merely kept living whether time was moving frontways, backways, sideways or at a most uncomfortable angle.

I had no choice but to carry on no matter where I found myself, although as everyone who knows me knows full well, I am not a person who does what other people tell me to do. Even when my head hurts like it's been crushed by a hammer.

Gwendolyn has said, more times than I can count, "I am alone in the world, Charlotte. No family at all." (Or friends) "I lost my only brother, Charlie, whom I adored" (more accurately despised) "when I was a mere child, and I have wandered the world a solitary soul" (if you don't count two failed marriages) "only to end up back in the city of my origin, content to live out my days simply and quietly." (In a skyscraper luxury penthouse, with chauffeur, charge cards, and wads of cash)

The significance is this: Gwendolyn is not quite as alone as she would like to think.

And finally, there is PROBLEM THREE: the photograph that appeared mysteriously in the Tower Room after Henry and me located Gwendolyn's missing broach. This snapshot (taken by the universe – there is no other way to explain it) refuses to stabilize even when I stand in front of it and say Get on with it, already. One day I'll see what I think might be Old Mister Weeping Willow Tree and a bunch of children (maybe) and Charlie, centred and grand, taking on a bunch of wavery objects that look like pigs and the next day lots of people (what else could they be) with arms and legs all akimbo (new word) in what might be Dilys's living room on the Island. These photographs are altogether weird and slantwise, upside down and distorted and mostly a huge muddle with the one exception of CHARLIE who is completely in focus and so real I know I can reach out and touch him EXCEPT I get this dizzy feeling when I peer too closely, almost like I am seasick and about to heave.

Leo will only say my work is not done. That's why the photograph is a mess. Give me a break! I found the brooch, I found Gwendolyn's relatives, come on already. I'm not superhuman even though I pretend I am.

What went wrong, Hilroy? Doesn't Gwendolyn now have everything she wants or will she settle for nothing less than the entire world?

DAY: same day, same place, more mosquito bites, etc. etc.
TIME: 12:15 PM

Gwendolyn is, at this very moment, having a steadying chat with Leo in my kitchen while I sit in chair scribbling furiously. We are all on our way to Henry's house to try and convince Henry's parents to allow him to fly across the ocean. His parents are rarely in town and rarely see Henry since they travel the globe continuously – accumulating brass artifacts and whatnot for their coffin manufacturing business.

Henry to me: "I think my parents like the idea of having a child in the abstract."

Whatever that means.

I lost my point.

Oh yes: Gwendolyn.

Leo is reminding her how to behave when she meets Henry's parents – Ha! That is a lecture he usually heaps on me. Gwendolyn MUST behave normally otherwise Henry won't be allowed to go which means I can't go because I am not leaving him behind.

Sneaking to the door I hear her say: "I wasn't born in a barn, Leo. I do understand the basics of social niceties."

"You better. I'll be watching."

The hair rises on the back of my neck. Leo's voice sounds… MENACING!

What hold does he have over Gwendolyn, and WHY don't I know what it is?

Chapter One

"Thank you for coming, Mrs. MacFarlane," Doris Jacobs said. She held the door open with one hand and, with the other, anchored a stray wisp of hair beneath the bun anchored to the top of her head.

Gwendolyn blinked. She had rarely seen such an unattractive hairdo, although in her daily perusal of fashion magazines she had seen some that came close. The strain of all this hair being pulled and forced into an unnatural position gave Doris a bug-eyed appearance, and right before she caught herself staring and dropped her gaze, Gwendolyn saw the resemblance to Henry, whose eyes also looked like they were ready to pop out of their sockets.

"Or is it MacFarlane-Fenton?" Doris asked, pumping Gwendolyn's hand (which had to be picked up from her side and placed back once the formalities were over). "There appears to be some confusion, as Henry calls you one thing and Charlotte, another."

She laughed, but it was out of embarrassment more than humour, Gwendolyn quickly noted. After running her eyes from Doris's shoes to the tip of her head, Gwendolyn summed her up thusly: Overachiever, social climber, possible eating disorder. The woman was like a three-dimensional geometric construction of overlaying triangles, her body ending in far too many sharp points. Gwendolyn managed to avoid touching any of these points by sweeping forward regally and pausing when she was six feet away from Doris.

"Gwendolyn will be fine," she said. "I wonder where you heard all these disclaimers."

"From Charlotte, of course. She has told us all about you."

"Dear Charlotte," Gwendolyn said with a frosty smile. The child was far too involved in Gwendolyn's life, and this was strictly because Charlotte had no life of her own. "Thank you for having me," she added, remembering she was here to charm and not annihilate.

Gwendolyn had far more experience with the later, but she could put on a different face when she chose to do so. She added an insincere smile and beckoned to Dragos, who was lingering on the threshold, arranging the cuffs on his military jacket.

"And this would be?" Doris asked, as Dragos bowed low and kissed her hand.

"My driver. He will be taking us to the airport, so I assumed you would like to meet him."

One eyebrow rose slightly as if daring Doris to say Henry was not allowed to fly across the ocean. In truth, one which Gwendolyn chose not to reveal, Dragos was only her occasional chauffeur and not her "driver" because he was a man who refused to be pinned down to one person. Principally he was Leo's best friend and was being paid to lend the meeting an air of authority and make certain that everyone understood Gwendolyn was a woman of means and status.

Although no one would dare say this to Gwendolyn's face, she could be summed up, too, and it gave her some pleasure to know the words would be: Privileged, disdainful, and cold as ice.

Gwendolyn continued her onward sweep into the living room and noted that Henry was standing frozen in front of the fireplace. As if drawn by an unknown hand, she walked closer to examine a painting above the mantle, a pictorial antithesis to Henry's lifeless demeanour. Here was a young woman, fey and otherworldly, with flaming red hair and wearing a multi-coloured robe. She held a painted bowl in her hands and was reaching forward, as if making an offering. The painting reminded her of *Lady Lilith* by Dante Gabriel Rossetti, and yet it was more sardonic. The woman appeared to be smiling inwardly as if remembering a joke.

"This can't possibly be Rossetti," she said, turning to address Doris.

"It's a Richard Dadd," Doris said. "And extremely valuable. We purchased it when we were in London many years ago. Dadd was one of the most famous painters of pixies and sprites. Do you like it?"

Gwendolyn said nothing and wondered why Henry's father did not join in this litany of praise. If anything, he looked slightly caught out, his hands clasped, thumbs twirling. She neither liked nor disliked the canvas, but there was an artistry she could not deny.

"We have many great works of art from our travels. Mostly sculptures as you can see," Doris said, indicating that Gwendolyn could peruse the *objets d'art* at her leisure.

The room abounded in statues: a hodgepodge of African, Greek, Roman, and a miniature collection of playdough figurines that Henry must have manufactured at school and then put in the freezer to set, as they all had an icy chill about them and were uniformly grey in colour. And yet, they were bizarrely beautiful and if one squinted, they resembled a heavily burdened family of ethnic origin desperate to find a way out of the Jacob's residence and return to the stark and bleak lands where they belonged.

"You are admiring our Inuit family?" Henry's father asked.

That word *Inuit* rang a distant bell and reminded Gwendolyn of the Arctic cruise she once (foolishly) thought she might like to take, and then rejected when the list of necessary clothing arrived along with the size of her accommodation on the whaling ship. The room had been no larger than a closet!

She saw Charlotte staring at her and immediately frowned. Gwendolyn knew that Charlotte had caught her out. Charlotte always caught her out, which was one of the many reasons Gwendolyn despaired of having made the promise to take Henry and Charlotte to London. And how did Charlotte arrive at the Jacobs residence before Gwendolyn? She had been playing hopscotch on the street (dangerous) while Gwendolyn gave instructions to Dragos. It was no accident that Charlotte beat Gwendolyn. Charlotte was always manufacturing games, most of which Gwendolyn had no awareness of.

Charlotte's lips moved quickly, but Gwendolyn could see they opened and then moved horizontally, the exact shape to the words she heard in her sleep: "I won."

"And you would be Mr. Jacobs?" Gwendolyn said, turning to face the owner of the husky voice beside her. And in doing so, banished Charlotte to the dustbin. Two could play, she reminded herself, and then caught Leo standing at the bay window regarding her sternly. "I've heard so much about you and your wife from Henry."

"You have?" Henry's father stared at her blankly. "Henry is a boy of few words. The fewer the better," he chuckled, manfully punching his son on the shoulder.

Henry blinked by way of response. "Hello Gwendolyn. This is my father, Aaron."

"And you look just like him, dear," Gwendolyn said, feeling Leo's eyes burn a hole in her back.

Henry *might* look like his father if someone slapped 150 pounds onto his frame, added an abundance of curly brown hair to scalp and face, and thawed him out in an oven set to 175 degrees so he could slouch and smile and appear to enjoy his life rather than simply endure it. There was an ease to Aaron's bearing and manner that Gwendolyn approved of. He wasn't scared of her (unlike his wife), and there was a mischievous expression in his eyes that informed her he was onto this charade. He was not the one she would have to convince of her suitability as chaperone to their only child.

"Take a seat, why don't you?" Aaron said. "You can join the argument."

"Argument?" Gwendolyn asked.

"Doris doesn't want Henry to miss the first day of school. In theory, I get it, but let's be honest: we are dealing with a kid who could miss the entire year and still come out ahead of all his classmates. Henry's got smarts, don't you?"

"Whatever you say." Henry's agreement came with a total lack of inflection.

"A trip to London, England, is very educational," said Charlotte, "and we already have Mr. Hemmingsworth's permission to go."

She sat cross-legged in front of the fireplace, the outline of her Hilroy notebook showing through her dirty cotton T-shirt. The child scribbled continuously, meaningless observations on life in general and was far too precocious to be liked and admired.

"And who is Mr. Hemmingsworth?" Gwendolyn asked.

"The headmaster of The Learning Academy," Doris answered quietly, with a certain grit in her tone (and this *grit* suggested the school was costing a lot of money, and she didn't want to waste it). "It is an exclusive private school to which Henry has gained admission."

"I gained admission, too," Charlotte added. "I told them during my interview that any school that called itself by the name of what they were supposedly offering was a mistake, and they agreed to take it under consideration. Henry and me think that they should shorten the name to "the Academy" because it makes it more mysterious and also releases them from any lawsuits should learning not occur – and believe me, there isn't much learning that occurs in public school, so why is private school any different?" She paused to consider all the eyes that were upon her. "In truth the only difference between private school and public school is that private school has 132 days of bona fide learning opportunities whereas public school has 187. Plus, there is the money factor, but that doesn't matter to me."

"Charlotte got a scholarship," Henry informed the avid audience.

"Way to go," Aaron shouted, giving Charlotte a high five.

To give Charlotte credit, she did not gloat over her achievement. But on the other hand, she treated it as if it were her due, which rankled Gwendolyn. Charlotte was not that special.

"I don't remember Henry being given the opportunity to apply for a scholarship," Doris said, smiling anemically in Charlotte's direction. "Henry's test scores were perfect."

"We can afford it," Henry replied, staring straight ahead. "Besides, Charlotte is more of an asset than I am."

"Why, Henry," Doris said, her pale lips closing in a frown over her pale teeth. "How can you say such a thing?"

"Because it's true," he said, reverting to his usual three-word answer.

"School starts on the seventh," Leo said gently. "And the children will return to Toronto on the eighth. They won't be missing any school except for the Monday get-acquainted day. But I have been told the get-acquainted activities can take up to a week. All is well on that front."

"I'm still against it," Doris said staunchly. "I'm very sorry, Gwendolyn, but we don't know you, and we can't allow Henry to go so far away in the company of a stranger."

"And that is exactly why we are having this meeting." Aaron picked at his beard the way a pileated woodpecker picked at the bark of trees for insects. "To get to know one another. Please take a seat, dear lady," he added, indicating a plush chair by the window. "What can I get you to drink? Tea? Coffee? A glass of wine? Or perhaps champagne?"

Gwendolyn pretended not to hear him and inspected the chair closely. She was dressed primarily in black and was wearing enough pearls to disrupt her posture. But after years of masquerading in this exact costume, Gwendolyn could wear a grand piano around her neck and still stand upright, her eyes looking down on everyone around her.

"What a marvellous piece of furniture," she said, deciding it was time to warm Doris up with a few lies masquerading as flattery. "The stunning black and gold inlays. The clean, graceful design. The purity of the natural grain of wood." She ran a finger along the chipped surround that meandered across the back of the chair. "It's a Biedermeier, is it not?"

"Exactly what I thought when I purchased it from a neighbour last year," Doris answered excitedly.

"It a piece of junk," Henry's father muttered just loud enough for Gwendolyn to hear.

"I had it appraised by Sotheby's, of course."

"And what did they say?" Gwendolyn asked, her eyes all innocent and bright.

"Sadly, it is not. But it could be."

"As could I," Henry's father said, by way of aside.

"Tut, tut," Gwendolyn replied. "It's the impression that is important. If it looks like a Biedermeier, then it is a Biedermeier."

Gwendolyn ignored the pretender and sat down in a straight back chair. She fingered her pearls, adjusted the cuffs on her white silk blouse so that they were evenly aligned with the braided cuffs on her black jacket, and lifted a finger in Dragos's general direction. He immediately crossed the room, removed a large white handkerchief from a pocket hiding beneath an army of buttons and fictious medals manufactured by one of his many sons-in-law, and placed it on Gwendolyn's lap.

"I can understand your doubts at the thought of allowing dear Henry to accompany me to London."

Henry's mother began backpedalling furiously, saying that she knew what an exceptional treat this was and how generous Gwendolyn was to suggest it, but was silenced when Gwendolyn raised her hand.

"As would I. As would any mother, I dare say." Gwendolyn was not now, nor had she ever been, a mother, but she appeared to understand exactly how that species would behave. "After all, who am I? A stranger who wishes to whisk your son to London for a week. If I were you, Doris, I would be appalled and would refuse outright." Her lie was stated with the utmost sincerity.

"I'm so glad you see our point of view, and I apologize for the inconvenience of this visit."

Gwendolyn turned to Henry's father. "Aaron, dear, some water please. My throat is dry. And now, if you don't mind, I would like to tell you a story about your wonderful son."

Leo cleared his throat furiously, but Gwendolyn ignored him. He might think he had a hold over her, but no one was allowed to control the flights of her imagination. It was now time to perform.

"The first time I met Henry," Gwendolyn reported, her eyes misty with recollection, "I was sitting in a park minding my own business when I was suddenly accosted by this wild-looking mongrel who thought my leg was a stick." She purposely kept the story vague so as not to be pinned down with bothersome details like what park, what day, what time and what year and the fact that she would never be caught dead sitting on a bench in a park. "Do you remember, dear?" she asked, fixing Henry with a piercing stare.

"He remembers," Charlotte said when an uneasy silence filled the room. "Action sort of clouds Henry's memory bank."

Charlotte lied as effortlessly as Gwendolyn. It was the only thing they had in common.

"He was so brave," Gwendolyn rhapsodized. "He chased the dog across the park, banishing him into the nether regions, and then returned to see if I was injured."

"Why, Henry," Doris said proudly, her bug eyes widening. "You never said a word."

Everyone in the room was suitably impressed by Henry's courage, including Henry himself. His chest puffed as he mentally chased the mythical beast across the park, scurrying back to lay a severed tail at Gwendolyn's feet.

"We got to talking," Gwendolyn continued. "And I was astonished by his formidable intelligence."

That she never talked to anyone unless she was forced to do so was omitted from the tale.

"We became friends, and he visited me at the penthouse once a week. I came to rely on his advice and guidance."

"His what?" Aaron asked incredulously. "I can barely get him to say three words in a row." He instantly became suspicious. "And what advice did you give, Henry?"

Henry remained frozen, never moving a muscle, until Charlotte coughed loudly, and he responded by lifting one puny shoulder.

"He's a mathematical wizard. He has remarkable organizational skills. And he studies the financial news and understands the market."

This bit was completely true, although Gwendolyn had not shared the details with a soul. No one would believe her if she did, and besides, her life and her choices were hers alone and not fodder to be chewed on and spat out by her acquaintances.

In truth what had happened was this: When Henry had been delivering a parcel for Gwendolyn (as a favour to Dragos) he had slipped on a Persian rug in her vestibule and righted himself by grabbing the corner of her side table, which held her mail. Once again perpendicular, he had turned to face Gwendolyn.

"That mining stock prospectus you ordered is not a good move. If I were you..."

Instead of dismissing him immediately, she had invited him in, poured him a glass of orange juice, and sat down and listened. She had paid handsomely for his advice (twenty-five dollars) which Henry had refused to accept (a mark of good breeding). Gwendolyn had then hired him to set up a template for her accounts and general bookkeeping, and it was vastly superior to the one given her by her accountant.

Clearly, Henry was gifted, but he had another special trait – complete disinterest.

"The stock market is a fool's game," he had told her, repeating verbatim words he had heard his father utter. "But it can be an interesting experiment if you are patient and cautious and not greedy and foolhardy."

He'd mentioned the mining stock, he went on to explain, not because he cared one way or another if she took his advice, but because he had extrapolated from a mishmash of data in an article from the *Financial Times* that most mining stocks were risky. The newspaper had been discarded on the seat beside Henry while he waited to see the eye doctor in the clinic on Bay Street.

"I was bored," he'd told Gwendolyn. "I have no current interest in mining, but once I read something it sticks in my brain whether I want it to or not. I set up an experiment with various predictors and in two weeks lost twenty percent of my fictious investment. That was pretty boring, too."

"Do you dabble yourself?" Gwendolyn had asked. "For real? Or is everything you do an experiment?"

"Life is an experiment," he had reported. "I read that, too. But it's probably true. Most risk-avoidant people are missing out." And then he had fallen silent while he shifted through a few channels in his brain. "I have a small account with my father. My holdings have increased by twenty-six percent in four months, but I don't take it seriously."

The perfect response from a boy she never would have looked at twice if he passed her on the street.

Gwendolyn had no idea what Henry saw in Charlotte. He was a more suitable companion for Gwendolyn, no matter the large discrepancy in their ages.

"Henry is one of a kind," Charlotte said, muscling her way into the conversation. "Isn't that right, Leo?"

"It most certainly is. You have raised an admirable child," he told the couple.

The admirable child cranked his head in Leo's direction. "Thank you."

Charlotte carried on. "We've had some amazing adventures together. He'll be a real asset at Sarah's theatre school in London, I can tell you that. We've already been invited to attend every day we are in London and what better education could that be? We can write a play, can't we, Henry? Sort of like a *theatre of the real*, in which Henry and me discuss what it is like to find ourselves in London, England. And we can have real-time conversations during which we explain the differences we encounter. With Gwendolyn supervising us, of course." She added as an afterthought.

"Does that appeal to you, Henry?" Doris asked.

Henry shrugged. "It does," he admitted, braving a small smile. "Charlotte always has such interesting ideas. I knew that about her the first time we met."

Gwendolyn watched as Charlotte scribbled furiously in her dreadful Hilroy. She was *still* taking notes, and for what earthly reason? She'd like to get her hands on that Hilroy and rip it to shreds, but it was never, not even for a second, out of the demon child's possession. "We have been friends from the first time we met. Isn't that so, Charlotte?" Gwendolyn asked innocently.

Charlotte cast a glance her way, the look on her face unequivocal if fleeting. *Absolutely not. We have been staunch enemies for decades.* She turned to face Doris and smiled.

"I run errands for Gwendolyn, and in exchange she tells me about her travels."

"Now, Charlotte, I'm certain no one is interested in the details of my life." Gwendolyn simpered unconvincingly.

Henry's mother crossed her legs with the swishing sound of palms being rubbed together. She drew breath to beg Charlotte to continue, but before she could, Henry's father reappeared carrying a glass of water which he handed to Gwendolyn.

"What is this?" Gwendolyn asked, her tone a bit edgy.

"The water you requested."

"That was so long ago I barely remember."

Leo cleared his throat, and Gwendolyn apologized nicely. She then took the glass and moistened her lips.

"A boat train down the Euphrates," Charlotte stated, holding up a finger to enumerate. "That was in her second or third decade."

"A *boat train*, you say." Aaron smirked and glanced over at his wife. "I think perhaps you should see to those canapes," he added, alerting Doris to the growing smell of almost burnt pastry that was floating into the living room from the kitchen.

Leo followed her to the kitchen, adding reassuring words that he was well acquainted with the smell of burning pastry and it had not reached nor come close to that level.

"Yes," said Charlotte, "a boat that is also a train. After the camel caravan in Egypt, she crossed over to New Zealand where she stayed for a while, and then moved on to Australia where she worked for a newspaper."

"It was volunteer work, you understand," Gwendolyn added. "The paper was in a shambles, and I merely put it right before moving on." The paper was a hangover from one of her deceased husbands, who had run it into the ground through mismanagement and neglect.

"What was the name of that paper?" Henry's father asked. "I once knew the editor of the *Melbourne Express*. We met him in Bavaria. Decent chap, mountain hiker, quite a catchy accent."

"I think it is far more productive to discuss our upcoming trip, as I do have a committee meeting to attend," Gwendolyn stated, glancing at her watch.

Gwendolyn wouldn't be caught dead attending a committee meeting on anything as she despised groups, causes, and most of humanity in general. The glass of water had been dispatched to Dragos, who, forgetting his role, drank it down in one healthy gulp.

"Oh, there you are, Leo. I think it's time to tell these lovely people about Sarah, the house where she lives, her incredible accomplishments." Gwendolyn gave a crisp smile as Leo re-entered the living room carrying a platter with an assortment of overheated, factory-made appetizers. Doris followed closely behind carrying plates and party napkins. The smell of melted camembert and seafood assaulting her delicate nostrils, Gwendolyn refused the offerings until Leo nudged her foot, and she sighed.

"I rarely eat between meals," Gwendolyn explained. "It's how I keep myself fit."

"Really?" Doris's triangular eyebrow creased her forehead, and Gwendolyn knew her womanly contours were under scrutiny. Gwendolyn had weighed the same for five decades and was extremely proud of her statuesque figure that could still turn a few eyes as she paraded from her penthouse to Holt Renfrew and back every day.

"But I will indulge, just this once," she said, choosing a piece of asparagus that had been confined in pastry. She took one bite of the asparagus tip and immediately felt overfed.

"I'll finish it," Charlotte volunteered, and Gwendolyn handed her plate and napkin to Dragos who placed it in Charlotte's greedy little hand. Charlotte had developed an unfortunate habit of believing that everything Gwendolyn had belonged to her, but there were times when this came in handy.

"I'm simply too excited to eat," Gwendolyn explained prettily, cleaning the grease off her fingers with the handkerchief Dragos had long ago placed in her lap. "I'm sure Leo mentioned that we will be guests of Sarah Nyman, my late brother's... wife," she stated with uncertainty, not knowing whether Charlie and Sarah ever married. Gwendolyn's dislike of Sarah ran neck and neck with her dislike of Charlotte. "In days gone by, Sarah was a frequent visitor to the house in Rose Park where I lived. Sadly, that house is no more," she said, the first real emotion she had expressed since arriving. "It used to be three houses down from this very one, where that modern monstrosity now takes up space. I remember very well..."

Leo cleared his throat once again and Gwendolyn stopped her jog into the past – which she herself had stated did not need to be discussed. "Sarah was my tutor when I was younger than Henry and Charlotte are now," she said, smiling falsely.

Charlotte's face turned red, and Gwendolyn knew she was steeling herself not to say that Gwendolyn was eleven years old when Sarah was her tutor, not ten or nine or eight or three.

Gwendolyn always shaved years off her life. Currently, by her steadfast whittling, she was a mere child lurking beneath a crumbling façade.

"Sarah has resided in London since the start of the Second World War. She always meant to return to Canada but one thing and another," Gwendolyn said vaguely, lifting a limp wrist and then releasing it to hibernate on the white handkerchief in her lap. "We never lost touch..."

Except for a measly sixty-plus years.

"And she explained that life was somehow more congenial in Britain."

"Well, I don't know about that," Aaron said, stopping the monologue. "I don't think anyone truly appreciates what a great country we live in. There's always this nonsense about how much better it is in Europe or Britain or, God forbid, the United States. Isn't that right, Henry?"

"I don't know," Henry stated. And then he tilted his chin in an upward direction. "I've never really gone anywhere. I like Toronto well enough, but I would like to see more of the world in which I live. Gwendolyn is offering me a special trip, and I think it would be rude to say no."

Gwendolyn silently applauded. It was about time Henry started lobbying on his own behalf.

"Sarah owns and manages one of the most prestigious dramatic academies in London and raised her daughter by herself. Charlie never returned from the war, his plane shot down over a distant battlefield." If Gwendolyn had ever known the truth of Charlie's passing, she had supressed it as another heartache that life, callous and indifferent, had heaped on her person. Ensconced in her own misery as a child, she missed World War II altogether.

Briefly, a whiff of real emotion fragranced the room and everyone bowed their heads in respect for Charlie's long-ago demise.

"All this in the days before it became fashionable for women to forge their own way in the world. Sarah had no choice. And I give her credit for that."

"She must be quite elderly," Doris said. "How old is she?"

"I suppose she is in her nineties. Her daughter attends to her needs." Gwendolyn had forgotten the name of her niece if she had ever known it. And she also neglected to say she would not be staying in the Mews House but had booked herself a suite at the Savoy. This was a secret which she meant to keep under wraps until she was safely in London. Sarah and her entourage could look after the children, and Gwendolyn would see her relatives if she chose. Too much togetherness was like a prison cell, and Gwendolyn would not be forced to endure family meals and chit chats unless she initiated them herself.

"Sarah has already arranged many outings for the children, and they will participate in the after school classes she runs for young thespians. It is, if you forgive the hyperbole, the trip of a lifetime."

"A telephone call to Sarah... just to go over a few details..." Doris was starting to bend in the right direction. "Could you leave me her number?"

"Leo?" Gwendolyn asked (or ordered). "Add this detail to the list."

"I must go over Henry's allergies."

"I don't *have* any allergies," Henry said clearly, refusing to be coddled. "I got over them at Camp Highland. The doctor at the camp said they were all exaggerated."

"Nonetheless, a telephone call is necessary," Doris said. "What would Sarah think if we didn't reach out?"

"You may try, of course, but Sarah keeps most irregular hours, and there is the time difference to consider. The Mews House dates to the time of Henry VIII, and the telephone wires do not always function as they should," Gwendolyn lied. "Something about a burial site, I believe, but it is all so vague." She rotated her wrist and straightened the cuff on her blouse. "Henry will be able to report routinely, as I believe there are a few pedestrian phones on the street. I think it will be best if we call once we are settled."

"Pedestrian?" Henry's father inquired. "What kind of phones are these?"

"Pay phones," Leo explained. "And a telephone call *is* in order," he added, contradicting Gwendolyn. "I will give you the number of the theatre as well, if you can't reach Sarah at home."

"She still works on a daily basis?" Doris asked, clearly flabbergasted that a woman in her nineties had the stamina.

Leo nodded. "Apparently so."

"And why aren't you going on this trip?" Doris asked. It was clear by her expression that she trusted Leo and still wasn't altogether certain about Gwendolyn.

"Someone has to stay with Peabody," Charlotte stated. "It wouldn't be right to leave him with a stranger, and he can't come because dogs are locked up for six weeks when they arrive in England, which isn't fair, but there is nothing I can do about it. He would pine and most probably die without one of us, and you wouldn't want that on your conscience, would you?"

"We can look after the little fellow," Aaron volunteered.

"No, we can't, Aaron. We leave in three days for Turkey. I'm going to have to think about this."

Gwendolyn ignored this entirely. "Tomorrow, at your convenience, Celeste, my great niece, daughter of…"

"Ariel," Leo said quickly while Gwendolyn pretended to cough.

"My brother Charlie's only child," she said, pressing the string of pearls that covered her heart. "Dear Ariel. Mother of Celeste. It's all rather confusing, isn't it? Even to me. But never mind. Celeste will be coming to visit, and she will be able to answer all the questions we have not. The dear girl grew up in the Mews House and has lived with Sarah for all but the past year of her life. She married a Canadian and emigrated and would be with us today, but she had an appointment at her obstetrician. She's expecting twins."

Henry's face took on a radiant glow that had nothing to do with sunlight beaming into the room. "She's promised to name them Charlotte and Henry if they are a boy and girl, and we will be hired as babysitters."

"Why have you never shared any of these adventures with us?" Doris walked over to Henry and ruffled his hair. He took a step back and scratched his head.

"You're never here," Henry answered.

"We have to travel for work," Doris explained to Gwendolyn, mistaking the woman as someone who could give a hoot how Henry was raised and whether his parents were in Toronto or Timbuctoo. If Gwendolyn had been a parent, she would have arranged not to be present during the nine-month pregnancy and subsequent birth.

"It worries me that I have had to miss so many of Henry's events at school, but one must make a living. I'm sure you understand," she said, looking to Gwendolyn for confirmation.

The lady herself was busy reinstating the razor-sharp pleats in her skirt by ironing them with her fingers, her mind elsewhere. When Leo cleared his throat, she responded with a slight forward shake of her head, and after a second or two, she furrowed her brow. Her response was predicated on absolutely no idea of economic imperative. Gwendolyn had never had to work a day in her life, and did not live on the same planet as working parents.

"I give you immense credit for something I never had the courage to do. With that in mind, I can promise I will look after young Henry as if he were my own." And after a moment added: "And Charlotte, too, of course."

"I'm inclined to say yes," Doris said, looking at her husband.

"I've said yes from the start. It's a damn good idea," Aaron said, giving the thumbs up to Leo. "Henry needs to get out and about and get a taste of life."

"That's not what I mean," said Doris, tossing a dagger with her eyes and alerting the guests to the tensions present in the mother/father dynamic. "But now that you mention it, Lena might be a problem. Lena is Henry's nanny," she told Gwendolyn. "Since a week after he was born," she added, proudly. "From what I understand most nannies never stay that long."

Gwendolyn's eyes were closing in boredom, but they snapped opened immediately when Dragos stepped on her foot.

Henry drew the flat of his hand across his neck. "I used to be easy to manipulate," he explained to the room at large.

No one expressed surprise at this announcement, least of all Henry's mother, who nodded complacently. "You were always a good boy, Henry. That's why we loved you so much."

"Speaking in the past infers that the person discussed is no longer present," Henry said, a hint of rebellion.

"We'll interview Celeste," said Aaron, "but as far as I'm concerned, Henry is already packed and boarding the plane. This is a sterling opportunity. Doris and I will discuss the particulars between us."

Doris, clearly offended at being denied the opportunity to further protest, capitulated gracefully when Henry spoke.

"Thanks, Dad. This is an important step in my personal development."

"Henry?" Doris inquired sadly.

"Yes?"

"Don't you want to thank me, too?"

Henry's expression said: For what? But the words out of his mouth were: "Thanks, Mom. This is an important step in my personal development."

As with anything repeated, the glow was not quite as intense.

"We will pay for Henry's airfare and incidentals, as I do not want you to be out of pocket," Henry's father said, offering Gwendolyn a hand.

"That is not necessary," she said. "Henry has performed a service which more than covers the trivial amount of money spent on an airline ticket."

"Do you mean the dog?" Doris asked. "But really—"

"What dog?" Gwendolyn interrupted, momentarily mystified. "Oh, yes. *That* dog. I refer to a different service entirely. Charlotte and Henry found a brooch I had lost sixty years ago. I'm sure he told you."

"They couldn't understand how I recognized it," Henry said succinctly.

"Wait a minute," Doris said. "Are you telling me that story of Henry's is true? That he lived in your house in 1939 and met your brother who—"

Gwendolyn stood, went to the couch where Doris was sitting, and overcoming her revulsion, picked up the woman's hand, holding it tightly in her own.

"My dear, of course I don't believe that story. But the children did locate my missing brooch, a family heirloom. You will see it tomorrow when Celeste comes visiting."

"But if Celeste has the brooch now, then your family in England must have always had it, and since your family had it and you were in contact with your family, it was never lost at all."

The wheels of logic were ticking away furiously in Doris's brain, and even Henry's father looked a trifle confused.

"Details," Gwendolyn said, dropping Doris's hand and fluttering her fingers through the air. "All totally irrelevant. I had lost touch with Celeste and had no idea that she was in possession of the brooch. Henry and Charlotte, through some twist of fate or happy accident, found Celeste wandering through St. Lawrence Market wearing the very distinctive Tree of Life and brought her to me. Have you never misplaced a relative?"

"There's a few I wouldn't mind losing," Henry's father muttered.

"How did you recognize something you've never seen?" Doris turned to Henry for an explanation.

Henry's powers of invention were not a match for Charlotte's, so she spoke on his behalf.

"Leo told us all about it when we were putting things together for the Millennium Project at school. You know how many old people we interviewed for that project?"

"*Elders*," Leo said, correcting Charlotte.

"We interviewed thirty-six elders, and the histories started colliding and the MacFarlane name was mentioned all the time."

"We were quite a prestigious family," Gwendolyn agreed, dipping her head to acknowledge a wave of silent clapping. "Everyone has always talked about us."

"And Gwendolyn refused to be interviewed..."

"I wasn't asked," she said huffily, "and so did not have the chance to refuse."

"We had to do a lot of research in the reference library and one thing led to another, and Leo told us about the brooch. It's one thing to hear about it but seeing the brooch in the flesh is a whole different matter."

"Was this before or after you met Henry in the park?" Doris asked, eager for a timeline she could comprehend.

"Since the children never thought to interview me, I would have to say the incident in the park occurred at some point in time that has no relevance whatsoever to the discovery of the brooch. I wonder that you might think it did?" There was just a suggestion that Doris was not quite up to the mark. Who cared about a fictious dog? "Now, I really must go," Gwendolyn concluded.

Gwendolyn had been born with many special talents. She held forth, she did not speak; once every year or so, she pretended to listen to what a person had to say, but she never heard a word, and she believed, steadfastly – with all the heart she did not have, and without having any facts to back this up – that she was smarter than anyone who dared to come within range of her being.

"We depart in two days, and since you will be abroad yourselves, you will not be missing Henry in the slightest," she added in a reassuring tone. "Leo will deal with the small details of passport procurement which I understand, for a price, can be expedited. Possibly a note of authority must be given to allow me to look after Henry. And Charlotte," she said, after a moment of distasteful reflection. "Henry will, under my tutelage, keep a journal of his impressions. Isn't that right, Henry?"

"Of course," Henry responded with a noticeable lack of enthusiasm.

"Dragos has my card should you have _any_ concerns, but I'm certain we have covered the essentials. Dragos?"

"What you want?" Dragos had lost interest in the proceedings and was staring out the window.

"My card, please."

Dragos displayed his beefy fingers for all to see and shrugged his massive shoulders. "Have my card," he said, reaching inside the breast pocket of his tunic and extracting a slim silver case which he flicked open. "Not have your card. Why you bother having card? You no work."

"Dragos," Leo interjected gently, patting his friend on the shoulder. "People have calling cards. You know that."

"I not," he said huffily. "Person speak for self, no need card to say what mouth can do. You agree?"

Dragos directed his question to Charlotte who nodded with enthusiasm.

"Waste of whole tree, maybe more. End up in garbage. Or maybe in wrong hand and then trouble start."

"Fine, Dragos. I'm certain we all appreciate your thoughts on the matter. Please give Henry's parents *your* card because we must depart at once."

Gwendolyn swept towards the door showering praise on Doris for maintaining such an accommodating space in which to receive visitors and suggesting that they meet for tea at her penthouse at some unspecified date far into the future.

Henry's father studied the business card he held in his hand. He tapped the corner with his thumb and asked: "You own town cars?"

"Fleet," Dragos answered at once.

"What? Like a hundred?" Henry's father questioned, impressed.

"Seven," Dragos said proudly. "All tip-top shape. Useful for any purpose, free water and newspaper. Affordable rate. Always on time."

"Probably a hell of a lot cheaper than leaving the car in long-term parking at the airport. Much appreciated," he said, tucking the card in his pocket.

"Plus, bodyguard," he said, pointing to Gwendolyn. "Those who need. Special rate."

"Intriguing," Henry's father said. "Is there a particular reason she needs a bodyguard?"

"No reason. Maybe atmosphere?"

"She's frightened of the atmosphere?" Henry's father pressed the point, suddenly wary of Gwendolyn's suitability as Henry's chaperone.

"It's for service," Charlotte explained. "Carrying groceries, holding the door, escorting Gwendolyn down the sidewalk, making sure she is first in line. That sort of thing."

"That sounds about a hundred years out of date. Gwendolyn will fit in quite well in London."

"Gwendolyn is extremely careful. Which is why she will make an excellent chaperone," Charlotte said. "Celeste told me that Sarah has a dogsbody, too, so we will be in good hands."

"A dogsbody?"

"A person to boss around, look after watering the flowers, locating missing housekeys, preparing the tea tray. Sounds okay to me."

"Me as well," he said, winking. And then he pulled Charlotte aside for a private word. "You'll look after Henry, won't you? I know you are his best friend, and you have a lot more get up and go then the boy has, although this recent stint at Camp Highland helped him become more independent. Just between you and me, I am going to give Henry the name of an old colleague and friend, a man of discernment and refinement, trustworthy. We don't need to let Doris know, but if either of you have any questions or concerns you are to call him at once. You understand?"

"Perfectly," Charlotte agreed, smiling. "But you have nothing to worry about. What can possibly go wrong in a week?"

Chapter Two

The house at #2 Rose Park Avenue, Charlotte and Leo's home, was deeply rooted in the past. The black and white subway tiles in the front hall were scratched from hobnail boots, hockey sticks, and ice skates. Decades of cigar smoke exhaled by former resident Gus Frank had turned the white tiles a sickly yellow that no amount of scrubbing could remove. Dust motes swirled two storeys high, collided with the high ceiling, and descended. They never really came to rest on anything since the front door was constantly ajar, stirring up motes in tiny tornado formations. If a person squinted, the air itself appeared almost flaxen, with the promise of wheat fields and long swaying grasses just beyond the reach of the doorway leading to the kitchen.

Charlotte could never locate her key, and it was easier to leave the door off latch because there were always people in and out of the house. Some who needed a strong cup of coffee before they could face the day, others who were drawn by the medicinal smell of chicken soup simmering on the stove. And a few brave souls had appointments with the elder resident, Leo, to drink a cup of tea and talk things over in the Tower Room – from which they would emerge, an hour (or a century) later, with new expressions of hope on their faces, their voices stronger, their backs straighter.

Not everyone was a candidate for a visit to the Tower Room, and there were those who failed to see a window opening as they sipped the smoky tea Leo offered, but even these few found a momentary respite from what was troubling them and came away wearing a more cheerful expression.

Sometimes this feeling of satisfaction did not persist, and in those rare occasions, Leo had to step forward and whisper a word of advice in the recalcitrant person's ear. Such a one was Gwendolyn MacFarlane, who was currently being discussed in the vast and cavernous kitchen – the only room in the house, according to Charlotte, where magic appeared every time Leo opened the oven door.

"Gwendolyn booked herself a suite at the Savoy hotel in London. Sarah thought she might do something like this, so I called her and let her know. She'll be taking care of it at her end."

"How come you didn't tell me earlier?" Henry asked, from his seat at the kitchen table.

Charlotte shrugged. "I didn't have a chance. I talked to Sarah about ten minutes ago."

"At my house?" Henry's facial expression had not changed at all, but his tone of voice hinted at outrage.

"What's a measly long-distance call to you, Henry? You can afford it. I've used up almost all the money Leo has saved for me." Charlotte's allowance was split between her greedy palm and the cookie jar because Leo was trying to teach her how to save for a rainy day. "How much do I have left?" she asked.

Leo gave it some thought. "A couple of dollars? And Henry, I will compensate you for the phone call. Charlotte shouldn't have done that. And she knows it." He waited patiently until Charlotte apologized and then resumed making lunch.

"Don't worry," Henry said. "My parents will never notice. Or they will think they made the call themselves."

Henry was able to converse normally when he was not in the presence of his parents. Leo suspected that Henry had developed this strategy to free himself from their cloying presence on the rare occasions they were at home because, as he had stated with absolute certainty, *They have this preconceived idea of who I am, and I have no interest in changing their minds.*

"The real problem," said Charlotte, "is that Gwendolyn meant to ditch us the minute she landed in London. And you think my behaviour is awful. I'm just looking out for us."

"Really? Or are you attempting to control Gwendolyn's every move?" Leo asked.

"Well, that, too," she stated emphatically. "I'd like to be free of this responsibility once and for all, and I can't do it if Gwendolyn won't cooperate."

The responsibility to which Charlotte referred was a direct result of her trip to the past, a trip that took place in the spring a mere four months ago. She was burdened with a tremendous responsibility all because she had been where she was not supposed to be, underneath the table in the infamous Tower Room – a room that held magical abilities of time transposition and was part of her family heritage. Although, as Leo had pointed out repeatedly, she was far too young to be involved in that heritage and was forbidden to enter the room.

Leo should never have used the word *forbidden*. Henry, acting out of concern (and fear) had confided all to Leo. Charlotte had visited the room whenever Leo was not at home, having easily located the key in Leo's dresser. And she had described her experiences, which Henry repeated verbatim: The room was bright and airy and filled with an array of black and white photographs taken by the long deceased Great Uncle Gus Frank. The pictures had a way of staring at Charlotte more than she stared at them, but she took that as her due because she was interesting and special and cute and deserved the attention.

'As *if*,' Henry had said dismissively.

But once, because of her intense dislike of Gwendolyn MacFarlane (a recent friend of her grandfather's) she had dragged Henry to the third floor and forced him to hide beneath the cloth which covered the old round table, so she could eavesdrop on their conversation and figure out how to get rid of Gwendolyn once and for all.

Big mistake!

And one she was still paying for, because the magic that existed in that room had dragged Henry and Charlotte through a vortex of rushing sounds and tornado-like propulsion to Gwendolyn MacFarlane's very house way back in 1939 and left Charlotte – not Leo, who was the intended guide – to sort out the mess Gwendolyn was currently making of her life.

And now Charlotte was left to figure out what she did wrong – which was *nothing*, she'd told Leo firmly, because Gwendolyn was now an elder mess instead of an adolescent mess, and how could she ever fix the unfixable?

Leo had realized he had to step back and try to help Charlotte understand what must be done. He was no longer in charge of the Tower Room and its varied transpositions.

Charlotte was currently, under Leo's tutelage, decoding some notes of her Great Uncle Gus (the first and most mulishly difficult of travel guides) and she was coming to understand that magic did not just make things right, wash its hands, and disappear. No way, José. Magic was far more subtle than that. Otherwise, she and Henry would never have found Celeste and the Tree of Life brooch that Gwendolyn insisted was hers, and they would not be travelling on a less disruptive time flow to London, for Gwendolyn to reunite with a family she never thought she had and clearly had no interest in getting to know.

This problem was Charlotte's to solve, and Leo had the utmost faith in her, because she was a descendant of the great Frank-Becker line and fearless in the face of adversity.

"Leo, how did you get Gwendolyn to come to my house?" Henry asked. "That was bloody awesome."

Bloody was a recent addition to Henry's vocabulary, as he was practicing inserting British words and idioms into his sentences in anticipation of not feeling odd man out when he landed on those distant shores. Charlotte had told him his parents would capitulate and allow him to go, and because she had more faith than he did (or at least pretended to have more faith) he had begun to prepare. Learning the vocabular was part of his plan. "It was pretty bloody amazing that she stayed as long as she did, too."

"Coo Limey," Charlotte added, tucking into a liver sausage sandwich on crusty white bread that was merely two hours old.

"You can say that if you want," Henry told her, swiveling his head to look in her general direction. "But all it means is 'awesome Brit', so it is hardly relevant."

"Yeah? Really?" Charlotte's inflection suggested that she did not care whether anything she said was relevant. She eyed Henry with suspicion.

Leo put another plate of sandwiches on the table. "More British vocab, Henry?"

The boy nodded. "Fancy is a good one. Instead of saying I want a bar of chocolate, a British person says: I fancy a bar of chocolate."

"Got it. I fancy this liver sausage sandwich," Charlotte said.

Henry's face went blank (or blanker than normal), and Leo knew he was busy projecting a page from his notebook on the table beside his plate.

Any blank surface would do, but Henry liked to have a wall or a table-top close at hand to project his files. His eidetic memory allowed him to remember every page of print he had ever absorbed, in complete photographic perfection, and was one of the reasons that people thought he was extraordinarily smart.

"Knackered, cheeky, cuppa", Henry reeled off immediately, reciting from the top of his list. "*Mate* is a good one. Everybody says mate, like, 'Hey, mate, what do you want to do today?'" Henry also liked tickety-boo, which Charlotte said sounded like the name of an insect. "You're whing-ing," he told her.

"I am not," she stated. "I am sitting up perfectly straight."

"Whinging means whining," he said, gazing at her with his usual deadpan. "Little nippers do a lot of whinging. Grousing and grumbling are close cousins but not particularly British. Perhaps I do you an injustice," he added, reflectively.

"Yeah, you're always doing that when I'm busy saving your butt."

"Fair enough. It might be more appropriate to say you are full of beans."

"I'm not the one farting up a storm. That would be you," she said, pointing a dirty finger in Henry's direction.

"Charlotte," Leo warned. "That's rude."

"Didn't mean it," she said, ducking her head. "Henry knows that."

Leo was impressed by Henry's recent and quick study of all things British. Charlotte would survive very nicely when they arrived in London, but Henry would be closer to understanding the history and the sheer magnitude of the place. Henry told him he had already inputted *Little Dorrit, The Way of All flesh, Bleak House, and The Mayor of Casterbridge*, none of which he attempted to understand, but he did come away with a small morsel of food for thought. He stated the most obvious facts: "The men are either obese or chronically drunk, or both, they get beaten up routinely, and they then beat up their wives. Brothels, which are these questionable shelters for women, are everywhere, and orphans positively litter the streets."

Henry had also dragged Charlotte to the reference library, and while she rode the glass cage elevator up and down and up and down he paged though two issues of *Tiger Beat*, and a few copies of the *Observer* and the

Sun, a daily rag that was the biggest selling newspaper in Britain (according to Sandra, the librarian who had taken a keen interest in Henry's research and reported back to Leo just so he knew what the children were doing).

"We are mates," Charlotte said, taking another sandwich from the platter. "I fancy that."

She transferred the crusts on her plate to the edge of the table where Peabody, the wire-haired terrier, sat on a chair with a napkin around his neck. Leo had tried to explain to Charlotte that a dog did not have a place at a kitchen table, but since the dog in question was neater when he ate (leaving not a crumb behind) and less vocal than Charlotte, he decided to let it pass and just gave the table a good swipe with a clean cloth when everyone had departed.

"*Narky* is another and, *arsed* (as in can't be bothered)," Henry said, adding parentheses with his hands. "You don't use *arsed* to describe yours or a person's rear end."

In their nightly telephone debrief, Charlotte had learned that Henry's new vocabulary had caused a bit of trouble at home. Without thinking, he'd used *arsed* when his mother told him to take out the garbage. "I can't be arsed," he had replied, lost in his role of a more cosmopolitan Henry, and Henry's father had immediately been summoned to explain to the lad that a properly brought up person did not speak to his mother (mum, mam, mater) in such a rude fashion and what did he have to say for himself.

"I'd give you my entire list of words," Henry told Charlotte, "but you'd probably just lose it."

"Cheeky bugger," Charlotte said, nodding her head in agreement.

"You distracted me," Henry said, remembering where he was in question period before he got sidetracked by showing off his British proficiency. "Leo, how did you get Gwendolyn to agree to come to my house? When I saw her yesterday, she was talking about cancelling the trip. She said that her mind had been 'twisted into some temporary aberration,'" he said, quoting the women herself. "She only wanted to see the Tree of Life again and had no interest at all in Sarah or her niece Ariel, and Charlie was long dead and gone, and she had never really liked London, and if she had she might not have gone to New Zealand and her life would have been entirely different and she was too old to start again." There were several unpleasantries regarding travelling with Charlotte, but for Charlotte's sake Henry decided to keep those private.

Leo was about to answer, when the back door burst open and Dragos entered in a huff.

"That woman," he declared, slamming his fist on the table. "Dragos this, Dragos that, like I be her servant." The sound disturbed Peabody, who raised his lip and snarled.

"Dog no belong at table," Dragos muttered. "Belong in cage. Like chicken. Charlotte think you be ghost of old man who she knew as boy, but I say this: You be dog. Get that through thick head."

By arguing with Peabody, Dragos was complicit with Charlotte's theory that Peabody was Lukas – Henry's best friend in 1939 – incarnate. "I helped Helen clean out Lukas's house," Charlotte said. "I found the note he left for Henry. I rescued Peabody from the shelter. None of these things would have happened had I not been divinely guided." Charlotte loved sparring with Dragos, and next to Leo and Henry, Dragos was her favourite person in the universe.

"Sneak is all, and no guide need be sneak. Why you let dog sit at table, Leo?" Dragos asked, shovelling half of a sandwich into his mouth.

"Because he never argues, never eats anything except what is on his plate, and never spills on the tablecloth," Charlotte answered before Leo had a chance to open his mouth. Crumbs, mustard splatters, and bits of pickle surrounded Dragos's elbows which were firmly anchored on the table. "And he never, ever, pees on the floor. I know a woman who walks her dog around the kitchen table. She is too lazy to take him outside and when he does his business the housekeeper cleans it up."

"That's not true," Henry said. "No one walks their dog around a kitchen table."

"Oh, yeah? You'd be surprised what people do, Henry. But then you'd have to really open your eyes and look around."

Dragos bristled. "That woman belong in cage. Keep Gwendolyn company. Maybe you not be so bad," he added, pointing to the terrier.

Peabody lifted his upper lip, exposed his baby chicklet teeth, and jumped down from his chair to curl into a tidy little ball in his bed by the fireplace.

"Why you go to London with nasty old woman?" he asked. "I come and protect. Besides, you miss Friday night movie with Leo. Important event. More important than trip to London."

As a learning exercise, Leo had instituted the Friday night at the movies three months ago. Leo believed anything old had merit, and he spiced the event with Hamburger Helper and heaps of buttered popcorn. *The Guns of Navarone, The Dirty Dozen, The Great Escape,* and *A Bridge too Far* had all been screened for Henry and Charlotte, and Dragos was equally mesmerized. The quartet had been working their way through all the best war films in Leo's library before he switched them to what he called screwball comedies. After their recent adventure back in time, he decided it was appropriate that Henry and Charlotte understand – through fictional rendering – an important historical period.

"Leo's promised a triple bill when we return."

"Have I?'

"Yes," Charlotte insisted. "I'm sorry, Dragos, but we have to go on this trip, and you have to stay here and keep Leo company. We will be fine. Henry will protect me, wouldn't you?"

"Of course," Henry answered automatically. He knew Charlotte was kidding. She was the protector in their constellation.

"Here's something weird," Charlotte reported, while rinsing the plates. "Sarah wants to see what my handwriting looks like."

"Why?" Henry asked. "Have you been blackmailing someone?"

"Of course, I haven't, Henry. She's very cagey and won't say why, so it's a mystery. Why do you think, Leo?" she asked as she stacked the plates in the dishwasher.

"I couldn't say," he replied, shrugging his shoulders.

"She also wants to know what kind of tea Gwendolyn drinks and what she likes for breakfast."

"You see?" Dragos shouted. "Why people go out of way to be nice to person who not nice?"

"She can be nice," Henry argued. "She paid me for setting up those accounting templates for her."

"You never do for me," Dragos said, immediately wounded. "And I run business. That woman just spend money given her free from universe."

"How much did she pay you for the templars?" Charlotte asked, carrying the freshly made strawberry shortcake to the table and handing out new plates and forks.

"Templates," Henry corrected automatically. He pondered, his thumb and forefinger caressing his lip. "I billed for five hours, and it only took me thirty minutes. She paid me four dollars an hour which was quite fair. I made eighteen dollars more than I earned, and she didn't question the bill. Besides, I don't really need the money. I made a small fortune at camp this summer."

Henry had a neat little racket going at Camp Highland selling contraband candy and charging money to touch some idiot whose body temperature dropped to 36 degrees Celsius while he slept. Not only that, he had manufactured these businesses while malingering in the sick bay so he didn't have to participate in any legitimate camp activities. Dragos repeated this story to everyone he knew, but he had not heard about the business with Gwendolyn.

"Worm pickers get four dollars hour, Henry," Dragos pointed out. "I know this because when I first come to country, I get twenty-five cents hour and I keep track of current rate. You not worm picker. You undercharge. She take advantage, Henry. Most people take advantage. Learn lesson now and you not end up in poorhouse."

"Thanks," Henry said nonchalantly. "But what's done is done."

Charlotte bristled instantly. Henry may not need the money, but she did and what was his was hers and vice versa. "We could use that extra money for our trip. I am almost completely without funds," she added, an ongoing dilemma that everyone at the table knew very well.

"I shall advance you a small amount," Leo told her, patting her shoulder. "More than enough to keep you afloat in London where you will have no expenses."

Charlotte pouted and cut a piece of strawberry shortcake for Henry that was half the size of the one she'd offered Dragos.

"You never answered my question, Leo," Henry said, thanking Charlotte nicely for the meagre offering. "How did you get Gwendolyn to agree to go once she changed her mind?"

"I told Gwendolyn that her travelling days were not over. I mentioned that the effects of the Tower Room would linger and disturb her equilibrium until she completed her journey."

"And that's my job to complete," Charlotte said, her mouth full of straw-berries and whipped cream. "But what is my job, Leo?"

"Do not speak with your mouth full. And as to your question, I have no idea."

"Yes, but you've been in this position before. You told me so." Her eyes were accusing.

"Every case is different. Sometimes a person is forced to quit their job before sanity can return. Sometimes people must leave their homes and live for a while on the road. Other times a person must learn to forgive themselves."

"But Gwendolyn doesn't have a job. And she would never stoop to forgiving herself because she doesn't believe she has ever done any-thing wrong."

"As I said. Different people, different outcomes. I am not being obtuse. I simply do not know."

He wished he could be more specific, offer guidance to Charlotte, but he had none at his disposal. His own adventures had taught him that logic and transformation were not intrinsically connected. And, unfortunately, he had also learned that change often first brought pain and hardship. But Charlotte would not be alone. Sarah would look after her if Gwendolyn wouldn't, and Henry had a practical dogged side that would come in useful. To complete her journey, Charlotte must first go to London. There was no way round it.

"I wish you were coming. It would be altogether better if you came. Sarah wants you to come," Charlotte said, wiping her fingers on her T-shirt.

"And I would like to journey abroad if flying did not make me so uncomfortable," he explained, passing her a napkin. "And there is the ques-tion of Peabody. Someone must remain behind to look after his needs, as you so clearly stated earlier in the day."

"Okay. Fine. But am I allowed to take Gus's journal with me? I have to learn from somebody if this is to be my lifetime occupation," she added, kicking Henry's leg when he lifted his eyebrows. "I will know what all this travelling means and be better placed to understand my role in future expeditions."

Henry interrupted Dragos's tale of how everyone in Romania believed in magic and how the Tower Room was a pale imitation of what went on in his home country every minute of every day. "But this upcoming trip is more important than ones you may or may not take in the future, Charlotte. And I think we both need to understand how Leo got Gwendolyn to lobby on my behalf."

"I told her that she had no choice. She had to get over her misgivings and go, and if nothing came of it, she could blame me upon her return."

"She must have liked that," Charlotte said, grinning.

"She did. But I also said she must never forget to treat you and Henry with great respect because you both have already helped her immensely."

"Knowing Gwendolyn, that still doesn't seem like enough."

Leo made a steeple with his fingers. Henry would not give up. Leo had no choice but to answer.

"I also told her that, if she reneged on this adventure, Dragos would no longer care to work as her personal chauffeur..."

"Now you talk sense," Dragos responded with a big grin. "Hit where counts."

"... and that the weekly deliveries of baked goods, quiches, stews and soups, all made in this very kitchen, would stop and never again resume."

"You blackmailed her," Charlotte said, wiping her lips on her napkin.

"If you wish to put it that way, I suppose I did."

Chapter Three

Far across the ocean, in another time zone, two people laboured intensely on Gwendolyn's behalf, remaking a child's bedroom into an oasis of comfort for a finicky old woman.

"Do you think we should bring over more pillows from the main house, Grandfather?" Jeremy asked.

He couldn't recognize his old room, neither tactilely nor visually. The bed, vastly transformed, was now covered with a pale pink satin duvet cover. The sheets, used only for special guests and made by a company called Frette, were as soft as cotton balls and moss – sweet-smelling moss only found beside a very private lake in the country.

This corner room in the Mews cottage, a room overlooking a tiny but still flourishing fall garden, had been until this very morning, Jeremy's. All his books, clothes, archaeological artifacts and miscellaneous posters and pictures had been temporarily stored in the attic, a rather spooky, cobweb-ridden place that Jeremy would only enter if his grandfather stood at the bottom of the ladder and called up to him every five seconds to make certain he had not been ambushed by ghosts.

It had been much easier to turn Oliver's bedroom into a sitting room for Mrs. MacFarlane-Fenton, because it had a daybed which could masquerade as a chaise lounge and only needed an abundance of flowers to decorate its rather spartan appearance. Besides, Oliver's bedroom was off the laneway and sometimes cars drove by disturbing the peace of the night. Although it was more work to convert Jeremy's into a facsimile of what might be found in one of the higher-end hotels in London, it had been worth the effort. Chairs, tables, curtains, Persian rugs, and restrained oil paintings of the British countryside had been borrowed from the downstairs and from the main house, and the room was now both elegant and warm. It was a shame Oliver did not have time to sand and repaint the walls, but there was nothing to be done about that save hanging the pictures over one or two dents made by an overzealous kicking of a soccer ball.

The toiletries and clothing Jeremy would require had been moved by garden dolly to the basement apartment in the front house, where he would live in comfort with Oliver and bask in the glow of having Sarah only one floor above him.

"About those pillows, Grandfather? I could be back in less than a tick. Sarah said Mrs. MacFarlane-Fenton is very particular, and she might want to have a selection to choose from."

"It is always better to err on the side of less is more, Jeremy." Oliver arranged a vase of white mums on a table by the window. "The cleaning service is arriving in an hour, and our work will soon be done."

"Look at this, Grandfather," Jeremy said, his hand cupping one of the chrysanthemums. "It's white but it looks touched by fire like it is absorbing all the colours in the room."

Jeremy continued to stare into the heart of the flower, his shoulders slumped.

"What is it, lad?" Oliver asked gently. "Something is troubling you."

"Do you think Henry and Charlotte will like me, Grandfather?" Jeremy asked, lifting his eyes to meet Oliver's. Oliver tried not to flinch when he looked at his grandson's battered face.

Jeremy's black eye from his last beating had faded into shades of yellow and green, and he still wore a soiled white bandage around his wrist. In keeping with a time-honoured tradition Jeremy had refused to rat on the classmates (he had a brilliant explanation for this and shared it with Oliver over the course of twenty-five long, agonizing minutes) who had participated in this last assault, and the headmaster's hands were tied – although Oliver had told him that if the man did not untie his hands soon, Oliver would see to matters himself. To this end, the Latin tutor had been put on hold and a respectable – if somewhat battered – pugilist from Oliver's distant past had been hired to teach Jeremy a few tricks of the trade.

"The kid never shuts up, which is his biggest problem," Arthur had told Oliver when they sat in the garden, discussing strategies and drinking a decent single malt scotch. "In my opinion that's why he gets all these beatings. Plus, he looks like a mashed-up bag of bones which is going to offend most of them arse-wipes, the ones in training to be toffs. I seen 'em when I collected the kid last week at school. Here comes Jeremy, slouching down the stairs, his mouth moving non-stop even though there's nobody within earshot except for this group of tossers waiting by the stone lion – say, is that lion supposed to be Cromwell?"

"I think it's supposed to be a lion," Oliver had replied softly, letting the scotch roll in his mouth and burn his tongue.

"What does a lion have to do with some swank boy's public school?"

"What does Cromwell?"

"You've got a point. Carrying on, I think it was the sound of Jeremy more than anything else that set the stage – the air changes colour when a fight's about to begin, you ever notice that?"

"Can't say that I have," Oliver said, wondering if it was prudent to remove Jeremy from yet another school. But how would this help the boy learn to survive in the world?

"I tell you, Oliver, if I hadn't gotten there fast, the kid would have been laid flat and thrown into the street like he was a dead dog, 'cept a dead dog would be treated with more respect because we Brits care more about our dogs than we care about people, don't we? It's going to take some time, but I think I can slap some sense into Jeremy, teach him a few tricks."

"Whatever it takes, Arthur. I am at my wits' end."

"I mean no offence here, but Jeremy doesn't walk so much as slink, and he always looks like he's up to something."

"And that's because he always is."

"And he doesn't have one friend that I can see. Crazy thing is, the kid thinks I'm his friend. I'll tell you this for free. The kid is good on his feet, I'll give him that. Reminds me a bit of Lenny McLean, the way he can move. You remember him?"

Oliver felt a prickle of interest. "Was he the one who handled security at the Lamplighter?"

"One and the same."

Oliver had done a stint as the doorman at this club, mostly because he loved the uniform – navy blue, doubled-breasted, with brass buttons and epaulets. He enjoyed standing at attention and surveying, with an expressionless face, his temporary domain. He'd gotten the job easily enough because he didn't require a salary and agreed to pay for his own uniform. He remembered Lenny, built like a brick shithouse and 1.85 metres in height; he used to slap Oliver on the back when he entered the club.

McLean had favoured cigars and buxom brunettes, and occasionally Oliver would smell his cigar smoke on one of the patrons who flew headfirst from the doors, landing in the gutter and moaning. Oliver always helped the wounded, brushed off their jackets, and saw to their flesh wounds with a first aid kit he kept in his limousine (which was parked illegally at the curb).

That Oliver had the resources and money to behave in such a peculiar fashion bothered him not in the slightest. He had paid his dues in the way the British upper class was trained. He had completed an education, read anthropology at Cambridge (it was all a game to Oliver: masquerading as a student, flitting around campus in a long black gown, steadfastly reading into the night by the light of a candle – a conceit that he embraced wholeheartedly even though electricity crackled around him) and even worked for a time in the British Museum until he decided his talents could be put to better use elsewhere.

"Lenny passed on last year. Pity that, but he taught me a few things. It's not about who lands the first punch, it's more about wearing out your opponent. Between the mouth on Jeremy and his dancing feet, if he continues to grow the way he's been doing we might have something to work with."

When Jeremy noticed his grandfather's stare, Oliver dropped his eyes.

"You will be the best of mates. I can assure you," Oliver answered with conviction.

He had been present when Sarah had talked to Charlotte on the telephone, and he was impressed by both her precociousness and deviousness in discovering the reservation at the Savoy. He didn't quite believe Sarah's tale of having *possibly* met both Charlotte and Henry more than sixty years ago, but this belief was in keeping with how fey and capricious Sarah had become of late – it was almost as if she were experiencing a second childhood, not uncommon for one who had spent her life in the theatre. Oliver himself didn't believe that growing up and behaving like an adult were strictly necessary, although he leaned heavily on responsibility and loving behaviour and always had.

Oliver had not seen Sarah so keyed up since the Motley Players received a reserved-yet-favourable review for the avant-garde staging of *Pericles* where the entire production was supposed to take place beneath the sea. He himself had helped build the sea palace and hand painted more than a hundred fish, including rays, grunts, batfish, seahorses, and angelfish.

The building which housed the theatre company and the cost of keeping the Motley Players afloat had been Oliver's to bear since that glorious day, fifty years in the past when he had driven by a ramshackle building abutting a small square and seen Sarah depositing trash in a can by the curb. He had slammed on the brakes, twisted in his seat and, as far as he could tell, had never twisted back. Their meeting had been fortuitous and emotional. Both had cried; he because she had saved his life, burrowing through the rubble of his family home after a bombing raid in London; she because Oliver was the first person she had driven, by ambulance, to hospital, having only started her volunteer tour the day before. Taking over the care and feeding of Sarah and a difficult, out-of-control, soon-to-be teenage Ariel had been Oliver's salvation.

At first, neither had been interested in his gifts.

"We are very happy here," Sarah explained touring Oliver through the rooms above the theatre that she called home. One large room with two pallets on the floor, a hot plate on the window ledge, a desk, and two dilapidated leather chairs on either side of a gas fireplace; another room filled to overflowing with sewing machines, fabric, half-empty paint cans, and who knew what else. And a rabbit warren of smaller rooms that Sarah had not gotten around to emptying, full of rubbish belonging to the former tenant.

And making do, as he was later informed, on a small pittance left to her by her mother and begging favours from people who "loved" the theatre.

"Bugger off," Ariel had informed him when Oliver asked her name. Followed immediately by: "Is that a death masque or have you been mauled by a savage dog?"

Oliver had been instantly charmed.

Sarah had not.

"Leave us to our bohemian ways, Oliver. It is not possible to tame us."

"You mistake me, Sarah," he'd said, bowing from the waist. "I do not wish to tame you. I wish to join you."

"Crazy bugger," Ariel whispered – she had retreated only as far as the door. "What's on offer?"

Inserting himself into the lives of the people who inhabited the theatre, where the rent was always paid late and dinners were eaten at noon, midnight, or not at all, had allowed Oliver to indulge his eccentricities. He was currently in costume of one of his favourite characters: that of faithful retainer and servant, dogsbody and protector. It was no accident that his two marriages had not survived more than a few years each, because the gravitational pull of Sarah and Ariel was too strong to resist.

He had asked Sarah to marry him countless times, and she had always steadfastly refused. First citing the difference in their ages, next the social stigma he would feel being married to a Jewish woman, and when these two tactics did not work, she told him she was impossible to live with and wasn't it better that they simply remain the best of friends?

His family of birth (all long deceased and largely forgotten) maintained that Oliver was *different* because he had been injured in the war. A bombing raid had caught the studious young Oliver in the library (where he was not supposed to be, because the sirens were screaming and the rest of the family had sought shelter in the old wine cellar) but young Oliver considered himself to be invincible, beyond the range of any bombs that might fall nearby or directly overhead. He had been charged with the sort of adrenalin that belongs mostly to the young, and he'd decided he had to get Thackery's *The Luck of Barry Lyndon* from the polished mahogany shelf in the library, and he could outrun any disaster if and when it should occur.

He'd made a great error of judgement.

His young limbs had been unable to propel him out the door, and when the bomb hit, he could not escape and lay trapped beneath a considerable amount of rubble, largely unconscious but mewing a programmed response – *help me... help me... help me...* – that had served so well with the numerous misjudgements already committed during his scant time on earth. And because he had been saved so often before, he had no doubt that he would once again see the bright light of day and the limbs that had been broken and mangled would repair themselves almost at once.

Oliver was born an optimist, and an optimist he remained.

"What injuries?" he asked, upon waking in the hospital. When he learned he had two broken legs, a broken elbow, a shattered collarbone and three mangled fingers, he said he was lucky to have escaped mostly intact. And when he was also told that a broken piece of timber from the magnificent library walls had cracked his cranium and left him with a scar that stretched from the corner of his chin, zigzagged its way across his left cheekbone, and came to rest mid-skull, his response had been to cry "Zorro!"

And then faint from the pain of his excitement.

At the age of eight, Oliver had been convinced that he was, in fact, Don Diego de la Vega, the only son of the richest landowner in California. That he lived in London and in the family estate in Surrey was irrelevant, all the other details were accurate. He had read *The Curse of Capistrano* so many times, he had it memorized. A masked avenger with a double identity was as deeply appealing to the elder Oliver as it was to the young Oliver, and he had never truly shed his secret identity. If his biography had been available for common consumption, it might argue that Oliver's strangeness predated his terrible accident, and instead of changing it had merely reenforced it.

The "Zorro" cry and escalating aberrant behaviour had deeply disturbed his parents, whose worse fear in the world was embarrassment. But the doctor did confirm to the distraught couple that Oliver's brain had been damaged in some mysterious and unsolvable way. And that he would just have to make do.

"We *all* must learn to make do," the doctor added, his expression rather steely when Oliver's stepmother whimpered and pulled at her handkerchief. "Buck up."

Sarah had found him the day of the bombing – had heard his pitiful cry and kept the workers digging, and Oliver had emerged, dehydrated, nearly dead but alive enough to see the smile that illuminated Sarah's dirt-streaked face.

In his debilitated state, he thought Sarah was an angel, and he never lost this marvellous sense of deliverance. He demanded, once he regained the power of full (if somewhat halting) sentences, that his parents' honour and reward the person who was merely doing her job and expected nothing in return.

The only problem had been that Sarah had vanished. He didn't know her last name, her age, her status. He remembered nothing except her eyes, her smile, the long, graceful curve of her neck, the midnight blue-black colour of her hair.

Oliver wanted to say "Hello" and "Thank you" the first time he saw Sarah's face through the haze, but he was unable to speak and then unable to fend for himself for almost a year.

This had given him a lot of time to think.

His emerging sense of who he was and what he was entitled to had changed utterly. He remembered vividly (and always would) the first sight of his face in the looking glass.

He looked singularly transformed.

He no longer resembled a boy nor a *young gentleman,* as his father had insisted he call himself. No, indeed. Oliver looked like an elf or a gremlin – he couldn't decide which because he no longer remembered the difference, and he was not at all distressed at what he saw. With the right side of his face hitched high and out of symmetry with the left, a permanent expression of rapscallion delight was embedded in his countenance, and he had realized that he looked, for the first time ever, ridiculously happy. He never tired of gazing at this transformation. And he had convinced himself that this reconfigured image was who he truly was meant to be.

"It's not acceptable to behave in this cavalier fashion, Oliver," his father had repeated over and over throughout the early decades of Oliver's life – but the boy was so agreeable, so terribly brave in the face of his disfigurement, that no amount of criticism could make him change his ways.

"We both look like warriors, don't we, Grandfather?" Jeremy asked, shocking Oliver out of his recollections. "Like twins," he added, staring at himself in the mirror. "My face now has character and determination, just like yours always has.

"Do you think it would be terribly boring to be normal?" the boy continued. "I keep hearing all the time that I'm weird and a freak, but most of the people around me are just deadly dull and stupid. Is it wrong of me to think that?"

Was that why the boy rarely complained as ice packs were placed on his eyes, his forehead, his cheeks, his split lips? "Are you advancing in your boxing techniques?" Oliver asked, instead of answering the question.

"My footwork is excellent," Jeremy answered, dancing around the room on the balls of his feet and shadowboxing with the air. "I think my jab is stellar, but Arthur just frowns. When we tried the haymaker, I wrenched my shoulder. He says I must fatten up and then start working on developing muscle. I do my routine three times a day, and I feel stronger every second." Jeremy's arms had the shape and consistency of a birch twig, and although the child ate everything put in front of him, he did not gain an ounce.

Oliver sighed, and then remembered to praise Jeremy's footwork. When the boy stopped moving and his shoulder slumped, Oliver had an idea what was coming.

"Are we ever going home?" Jeremy asked, his voice instantly stripped of all expression. He peeked at Oliver through lowered eyelids.

Bingo!

Any change unnerved Jeremy, and although he expressed delight and gratitude at the temporary move to the front house, anxiety lurked in the tightness of his forehead.

"I think not," Oliver said gently. "I think it is better that we stay right where we are."

Jeremy leapt from hiding with a hearty shout. "Hooray!" he cried. "That's wicked, Grandfather. Double, triple, quadruple ACE!" His shoulders straightened, and his fists reached for the ceiling. "I would like to stay right here for all time, if that is all the same to you."

44

"It is." Oliver moved the vase of flowers to the exact centre of the table and looked at his watch. "We have shopping to do and menus to prepare. Would you like to turn the car for me?"

"Yes, please and thank you, Grandfather. I will be most careful as you know I always am."

"The keys are on the hall table."

Oliver stayed to straighten the crease in the drapes. He watched Jeremy tear across the garden and disappear into the laneway between the house and the fence. He ran so fast the navy and white stripe of his shirt remained burned in Oliver's retina long after the boy himself had vanished.

Chapter Four

Gwendolyn sipped a glass of champagne and averted her gaze from the line of tourist class passengers who were blocking the aisle in the Boeing 727 soon (but not soon enough) departing for London. There were far too many people still waiting to claim their seats, and Gwendolyn wished to fly on without them. Most fidgeted, adjusted boaters and beanies, pulled at their pants, devoured bags of salty crisps that would immediately cause intense thirst, consumption of polluted water, and several trips to the washroom. All were dressed inappropriately for long-distance travel – a predominance of short sleeved shirts and blue jeans assaulted her eyes. And most carried their luggage, curious canvas bags with far too many side pockets and clasps, on their backs, pretending they were Sherpas. What she saw was a total lack of decorum and sensibility. Black was the only colour to wear when travelling and silk preferable to cotton. As for luggage, no one with any sense carried their own.

Gwendolyn had purchased two first class seats for herself, thereby eliminating the possibility of being forced to listen to the pointless chatter of a stranger. The second seat she used as an open suitcase, and it housed her cashmere shawl (black), reading glasses, and a package of hand wipes to remove the unhealthy air from the tips of her fingers, air that had already begun to settle on every exposed area of skin.

She heard rather than saw Charlotte in the line of passengers, grandly orating to a perfect stranger a litany of what she had seen, done, and bought (with Gwendolyn's money) since their arrival at Pearson International two hours before.

"…three bags of Skittles, a terry cloth washcloth, a pair of sunglasses shaped like the CN tower and my Hell-o Kitty bag. Besides all that what is astonishing is that my friend Henry has never been on a plane before even though his parents travel the entire world on a routine basis. Henry doesn't speak, so don't bother asking him any questions. If you want to know anything, anything at all, just ask me. Now, as I was saying…"

Gwendolyn noticed that Charlotte did not bother saying she, too, had never been on a plane.

This was typical behaviour, but then Charlotte always claimed to be far grander than she was.

Charlotte's voice was amplified, condensed and sharpened by the metallic tunnel attached to the door of the Boeing. The child had no sense of discretion and no idea that strangers were not interested in what she had to say. She blocked out the rest of this strident monologue and checked to see whether Charlotte was in view. She supposed it was only decent to greet the child. She had already explained why she was boarding the plane first and why it was so very much better that Henry and Charlotte sit in the back of the plane and how they would join up once the airbus landed in Heathrow, and so many other details that she was exhausted trying to remember.

The absence of Leo presented a problem because there was no way Gwendolyn was going to chaperone Charlotte. If it were just Henry, she wouldn't mind, because Henry was smart and rarely spoke and could memorize important details like where the food section was to be found in Harrods and how to convert the British pound into its Canadian equivalent.

Gazing steadfastly into the future, Gwendolyn decided that Henry would look just fine in the junior-size black tuxedo that Gwendolyn would purchase for him, and his behaviour would be impeccable, thereby making him a respectable partner when they went to the opera.

Gwendolyn had no intentions of taking Charlotte to the opera.

Charlotte could amuse herself elsewhere. Perhaps with one of her many new friends waiting impatiently for their seats, falsely believing that once they were seated, Charlotte would stop bothering them.

For a brief period, perhaps two or three days – she couldn't believe it had lasted that long – Gwendolyn had treated Charlotte with respect and deference and even (now shuddering at the thought) called her "dear one" or something else sickeningly inappropriate.

But that all came to a crashing end when Charlotte (eleven), started lording her 'special powers' over Gwendolyn (seventy-one). Gwendolyn (Sr.) realized immediately how much Gwendolyn (Jr., circa 1939) would have despised Charlotte had such a ludicrous meeting ever happened. And yet there was something eerily familiar about Charlotte's bossiness and strident voice, and the child knew far too many details of Gwendolyn's life as a child to be discounted entirely.

Gwendolyn took another sip of her champagne and lifted her glass to show she wanted a refill, but the steward, or fly attendant or whatever they called themselves now, had disappeared. Likely hiding out in the washroom, the curtain drawn, until the aisle cleared and peace once again reigned.

"... brand new private *very exclusive* school where you have to be really, *really* smart to go ..."

Charlotte's voice had developed a presence of its own and delighted in emphatic flourishes merely, Gwendolyn knew, to torture her.

"... and Henry has already inputted the *entire* curriculum, so it doesn't matter if we should happen to miss the first day or week of school and *furthermore* ..."

Still, there was no sign of a body belonging to this constant blast of worthless information, and Gwendolyn began to wonder if life would ever be truly her own again. There was something completely wrong with Charlotte, but Leo refused to consider the help of a therapist. *'There is nothing wrong with Charlotte,'* Leo had said calmly, waving aside the suggestion of a "grandiosity complex" and refusing to ask what it even meant.

"... three *tons* of gravel to fill the stadium, and I personally believe that is ..."

What stadium? Gwendolyn wondered. She noticed a drop of something on black skirt. Champagne perhaps. She blotted at it with a handkerchief she carried, folded up, in the sleeve of her blouse.

"... Henry says that it could be done in a much simpler less *expensive* way, but no one will listen no matter how many letters I write. Do you want to know what I *really* think?"

48

Gwendolyn closed her eyes and pretended to be asleep. The voice was coming closer and soon there would be no avoiding a brief hello (very brief).

"... lots and lots of catching up to do because while Henry and me have only had four months to pull ourselves together, Sarah had over sixty years, so the way I figure it, she has more stories than I do although you'd be very surprised at the strange things that happen to me *every minute* of every day."

Gwendolyn shuddered because she knew this was true. The Sarah she remembered never stopped talking, and it gave her a headache imagining that non-stop raspy voice warring with Charlotte's hysterical, high-pitched shrieking.

"... will be attending a large and extremely *famous* theatrical academy in London where Henry and I have recently gained admittance and furthermore ..."

This was news to Gwendolyn. When had Henry and Charlotte received admission to the (no account, decrepit) theatre school that Sarah ran out of the back of a drop-in centre for juvenile delinquents? Did this mean Gwendolyn would have to pay to have the two of them air bused back and forth across the Atlantic every weekend so they could participate in acrobatics or tight rope walking or whatever current craze Sarah deemed necessary for the development of a true thespian?

And more to the point, what was a woman in her nineties doing still working? Why was she not bedridden and demanding and crotchety as Gwendolyn knew she would be when she assumed the role of a nonagenarian? Hadn't Sarah chain smoked? Gwendolyn remembered trailing stinking lines of whitish grey following Sara wherever she went. By all accounts she should be long dead.

"...*killed* in the war, shot down and presumed dead which was totally unfair because he was the *best* person and very funny, and he taught Henry and Lucas how to drive his roadster, not to *mention*..."

Why was Charlotte still talking? The line had stalled, and the first class compartment had become congested with people who smelled like a combination of ripe apples and blue cheese. Everyone within hearing range of Charlotte had a desperate look in their eye.

Gwendolyn knew that feeling only too well.

"...can't come because she is eight months pregnant – with *twins*, by the way, and it's dangerous to fly, which is hardly a valid reason because if the babies decide to arrive over the Atlantic, Henry and me could take care of it. Do you have any idea how *many* times we've had to deliver babies?"

Gwendolyn felt she might expire from embarrassment, but so far no one had connected her to Charlotte. Quickly eliminating her decision to greet Charlotte with a brief hello, Gwendolyn decided she would pretend she didn't know the child.

"...once in the middle of a sandstorm in the Mohabush Desert where you could *barely* see the fingers in front of your face. If it's a boy and a girl they'll be called Charlotte and Henry. Two boys will be Charles and Henry and two girls will be Charlotte and Henrietta, and we'll be babysitting after school and on the weekends and *whenever* school is closed which is almost *always* because, as I already mentioned, we are attending a *very* exclusive private school which means the school is closed more often than it is open. Henry has inputted our time off, and get this, we are in school for only 123 days out of 364. If you round that out into weeks and then months, which is a mathematical exercise I have *mastered*, that means we are in school less than half a year, which, by the way, I think is far too *long* to be cooped up in a building reading books and holding discussion groups, when it is imperative – that's a new word I learned yesterday, I learn twenty new words a week – to be out and about in the world..."

Why had Gwendolyn ever allowed herself to be bullied into allowing Charlotte to have a coffee?

This gross error in judgement had been the fault of the security clerk, who had insisted that Gwendolyn empty her purse so the woman could paw through all the tiny, impeccably packed, pale blue Longchamp bags that she had placed into a larger black Longchamp bag used exclusively for travelling.

"You label these bags?" the odious woman had asked, looking at the bold type which stated clearly: Cleaning Products. "Amazing."

And then she had proceeded to unzip every single one and comment, unnecessarily, on Gwendolyn's good taste and judgement.

"Most purses? Heaped with garbage," she said, laying on the counter Gwendolyn's travel toothbrush and small tube of Sensodyne. "One thing thrown on top of another. If their purses look like that, I know what the inside of their houses look like." She closely inspected three tubes of Chanel lipstick, nodding her head in appreciation of the label marked: Cosmetics. "Clothes thrown all over, dirty dishes, nothing swept, filthy cat litter, mail piling up."

Steering her body immediately to the first class lounge after this insult to her sensibilities (the crush of tourists in the cavernous arena of Pearson International had given her heart palpitations) Gwendolyn had swept through the entrance imperiously, demanding, at once, a private room and a warm fragrant towel. There were no such privileges to be had, she was told, but a table by the window could be arranged.

Gwendolyn shook her head in disbelief. What had happened to luxury travel? It had disappeared overnight, she decided, even though it had been over twenty years since she had set foot out of Toronto. Mercifully, Dragos had checked in for her, and disposed of her luggage while she had fanned herself with a linen handkerchief and tried to ignore Charlotte. The girl's eyes had been as big as saucers as she'd spun in circles, her arms wide, trying to take it all in when Gwendolyn wanted nothing more than to shut it all out.

As Gwendolyn began the long walk towards the area of least habitation, the odious attendant stopped her by the sharpness of his expression. "Aren't you forgetting something, Madam?" he asked, smirking.

Smirking!

British Airways would hear about this.

"The children?" he asked, his eyebrows lifted.

And there at the doorway stood Henry and Charlotte, both looking like they had arrived from some orphanage with no one on hand to greet them.

"Put them in the children's section, please." she requested, barely giving them a glance.

"There is no such place, Madam, and children must be accompanied by an adult at all times."

Gwendolyn beckoned with her fingers, and Charlotte raced to her side, Henry arriving once he got his feet to pay attention to what his brain was trying to tell them.

She had no memory of ordering a coffee for Charlotte, but then no one ordered anything in the first class lounge because it was self-serve. She rejected everything on display except a cup of Earl Grey tea for herself and a glass of skim milk for Henry (who looked like a glass of skim milk himself, all pale and slightly blue around the edges).

There had been nothing on that tray for Charlotte because Charlotte was already being punished for being difficult and loud and insensitive and rude, and when Gwendolyn had arrived back at her corner table, Henry carrying the tray and spilling half her tea and most of his skim milk, there, as if by magic, was an oversized cup of espresso with a mountain of frothed milk. Charlotte had downed it in two seconds, burning her throat and gagging, all before Gwendolyn had time to adjust to her uncomfortable seat and tell Henry to find some napkins to clean up the mess he made.

There had not been a word of thanks before Charlotte had dashed off to purchase some totally unsuitable Hello Kitty garbage, a pair of sunglasses resembling the CN tower, and a gossip magazine concerning what fools the royalty had currently made of themselves so that Charlotte could speak with assurance and knowledge when introduced to the queen.

Who on earth was she kidding?

If Charlotte was able to sneak by the thousands of armed guards standing sentry day and night outside Buckingham Palace, it would be a matter of mere seconds before she was discovered writing graffiti on the wallpaper adorning the entranceway, and she would be stuffed into prison and Gwendolyn would be called upon to bail her out.

Gwendolyn had no intention of intervening on Charlotte's behalf.

"Get your feet off the table," she had said.

And then Charlotte had screamed because their plane was boarding and Gwendolyn had missed her chance to get on first – age, class, and money dictating who set feet first on the thin tubular structure that sucked people on board the Boeing 747 – and she had to settle for being second in line.

"… two hardboiled eggs, six minutes so the yolk is not hard as a rock, and *homemade* mayonnaise, not that bottled kind although that stuff is okay on turkey sandwiches… wait a *minute*, just a minute here! How come you have two seats?"

Gwendolyn opened her eyes and there before her was Charlotte's face and the rest of her body. Both were taking up far too much of Gwendolyn's air space and she sank back in her chair, the groan of the leather blotting out, for a brief second, the grating sound of questions, questions, questions.

"You're holding up the line, dear," Gwendolyn told her sternly, fanning the air furiously with her hand. Charlotte smelled like a mixture of spun sugar and chili peppers. "Move on. There's a good girl."

"How 'bout I stop here instead?" Charlotte clambered over Gwendolyn's legs and sat down on the vacant seat near the window – but first she brushed the shawl, glasses, and wipes to the floor. "Save me a seat," she said to Henry.

"We have assigned seats," he said, staring at the boarding pass in his hand. "I'm forty-nine J. I think we might be sitting together but let me check your pass. There's a million seats back there." He peered into the distance and blinked. "You'll never find me."

"I don't have a pass," Charlotte said nonchalantly. "Or if I did, I lost it."

"Give me that," Gwendolyn said, picking up her cashmere shawl. "You have a boarding pass, Charlotte, or they would not have let you on the plane."

Charlotte spilled the contents of her Hello Kitty backpack onto her lap and Gwendolyn had to look away. A sea of gum wrappers, pebbles, sticks, hairbands, used Kleenex, a huge First Aid box with the word Essentials labelled in Charlotte's messy script, and God knew what else. After digging through the litter, Charlotte produced a boarding pass, quickly folded it into a paper airplane, and sailed it in Henry's direction.

"Forty-nine K," she called out.

Henry was getting swept past first class by a tidal wave of tourist passengers. Gwendolyn could have sworn Henry stared at her accusingly, but it was a normal feature of his eyes, magnified twice their normal size by the glasses he wore. Henry was legally blind, but he managed to get around just fine, thank you very much, and did not carry a stick, much to his credit. Gwendolyn approved of grit in the face of adversity. Never having to suffer such herself, she admired those who did.

"We can visit once the plane is aloft, Charlotte," Gwendolyn told her, watching the child put every piece of rubbish back into the garish bag Gwendolyn was talked into buying. "I need to get my bearings and review our travel itinerary, perhaps close my eyes for a minute or two, and then I will get permission for you and Henry to sit with me for ten minutes."

"How come you didn't get us all seats side by side?" Charlotte asked.

"As you can see, there are only two seats in a row here and it is much more comfortable for children to sit in the back of the plane."

Charlotte scratched her neck until it started to bleed. "Mosquitos," she explained.

Gwendolyn gave her a tissue. There was no thank you, just the typical grab as if she were entitled to this attention.

"You have two seats and Henry and me can fit in this one just fine."

"That seat is booked."

"There's no one in it except me."

"The passenger might be late, and board at the last minute."

"I'd believe you if I didn't know you booked both those seats for yourself. Gwendolyn MacFarlane, row 5, seats A and B."

"Have you been going through my purse, Charlotte?" Gwendolyn held her champagne glass aloft but there was still no one around wearing a uniform who could fill it.

"That's a terrible thing to say. Why would I do that? I saw those tickets in your hand when you stood up and left us behind in that arena back there. I can read upside down," she added proudly.

"Bully for you. Now go."

To the child's credit she did not say if it wasn't for her, they wouldn't be going to England and Gwendolyn would be sitting in her penthouse apartment in Toronto all alone with no family and no friends. The quiet of the penthouse apartment seemed particularly appealing now.

"*Bully for you* is something they say in England. Henry has a whole list of expressions and we have been practicing them. We both want to fit in and not be treated like foreigners. They drive on the other side of the road and the subway is called the Underground or Tube and people say righty-o quite a bit."

Perhaps, when the plane reached London, Gwendolyn could re-board another plane, under cover of pretending to freshen up in the washroom and fly back to Toronto. She could leave Charlotte and Henry in the extremely capable hands of Sarah, a woman far more persistent and devious than Gwendolyn could ever pretend to be. Maybe the children would never come home and take up permanent residence with Sarah and her daughter and Peabody, that yappy little dirty bearded terrier, would join them (courtesy of Gwendolyn's deep pocketbook). And then the serene, non-eventful life that Gwendolyn had so carefully crafted for herself would return, and wrap itself around her with the comfort and warmth of a greatly-loved blanket.

But then she would never hear what happened to Charlie, her long-lost brother.

'I'll tell you the whole story when you arrive, Gwendolyn,' Sarah had said, long-distance, the minutes ticking by flashing very large dollar signs. Sarah's voice had been deep and scratchy after a million years of cigarette smoking, but it had lost none of the famous resonance that had so cowed and angered the young Gwendolyn – whom nobody loved, not even her father who was supposed to love her. Or her mother who deserted her by dying so young. Or Charlie who treated her with the contempt only an older brother can show. And poor Gwendolyn, the smartest, kindest child in the universe, was alone. Completely alone.

"You are giving me a headache," Gwendolyn complained, willing Charlotte to disappear and never return. She folded her shawl and aligned it across her knees.

"Righty-o," Charlotte said. "I'll be back."

How would she survive this? Gwendolyn wondered. At least she wouldn't be staying with Sarah. Gwendolyn had booked herself a suite at the Savoy in the city of Westminster, and had arranged for a driver to ferry her here and there when she felt like visiting her relatives and not the other way around. Gwendolyn needed to arrive and depart on a moment's notice, and she felt no need to alter a lifetime's habit just because she had suddenly found she had relatives when she assumed she had none.

She fought with and overcame the desire to organize the contents of her purse. She had performed this job three times already since leaving her penthouse, and there was nothing in it left to throw out. Instead, she mentally straightened the tie on the man sitting to her left on the aisle and mopped the drops of champagne he had spilled on his tray. Why did people not see the mess they created around themselves? Had they no self-respect? Gwendolyn prided herself on order and neatness, for it was within these measures she found contentment. When she died, she imagined the look of surprise and gratitude on the faces of the cleaning service the condominium would employ on her behalf. "She was so clean and tidy," one of the men would say, looking around in amazement. "A real lady," another would say.

Nothing out of place and no loose ends. The credo by which Gwendolyn lived her life.

Except for the "new" family she found herself burdened with.

Upon reflection, her life had been easier when she had been unencumbered with familial obligations. Her husbands (both hideous mistakes) had departed her presence rather early in the relationship, preferring death to the forceful superiority of person she habitually inhabited. Gwendolyn couldn't help who she was, she had said on numerous occasions, and the thought of changing had never once entered her mind.

Gwendolyn firmly believed that most people were terrified of being alone. This fear, if unchecked and left to run wild, escalated with age – and resulted in a legion of bewigged and wrinkled elders choosing some dreadfully unsuitable partner largely because they were frightened of entering a museum or a restaurant on their own.

Pathetic!

Gwendolyn existed in a different universe, a serene and happy place. Until now.

From the Hilroy of Charlotte
Lisa Hansen

DATE: MONDAY, AUGUST 30
TIME: 10:22 PM
LOCATION: At the window of a British Airways 747 (SEAT 49 K, Henry is beside me in 49 J)
NOTES: Seatbelt signs are lit, and our trays are in an upright position. Luckily, I am adept at writing on my lap.

Before the plane roared those mighty engines and started to roll down the runway the man in 49 L looked at Henry and me and said: "Where are you parents?"

Henry said: "In Romania."

And I said: Dead.

He requested a seat change immediately, so now Henry and me have three seats in which to lounge, eat, fight, and discuss essentials for many, many pleasant hours.

Once aloft, which took far too much time in my estimation and caused my ear channels to block and my body to feel like it was being crushed into itself, we reached cloud level and evened off, allowing me to blow my nose strenuously (new word) until the channels unblocked with a loud pop. I had to press my feet against the seat in front of me for leverage and received a nasty look from the woman in occupation. I braced for another round of questions, but I don't think she could properly see me, as she kept squinting and telling me to cut it out or she was going to report me to some authority who patrols the narrow aisles of the plane.

Impression: Being on a plane is rather like being in school. There are all these rules which are ridiculous, and people are forced to sit far too close to one another and try to get along. I explained that my ear tubes were blocked and launched into the beginning of a story about why I was on the plane and my very important mission. She held up a hand (exactly like school again) and told me she was not interested and to stop pressing against her chair or I would be in trouble.

Henry deserted shortly after our dinner trays were taken away. Before that, he stared straight ahead and seemed to be projecting something on the back of the seat in front of him. Since I do not have this peculiar eidetic memory that he has I was unable to read what was invisible, so I punched and prodded him for a while, ate my dinner, threw up in this neat little brown bag, and got comfortable by taking off my shoes.

Henry put away whatever unseen material he was reading and told me he wanted to talk to Gwendolyn but would not tell me why. I suspect he is asking Gwendolyn to loan me money because he refuses to do so and ALL because I want to do the decent thing and buy a bottle of Shalimar perfume for Sarah. It's not like the money is for ME.

I decided not to follow him as I had serious work to do, deciphering one of the journals of my long dead Great Uncle Gus Frank for clues regarding my job once we hit the town of London, England. His penmanship is appalling, and the pages are paper thin and stained brown and yellow and black (I don't want to know why – even though I need to know everything).

Interesting point here: Dilys told Leo that her father never kept journals because he couldn't write properly, whatever that means. Not true. I happened to find a pile of disintegrating journals hiding behind a stone, which I removed by accident, in the basement wall of our house. Why were these journals stuffed in a cavity where mice could eat them? Was Gus embarrassed at his poor penmanship? Baloney. Even if he should have been, nothing embarrassed Gus, who, I am told, lived exactly the way he wanted to live and which I strive to do on an hourly if not minutely basis.

My job, among many, is to decipher this journal and find out what I did wrong and how to make it right. Not that I care that much about Gwendolyn. I care about learning my trade, because I suspect I will be travelling for the rest of my life.

Chapter Five

The euphoria that had overcome Gwendolyn when she realized that Sarah was still alive and that she and Charlie had had a child, and this child – her niece, she supposed – had her *own* child, and *that* child was now expecting two more children… well, that euphoria had vanished utterly, leaving Gwendolyn little more than a prisoner in the first class compartment of an airplane that had clearly seen better days.

She had no intention of living out the rest of her days a puppet of Charlotte's manufacture, pretending to be grateful for the sudden appearance of some ramshackle family who would beg, wheedle, cajole and demand her time, her energy, and worst of all – her money.

This was a mess she had been unable to untangle, principally because she had *promised* (the real Gwendolyn cared nothing about promises) and subsequently been threatened with the removal of her very small comforts; Dragos and his limousine, and Leo and his baking. The utterly false Gwendolyn pretended to believe (weakened by Charlotte's insistence) that she had first met Charlotte and Henry in the summer of 1939, when she, Gwendolyn, had been eleven years old, the same age as the terrifying children who now sat in the back of this ancient, creaking airplane.

Charlotte had forced Gwendolyn (temporarily unbalanced by the reappearance of an heirloom brooch lost for more than sixty years) to recognize that this totally unsupportable fairy tale was the truth and, furthermore, that Peabody's flea-ridden body housed the spirit of Lukas, a rather nondescript, shy, easily manipulated little boy that Gwendolyn had pretended to like but really used as a personal slave when they all lived together in Rose Park before the start of the Second World War.

When Gwendolyn had met and closely questioned the young woman who was in possession of the Tree of Life brooch, she had to believe that *something* strange was afoot – because Charlie, her older brother whom she had mostly despised when she was a child, was indeed grandfather to Celeste (totally *ridiculous* name). Sarah had looked and looked and looked for Gwendolyn, Celeste had told her, but she had disappeared without a trace. The real Gwendolyn didn't believe that either. The real Gwendolyn believed that, if Sarah had wanted to find her, she could have.

It didn't matter that a far younger version of the real Gwendolyn (who now sat uncomfortably in her phony leather chair in first class) had destroyed every letter Sarah had written to her and refused to answer. Because she was punishing Sarah for deserting her, and punishing Charlie and her father for dying and leaving her alone.

Upon attaining her twenty-first birthday and the sizeable inheritance she received from her nine-years-dead father (who had always loved Charlie more even though he wasn't even Charlie's *real* father) Gwendolyn had left Canada in a pique of defiance to live in France, England, Switzerland, New Zealand, Australia and other countries whose names she could not remember.

The real Gwendolyn was mulling through all these details as she removed, with a fake silver fork, tiny morsels of the dinner put before her. She had no idea what time it was up here in the nether, but she was sure it was changing back and forth every second.

A morsel of *foie gras*, a taste of carrot, a sliver of beef tenderloin and she was full. She arranged her tray in perfect order, wiped her fork clean, folded her napkin and dearly wished she could open the window and dispose of the tray so she no longer had to look at it.

People ate far too much and never knew when to stop.

The real Gwendolyn did not believe in letting herself go just because she was old. She weighed the same now as she had when she was forty and the world had been before her. Well, it might have been before her, but the world turned out to be just one huge disappointment after another, and she couldn't shake the feeling that these new relatives were going to be the same.

She bent gracefully from the waist and sent her fingers exploring until they located the handle of her purse. She moved the purse so that it nestled against her right foot. A person had to keep their belongings close, otherwise there was no telling what could happen.

Upon reflection, Gwendolyn realized she had never liked Sarah, all those long, tedious years ago when Sarah had been her *tutor* – please! Gwendolyn had always been far smarter than anyone she knew, and that included Sarah, who had been foisted on the family because she was a friend of Charlie's. Gwendolyn immediately got Sarah's number. Sarah was bossy, controlling, and superior, and now, firmly ensconced in her nineties, these unacceptable personality traits would issue out of the wrinkled mouth of a now imperious and impossible to please elder.

Gwendolyn did not approve of the license people took when they became senior citizens and believed that most, if not all, should be shut away – so as not to run over the unsuspecting with their motorized wheelchairs and walkers and sense of entitlement gained merely because they had outlived their friends.

All the better she had her own suite of rooms and a driver. Perhaps she wouldn't even visit her new relatives. Mercifully, Henry and Charlotte had been offered rooms in the house where Sarah and her family lived and would be off Gwendolyn's hands as well. She could spend her time leisurely strolling the streets of London, have high tea every day, buy whatever she wanted, go to the real Sotheby's (not the facsimile that existed in Toronto) and perhaps, if the mood overtook her, purchase an apartment to house her during the visits she would never make.

A vibration in the air caused Gwendolyn to look up and over.

Henry was standing in the aisle, staring at her.

"Are you alright, Henry?" Gwendolyn asked.

He looked rather sick, but then Henry never looked any different. Henry had many free-floating problems, near blindness, anxiety, a crippling kind of paralysis that made him resemble a poorly made statue, but the most significant, according to Charlotte, was his refusal to allow events to unfold in their proper time and to be present to the moment. Charlotte was soaring across the Atlantic with a Hello Kitty backpack and an old laundry bag as her only luggage, while Henry had a vintage *American Tourister* to which his parents

61

had affixed brass cornices and a leather strap, a suitcase that was almost as large as he was, plus a briefcase, a black facsimile medical bag carrying essentials – in the event his *Tourister* flew on to Shanghai without him.

Gwendolyn knew this because Charlotte told her while Gwendolyn tried to organize her own packing.

"Do you really need all these suitcases?" Charlotte had asked, lounging on Gwendolyn's pristine white couch and sucking on a tube of paper that housed sugar flavoured powder.

Odious, odious child.

"Henry?" Gwendolyn asked, starting to feel concerned. All she needed was for one of her charges to develop malaria or fall apart completely. Henry looked like he was having some deep crisis and if this was the case, she would turn him over to one of the uniformed personnel flitting about the plane and pretend she didn't know him.

"I'm fine," Henry said in a monotone, blinking rapidly to ground himself. "Charlotte ate too much, got sick, and is now getting ready to work, or at least that's what she said."

"Work?" Gwendolyn asked, raising an eyebrow. "On what?"

Henry shrugged. Even though Charlotte was his best friend and he cared what happened to her (more or less) there were times – many – when he could not stand to be close to her. "She probably just wants to sleep but won't admit it."

Gwendolyn glanced at her watch, a diamond encrusted Panthère de Cartier she had purchased for herself a year ago because she felt she deserved a present and ascertained they had been aloft for merely two hours. It felt like two decades, and they still had six hours before they reached their destination. Gwendolyn straightened her back.

"How curious."

Charlotte never slept, or so she said. She was far too busy travelling, at breakneck speed, in and out of different decades and bothering people who simply wanted to be left alone.

Henry stared at something to the right of Gwendolyn's head.

"She ate all her dinner and then she ate mine and then she said she didn't feel so good and threw up in that brown bag that was hanging off the back of the chair in front of her and then…"

"That's enough, Henry." Why did people insist on all these unnecessary details? Yes and No were respectable, uncluttered answers to almost any question asked. "You've said enough," she told him. People would eat anything put in front of them and Gwendolyn could not understand how most managed to survive. "Why don't you sit down for a moment?"

"May I?"

The boy had been raised properly; Gwendolyn had to admit that. He never presumed and waited to be asked.

"Thank you," Henry said, sliding into the seat and sitting on the edge as if he suspected he might be ejected at any moment. "I promised Charlotte I would ask you a question."

Gwendolyn sighed deeply and braced herself.

"I don't really want to ask but I promised."

"Well, then, Henry, carry on. A promise is a promise."

"Charlotte wants to know if she can borrow fifty pounds." This was the truth, but Henry knew Charlotte had forgotten it the minute she asked. Asking people for money was standard Charlotte behaviour.

"No, she cannot." Gwendolyn took a sip of champagne. Charlotte had no concept of the value of money, nor did she understand that people who possessed it in great quantity were loath to give it away.

"That's what I told her you would say," Henry replied in his careful monotone. "She wants to buy a bottle of perfume she saw in the duty-free catalogue as a gift for Sarah. Shalimar Eau de Parfum," he added, consulting his eidetic memory. Her excitement upon locating this tiny glass bottle in the in-flight magazine had disturbed all three people sitting in front of them. But then dinner arrived, she ate far too fast, vomited, and seemed to forget all about the perfume.

"Charlotte has money," Gwendolyn told Henry. "If she wishes to waste it on a bottle of perfume that no one will use, that is her business." Gwendolyn knew Charlotte had money. Her grandfather Leo had given her fifty pounds to spend at her discretion. Fifty pounds was an outrageous sum of money to be entrusted to one whose approach to anything monetary was extremely cavalier.

"Charlotte must learn to temper her desires. I have spent a lifetime doing the same, and it has brought me nothing but contentment." Gwendolyn stated clearly, spiking an errant piece of dust, lodged into the seam of the leather seat, with her painted fingernail. "Do you enjoy the opera, Henry?" she asked.

"I have no idea, but I think I probably wouldn't like it," Henry responded immediately. "My father says opera is like life magnified a thousand times, and the screaming gets on his nerves."

Gwendolyn chuckled. Henry had given the perfect response. He had no pretentions whatsoever, which, if she were honest, was the only thing she admired about children. They didn't care who they impressed, and they were politically incorrect all the time. She and Henry would have a wonderful time in London and perhaps together, they would ignore Sarah and family completely.

Gwendolyn lifted her hand imperiously beckoning the airline attendant to approach.

"Steward," she announced, "the boy will have his meal now. Perhaps a sausage and a glass of water. Does that sound good, Henry?"

"I don't want a sausage, thank you. I want what she had," Henry said, pointing at Gwendolyn's plate. He was hungry because he refused to eat the food they served to him in the back of the plane. He could not identify the animal from whence it came and it smelled ripe, like the barnyard at Riverdale Park. "That looks like liver paste, and I love liver paste."

"Get the boy what he wants," Gwendolyn directed, waving her hand dismissively. She adjusted the cuffs on her blouse until aligned symmetrically, a millimetre above her bony wrists. "And a ginger beer. Do you like ginger beer, Henry?"

Ginger beer sounded very British, so Henry nodded in agreement.

"We don't usually serve children *foie gras*, Madam, as the dish is very rich, and children have a tendency to get sick."

"Just get the boy his dinner," Gwendolyn said sharply. "Whatever he doesn't eat we'll just pass along to Charlotte."

Gwendolyn used her napkin to remove every crumb from her tray, motioned for the attendant to remove her dinner, and demanded a hot towel at once. She held her hands aloft until the attendant returned and then proceeded to scrub her fingers until they turned red.

64

"Once Charlotte wakes up and finds I'm missing, she will tear the plane apart. On the other hand," Henry said reflectively, "she does have work to do. I think she is probably trying to decipher one of Gus Frank's old journals that Leo gave her."

"Gus Frank?" Gwendolyn dove into her memory and emerged with the picture of a dissipated old drunk who once burned her (and not by accident, as her dear mother had said) with the tip of his cigar. She had been taken by her mother – *dear Mother, how I miss you still,* her brain repeated for the millionth time – to the Frank residence so she could have her photograph taken by the creepy, fat, gin-swilling old man.

The portrait of her with her mother was Gwendolyn's most prized possession. The only photograph she had of her mother, and although she wanted to hate the old man (Gwendolyn's grudges never went away, for they improved and ripened with age like vintage wine) she was beholden.

"Gus Frank is Dilys Frank's father and Charlotte's second or third cousin twice removed."

"And who is Dilys Frank?" Gwendolyn knew *exactly* who Dilys Frank was because Charlotte mentioned her name at least five times a day. But she pretended ignorance for her own amusement. She wanted Henry to understand that, although she was involved in their little time travel game, she was also removed from it.

Henry remained silent, staring inwardly with his strange, crossed eyes. And sighed.

Gwendolyn hated people who sighed.

"Dilys is Charlotte's great aunt," Henry explained patiently.

"I know," Gwendolyn replied peevishly. "But what I don't comprehend is why Leo gave Charlotte a journal written by a con man. You realize, don't you, Henry, that Gus Frank said he won that house in a poker game, but did he? Do Leo and Charlotte really own the house they live in? Imagine being turned out at Leo's age. Where would he go? What would he do? I'm not concerned with Charlotte. She is a survivor. But Leo? Oh, it's too dreadful to consider."

"A Frank has been in attendance in that house for seventy years. They have squatters' rights. I don't think there is any reason to be concerned,"

Henry replied mechanically, parroting the words he had been taught by Charlotte.

Gwendolyn spent a moment gazing out the window. The cloud formations below looked the same as the ones they had passed over ten minutes previously: large, disorganized masses of gauzy white with disquieting irregular black lines zig and zagging across the surface. Was the plane flying to London, or was it frozen in time, steadily maintaining altitude above the same endless stew of thickly layered gaseous outbursts (what were clouds anyway – Henry would know) merely to torture her?

Gwendolyn felt a shiver of fear. What if Charlotte was busy orchestrating some other trip to the past, a trip that Gwendolyn wanted to go on about as much as she wanted to go to England?

"What are clouds, Henry?" she asked, fiddling with the handkerchief in her lap. She noticed creases in the fabric that had not been there before and tried to iron them out with her fingers.

"Excuse me?"

"You heard me. If ever I knew I have forgotten."

Henry spent a moment paging through his eidetic memory for the dictionary definition of clouds. He recited: "A cloud is a visible mass of condensed water vapour floating in the atmosphere, typically high above the ground."

"Look at that," Gwendolyn said in satisfaction, forcing Henry to peer out the window. "Your words transformed into reality."

Of course, they *weren't* his words, but Henry smiled modestly.

"I would like to plan our time together, Henry," Gwendolyn told him, pulling a large day planner out of her bag. She extracted a gold pen from the second smallest Longchamp bag in her purse and readied it above the page. "We will go to Covent Gardens. At least once. Just the two of us. It won't be necessary to invite Sarah or the rest of the entourage."

"I don't have the proper clothes," Henry protested.

"Not to worry, Henry. I will outfit you. Tuxedo, cummerbund, black patent leather shoes. Perhaps a top hat."

Henry's shoulders slumped in defeat and then, after a curious moment spent staring at the back of the seat in front of him, he said with relief:

"Convent Gardens is closed for renovations."

"No." Gwendolyn breathed in sharply through her nose and exhaled through her mouth. "How do you know this, Henry? Surely you are wrong."

"I'm not wrong," he stated. "I've memorized most of the Fodor's guide I found in my parents' library."

Gwendolyn, who had done no preparation for her trip besides organizing her clothes and jewels, was deeply disappointed. She plucked, kneaded, and ironed her skirt with her fingers.

"How come you are always straightening things?"

"Whatever do you mean, Henry?"

"I notice you do it in your penthouse when I am working in the office. You come in and ask me if I want a glass of water and then you adjust the lamp shade or fluff the cushions on the chair or set all the figurines at right angles. You're doing it now," he said, watching Gwendolyn adjust her Day-Timer exactly in the middle of her tray. If Henry had a ruler on his person, he was willing to bet the book was centred to within a millimetre on either side.

"I take pride in my possessions, Henry. Very few people respect the space in which they reside and treat all objects that come within their reach with careless disregard. I pride myself on creating a tiny oasis of calm in a congested and noisy world." Gwendolyn stopped herself from readjusting the Day-Timer and willed her fingers to stop ironing her handkerchief. "You may return to your seat now, Henry. I would like to close my eyes."

"But I haven't gotten my liver paste yet. I think she forgot about me. Could you ring your bell?"

"When, and if, that person arrives I will direct her to your seat. Now go."

"Okay," Henry said, most agreeably for a boy who showed no emotion whatsoever. He did not say thank you nor did he say goodbye. He just stood up and left.

Gwendolyn was glad that Covent Gardens was closed. Henry did not deserve this special treat. No one had ever had the presumption to question her behaviour before, and she would not be felled by a small, insignificant, half-blind boy. She folded her handkerchief into concentric squares and placed it in the pocket of her purse.

Although she would never say this out loud, perhaps Henry had a point. She had noticed that if everything in her life was not perfectly arranged, she felt like screaming.

Or crying.

She wondered what Henry and Charlotte were doing in steerage, what they were discussing – *her,* no doubt. All her peccadillos and oddities and pretensions.

How *dare* they?

In a rush of rebellion, Gwendolyn upended her purse in her lap and felt a flutter of anxiety in her chest.

There was a used tissue caught in the neck of her glasses case that she had not thrown out.

Chapter Six

"If Gwendolyn won't give me the money to buy the perfume, then do you think you can talk her into buying it for Sarah?"

"No."

"Does that mean you won't even try?"

"Yes."

Charlotte lowered the arm rest that separated her seat from Henry's and moved closer to the window. She drew a heart and wrote her name and Sarah's on the inside, but it was invisible since there was no condensation.

"Don't you remember the way that Sarah used to smell?"

Henry's memory didn't record smells, tastes, sounds or emotional responses. He remembered Sarah was tall and skinny and smoked continuously and laughed like she really meant it. Other than that, his files presented no further information.

"Shalimar. She wore Shalimar. Leo told me. He is very good at recognizing perfumes. And look," Charlotte said, pressing the duty-free magazine into his lap. "There it is." A grubby finger tapped a picture of a perfume bottle. "I'm sorry I didn't think about it before we left because this is concrete proof, proof that *cannot* be denied, that we were with her in 1939. Imagine how impressed she will be that we remember."

Henry regarded the magazine with disinterest, closing the steel trap of his brain with determination, so that the items for purchase would not imprint themselves in his cranium, more useless rubbish to cart around daily.

"You could loan me the money."

"I could," Henry said reflectively. "But I don't want to. Besides, you have fifty pounds."

Charlotte bristled immediately. No one was allowed to bully her into spending her own money. "How do you know I have anything at all?" she asked.

"You told me." Henry said, reflecting, "You gloated about it."

Henry, frugality personified, had double that amount strapped to various parts of his anatomy and hidden in his luggage so that Charlotte could not get her hands on it, *plus* a letter of credit to Lloyds of London authorizing a thousand pounds to be put at his immediate disposal. This outrageous sum of invisible money was to assuage Henry's father's fears that Henry might be hit by a bus and linger in the public ward of some filthy hospital before word was sent out across the airwaves that his son was in trouble. The credit note, along with twenty-five pounds of 'mad money,' was stuffed into the toe of Henry's shoe. This was quite uncomfortable and, given the circumstances, totally Charlotte's fault. Also, to be on the safe side, an address was entrusted to Henry of a British citizen who would be able to contact Henry's parents through the Canadian Embassy in Romania (should such a place exist). This kind gentleman and his staunch wife ("not *at all* liked by the old mater") would look after Henry in the interim and give him shelter should his life be at risk.

Henry told Charlotte what he had observed during his twenty minutes with Gwendolyn and asked for her opinion.

"Why is she forever straightening and fussing and cleaning things that are already clean?"

"Do you mean it has taken you this long to figure out the obvious? Gwendolyn is weird. End of story."

Charlotte balanced her feet against the seat in front of her and stretched her legs, so her knees locked. A section of a face wearing dark glasses and a frown appeared immediately in the space between the chairs and before a word was spoken Charlotte lowered her feet and lifted her hands in apology.

"How many times have you bothered this person?" Henry asked curiously. The speed with which the face appeared, and the frown were all indicators that this was not the first time Charlotte acted like she was the only person in the universe.

"I don't know. Once or twice."

The area below Charlotte's seat was a landmine of rubbish: her Hello Kitty backpack, her sneakers, her coat, half eaten bags of Cheetos and Doritos, blanket, pillow, empty milk container. And that was just what was visible on the top layer. The notebook that Leo had given her was in her lap, and her fingers were tightly curled around the spine.

"Can I see that?" Henry asked.

"No," Charlotte replied, tucking the book beneath her thigh.

"Is that Gus Frank's travel journal?"

"It's one of ten journals," Charlotte said, correcting Henry with asperity. "This is a prediction of my future, Henry – and yours, too, should I decide to include you in my upcoming travels. But I need to absorb all the data first. These are *real* adventure stories and not the usual fictional garbage that you read. Besides, I happen to know that you will immediately make fun of the fact Gus can't spell."

A toddler, free from the restraint of the parental arms, careened down the aisle with an expression of delight. He burst past Henry like a cyclone.

"You can't spell either, so how would you even be able to tell?" Henry asked, feeling a breeze of stale air touch his face as the toddler passed.

"He spells the way I do, which is a very large indicator that we are related. Look," she said, peeling the notebook from beneath her thigh and thumbing through a couple of pages until she found what she was looking for. "Take a gander," she said, and Henry willed his face not to show a smile of satisfaction. Charlotte had no idea how easy she was to manipulate.

He backtracked at once when he tried to read the words on the page. The paper was yellow and brittle with age, there were indeterminate stains obscuring some of the print and a sharp astringent odour made Henry's eyes burn. Although Henry knew this was impossible, the words he was looking at and the way they were seared on the page, seemed to have a presence and personality usually not found on old pieces of paper.

He squinted, breathed through his mouth, and lowered his head closer to the page careful not to allow himself to be sucked into the vortex.

He managed to decode a fragment of a sentence:

Sandstorme hit at 23:00 hours no warnning and dug like a rat to make a whole but filed in fast like death preasurring my head near explosive...

"A Bedouin tribe was crossing the Sahara and Gus had to help deliver a baby – which if you consider the elements is pretty astonishing."

This narrative was not in evidence on the page, but Henry could only trust that Charlotte's ability to read Gus Frank's words far exceeded his own. It also explained Charlotte's cryptic remark to a total stranger that she had delivered a baby in the Sahara (or the Mohabush, which didn't exist). And he, Henry Jacobs, had been in attendance. She had mixed up her own fantasy experiences with Gus's fantasy experiences.

"Why was Gus there? Who was he helping?"

The only thing that Henry partly understood about the spooky business going on behind the walls of the Tower Room was this: if a person travelled back in time, it was strictly to help someone else. It had nothing to do with a nostalgic yearning to be in another time zone. It was all about service.

"I haven't gotten to that part yet. My relative is an emotional person, unlike you, and he needs to understand what he is feeling before he can launch into facts and figures."

Henry liked facts and figures. They were tangibles that a person could trust and respect.

"Once I translate Gus's entire text, I will let you in on a few secrets such as how to survive in an alien universe and, more importantly, the real purpose of this cross-century travel we will be doing quite a lot of in the future."

The flight attendant arrived with Henry's plate of foie gras and a blanket. Her eyelids were listing starboard, and Henry assumed she had just spent a few exhausting minutes with Gwendolyn.

"Your grandmother says you are to eat this slowly, and if you don't like it, you are to ask for a hotdog. I'm telling you right now we don't have hotdogs and if she hadn't threatened to alert my supervisor you wouldn't be getting this tray at all."

Charlotte leaned forward and poked her finger in the middle of the duck liver. "Ooh, it's good," she said. "You're going to love this, Henry. Try it."

With Charlotte's permission, Henry tasted a small piece of the liver. He moved his tongue slowly and felt his chest muscles tighten. This was not the liver paste he longed for. This was unnaturally rich, cloying and there was no way he could swallow it.

"Spit," Charlotte instructed, holding a napkin to his mouth. "Do you mind?" She asked, passing the soiled linen to the flight attendant.

"Could I be moved to another seat if she vomits again?" Henry asked, tugging on the flight attendant's sleeve. "I thought riding on a plane would be fun, but it's getting to be a chore."

"No," the attendant answered, dropping the soiled napkin on Charlotte's lap.

When she departed the two children shadowboxed over who had to dispose of the napkin (Henry lost) and the sliver of a face appeared once more in the space between the two chairs in front of them.

"I can't wait to see Sarah again. I've already talked with her three times."

"When?" Henry asked, angry that he was excluded from these conversations. He loved Sarah.

"The longest conversation we had was when you were out with your father buying new T-shirts."

"Did you call again from my house?"

"Of course. Leo can't afford transpacific calls."

Henry chose not to correct her. "You know I will be blamed."

"There's really nothing I can do about that, Henry."

"Jesus," he moaned, thinking he could get in a swift punch and then curl into the shape of a hedgehog before she had time to react – but the reminder of that ghostly face in the space between the two chairs mercifully saved him from acting.

He noticed that the lights had dimmed in the plane.

The couple to his right covered themselves with a blanket and lowered their seats as far as they would go. And then a minor skirmish broke out as to who had more of the blanket.

Occasional dots of light further ahead to his right indicated some were still watching movies, and above the hum of the engines, Henry imagined he heard the sighs and shifting seats of people determined to at least try and be comfortable.

Charlotte's voice droned on, but Henry barely listened.

"Maybe, just maybe," he thought he heard her say. "We are meant to move to London permanently, and we will transport Leo and the house and Peabody and establish ourselves like we've always lived there. Our purpose, Henry, will be presented to us, but so obscurely – that's a new word – that we will have to be hyper-alert to all the signs that we stumble across, so what I need you to do, Henry is…"

By the time Charlotte had finished listing all the jobs that Henry had to undertake to make sure they never left London, he was asleep.

Chapter Seven

A black, highly polished Rolls-Royce limousine slid to the curb at Heathrow International Airport. A baggage clerk wheeled his trolley towards the driver, who had exited his seat and was busy straightening the lapels of his livery jacket. Words were spoken, money changed hands, and a sticker was placed on the dashboard allowing the limousine to rest in place for an hour. Having transacted their business, the two very different attendants stared at the sky and commented on the quality of blue that was rarely seen.

"Warmer than usual," one said.

"Most agreeable," said the other.

"Think it might rain later?"

"Always a possibility."

"Picking up international, are you?" the first said, motioning to the doorway.

"One could argue that we are all international."

These utterings might have continued had the back door not been flung open, clipping the baggage attendant on the leg.

"I'm so very sorry, you'll please excuse me but, Grandfather, Sarah needs assistance."

An elderly head with wild dishevelled white hair poked through the open door, the rest of the body bent over in what appeared to be some type of internal crisis.

"Wheelchair?" the baggageman asked, snapping to attention. "Medico?"

"None of the above," the woman replied, wiping her eyes. "Unless Jeremy qualifies as an errant virus that must be contained. Honestly, Oliver," the woman said, exiting with the help of two pairs of hands. "He has to stop telling me jokes, or he'll be the death of me."

"I didn't think what I said was all that funny," Jeremy apologized, slipping his arm around Sarah's waist until she found her balance. "It was just the old chestnut about elephants having flat feet."

Sarah's nose tickled and she felt she might descend into the madness of out-of-control laughing once again. She ordered Jeremy to go inside the terminal and do reconnaissance, check the arrivals board, commandeer a chair and, if possible, locate and deliver two very strong cups of tea.

"I know that joke," Oliver said, walking Sarah slowly towards the sliding doors. "It's amusing, but only just."

Sarah agreed. "It's nerves, Oliver. Gwendolyn can do that to a person."

"Surely she has mellowed with age."

"I've already spoken with her. She has not."

Jeremy, semaphoring from the distance, was holding two chairs captive and urging his grandfather to hurry.

"Does he think someone will take the chairs away?" Sarah asked, peering into the distance.

"He's excited," Oliver said. "He has already assigned best friend status to both Charlotte and Henry." Oliver crossed two fingers of his right hand. "I hope this comes to pass because it is exactly what he needs."

The duo passed a young girl holding a bouquet of flowers. Unseen by her mother she was picking the petals, one by one, from a bunch of wilted daisies, and secreting them in her pocket.

Sarah caught the child's eye and grinned, but the child stared back, wide-eyed and expressionless.

"I don't know," said Sarah. "I have a bad feeling about this. I promised to look after these children, not lead them astray. After all, if it weren't for them, I would not be within minutes of meeting my old adversary. But it is some consolation that I will finally be able to honour Charlie's wishes and give her what he left behind."

"You believe that story, don't you, Sarah?" Oliver said, gently touching her hand. "You believe that you've met these children before."

Sarah stared off into the distance and her face became tranquil.

"Two children and an elderly man did arrive at the MacFarlane residence over sixty years ago when the house was in crisis. The elder, Leo, said he had been sent by a service to help in the kitchen, and why should anyone disbelieve him?"

"In those days, the means were limited on checking credentials, that is true."

"Besides, why would anyone want to? He was a gem and took over all meal preparation. The king and queen were to arrive in Toronto in less than a week. Gwendolyn's father was a man of standing in the community and expected to entertain. The only anomaly were the children. They had their own story of arriving by train and losing their luggage, and were found underneath the table in the summerhouse in a state of some disorientation. Charlotte maintained they were hiding, and who was I to disagree? I was a servant."

"You were never a servant," Oliver said, patting her hand.

"I've always been a servant, and I like my position, thank you very much. You only masquerade as one," she said stroking Oliver's jacket.

"I offer service. What could be more noble?" he answered calmly.

"As if," she sniffed. "It gives you great access to observe the human comedy. But to continue, the discrepancies or oddities of the trio's arrival increased once I got to know Charlotte. Gwendolyn hated her on sight and wanted her removed from the house, but she did not have the authority. Do you know," she mused, "Charlotte told me she once helped Amelia Earhart fold bandages at a hospital in Toronto?"

"Amelia," Oliver said with great fondness.

"Charlie's hero," Sarah added. "One of the great benefits of achieving the age I am now is the willingness to believe in what cannot possibly be true. For instance, how did I get to be so old? I never thought I would reach my current age, and yet here I am. Something that could not possibly be true has become a fact."

Sarah stared straight ahead at the arrival door and the opaque glass dividers remained closed. There were no shadowy signs of activity, and yet the arrivals board indicated that the plane from Toronto arrived twenty minutes ago.

"Yes, but our ages, our health, our thoughts, our well-being, are merely transitory realities which can change in the flash of a second. Perhaps I will stand up and fall over dead of a heart attack."

"You'd better not. If you leave me alone, you will be stuck in purgatory eternally."

Oliver chuckled. "And now you believe you will recognize the two children who will soon pass through the doors."

"I believe more in the existence of Henry and Charlotte than I do in some notion of where we will go when we leave our bodies behind. Many of the things that Charlotte confided to me on the telephone coincided with my own memories of long ago."

Sarah shifted in her chair and tried to get comfortable. Her muscles were weak, her bones fragile, and she accepted these signs of aging with equanimity and was never one to complain (as did so many of her contemporaries). She was an observer now, both of others and herself, and she indulged without guilt in habits and tastes that she had been told would shorten her life. Reaching inside her bag she unwrapped a Cadbury chocolate bar, broke off a piece and put it in her mouth. The sensation of the chocolate slowly melting on her tongue gave her deep satisfaction, and she broke off another square and offered it to Oliver. He accepted it good-naturedly, held the square between thumb and forefinger and then with a flick of his wrist popped it into his mouth.

Oliver scanned the waiting room for his grandson. "If he doesn't show up soon, I suppose I must go looking for him."

"Nonsense. He's exploring, just as you said. Do you wish me to raise my voice and call for him?"

"Please, no," Oliver replied, bowing his head and placing his hand on his chest. "I don't wish to frighten these poor souls who are waiting patiently. Why don't you finish telling me why you believe this strange story Charlotte told you?"

Sarah crossed her ankles and stretched her back. "Whether it was Charlotte's impassioned description of our time together, or some rearrangement of these tired old brain cells, something clicked, and I said to myself, *Sarah, how does this child know details of my life that she could never access unless she was there?*"

"For instance?" Oliver persisted when Sarah lapsed into an extended silent reverie.

"My performance in *The Sea Gull* on Toronto Island sixty years ago. The afterparty at Dilys Frank's cottage," she said ticking off items on her fingers.

"The taking down of those hateful anti-Semitic signs, the note she left Charlie when she found the brooch Gwendolyn had hidden. Charlie gave me that note, and I still have it, Oliver." Her voice was triumphant. "And I have asked to see an example of Charlotte's handwriting. If it matches, I need no other proof. And there is one other thing. How could she and Henry have recognized the brooch that Celeste was wearing? What child notices jewellery? They both saw it, they both acted. Ergo, they were present during my early years and how or why that is possible I do not know."

"Yes, but all those details could have been told to Charlotte and Henry by Gwendolyn – including the description of the brooch."

"I agree," Sarah conceded. "But why should the Gwendolyn I used to know confide any of these details to these children? And besides, there is still the note. Even putting the handwriting aside for the moment, Oliver, Charlotte knew of the note. Gwendolyn *certainly* didn't. By the way, you did cancel her reservation, didn't you?"

"I saw to that two days ago. I told you."

"And the car, you cancelled the car?"

"Yes. It's fortunate that Charlotte told you the plans Gwendolyn made, otherwise I don't know how you would have convinced her to stay in the cottage."

Sarah's eyes widened with delight. "Charlotte has always been a sneak and totally heedless to other people's privacy. I knew I could count on her to let me know if Gwendolyn was going to be staying off-site. Which," she added, poking Oliver in the stomach, "is another reason why I must have come across Charlotte in the past. How else would I know how she would behave?"

"There he is," Oliver said, standing abruptly and telling Sarah he would return.

Sarah watched as Oliver marched across the arrivals lounge and captured his grandson by putting his hand on his shoulder. Jeremy turned with an agreeable smile.

Oliver was a saint, Sarah thought, watching the reunion of grandfather and child. The same could not be said for the rest of his family members. Jeremy's parents had abdicated responsibility more than five years before, when they had both found spouses more to their liking and decided to settle in Scotland and Spain respectively. Oliver had stepped up when the boy had been left behind one too many times in a train station in Aberdeen, but he had neither the interest, patience, nor stamina to be anything more than a tolerant and kind guardian. Whatever outings Jeremy had enjoyed had been due to Sarah's interference. Otherwise, Jeremy spent his days in a stuffy public day school and his summers under the watchful eye of his fencing master or classics tutor.

Jeremy was clever rather than smart, an incendiary risk considering his other shortcomings, and it was Sarah who asked if Jeremy could miss a few days of school so that he could spend time with Henry and Charlotte.

"I was making enquiries about a bus tour through London," Jeremy explained to Sarah, his eyes wide with excitement. "I was about to purchase three tickets when he came and prevented me."

Jeremy flopped down in the seat beside Sarah and pointed an accusing finger at his grandfather.

"You have no money, Jeremy, and even if you did, it is an unnecessary expense. We have the limousine."

"Anybody can drive around in a limousine. How many people get to ride the bus?"

"More than you might think," Oliver answered, exasperated.

"Yes, but I just discovered that if you ride on the bus, you can get off and get back on whenever you want. It's a hop bus," he explained to Sarah, twisting in his chair. "You hop on and hop off whenever you want."

"As you can in a limousine, Jeremy."

"No, you can't," the boy pouted. "I can only get out when you stop, and you only stop when you want to stop, and how is that fair?"

"And how did fairness enter the equation, Jeremy?"

"Fairness is important," Jeremy declared, his eyes narrowing to slits. He leapt to his feet, widened his stance, and took a deep breath, his right hand placed over his heart. "Fairness embodies our very being, Grandfather. As a British citizen and a man of standing – although *you* steadfastly refuse to acknowledge you have any standing at all – you must find room in your heart for fairness on all levels, not just the ones you choose to embrace."

"You mean like the one you have chosen to embrace?"

"Make fun if you wish, but you would do well to remember this: Gordon Brown said that British history is defined by our belief in tolerance and liberty, and this comes from a commitment to fairness and fair play."

Oliver drummed his fingers on the back of the chair while Sarah beamed a smile at Jeremy. "I don't believe that our former Prime Minister meant this to refer to one's desire to get in and out of a limousine at will," he said.

"That's the thing about quotations, Grandfather," Jeremy said relaxing his stance and dropping his hand. "Quotes are merely a series of words strung together in a certain order, and while it is true that the words that make up the quote cannot be rearranged or refitted, like the spark plugs in your *limousine,* forgive the comparison, the meaning or essence derived from these words cohabitating, so to speak, is malleable, and as such can be applicable to a variety of situations and circumstances." He smiled smugly and tilted his head to the side, waiting for Oliver's response. It was a game the two played routinely and although scores were not kept Jeremy was usually a few points ahead of Oliver.

"Is it fair that you are excused from an entire week of school when all your classmates are not?"

"Of course, that's fair. Nobody else that I know has people visiting from abroad. Am I right, Sarah?"

Sarah refused to get too involved in Jeremy's debates. They were sparring matches between he and Oliver. A small dose of applause was all that was necessary. "On that point, I suppose you are – although I haven't interviewed any of your classmates, so I can only assume you are telling the truth," she said.

"But why would I lie? And more to the point, why would you want to talk with any of those tossers, Sarah? They would sneer at you behind your back because you are old and wear the bottoms of your trousers rolled," he quoted, the world's youngest Prufrock fan. "And they would never answer any question you asked because they would mime this charade back and forth, hands tucked behind their ears, and while they might *pretend* to be solicitous, what they would really do is take your arm and abandon you by the dumpster that's hidden behind the row of yew trees. You know the yew trees, right, Grandfather?"

Oliver nodded, but he was clearly unable to follow Jeremy's train of thought.

"They think I am blind, but I see all of it. These classmates of mine, Sarah, are mean and vicious and cruel and frankly, in my extremely humble position, they do not deserve to live." Jeremy's face had reddened, and his voice trembled with emotion. "They don't do good deeds. And fairness is not a word in their common vocabulary."

Sarah understood Jeremy's anger all too well. His classmates used him as a punching bag because he was different. As a Jew living in Toronto in the 1930s, there had been many doors closed to her. She took it as a challenge to get ahead no matter what and largely succeeded. Jeremy did not have to suffer religious persecution but only the *illusion* of poverty, with his grandfather a common chauffeur. Class, ethnic, and religious differences still percolated right below the surface of British society, and it was a challenge that Sarah knew Jeremy would meet with asperity.

Oliver said, "I will give some thought into allowing you and Henry and Charlotte to tour by bus one afternoon. Do you feel that is fair, Jeremy?"

"Oh, thank you, Grandfather," Jeremy gushed. "We will have the most marvellous time. I am well versed in British history, as you know, and there are many places of interest well off the beaten track."

"In exchange, Jeremy, I need you to remember what we have discussed. It is important that our guests do not know any of our particulars. There's a reason behind this, isn't that correct, Sarah?"

"It is," she said. She stood up and walked a few steps forward to ease the pain in her joints. "It's a charade. Rather like one of the exercises you do so well on Saturday mornings at the theatre."

"I am perfectly capable of keeping a secret, thank you very much, Grandfather. You are a humble servant, and I am the boy who is always lurking about – but it will be difficult for me to maintain the proper air of subservience that may be required. I'm thinking more in the lines of a savant, a very bright person who has no social awareness whatsoever."

"I think that will be fine, Jeremy. You can assist with the luggage."

"I am terribly strong," he said flexing a muscle in his arm that put in a brief appearance before deflating. "Leave it to me. Oh, look," he said, excitement raising his voice an octave. "They are soon to appear, Grandfather."

The doors of the departure lounge slowly opened, and an elegant woman with a disdainful look walked forward slowly, blinking under the harsh fluorescents.

"Is that her?" Jeremy asked, dancing on the balls of his feet.

Oliver glanced at Sarah for confirmation and saw the slight nod of her head.

"Are you certain this is a good idea, my dear?" he asked softly.

"I'm too old to consider the consequences, Oliver. We are pushing on with the plan no matter what." She lifted a hand in greeting and walked forward slowly, seeing not the older Gwendolyn, but the brash and rude youngster who had enlivened her life so many long years past.

Gwendolyn came to a dead stop just beyond the sliding glass door, inconveniencing those who were eager to move forward and greet friends and relatives or just get the hell out of Dodge. Sarah's pace had slowed considerably, and there was still a great distance to be closed before she came near enough to Gwendolyn to offer her hand.

"It's like predators in the jungle, Grandfather," Jeremy whispered, keeping his distance when he saw Sarah's hand motion him back.

"Contain yourself, Jeremy," Oliver suggested, placing his hand on the boy's shoulder. "We are here to assist Sarah, not cause a scene."

Gwendolyn slowly advanced, wearing a tight smile and clutching her handbag fiercely.

"Sarah," she said, offering her cheek for either inspection or a kiss. She looked Sarah up and down with an emotionless eye. "You look well enough."

And Sarah replied: "*You are old, Father William…*"

About to retort with something equally insulting, Gwendolyn said instead: "*And your hair has become very white.*"

"You remember," Sarah said, reaching forward to gently hug Gwendolyn.

"Our afternoons on the grassy mound in my backyard, near the fishpond where giant goldfish lazily drifted through the water." She quickly released herself from Sarah's embrace and corrected her posture. "Did you know that goldfish have no short-term memory and as a result they never get bored? Each repetitive circling of the same small pond is always new to them."

"Time has been kind to you," Sarah said.

Gwendolyn waved the compliment aside. "When a person ages the middle years disappear entirely and all that is left is memories of what it was like to be a child. I have no use whatsoever for my middle years – nor the supposed 'idyllic' years of childhood."

"Speaking of children, where are they, Gwendolyn. Where are Henry and Charlotte?"

"Oh, back there somewhere, I don't know." Her fingers fluttered through the air. "Charlotte was making a scene because she forgot something on the plane. She and the boy are being looked after by attendants, and I daresay they will appear in time."

"What have you done with Charlotte and Henry? Why aren't they here? Has something happened?" Jeremy demanded, placing himself squarely in front of Gwendolyn.

"Who is this person, Sarah, and why is he staring at me?"

"He is my grandson, Madam," Oliver said stepping forward and bowing slightly from the waist. He pretended to cuff Jeremy behind the ear and leaned forward to whisper: "Go find them," and pushed him towards the door. "He is eager to meet your young charges, or he would never act so presumptuously."

"My what?" Gwendolyn asked. Too many questions from people she did not know caused her to take a step back.

Oliver made his obsequious bow and Gwendolyn's eyes widened at the sight of his ghastly face. No embarrassment clouded the man's expression, and he stared straight into Gwendolyn's eyes.

"Who are you?" she inquired rather rudely. "Do you belong to Sarah?"

A small smile appeared and vanished at once. "At your service, Madam. I will be driving you and the children to Sarah's."

"But I am not going to Sarah's. I have booked myself a suite at the Savoy, and that is where I wish to be taken. I prefer having my own quarters."

Sarah pasted a suitably understanding expression on her face and replied: "Even though I was a bit hurt, Gwendolyn, that you did not wish to stay with me, I did appreciate your desire to stay elsewhere. Charlotte told us your plans. However, Oliver made inquiries yesterday regarding both your reservation and driver and found that neither had gone through. It is most perplexing."

"A very sad situation, Madam. I spoke up on your behalf but was told that there is not a room to be had."

Gwendolyn was speechless.

"On your behalf we canvassed the Dorchester, the Connaught, Blakes and Browns," Oliver told her, ticking off on his fingers, the grandest hotels in London. "None have a suite available at such short notice. And the Savoy requires reservations booked at least six months in advance – which is why the manager was somewhat perplexed when I told them the reservation had been made a few days ago."

Oliver folded his hands on his chest and bowed his head. "There is a standard room available at Bluebird's, but the hotel is also home to a super-market, fruit stand, butcher shop, several boutiques catering to those in their twenties, and a discotheque which does not close until three am. I inspected the hotel, of course, on your behalf, and it simply was not suit-able for someone of your rank and standing. The window looked out on a factory building and in the evenings the alleyway is used for trysts."

"For what?" Gwendolyn asked, fanning her face with her hand.

"Assignations?"

"Yes, yes I know what trysts are, I am not—"

"It is not as bad as you think Gwendolyn," Sarah added, peering anx-iously at the glass door. There was no sign of Jeremy, Charlotte, or Henry. "Oliver, do you think we should make enquiries as to the location of the children? I believe all the passengers have now come through; I haven't seen anyone exit in more than a minute."

"I shall investigate at once," Oliver replied, scurrying through the door. "If I don't return in half an hour, send help," he called over his shoulder.

"Now, Gwendolyn, you and I are going to sit down over there on those comfortable chairs and have a little talk."

"I don't wish to talk. I want to go home."

Gwendolyn was rooted to the spot, and it took some gentle prying and poking on Sarah's behalf to get her to move the twenty required steps, press her into a chair, and hand her a handkerchief.

"Who is that person, Sarah? He looks like he recently escaped from some institution, and you, how can you smile and appear so carefree when you know I am very upset?" She paused for a moment and then added:

"And your clothes? They are more suitable for an eccentric in the prime of their life, not one who is staring death in the face."

Of all the things that might upset Gwendolyn, Sarah had never considered that the clothes she wore might be one. She dressed as she always did, in comfort more than style, preferring cotton or wool to synthetic and, thanks to her daughter Ariel, had a closetful of colourful items to choose between. Today she wore a soft white blouse beneath a dramatic red velvet smoking jacket (Ariel often removed clothes from Oliver's closet and transferred them to Sarah's) a pair of forest green velvet bell-bottoms and striped knee socks beneath a pair of navy blue Mary Janes.

"Are those Mary Janes?" Gwendolyn asked, staring at Sarah's feet.

"Perhaps. I call them shoes."

"I wore Mary Janes," Gwendolyn said. And then pointedly added: "When I was eleven years old."

"What you see is me being glad to meet you again, Gwendolyn. And amazed at how... *recognizable* you are. As for my clothes, I have never dressed otherwise and feel no need to do so now that I am not, as you so kindly pointed out, in the prime of my life. Would you like a description of where you will be staying?" she added. "I think you will like the accommodations very much and you will be given as much privacy as you desire."

Gwendolyn breathed out dismissively through her nose.

"The children will be staying with me in the main house, but the cottage where you will be staying – alone and unencumbered – dates to the seventeenth century. Imagine! So much history always surrounding us."

"Do you own this establishment?" Gwendolyn inquired.

"Ariel and I are allowed to stay for the rest of our lives."

"Exactly what does that mean? You either own your residence or you do not."

"It's a very long story, Gwendolyn. Perhaps I will share it one night when we sip wine in front of the fire. The fireplace mantle is original, by the way. I believe you will love the hearth. It is very cozy. Rather like the old inglenook in your childhood home. Up until a few years ago I tended to the garden myself, and you will see a beautiful display of Gentle Hermiones, Claire Austins, Floribunda, Rambling Roses, Foxglove, Wisteria, Hollyhocks—"

"Did you and Charlie marry, Sarah?" Gwendolyn asked, hoping the non-sequitur would turn the monologue away from nature and hoist it back into the practical world.

"We were... *together*. Call it what you will."

"I want to know about Charlie," Gwendolyn stated, turning to face Sarah. "That is the reason I made this journey. I want facts about my brother, when you saw him last, what he had to say about me, why he insisted on leaving Canada to fight a war that had nothing to do with him. I blame you, of course, for stealing Charlie away. It was your fault entirely that he vanished completely from my side."

Sarah took no offence at the attack because none of it was true. In time she would reveal what she knew, but not in a crowded airport terminal. Gwendolyn had never been a patient person but now she had no choice but to wait.

"Actually, most events in life are grey, Gwendolyn, not the stark black and white you prefer."

Sarah's voice had suddenly taken on a strong British accent. Gwendolyn called her on it immediately.

"I can't help the way I speak, Gwendolyn. I have lived here most of my life."

"That is no excuse."

"Have you never noticed that one adapts to changes in life? A person cannot swim against the tide continuously, wouldn't you agree?"

Gwendolyn fussed with the pleats in her skirt and refused to answer.

"I sense that you disapprove of something I just said but I admit, I have no idea of what that might be." Sarah laid a gentle finger on Gwendolyn's arm.

Gwendolyn flicked it away. She was not a flower that needed to be pollinated, and Sarah's finger had the unpleasant aspect of a stick insect.

"Leave me be, for a moment, please. I have things on my mind."

Sarah noticed Gwendolyn iron the pleats in her skirt with her fingertips and rearrange the rings on her fingers, so each jewel sat perpendicular to her knuckle. And there was tension in her check, indicating she might be biting the soft interior skin.

"I promise I will answer all your questions when you have had time to rest and regain your strength."

"I am a rather particular guest, Sarah. Your 'historical' Mews Cottage may not be appropriate to my needs."

Sarah smiled. Gwendolyn had not changed one bit. She was still incapable of relaxing, and her need to fight and belittle were well-established in her personality.

"The cottage has its own kitchen, bathroom, sitting room and bedroom, plus a study overlooking a flowering crabapple tree. You will have complete peace and privacy."

A prickle of interest crossed Gwendolyn's face. And Sarah guessed it was the word *peace*. The Gwendolyn Sarah remembered was interested in discord above all else, but perhaps that had changed. Sarah caught the relaxing of a tightened jaw, the almost silent exhalation of a held breath.

"I think we should call the police," Gwendolyn announced dramatically. "It's clear that the children are being detained. And yet we all went through that part," she said, waving her hands dismissively, "where a man – it's always a man, isn't it – stares at your passport picture and then stares at you like it's some bizarre masquerade and the time has come to be caught out." Gwendolyn shifted in her chair and smoothed the cuffs of her jacket. "Charlotte said something, I have no idea what because the child never stops talking. And then before I knew it, she and Henry were gone. You'll be sorry you invited her, Sarah, as she will chew your ear off and then fry it up for dinner. And that man of yours has vanished as well. This is most irresponsible on your part, I must say; and it puts a damper on my arrival. I simply cannot be expected to handle my bags myself."

"Nor will you have to, Gwendolyn. Because here they come, all in one piece. Charlotte," she cried, opening her arms wide as three children ran across the crowded floor, tripping, yelling, and laughing.

Gwendolyn covered her ears against the onslaught and watched with jealous eyes as they lay siege to Sarah.

Chapter Eight

"Charlotte lost a priceless historical relic that was under her protection," Jeremy explained, dancing along beside Gwendolyn. "She called out to you, but you pretended not to hear. She had to find it, or else we are all doomed."

"I understand Charlotte returned to the plane, Jeremy. Thank you for your concern."

"Then how come you didn't tell us?"

Jeremy was oblivious to the signs of dismissal radiating from Gwendolyn, her rigid posture, the way her hands kept touching her face to see if it was still there, her refusal to look him in the eye. He was eager to ingratiate himself with Gwendolyn and assumed she could be broken down, as most people were, by his relentless chatter.

"They had to rush back inside the plane, which was very difficult as Henry and Charlotte were pushing against the masses desperate to get out. The Siege of Leningrad might be a suitable comparison but a bit dated," he added, pondering, his finger to his lip. "And then it took forever to locate this artifact as someone threw a bunch of rubbish all over the floor in front of Charlotte's seat. It rather looked like the aftermath of a wartime bombing which Grandfather will be able to tell you all about since he was the innocent victim of just such a catastrophe."

"Perhaps if you stop talking, we will get to where we need to go faster," Gwendolyn suggested, trying hard not to trip over Jeremy. The child had an unpleasant habit of either stepping right in front of her or subtly pushing her towards a wall, so enthralled by the sound of his own voice that he did not look where he was going.

"When Grandfather and I entered the plane, the cockpit door was open. Imagine!"

Gwendolyn's voice tightened, and it sounded like the words were having a difficult time making the passage from her vocal cords to her tongue and lips. "And how did you and your grandfather manage to blithely walk onto the plane?"

"I like that word. Blithe. Do you know what it means?"

An icy hand was placed on Jeremy's shoulder and pressure applied to place him an appropriate distance away, but his body – devoid of balance and control – immediately began to list to the right.

"Blithe *can* mean happy or joyous, but I tend to believe it defines a person who is pretty much indifferent to rules and regulations but always keeps a cheerful countenance so as not to offend anyone. Once you get to know my grandfather, you will see that this is exactly who he is, and ergo, explains our ability to board the plane."

"What you are really saying is money changed hands," Gwendolyn informed Jeremy.

"Never," the boy said, his face turning scarlet. "Bribery is rarely necessary unless a person is deeply in trouble. Friendliness works wonders. I've seen it time and time again. People respond to a smile and a cheerful voice."

Gwendolyn sniffed, imperiously. In her opinion the masses were easily manipulated.

"And *since* the cockpit door was open, we all got a complete and exacting tour of the console! One at a time, of course, because there is really very little room inside the navigational pod, but the seats are a treat, real leather and soft and squishy rather like the chair in Sarah's sitting room that I am allowed to inhabit – but only when she is not sitting there having tea." He paused, took a deep breath, and continued. "Of course, we were ravenous after our educational experience, and we all had to sit down and have a bite to eat, because there is always food left over that the passengers don't consume, and for a few minutes we all lounged in first class having what Grandfather would call a *chinwag*. It was most informative and has perhaps changed the course of my life because I am now considering a future in aviation."

"And you did not give one second's consideration to Sarah and me, waiting and worrying about what had become of you?"

"No. Your names did not come up so that must mean none of us thought about you at all."

To avoid the garbage can that suddenly loomed before her due to Jeremy's erratic manner of walking, Gwendolyn tripped – and was saved from hideous embarrassment and possible injury by the warmth of a firm hand gripping her upper arm.

"Steady on," a voice intoned, and she felt a rush of warm breath skirt her left cheek. "I thought it time to save you from your perambulation with my grandson."

Gwendolyn took back ownership of her arm, her voice icy cold. "That boy does not know when to stop talking, so I would hardly call that a conversation."

Oliver dropped his chin and looked suitably chastened and yet there was a look, lurking in his eyes, that triggered Gwendolyn's antennae.

"I meant walk, of course, so you may stop looking at me like I am an ignorant commoner." As he spoke, Gwendolyn was having difficulty breathing – which signified she was losing control.

"Are you feeling faint, my dear Madam?" Oliver asked in concern.

Gwendolyn's face was completely devoid of expression, and her skin had turned pale.

"Please let me collect your luggage," he said, "and then we will make our way quickly to the limousine where you can rest. Might I ask for your baggage claim slip? I am here to assist you in every way."

Gwendolyn rummaged in her bag and found a neatly folded sheaf of luggage claim slips and placed them, perfunctorily, into Oliver's out-stretched hand.

"You have five suitcases, Madam?" he asked, keeping his voice entirely neutral.

"Be extremely careful with the bag marked fragile, if you would be so kind," Gwendolyn said, finding a place with her eye that was the farthest away she could be from Sarah and the swarm of children that now made up her entourage.

Oliver waved to Charlotte, who waved back after attempting (and failing) to get Henry to dance with her. There were several lumpy articles wrapped around Charlotte's body, one resembling a burlap bag stuffed with kindling, another with a picture of a petrified cartoon cat.

The luggage had begun to arrive, inexplicably delayed by some internal dispute amongst the baggage handlers, and Oliver stepped forward to assume his responsibility and look after Gwendolyn.

Her bags were easy to spot, luxurious creamy leather the colour of Devonshire cream, each bag ringed with straps, bolts, and cornices of pure toffee. Bric's designed bags like this, and although they were hellishly expensive, they were made to last, usually longer than their owner. The bags announced their presence with an understated elegance, making everything that arrived in their wake resemble the tag end of a dog's dinner. And by some miracle of disgorgement, the bags entered the carousel in order of size: large, medium, cabin size, beauty case and one compact, marked fragile. Gwendolyn's luggage, arriving in an unbroken line, had an air of entitlement about it, as if the inanimate objects had taken on the personality of their owner.

"Let me help, Grandfather," Jeremy insisted, pushing his way between a couple waiting for their luggage. "I've got it," he said, grabbing the medium bag and then dropping it on Oliver's foot. Jeremy wended his way to the trolley, declining to take the direct route, which was at most three metres, thereby showing his mettle by adding on another five. "Grandfather, this bag weighs almost as much as that wringer washer I assisted you with last week. You remember," he said, wiping his brow with his fingers.

"May I enquire as to how much you had to pay for excess weight?" Jeremy asked, arriving alongside Sarah with Henry in tow, using his new friend as a kind of crutch. "It is my understanding," he said, staring unblinkingly at Gwendolyn, "that a person is only allowed a certain amount of poundage in their luggage and if this is exceeded, a tremendous financial compensation is required."

In the astonished silence that followed, Henry whispered in Jeremy's ear. After a moment of puzzlement during which Jeremy's face went through similar contortion to one having a tooth pulled, the boy nodded and said: "My mistake."

He looked up at Gwendolyn and said sincerely: "I am most very sorry, Mrs. MacFarlane-Fenton. I will steadfastly from this moment on endeavour not to annoy you with these bothersome questions."

"Dear boy," Gwendolyn murmured, meaning the exact opposite. Her hand lifted as if controlled by an invisible puppeteer and hovered, ghost-like, above Jeremy's head until she got herself under control and pretended the hand had merely lost its way to her own head, where it lingered, touching a shellacked wave on her perfectly coiffed head.

"Sarah, I have the most terrible headache," Gwendolyn said, no longer bothering to pretend that she was above the common mass of humanity that surrounded her. "I must leave soon, or I will faint."

"Henry, do you have your suitcase?" Sarah asked, taking Gwendolyn's arm and patting it reassuringly.

"Charlotte is standing sentry over there," Henry pointed at a black medical bag and suitcase standing forlorn and alone in the corner. This luggage might easily belong to an elderly doctor who, after receiving word from above on his own declining health, had closed his practice, packed his belongings, and sent them on without him.

Charlotte was nowhere to be seen.

"She *was* there," Henry insisted, blinking rapidly.

"Oliver, we just need to add Charlotte's bags to the trolley if you would be so kind? Does she have a suitcase?" Sarah asked Henry.

"Just her Hello Kitty backpack and an old laundry bag that she had with her on the plane. Didn't you notice how lopsided she looked?"

"Ah," Sarah said, her eyesight not what it once was.

Oliver packed up Henry's luggage, not thinking twice about why a young boy was travelling with a medical bag. Everyone needed a medical bag.

Just as the rest of the group reached the door, Charlotte reappeared, breathing heavily.

"This is all you brought?" Sarah asked Charlotte, looking at the garish duffel bag – not a laundry bag at all but a bullet-shaped object in lime green and pink that Charlotte had strapped over her shoulder. Her Hello Kitty backpack dangled from her fingers, dragging on the ground.

"I have everything I need and not everything I *don't* need like some people," she said, pointing at Henry and then, as an afterthought, adding Gwendolyn, who was being helped into the limousine by Oliver, in the gesture. "We are here for a reason. The Tower Room adventure is not over. We aren't done. And that reason has something to do with Charlie."

"I *think* that reason is called a visit, Charlotte," Sarah said dryly. "Ordinary people do that from time to time. They visit one another."

Charlotte smiled sadly and shook her head. "If that's true, why do you want a sample of my handwriting? You believe me, Sarah, I know you do and together we must convince Gwendolyn, or I will be bound to her forever, and you wouldn't want that on your conscience, would you?"

In the front seat of the limousine, Gwendolyn was studying her face in a compact. With her free hand she reached inside her purse and removed a lipstick. She made a moue with her lips and began to apply another coat of paint.

She approved of the Rolls-Royce limousine. It had far more room than the inferior model Dragos owned, and it smelled deeply of money. The double sized front seat was at least three feet from the driver, and in the back there were four bucket seats in rows of two facing one another. All the seats were soft black leather and, if she wasn't mistaken, had recently been buffed and polished with beeswax. An inside silver vase beside the window held a real red rose and the car was panelled with cherry wood or possibly mahogany, Gwendolyn couldn't be sure. But it hardly mattered. Wood was wood. There was also a panel which could be raised to block out all sound from the backseat. This would be useful when Gwendolyn was ferried about town with the children in the back, but now – although she would dearly love to insist that the panel be raised – she felt it might show a discourtesy to Sarah, who would be riding in the back. Gwendolyn brushed her shoes across the carpet and not a particle of dust was raised. The carpets had been vacuumed and the exterior buffed to a high shine. She looked at her reflection in her compact and felt she did the Rolls a service, simply by being who she was.

"She's putting on *more* makeup?" Jeremy remarked, his voice dancing up the register. He pulled Henry and Charlotte behind the limousine so they would not be overheard. "She already has so much on it's hard to tell what she really looks like."

"She looks a bit like Greta Garbo in her later years. My father showed me a picture," Henry explained when Sarah asked how he knew who Greta Garbo was. "He was really impressed when he met Gwendolyn. He said that not many people weather their years as well as she has. A relic," he explained to Jeremy, "that's been polished to a high sheen."

"What do you mean the Tower Room adventure is not over?" Jeremy asked Charlotte, thereby bringing the conversation back to the starting point of the previous minute.

"You know about the brooch?" she asked.

"Yes – no – I mean, I don't know, do I? You found Celeste because she was wearing Sarah's brooch, or at least that is what Grandfather told me, and Gwendolyn decided to come and visit, although how you managed to get her to agree to bring you both is another matter altogether and one I would not be unhappy to understand because it is very important to be able to fly the world on the coattails of another when you are our age and without funds to make the necessary travel arrangements without help. I have only seen England, Scotland, and a bit of Wales but I was far too young to remember any of it, and the world is so big, and I am so small that it might take my entire lifetime and beyond to get a hint of its significance."

"Exactly!" Charlotte said, clapping her hands.

"Charlotte has been insinuating that we have come all the way to England to solve the problem of the brooch, which has everything to do with Charlie but only incidentally," Henry told Jeremy, quoting his friend.

"That makes no sense."

Charlotte sighed impatiently. "I found the brooch back in 1939, the one Gwendolyn insisted was hers but wasn't," she whispered. "I got it back to Charlie where it belonged. I thought that was the end of it. But then it turned up, out of the blue, sixty years later, when Henry and I were eating sandwiches in St. Lawrence Market. Now do you get it?"

Jeremy slowly shook his head. "No."

"The magical reappearance is why this adventure is not over," Charlotte summed up. "But, in fact, our trip has nothing to do with the brooch at all. Understand?"

Jeremy continued to rotate his head back and forth.

"Just say *yes* and be done with it," Charlotte badgered.

"Yes. Yes, I do. I see it all. It is completely clear and makes perfect sense."

"Really?" Charlotte asked, coming close and staring him in the eye.

"No. I lied. I just said what you wanted me to say."

"That's what I thought." She walked to the front of the limousine, a swagger in her step.

"What was that?" Jeremy asked, turning to Henry.

"Charlotte," Henry said simply. "You best get used to it, mate."

From the Hilroy of Charlotte Lisa Hansen

DATE: TUESDAY, AUGUST 31
TIME: 10:55 AM according to the airport clock! My watch says it's only 5:55 AM (must get Henry to fix the time)
LOCATION: Behind money exchange booth at Heathrow International.

Two totally WEIRD characters accompanied Sarah to the airport, an old man and a young boy. The old man is Sarah's chauffeur (why do I not believe this?) and the boy is his grandson. It's kind of like a distorted mirror image of my life: Me and Leo matched up against Oliver (grandfather) and Jeremy (grandson). The fillings in these family sandwiches are missing, the filling being parents. But perhaps it is better not to have parents. Henry has parents and they are no earthly use to him.

Oliver's face is altogether strange but not repulsive. It looks like a third of it was removed by some jagged tool and replaced out of order.

But.......

When Oliver smiles there is something altogether right with the world.

He smells like cinnamon and lemon drops with just a whiff of pipe tobacco. He is hugely helpful and in charge of organizing the luggage and keeping Gwendolyn happy.

And then there is JEREMY!

Whoa!

Jeremy looks a lot like Wile E. Coyote, both in his posture (forward sloping shoulders, sunken chest, long nose, and brown bristly hair) and in his attitude (forever optimistic in the face of rejection and ultimate destruction). Much against my will I keep looking up to see what is about to fall on his head from the sky.

Usually, I don't like it when brand new people enter my trajectory and cling to the planet (Henry) that is always circling, but Jeremy is so completely odd and so unfailingly good-natured that I can't dislike him no matter how much I try.

Example: he has NEVER been on a bus!

How is that possible?

Even if his grandfather drives a limousine, the company that employs him would never allow him to drive his grandson about town on whim.

Would they?

Cause for investigation.

Jeremy never stops talking. He memorizes words from the dictionary (just like me!) and he tries to always be the centre of attention (ditto!). The only way in which we are different is he thinks adults (Gwendolyn) are interested in what he has to say which, naturally, they are not.

And then there is Sarah.

SARAH!

(I have only seconds because it will soon be noticed that I have deserted my post as Protector General of Henry's stupid luggage).

Tons of white hair with lavender streak all bunched up on top of her head. The Cody red lipstick has been replaced by a kind of purply brown which makes her lips look full and lush and not withered and puckered like Gwendolyn's when she is frowning at me and telling me to mind my own business. Sarah still smells of Shalimar and cigarette smoke and she stands on her own two legs… okay, so she's a bit bent over, and either I've grown (probable) or she's shrunk (totally unlikely) because now the top of my head reaches her shoulder. When she put her hand on my head and pressed and said, "Charlotte," I felt this glow that shot right down to the soles of my feet, and I tingled everywhere!!!

I already know this adventure will be stupendously wonderful and all will work out exactly the way it should, whatever that may be.

Hilroy: Check this out. Gus Frank's very own words written just for me, long before he even knew who I was.

Stop thinking altogether and dive in or else be pushed. No way round it.

Couldn't have said it better myself.

Chapter Nine

Sitting in the front seat of the Rolls-Royce, Gwendolyn made a mental comparison between Oliver's skill behind the wheel and that of Dragos. On the plus side, Oliver kept both hands on the steering wheel. He did not swear when other cars cut him off. He did not turn on the radio and add his own commentary to the news reports, nor did he hum, whistle or sigh deeply. He did not smell of garlic, onions, and stewing beef but instead, a very slight spicy smell radiated from his jacket, tickling Gwendolyn's nostrils in a pleasing way.

The Rolls hummed and purred its way through a largely dispiriting community made up of apartment towers, gun metal grey with cheap windows – some of which were cracked and broken. There were no balconies, no surrounding greenery to enliven the eye.

Gwendolyn shuddered.

The roar of a jet plane thundered overhead, and she looked up to see a red and white Boeing 747 skim the surface of the rooftops as Oliver accelerated past a street lined with two storey cottages all in desperate need of repair or demolition.

"That was *close*," Charlotte screamed. "Does this happen all the time?"

"It's near to the airport so it is safe to assume the answer is yes," Sarah answered, gazing at the airplane cutting a swath through the sky. "I'm sure the people living here get used to the sound."

"Hunslow," Oliver stated, noting Gwendolyn's discomfort. "A suburb of London."

"Very poorly maintained, I must say," Gwendolyn replied. "You don't see this type of housing development in Toronto."

"How would you know?" Charlotte piped up. "You never go anywhere real. There're all kinds of places like this in Toronto, and Henry and me will be pleased to take you on a guided tour when we return. Won't we, Henry?"

"Where is Hyde Park, Oliver?" Henry asked, ignoring Charlotte. "I've read about it in my tour guide. Will we be passing it on the way to Sarah's?"

"Hyde Park is three kilometres northeast of Sarah's and not on our flight plan for today, young Henry."

Gwendolyn frowned. She'd had enough of being on a plane to last her for three days at the very least.

"But tomorrow you will have a grand tour. I promise you that."

Gwendolyn shifted slightly. She was tired, and her eyelids were in danger of drooping. She needed a nap, not the long informative chat about Charlie that Sarah had promised once they arrived at their destination. She had brought nothing with her that had once belonged to Charlie because she had nothing. The house fire had destroyed all the family photographs save the one she had of her mother. There were no letters or school reports or childhood toys and few memories. She would have to invent some, or Sarah would think she had been delinquent in her affections. Ha! That most certainly had been the other way round.

"We will soon be entering Acton Town. Directly to the north is the former Rothschild family mansion. It's now a local history museum," Oliver announced.

Gwendolyn was heartened to hear a name she recognized, one of wealth and stature. She assumed the Rothschilds had fled the neighborhood once it started to decay and received a hefty tax exemption for donating a mansion that had, most probably, seen better days.

"I have no interest in museums," she said aloud.

"I am merely your tour guide, dear lady. To inform, to enliven, to captivate."

Gwendolyn shot him a look, saying quite clearly she did not wish to be enlivened, which Oliver ignored.

Acton Town was moderately better than the area they had left behind. There were no decaying motor vehicles by the side of the road, no twisted metal skeletons which used to be bicycles, and the sidewalks were not full of holes. Even so, Gwendolyn would never dare to wander these streets without her rape whistle and pepper spray, both packed in her Longchamp's bag and inspected with amusement by the odious security guard at Pearson International.

"I'm hungry," Charlotte whined. "Are we going to stop for lunch?"

Naturally Charlotte was hungry. All she did was eat. That was Leo's fault entirely for he spoiled the child with endless plates of scones, muffins, cookies, cheese straws, banana bread, ginger snaps. Leo's kitchen had a permanent smell of spun sugar.

Gwendolyn's mouth watered. She could do with a bit of food, but was loath to admit she, too, was hungry.

"We have a feast awaiting your arrival, Charlotte, my dear. Everything you could ever desire."

"That's true," Sarah added. "Cottage pie, brisket, roast chicken, garden salads, corn, peas, and trifle for those who need a sweet."

"You made these dishes yourself?" Gwendolyn asked, dusting the dashboard of the Rolls with her handkerchief. She did not bother to turn her head, so as not to embarrass Sarah with the scrutiny of her gaze.

"I don't cook," Sarah replied. "I never seemed to have the time, and now I do not have the inclination. Oliver prepared our meal."

"Grandfather is a chef extraordinaire and learned his skills in Paris as well as Barcelona, Ankara, and Cairo. In Cairo he worked in a bakery, didn't you, Grandfather?"

Gwendolyn swiveled her head to look at Oliver whose eyes remained fixed on the road.

"My grandfather Leo is a baker," Charlotte said, always eager to compare favourably with the competition. "He's the best in the world. Will we be seeing the castle where the queen lives?"

"We will try and fit that into the schedule," Oliver answered at once. "At the moment, all is fluid apart from a bit of rest time. Jet lag can be beastly."

"I rarely sleep," Charlotte said, in her piercing voice that entered Gwendolyn's cranium like a sharp knife. "There is just far too much to do to waste a second sleeping."

As Charlotte's voice dwindled to an irritating mosquito drone, Gwendolyn felt her chin jerk and her eyelids close. How humiliating! She immediately pinched the inside of her wrist, a signal to her body to wake up and pay attention.

"Many original historic homes were demolished in Shepherd's Bush to facilitate the building of this motorway," Oliver said sadly. "Such a pity."

"From what remains, I cannot imagine this to be much of a loss," Gwendolyn replied, observing yet another new neighbourhood that needed a face lift.

Here, at least, the people were somewhat better dressed and did not look like they were out to destroy the world or carry the burden of it on their shoulders. An elderly woman made her way along the sidewalk, walking a mangy terrier, and although the dog barked relentlessly the woman appeared to be at ease, chatting with a couple, the man carrying a child in a sack on his back.

Gwendolyn noticed a judgemental silence had entered the pristine confines of the Rolls, and she wondered if it was because of something she said. She reviewed her earlier remarks and had a brief tussle with what remained of her conscience.

"I do not mean to disparage, forgive me. I always feel disoriented after a long journey. I'm sure this is a beautiful community. I'm a bit tired, and this predisposes me to being direct and less than polite."

Charlotte whispered in the back seat, words that Gwendolyn was unable to hear. She suspected this muttering was far less polite than she had been.

"You can take a rest if you wish when we arrive," Sarah said, laying her hand on Gwendolyn's shoulder. Gwendolyn rotated her shoulders to banish the intruder and said she was fine.

"A nap in the afternoon is one of the blessings of old age."

"Thankfully, I have not yet entered that demographic," she said curtly.

Oliver chuckled.

"Did I say something that was amusing?"

"Everything you say, dear lady, is amusing. It is a gift that few possess."

"Demographic is a particular sector of the population in case anyone is interested," Jeremy announced. "For instance, there are shopping habit demographics, leisure time demographics, animal behaviour demographics, sleep demographics…"

"Jeremy," Oliver warned. "That's enough. We all know what the word demographics means."

"That is an assumption based on presumption rather than hard cold facts, Grandfather. For instance, if we took a survey of ten people who we now see on the street there will be a statistical variation that might surprise you. Take that gentleman," he added, pointing to an old man dressed in a disreputable mackintosh and tweed cap, slouching across the intersection. "How many of you think he would know what the word demographics means? I vote in the positive simply because he looks like someone who would not know the meaning, whereas, if you took a posh-looking person, they would definitely not know because they are so busy pretending they know everything that they don't have time to learn a thing."

Sarah started to laugh, and Gwendolyn felt her headache return in force. This child, orating from the back seat of a Rolls-Royce that his grandfather had no business driving (who owned this vehicle, that's what Gwendolyn would like to know) was worse than two Charlottes rolled together in one jagged, grimy boulder.

"Memorizing definitions from the dictionary does not necessarily make a person intelligent, Jeremy," Gwendolyn said without turning around. The back of her neck suddenly began to burn, and she suspected Charlotte was glaring at her.

"I agree entirely, Mrs. Fenton-MacFarlane, which is why I use every word I daily learn at least three times in a sentence, thereby forging a permanent impression on my brain. People who pretend to be intelligent create far worse damage than people who are stupid, because you can't really blame someone who was born with an IQ of 80 and punish them for not being as quick and witty as you might like, but people who have a modicum of intelligence and pretend they have a gargantuan quantity are really quite dangerous because they go around spewing a lot of prejudicial nonsense and delight in putting a person down. For example, take Mr. Hargrave, our music master who is quite a decent type of person who plays both the oboe and the piano with quite astonishing competency. Well, he—"

"Jeremy," Oliver warned but it was ignored in the fervour of Jeremy's recital.

"… he picks a piece of music each week and plays just the first thirty seconds and asks if anyone can identify the piece. It's a game which I quite enjoy, and I am rather good at it because Grandfather and I listen to classical music every Sunday afternoon, and Grandfather tells me about the composer and concerto form and symphonic form and atonal music, which hurts my nervous system, and I have been exposed to a substantial amount of musical data throughout my happy years in his company."

What could a chauffeur possibly know about classical music, Gwendolyn wondered. What cultural experiences had he ever had when it was clear, just by looking at him, that he had spent his life working non-stop? Not to mention the quizzical stares that would greet him everywhere he went as people examined his face and quickly looked away. Surely, he had no time to indulge in pursuits such as the study of classical music. Gwendolyn, for instance, might know far more than she did, if she had bothered to pay attention to the hundreds of recitals and concerts she had been dragged to during her lifetime. But music tended to bore her, as she could not see any point in sitting still while someone else postured on stage.

She preferred silence over sound, a preference not shared by the ranting youngster in the back seat.

"… Respighi's 'Light Airs and Dances' which I know so well because it is one of Grandfather's favourites and mine, too, so I immediately put up my hand, in record time, too, about eight seconds I believe, and when I announced the piece this terribly bored can't-be-bothered classmate, Ian Peters, said, 'That's too good for Respighi.' It was a moment, Grandfather, that I will never forget. Ian was humiliated."

Sarah clapped her hands, an audience of one for Jeremy's impromptu performance, and told Gwendolyn that "the lad" was the star of her after school theatre group principally because he was a quick study and was able to do "outrage" very realistically. As Gwendolyn tried, unsuccessfully, to block out this unasked-for assessment of Jeremy's acting ability, she was certain she saw the hint of a tear in the corner of Oliver's eye. Love for one own's flesh and blood was among the many experiences that Gwendolyn had avoided in her lifetime but even she felt the wave of tenderness that warmed the air in the car.

"Lad?" Gwendolyn asked. "Don't you mean boy?"

"No, Gwendolyn. I mean lad. It is a common word here in England. You might hear more common language as the day goes by."

"Cheeky," Henry volunteered, his voice louder than usual. "Mate, cuppa and knackered. Hey mate, I'd offer you a cuppa, but I'm knackered."

"That's good," Jeremy said. "Did you hear that, Grandfather?"

"I did," Oliver replied. "Well done, Henry."

"You are not British," Gwendolyn reminded Sarah returning to the conversation that mattered to her.

"Gwendolyn," Sarah sighed. "I was born in Manchester, in case you have forgotten. My feet touched down on Canadian soil only briefly. I am sorry you find me tedious."

"That is a really mean thing to say, and you should apologize," Charlotte said, her voice tense and shaking with outrage. "Nobody in their right mind could ever think that Sarah would be tedious. Not in a million years."

"Calm down," Jeremy whispered. "That was a bit over the top."

"Thank you, Jeremy," Gwendolyn replied. "That you for coming to my rescue."

"A person learns by example," Charlotte shot back. "And there have been a lot of examples floating around in this car that aren't so nice."

"Always genuine," Oliver murmured. "What is a day without a quarrel or two?"

"A quarrel is different than an insult. Gwendolyn insulted Sarah," Charlotte announced, her Groucho Marx eyebrows rising so high they were lost beneath her bangs. "Just like Ian insulted Jeremy. People are always insulting Henry because he is smarter than anyone else and he looks strange. Tell him how many times I have had to fight on your behalf."

"Please don't, Henry," Gwendolyn instructed. "And I apologize, Sarah, if only to prevent Charlotte from listing more of my faults. I spoke out of turn. You may talk the way you wish and use whatever words you like. Tell me, Oliver, how long will it be until we reach our destination?"

The landscape had changed dramatically, and the Rolls had finally entered a neighborhood where it, and Gwendolyn, belonged. She recognized Holland Park instantly.

"The landscaping here is magnificent," she breathed, admiring a row of well-established plane trees. All the houses they passed looked as if they had been painted a mere ten minutes before her inspection. The doorknobs were all highly polished brass, and the miniature front gardens pristine. "I stayed in Holland Park many years ago, as I recall. On Knightsbridge, at the home of Stanford Gosling. He made his money in oil but dabbled in the arts. We went to many galleries together."

She smiled in recollection of happier days. But the truth, which she remembered a few seconds later was a bit different. Stanford got on her nerves immediately with his boorish pretentions and his bushy eyebrows which he played with relentlessly, and she had been forced to check into a hotel on the pretext that the constant roar of traffic (quite minimal, really) had disturbed her sleep.

"I feel like I have been in this car forever," Charlotte said. "Are we there yet?"

"Our destination is imminent," Oliver said. "In fact, it is right around the corner."

Chapter Ten

Sarah's house was on a cul-de-sac off Gloucester Place in the borough of Marylebone, which sat neatly between the elegance of Mayfair and the lively, trendsetting community of Soho. There was a wealth of greenery to absorb the sounds and smells of cars and lorries, and there were no parked cars to clutter the stylishness of the setting. The house was at the end of the cul-de-sac, with gardens on both sides, setting it apart from the neighbours who did not have as much property. The house was like the eye of the cyclops, the only thing a person noticed because of its perfect proportions and design.

"Where do you put the Rolls, Oliver?" Gwendolyn asked, trying not to sound too impressed.

"In the laneway garage. Otherwise, it is on the road. Marylebone was badly hit during the blitz and many of the houses had to be rebuilt," Oliver said, returning to his role of historian. "The cottage is original, but updated, of course. The front house was knocked to smithereens, but the bones were strong, and it sprang back to life with love and care." Oliver did not add that this was the very location where he, too, had been knocked to smithereens.

"You seem to know a great deal about it," said Gwendolyn.

"As I said before, I am your tour guide and, also, an avid student of the varied ways we have all misbehaved over the centuries."

"The house is more vertical than horizontal because of land shortage," said Sarah. "Four floors, with lower ground floor."

"Surely you have a lift," Gwendolyn stated. And then corrected herself quickly: "Elevator is what I meant to say.

"Surely I do not," Sarah laughed. "Exercise is good for a person. And speed is not essential. I found that once I began to slow down, I noticed so much more. Besides, my rooms are only one floor up."

"There is a dumb waiter that travels from the lower to upper levels, and bells, of course," Oliver added, eliciting a flurry of questions from the back seat.

"Dumb waiters?" Charlotte asked, bouncing up and down. "Are they living and breathing? Or are they ghosts?"

"Bells?" Henry added. "Like church bells?"

"You'll see. I will show you everything," Jeremy promised.

"Whoa," Charlotte breathed, spying a few ancient hitching posts. "Where are the horse and carriages?"

"No longer, dear girl," Oliver said sadly. "But once they did abound, I have been told. The hitching posts are still present. I shall leave you to stretch your legs while I park the car and see to the luggage. Jeremy, take our guests down the laneway, and we will all meet in the back garden."

Sarah unlocked the garden gate and left her guests, promising to meet them in the cottage. The children raced down the laneway with Gwendolyn following at a more sedate pace. Perhaps this would be an agreeable place to pass the time before she returned to Toronto. It was private and quiet and well appointed, all attributes she ticked off on her fingers. The garden between the main house and the cottage, although small, was well-tended and divided into sections. A kitchen garden on one side of a stone path, flowers on the other, flanked by a crabapple tree. A well-established rose garden, filled with Graham Thomas yellow roses, pink and white moderns, floribundas in pink, and a scatter of white rambling roses took precedence. She knew this because Jeremy named each rose bush for Henry's edification.

"It's the perfect size for a cutting garden, Grandfather maintains, and with the moderns, there are blooms into the fall," he said, smiling at Gwendolyn. "We also have an abundance of dahlias." He pointed to a cluster of red flowers close to the ancient apple tree.

Gwendolyn wondered if Oliver was the resident gardener as well as chauffeur and chef. The number of questions she had to ask Sarah were escalating at a rapid rate.

How did Sarah manage to employ Oliver when she was nothing more than an underpaid worker bee, eking out a living as a drama teacher, instructing children who did not want to be taught when everyone knew that acting was a precarious profession at the best of times and one would be lucky to make three thousand dollars a year or less. By all rights, Sarah should be living in a bedsit, fretfully feeding shillings or pence (or whatever false currency masqueraded as real currency in England) into a space heater that dispensed an inadequate heat, thereby giving Sarah an endless case of chilblains and deformed fingers and toes.

"For the past two years, Grandfather and I have lived in the cottage," Jeremy explained. "It's extremely grand."

"My cottage?" Gwendolyn asked imperiously.

"Do not worry yourself, dear Madam. It has been thoroughly cleaned." Oliver, appearing out of nowhere, was busily stacking Gwendolyn's luggage near the door.

"You'll have to take a fire hose to it when Gwendolyn leaves."

There was a shocked silence.

"If she can be rude then I am only answering in kind," Charlotte said, getting an evil look from Henry.

"What I was going to say, Charlotte, is this: I am sorry to displace Oliver and Jeremy, and I would have said that if you had not interrupted."

"You didn't mean to say that at all, or you would have before Oliver spoke."

"Where did you used to live?" Gwendolyn asked, bestowing an approximate smile in Jeremy's direction and ignoring Charlotte.

"In the lower ground floor of the front house while the cottage was being redone. Our former place of residence is…"

"That's enough, Jeremy," Oliver said, neatly cutting the boy off. "Mrs. MacFarlane is not interested in our living arrangements."

"Oh, but I am," Gwendolyn protested, bending down to pick a weed from the garden.

"Do you like sorrel?" Jeremy asked immediately. "Grandfather makes this soup with sorrel and potatoes and lemons, and I'm sure he will make a pot tonight if you wish. There's probably just enough left in the garden for all of us to have a bowl."

"Sorrel?" Gwendolyn asked, examining what she thought had been a weed. She had never gardened in her life. Her bowls and vases of flowers arrived freshly cut every Monday morning, delivered straight to her door, and her vegetables (sans mud and insects) were hand-picked from the sanitized shelves at Pusateris. "You cook, Oliver, as well as garden and drive? You are a renaissance man to be sure. I wonder how Sarah found you?"

"We came across one another a long time ago and have been the firmest of friends ever since." Oliver's damaged face creased into an approximate smile, and he refused to elaborate.

Charlotte was sizing up two feral cats who appeared from beneath a low hanging bough and were advancing, bellies low. The encounter resembled a standoff between two warring armies, the cats swimming in slow motion across the ground, hissing, and Charlotte standing steady with tight fists on her hips. Two tabbies, one grey and white, the other gold and black, began to circle her feet.

Just as they were about to pounce, Gwendolyn shouted: "Be gone, you little devils," and advanced on them waving her arms. The cats disappeared into the shrubbery.

"I can take care of myself," Charlotte said. "But thank you for protecting me."

"I wasn't thinking of you," Gwendolyn said shortly. "Oliver, if you would be so kind," she said, motioning to the cottage door. "I would like to wash away the dust of the day and enjoy a cup of tea. And while I am about it, do something about those cats. I will not have them ruining my morning with their scavenging and my sleep with their constant screaming."

"Is she always like this?" Jeremy asked. Gwendolyn had vanished into the cottage, and he spoke without fear of being overheard. "Those cats are not a bother and can be quite friendly if you don't try to touch them. They refuse to be caged, and I respect that. They are an excellent example of survival in the wild."

"Right. This passes for the wild, a wild with kitchen scraps and water bowls," Charlotte muttered, crawling beneath the bush and finding no evidence of the cats.

Jeremy looked at Henry. "Is she always like this, too? I must say Canadians seem to have extremely *robust* personalities."

"Like what?" Henry asked innocently.

"Is she always so brave and fearless?"

"I am," Charlotte answered, removing herself from the ground and pinching an errant branch that had affixed itself to her hair. "I have immense respect for cats. They think only of themselves and couldn't care less if you like them. They aren't sycophants, like dogs. Cats have complete contempt for us. Sycophants is a new word, by the way."

"Appropriate," Jeremy mused. "The hallmark of true intelligence is how many words a person has at their disposal. It really doesn't matter if the person you are speaking to understands their meaning. Words create an invisible protective barrier in which you can move easily throughout the world."

"Hmmm," Charlotte said, thinking this over and marking the recent bruises on Jeremy's face. "I can't agree. I think words are like missiles that you fire at a person to get their attention and then, when they are cowering, you drop them to the ground with a few well aimed mud balls."

"Why are you smiling?" Charlotte asked Henry.

"I'm not smiling," Henry said simply. "I'm exercising my jaw muscles."

"As if." She sniffed, but grinned when Jeremy began to laugh. "Come on, let's go inside. I guarantee you haven't seen anything as knees up as this cottage."

"Are we having a party?" Henry asked, brow creased.

"Excuse me?"

"Doesn't *knees up* mean a big bash, an all-out throw 'em against the wall, type of event?" he asked. "I don't think Gwendolyn will approve."

"How did you learn so much about English slang, mate?" Jeremy asked, throwing his arm around Henry's shoulder.

"I studied," he said simply. "I discovered early on that the easiest way to learn anything is to study the subject."

"You're a ledge," Jeremy said, swinging open the door.

And that, in Charlotte's estimation, was the perfect description for Henry. He was as flat as a piece of concrete surrounding a balcony. And not only that, he could also be placed, by a man operating a crane with

111

large pincher grips, directly on the very edge of that ledge and just stand there, not moving, and stare off into space – thereby becoming dead easy pickings for redtails and eagles and other birds of prey. One of the larger raptors could pick him up with their razor-sharp talons and fly away with him and Henry would remain as flat and motionless as the ledge on which he had just been standing.

"Why are *you* smiling?" Henry asked, watching Charlotte cover her mouth with her hand.

"I'm not. I'm just exercising my jaw muscles."

"Very not funny."

"I'm gagging for a cuppa," she announced, crossing the threshold of the cottage. She was vying for Jeremy's attention, but he was busy conferring with Oliver.

Charlotte stopped, took a deep breath, and forgot to exhale. It was almost as if she had entered an entirely different time.

The front room held a modest but priceless collection of antique furniture, not dissimilar to some of the pieces residing currently in the basement of the house she shared with Leo. Those pieces used to adorn their oversized living room but had been moved, for safety's sake, into the basement, when Charlotte took up the exuberant sport of indoor kick ball.

She remembered very well Leo telling her she had broken the Canterbury, torn a hole in the English roll sofa, and chipped a leg on the Davenport desk.

Her only reply had been: "I didn't do it."

Leo, being Leo, had not punished her for her transgressions except to inflict upon her a lesson on the workmanship and quality of the goods he had transported to the lower level for safety's sake – until she reached the age of "appreciation", as he had termed it.

Here before her was a similar birch ball foot cabinet with beaded moulding, on which an alabaster goddess figurine stood wrapped in grape leaves. Four comfortable, braided upholstered chairs were gathered, casually, around a chequer-banded round table and the aforementioned (and remembered) Canterbury held a small selection of Country Life magazines.

Gwendolyn was seated on the English roll arm sofa, rubbing her hand across the back. "I've been looking for this very fabric for years," she said.

"Where did you find it?" she asked Oliver who had returned from delivering her luggage to the second floor.

"Oh, one never remembers details such as these," Oliver said vaguely. "Sarah mentioned that the design was a favourite of Charlie's, and she left no stone unturned, as they say."

"Charlie? My brother?" Gwendolyn gasped in surprise. "The Charlie I remember would not have known the difference between cotton and wool, let alone be able to recognize designer fabric. Besides, he died over sixty years ago. You can't tell me that Sarah has been looking for this fabric for decades?"

"Did I say decades? Memories emerge, dear lady, and they are not concerned with the vagaries of time as we know it."

Gwendolyn watched as Charlotte wandered over to the fireplace and sat down on the hearth rug. The only thing this tableau was missing was a lurcher, drooling and farting.

"Well, I must say, this is all very tastefully done. How many bedrooms?"

"Two. Each with a private bath."

"This must have been converted at great expense."

Oliver shrugged his shoulders elegantly, but it was too late. Jeremy launched into an exhaustive breakdown of carpenters, plumbers, electricians, architects, fees, overtime, replenishments and assorted, unclassifiable expenses.

"That's enough Jeremy," Oliver murmured. "It is not good form to discuss money."

"I can't possibly have heard that correctly. Did you say in excess of two hundred thousand pounds?"

"Over many, *many* years," Oliver lied – the cottage had been refurbished a scant two years ago and no expense had been spared.

"I think this will do nicely," Gwendolyn said, bestowing her seal of approval. "I would like to rest for a moment and have a cup of tea and some sandwiches. Jeremy?" she stated, raising her eyebrows. "Perhaps you could help Oliver?"

"It's all ready, Oliver," Sarah said, entering the sitting room from the kitchen. "All you have to do is boil the water."

"Why, Sarah," Gwendolyn remarked in surprise. "I thought we left you in the front house and yet, here you are, entering from the rear. How curious."

"I forgot my bag in the car," she said, displaying a patched carpetbag that had seen better days. "I wanted to retrieve it before I forgot about it entirely."

"Oh, my dear," Gwendolyn replied, patting the seat beside her. "Are you having memory problems?"

"Only the same ones I have had my whole life. It is hard to keep track of all that is going on and small things slip away." She sat on a cushioned rocker, stretched her legs, and nudged Charlotte with the shoe. "What do you think so far, Charlotte? Are you glad you came?"

"Like a thousand percent. Or maybe a million."

"And what, may I ask, is that bulge in the waistband of your pants?"

"My Hilroy," Charlotte said proudly, removing the black and white checked notebook and holding it aloft. "It is my memory bank. Henry has a paperless memory bank, which he says is vastly superior, but I'm not so sure. When I last saw you, I used a Matilda, and I might make one to carry while I'm here."

"A what?" Jeremy asked.

"It's from an Australian folk song, but technically it's how hobos carry their belongings," Henry explained. "They put everything in a red bandana, tie the bandana to the end of a stick and throw the stick over their shoulder."

"Like a backpack but far more colourful," Jeremy mused. "I like the idea."

"Ta, mate," Charlotte said nonchalantly.

"What is a paperless memory bank?" Jeremy asked, sitting cross-legged at the hearth. "That's what I really want to know."

Henry sighed and stared at Charlotte, who regarded him with wide-eyed concern.

"What? You don't want anyone to know? That's silly. What you have is very useful. You can help people."

"I have a kind of photographic memory," Henry said mechanically. "Whatever I see in print stays with me – I don't know, maybe forever. To retrieve data, I project it on the wall or the floor or a table and read it. It's a different kind of memory than what a grilled cheese sandwich tastes like, or how the air smells after it rains. It is supposed to be a great gift, but I think it is kind of abnormal myself. I am a bit of a freak."

"Bugger," Jeremy exclaimed. "You're no freak. Already you are my best friend, and when we put our two heads together there is no telling how far we will go. Am I right, Sarah?"

"Yes. You most certainly are. And I must remind you both that being different is just fine. Not being part of the collective can be of great benefit. You are your own observer, you analyze, evaluate, interpret, reflect. You create."

As Sarah spoke, Charlotte wrote feverishly in her Hilroy, eager to imprint all Sarah's lesson. Her tongue protruded slightly out of the corner of her mouth as it always did when she was concentrating.

"You are drooling," Gwendolyn announced, spoiling the instruction. "Charlotte, tuck your tongue back in your mouth."

All this nonsense about being different was a bore. Gwendolyn had spent a lifetime thinking for herself. She made snap judgements daily and did not waste time analyzing, interpreting, reflecting, or evaluating. And she was just fine, thank you very much, rarely wrong about anything and very, very happy.

"I was wondering, Sarah, dear, if you could answer a question."

Although Gwendolyn's posture didn't change, Charlotte immediately sprang to attention. Gwendolyn used endearments so rarely it was a signal she was about to ask something outrageous.

"You can ask, and I will answer if possible."

"You are at least two decades my senior, am I right?"

"Probably more than that. One tends to lose track as the years speed by."

"And yet you still smoke cigarettes."

Gwendolyn had the nose of a bloodhound, and she sat forward and sniffed the air.

"Occasionally. Does that worry you?"

"It's a disgusting habit. And you should know better. Do you wish to influence these youngsters to follow your dangerous path?"

"Better that than becoming a boring old snob who thinks she is better than everyone else." The words poured out before Charlotte could stop them and she had the curious sensation that something was speaking through her over which she had no control.

The air in the cottage crackled with uneasy silence until Oliver, entering the room with a folded towel placed across his forearm, cleared his throat, and laughed, breaking the tension. "Where would we be without our minor peccadillos?" he asked.

"I believe that, unless a thing is illegal, people have the right to indulge. Mrs. MacFarlane-Fenton might believe smoking to be disgusting, and Sarah might believe smoking not to be disgusting, and they will reach an uneasy alliance without destroying the comforting fabric of their ongoing relationship. Everyone who agrees, shout Yay!"

The children stood fast with Jeremy, raised their hands, and shouted.

Gwendolyn sniffed, unconvincingly, and dabbed at her eyes with a handkerchief. "You never got in touch with me when I was young and alone. You never once enquired as to my well-being."

Sarah protested with much waving of her arms. "I wrote *countless* letters." This might be an exaggeration, but she knew she'd written at least half a dozen to Gwendolyn. And possibly more than that. "I also wrote to your father before he died, but he did not answer. I expect he was too distraught over Charlie's death." Sarah said mildly. "When you didn't answer, Gwendolyn, I wrote care of your lawyer. Charlie left me these details in the event…" She dwindled off and gazed pensively at the fire. "I would most certainly have invited you to come to England to live had you answered me, but in truth, I had no standing to interfere."

"That fat pig never gave me one letter," Gwendolyn lied.

The lawyer was terrified of her, which was good, and she distinctly remembered him placing paper-thin envelopes on her mother's Queen Anne *Bureau Plat* in the morning room before quickly removing himself from her presence. And, she remembered viewing, straight down the tip of her nose, these offerings before picking them up and depositing them in the garbage.

If Sarah had wanted to get in touch and let her know about her dearly beloved brother (whose face she had not been able to call up in over fifty years) then she could have boarded an ocean liner and arrived at Gwendolyn's doorstep where she might – or might not – have been granted admission.

Gwendolyn held onto a grudge the way most people held onto their teeth but, in older age, teeth and grudges had a way of loosening. After all, here she was, perched on the edge of a William Morris fabric–covered couch in a most warm and welcoming room, so why did she feel the need to argue and fight and cast blame?

She was here to *get* information, not hand it out. That realization made her feel better. Sarah had a lot to answer for. She had stolen Charlie, ferried him away to another continent, ignored Gwendolyn (already, the flimsy airmail letters had never existed) and now pretended friendship. Well, one would see about that!

She glanced up and saw five pairs of eyes studying her. The children showed not the slightest hint of embarrassment in witnessing these revelations, but Charlotte's eyes looked straight through her, like the girl could recognize that Gwendolyn was lying and could see beneath the lies to the sad, slightly derelict mess that remained.

Damn the child.

Oliver's eyes, on the other hand, were more understanding, but of course, he was an old man with a sizeable collection of car wrecks in his past, and he could afford to be forgiving.

"The past is dead, is it not?" he inquired mildly. "Keeping it alive will merely spoil the advantages before us. Would you agree, Henry?"

Jeremy answered before Henry had the chance to digest the peculiar trajectory of this question. Clearly, Jeremy thought otherwise. "The past is significant only if one takes the opportunity to learn from mistakes. You have told me that, yourself, Grandfather, if I am not mistaken. For instance, every time I get beaten up – which is never my fault – I could take that old and tedious high road and register this, as I limped away in disgrace, as a lesson learned but unfortunately, I cannot stay quiet because of the universal question which dogs my footsteps. Should I keep my mouth shut and remain unscathed, or should I raise my voice in accord with the yearnings that come from deep within me?"

Philosophers' corner was abruptly terminated when Gwendolyn rose, majestically, and demanded sustenance.

"If I am to be forced to endure questions to which there are no factual answers, and answers which have no relevance to my own situation, then

I can only do so if I am fortified with food. Sarah? I've been told you were busy laying the table with treats. I see no treats. Where might they be?"

Sarah stood up and, taking her old foe by the arm, led her through the archway into the dining room where a substantial feast awaited. Jeremy and Henry followed quickly, leaving Oliver and Charlotte alone to engage in a staring competition. Charlotte won, which was normal, because no one could endure the penetrating gaze of her unblinking eyes.

"What do you know that I don't?" Oliver asked.

"I could ask you the same question."

Oliver tapped his lip three times and pondered. "Would it be utterly brash of me to say we are all gathered together to make amends?"

Chapter Eleven

After their late lunch, Jeremy and Henry left the house to explore the neighbourhood and Charlotte returned to the sitting room to keep track of Gwendolyn's behaviour. She was feeling a bit unwell, her stomach was unsettled and her head aching. Much as she wanted to run around the streets with Henry and Jeremy, she had a job to do. She settled on the rug in front of the fireplace, crossed her legs, and waited until the elders got settled and Oliver served tea.

"I suspect this is Charlie, and yet it can't be."

Gwendolyn was gazing at a photograph of a dashing young pilot. It had arrived in her lap after she regained her throne in the sitting room.

A tiny almost unseen lifting of Oliver's eyebrows alerted Charlotte's hypervigilance.

Sarah smiled. "And why would you doubt it?"

Gwendolyn levered the photo about two feet away from her face. "My eyes are not what they once were..."

The man in the photograph looked impossibly youthful, fresh, and impish, but from a vastly different time – a time Gwendolyn believed never existed. She had no photographs of Charlie, they'd been destroyed in the fire, and so there had been nothing to keep the image of her older brother from drifting on the subjective tides of memory. Seeing him for the young man he was shocked her.

"He looks... tired," she lied – trying, and failing, to regain possession of the photograph that Charlotte grabbed from her hand.

"I have his letters, and I have kept all his possessions because I wondered if I might come across you again before I passed away. You may have whatever you want once you go through the boxes." Sarah winked at Charlotte.

"Hmmm," Gwendolyn mused. Here, before her, were some of the answers she sought and yet she did not feel overly eager to mine the depths. "I suffer from allergies," she finally admitted.

A lie.

"Excuse me?" Sarah asked. "Dogs? Cats?"

"People?" Charlotte added, winning a truly evil stare from Gwendolyn.

"Mould and dust," she claimed. "Boxes of papers stored in attics usually irritate my sinus passages."

"Do you not want to see what Charlie left behind?" Sarah asked.

"Perhaps you could tell me instead, and then tomorrow Oliver might bring the boxes into the garden where I can view the offerings from a distance. The task is a sad one, I must admit, and any help would be most welcome."

"Your wish, dear lady," Oliver replied.

"Did he talk a lot about Gwendolyn?" Charlotte asked, breaking another layer of ice.

"He mentioned her, yes," Sarah said.

Gwendolyn bristled immediately. "Mentioned? My brother *mentioned* me? And how exactly did that come about? Did he say, I am so sorry to have left my sister behind without a word, breaking her heart which to this day has never mended? Did he say, she was the dearest young soul, innocent and fresh and vulnerable and I miss her greatly?"

"You were never vulnerable," said Sarah, regaining her long-ago role as Gwendolyn's tutor. "You tormented Charlie relentlessly. To be fair, as an only child, I do not fully understand this sibling dynamic."

Gwendolyn's answer was unexpected. "We are very strange beings, we humans. In a bid to get attention, children tend to do annoying things. Am I right in saying this, Charlotte?"

"Yes. I think we are kind of like cats in that regard."

Gwendolyn crossed her legs and gazed into the past; a murky place, to be sure.

"Imagine if you will a neglected child, her mother long dead, her father without the basic attributes one generally expects of a human being, attributes such as warmth and affection and concern. Imagine a carefree, rather selfish brother, near ten years her senior. A housekeeper, a paid servant who was both dismissive and controlling. Add to this an empty, barren, echo-filled house and, in this, please place if you would be so kind, an intelligent, curious, affectionate eleven-year-old girl who wanted nothing more than to be noticed and loved. I believe, if you reflect on this scenario, you will conclude I was never the spoiled, entitled brat you believe me to be."

"You bullied everyone," Charlotte stated simply. Holding one hand aloft she began to raise fingers to tick off each name. "Lukas, Helen, Charlie, me, Henry. Oh, look I've run out of fingers."

Gwendolyn shook her head. "Charlotte has this curious little fantasy that she spent time in my company when I was but a mere child. I believe she does this because her own life is so uneventful."

"I won the award for audacity and bulldog courage the night we took down those horrible signs on the Island. You remember, right, Sarah? And I wore the Tree of Life brooch, and at the party at Dilys's house, Charlie carried me around on his shoulders."

"He did no such thing," Gwendolyn said sharply. "You make up these stories to annoy me, Charlotte, and I wish you would stop."

She tried to outstare Charlotte and failed.

"I appreciate the hardship you underwent, my dear lady," Oliver offered, clasping his hands.

"Thank you," Gwendolyn replied, a tear glistening in the corner of one eye.

"I have always believed it is the hardships in our lives that form us, and in that formation lies the universal choice."

"Which is?" Gwendolyn asked.

"Whether to turn away from all that life offers or to embrace it wholeheartedly."

"That's very easy for you to say," Gwendolyn replied sharply.

Oliver, being a gentleman and a kind person, let this remark slip away. He put another log on the fire and rearranged the embers with the poker. That Gwendolyn's remark had amused him was clearly indicated by a half-smile.

"Whether you believe it or not, you were pretty terrible to me," Charlotte offered. "You insulted every single thing about me, including my ability to chauffeur you around by bicycle while you comfortably sat in the sidecar."

Gwendolyn's lips became as thin as two slivers of ice. "As I have already stated, Charlotte believes it is fun to imagine she and Henry, by some magical intervention, appeared one day in May in the year 1939 at my house in Rose Park. Sarah already knows this, but I am telling you, Oliver, so you don't think that Charlotte is touched. She is completely lucid and competent, most of the time, but is burdened by this strange fixation."

Oliver turned his head slightly and winked at Charlotte. "You had a bicycle with a sidecar?" he inquired. "What a lovely coincidence. You didn't tell me that, Sarah."

"I forgot," she said, smiling in recollection. "It was a wonderful bicycle, and Gwendolyn was the only child in the neighborhood who had one. It was custom made at great expense."

"So?" Gwendolyn asked, all defensive.

"You will be interested to know that I, too, had a bicycle with a sidecar," Oliver said, leaning forward and resting his elbows on his knees. "It was quite simply the only way to travel. The sidecar was always filled with books as I ran an ad-hoc library service to those who were housebound. My father's library was substantial."

"Thank you for the meal, Sarah.," Gwendolyn said, ignoring Oliver entirely. She did not wish to know that Oliver performed a service with his bicycle because such a selfless act would never have occurred to her. "I don't wish to appear rude, but I would like to rest. Tomorrow, I don't wish to do anything but sit with you and read Charlie's letters and discuss his heroics. That is why I came." She walked to the staircase and paused. "And, of course, to see you, Sarah. It is curious, but I believe there have been many times in my life when I have missed you more than I missed Charlie."

"That I did not expect," Sarah said once Gwendolyn had disappeared in the upper realm. "I can't imagine that child missing anyone, me particularly. I thought she was glad to see me gone."

"Our memories are flawed," Oliver suggested refilling Sarah's teacup. "Can we really know how we felt sixty years in the past?"

He turned to Charlotte.

"Of course, *you'll* certainly know because you are recording everything. Many years from now all you will have to do is open this journal and you will be surprised at your reactions and observations. Time can smooth out the rough contours of our emotional responses to current events."

"Do you think that's true?" Charlotte asked.

"The odds are in your favour," Oliver told her, patting her head.

Sarah told Charlotte it was time to see a sample of her handwriting. "Let's get that out of the way, shall we?"

"Take a look," Charlotte volunteered, realizing as she offered her Hilroy, that Sarah was the only one to whom she would give such a gift. Her Hilroy was sacred, and even though most of her writing was deliberately pinched and crabbed to the point of near indecipherability, she rarely allowed another hand to touch any of her journals.

But Sarah was not interested in the gift. She asked Oliver to fetch a pad of paper and pencil from her desk. Once they were handed to Charlotte, she gave her instructions.

"Write as much as you can remember of the note you say you left for Charlie."

Charlotte sat back on her heels and grinned. Amongst her many attributes, her memory was sterling. She licked the tip of the pencil, crossed her eyes in concentration. "Probably won't be letter perfect but as close as I can make it," she promised, and set to work.

As she wrote, she remembered standing in Charlie's bathroom, breathing in the cinnamon smell of Old Spice. She picked up his straight edge razor, cleaned it until it sparkled and put it down. She arranged his toothbrush, and Ipana toothpaste, she plucked a few hairs from his comb and put them in her pocket. She then looked at herself in the mirror and held the Tree of Life brooch to her own chest so she could feel the warm radiating glow. She stared long at the picture she had created until her reflection began to wobble, stretch, and shrink and she no longer knew whose eyes were observing.

In those long-ago days, Charlotte had no one to help her make the right choice or even explain why this burden had fallen on her shoulders. She took a deep breath, then and now, and wrote from her heart.

I bet you didn't even know this brooch was lost again, but it was, hidden away in a very secret place that you would not have found.

Promise me, Charlie. You got to promise me. Keep this safe or give it to someone you trust to hold for you. I know you are going away. Gwendolyn told me when we sat together at Clayton's drinking sodas. I wish I knew whether you will be safe flying a British airplane all over the soon to be dark and dangerous skies.

Terrible things will happen if you don't keep the brooch safe. You know who to give it to. I can't tell you because you must figure it out all on your own.

I'll be seeing you, Charlie. Whether you and I are here, or there, or somewhere else we don't even know about I'll always be seeing you. Get USED to it!!!!!

By my mark, Charlotte Lisa Hansen, the Shadow

P.S. Don't show this letter to anyone except Sarah.

Charlotte passed the note to Sarah, uncrossed her legs, and stared off into space. Oliver stood behind Sarah, bent close to her shoulder, and they both compared the most recent offering to the one that was written sixty years ago. This ancient document – pen marks on a yellowed piece of paper with an inked thumbprint on the upper right corner – had been carefully preserved by Charlie, wrapped in muslin and then tied inside a handkerchief. By all rights the paper should have long disintegrated, the words dissolving and fading until finally they disappeared altogether. But because of the way he had preserved the note – or maybe because of magic – the words were as clear as on the day they had been written.

Sarah laughed quietly but it wasn't out of merriment. She dipped her head and remained very still until Oliver handed her his handkerchief. She dabbed her eyes and then blew her nose. "I wanted to believe it, but how could I when the whole idea of you being you," she said pointing to Charlotte, "in 1939, is the same as you are now in 1999."

Charlotte nodded solemnly. "I know. I don't get it either. Henry had a complete breakdown when we returned, and he wouldn't speak to me for weeks. He's completely fine now, but I think he might still be mad at me for forcing him to return to our own time."

"Where did Gwendolyn hide the brooch?" Sarah asked. "I have waited a lifetime to ask that question."

"In the secret compartment inside her sidecar," Charlotte answered at once. "It wasn't all that difficult to figure out."

"Do you think she cares at all about it now? I know it consumed her as a child," Sarah said. "It certainly is beautiful. I don't know that I've seen anything quite like it. I'm sure that's how you recognized it so easily."

"Yes..." said Charlotte lost in just the thought of it. In fact, when they'd seen it on Celeste, the sight of the brooch struck both her and Henry like a bolt of lightning.

She could see it in her mind's eye. Within a circle of gold was depicted an ancient tree intricately carved, its branches as delicate as a spider's web. The earth in which the tree was set was dark volcanic ore. Two white ivory doves were balanced on either side of the tree, fiery opals in their beaks, their wings lifting towards the sky. And on the compass points, rubies and emeralds.

When Sarah spoke, it was as though she were glimpsing into Charlotte's thoughts.

"Did you know that the first letters of the seven jewels present on the brooch spell the word *forever*. Fire opal, onyx, ruby, emerald, variscite, emerald, ruby."

"Yes, she told me that."

"Of course," said Sarah. "I imagine Gwendolyn knows this and many other stories about the brooch."

"Because of all the fairy tales her mother told her."

"That's right. And because it was the one thing she couldn't have."

"Did Charlie ever figure out who his real father was? The one who gave Eliza the brooch?"

Sarah laced her fingers, stretched her legs, and asked Oliver to put another log on the fire. "I don't believe Charlie cared. He loved Ian

MacFarlane." Sarah studied Charlotte and asked: "You remember him, of course."

Charlotte nodded. "His crippled leg and his sad face. My great aunt Dilys tried to cheer him up and failed. She was great friends with Eliza. Ian MacFarlane liked Leo and enjoyed reciting poetry in the kitchen while Leo cooked. But, in many ways, I think he was untouchable," Charlotte added, with a rare insight for one so young.

"And yet he worshipped his wife and would have done anything for her. He adopted Charlie before he was even born and loved him. Ian was his true father. In many ways, Charlie was a simple soul. He believed in laughing, having fun, and not looking too deeply into things that did not matter. He saw life as one great adventure."

"Which it is," Oliver confirmed, pouring more tea in Sarah's cup.

Charlotte slid closer to Sarah's chair and tapped on her on leg. "About that brooch? Gwendolyn certainly studied it when Celeste arrived at her penthouse with Henry and me. She even used a magnifying glass and took it to the window so she could see every little bit of it as clearly as possible. But she didn't demand it back. It was almost like she had found something she no longer wanted. Which brings up the question of why we are here at all."

Sarah didn't answer. She stared at both the notes in her hand, one so old it should have been crumbling into dust and the other brand new. She dropped both in her lap.

"I don't know. But this I do. You've come back. Can I, at least, have a hug?"

Charlotte didn't want to break any bones in Sarah's body, so she didn't hug her as hard as she wanted to. She wished more than anything that Charlie was in the room, too, laughing or playing a piano that didn't exist. Staring at her with those brilliant eyes that seemed to look straight inside all she kept hidden in her head.

"You watch everything, don't you?" Charlie had said to her once. "I can see you taking it all in."

"I don't know. Maybe," Charlotte had replied.

"And my sister has been a beast to you. Right?"

Charlotte had shrugged. "No more than I can take. And give back."

And that laugh. "She doesn't know how to be happy, poor kid. No more than she knows how to say thank you. Let's hope she grows out of it."

Charlotte wanted to report all this to Sarah but saw that the woman was lost in her own memories. "I only knew Charlie for a week. And that was only four months ago. For you it has been forever. It hurts my head because I can't figure it out."

Dizziness had overcome Charlotte, the room was spinning and tilting, the presence of Charlie so strong that she felt she could reach out and touch a solid person instead of the ghost she had created. She wondered again what it was she was supposed to do and thought that, if she stared at the facsimile Charlie she had created with her words and thoughts, he would mouth the approximate instructions. Instead, the image began to fade, and a ghostly smile preceded its final disappearance. The smile was not whimsical or sad, it was more a challenge. He was betting on her, and she would figure it out.

It was clear that Oliver and Sarah did not notice Charlotte's temporary absence because they were deep in conversation when she regained herself.

"We will win her over," Sarah said. "Or die trying. It's wonderful to be as old as I am," she confided to Charlotte. She rearranged the pillow behind her back and sighed. "Every possibility appears attainable."

"You seem pretty much the same to me."

This was true and not true, because there was this huge time gap of sixty years between her last minutes spent with Sarah and the here and now. Back then Charlotte was torn between trying to hold on to Sarah's hand in the Hart House Circle, circa 1939, and corralling the escaping Henry who thought it would be a nice idea to stay put with his best friend, Lukas. What Henry failed to realize was Charlotte's tenacity. She released Sarah, who turned to stone, and went after Henry and grabbed his ankle.

And lost the two people she never wanted to lose.

The Sarah Charlotte knew in May 1939 was wild and free, thin as a rake and daringly dressed in bright colours and berets and always wearing ruby red lipstick. She did not care a swat for what people thought of her and fought, always, for the underdog.

Here, the same Sarah remained intact, although a bit of her former colour has been stolen by the onward march of time, like fabric that had seen too much sun over the years. There was something regal and yet unsettling about it.

With Gwendolyn, the story was more complicated, because Charlotte first knew her as a crabby old woman, forever finding fault with everything and then met her again when she was eleven years old. The former impression was hard to shake because the child was so much like the old woman.

Gwendolyn the child merely explained Gwendolyn the adult, whereas Sarah today seemed an almost ghostly attenuation of the young woman Charlotte had first come to know in 1939.

"Henry and I travelled back to 1939 courtesy of the Tower Room in the house where I live," Charlotte explained to Oliver. "I know Sarah has told you about our time in Toronto, but she has never seen the Tower Room or felt what it was like to be inside a room lined with black and white photographs in which the people all seem to be alive. The entire house is haunted but the Tower Room is magical. It wasn't like I knew what was about to happen, and yes, I had been warned never, ever to enter the Tower Room when Leo had a guest, but I needed to know about Gwendolyn because she seemed to dislike me so much. This got in the way of the rules. I'm sure you understand. If I hadn't interfered, it might be Leo sitting in this room right now, instead of me."

Oliver nodded. He puffed on his pipe and observed a billowing cloud of smoke turn into a cumulus cloud above his head. "When a person is about to make a mistake, it is always wise to understand that consequences will occur."

Charlotte knew exactly what that meant and replied: "I got into a lot of trouble for interfering, and Henry absolutely didn't want to go and lost his best friend and almost lost his mind as a result, but magic doesn't ask anyone's permission."

"Yes, I have noticed that throughout the years," Oliver agreed, and for a second, he had the look of a necromancer about him.

"There's only one reason why Henry and I discovered the Tree of Life brooch in St. Lawrence Market, sixty years after it went missing. I think we needed to meet your granddaughter, Sarah, and Charlie's granddaughter, too, but Henry and Peabody and me are minor players in all this."

"Who is Peabody? And why isn't he here?" Oliver scanned the room.

"He is a wire-haired fox terrier, and he was banned from joining us, which is a crime, but one I had no time to fix," Charlotte pouted. "The authorities were going to put Peabody in quarantine for six weeks, and Henry and me are not allowed to miss six weeks of school so Peabody can't come. And that is why Leo had to stay home to babysit, although Leo is a major player in all this."

"A wonderful baker," Sarah mused. "A formidable man, as I recall."

"Peabody is really Lukas although he is a dog now, and he was Lukas's dog if you can believe that, and after I found out that Lukas died I rescued Peabody from the shelter where he was taken. And it was really Peabody who tracked down the Tree of Life brooch, because Henry and I were distracted and would have missed it altogether. By all rights he deserves to be here, but such is the way of law and disorder."

"Lukas is dead?" Sarah touched her hand to her heart. "But he was so young."

"Before Lukas died, he told Peabody the entire story because, apparently, Lukas saw me and Henry during our snowball crusade down in the ravine, and he recognized Henry although we hadn't met Lukas yet. And before you say I am dreaming or making this up, I was in Lukas's house and found his journal."

"So many people feel it necessary to keep journals," Oliver said, eyeing the bulge around the waistband of Charlotte's pants. "I have never indulged myself. Have you Sarah?"

"I have, of course, but now I find the sound of my own voice a bit tiresome."

"I will not ask how you gained admittance to Lukas's house," Oliver said, staring at Charlotte in a way that demanded an answer.

"Research. Investigation. Dogged detective work and the assistance of an old friend/enemy of Gwendolyn's called Helen. Nothing to it because it's what I do. All the time."

"Oh, I remember Helen," Sarah said, her eyes misty with recollection. "The only one who was ever able to get under Gwendolyn's skin."

Charlotte shuddered involuntarily. "Who would want to do that?" she asked, her eyes wide. "What if you could never get back out?"

And yet, as she settled back on her heels and watched as Oliver and Sarah exchanged a smile, she felt very uncomfortable because she knew that is exactly what she would have to do.

Chapter Twelve

Charlotte took her time exploring every inch of the front house before she settled into the bedroom assigned to her and Henry. In the basement she found a suite of rooms, two tiny bedrooms, a sitting room complete with a Nintendo station, full kitchen, and immaculate bathroom. Jeremy's clothes were scattered across the bed in one of the bedrooms, Oliver's shirts and pants and an assortment of colourful jackets hung in the closet of the other.

She inspected the dumb waiter she found in the kitchen, a curious box-type affair that was hidden behind a sliding wooden panel and attached to a system of ropes and pulleys. She climbed in, felt cramped, and climbed out again. The rooms smelled slightly of cherry pipe tobacco and roses. She ran her finger across the round oak table, inspected it for dust and found none. Why she cared was curious, because she was indifferent to dust and dirt and was allergic to making her bed. But she needed to know, as always, how other people lived their lives, what routines they followed, what they liked to eat, if they slept with their feet tucked under the blankets or uncovered, what soap they used and, if she could, how they comforted themselves when they were feeling homesick or displaced.

The bell box she found in the tiny vestibule; it was labelled with lights and room assignments: kitchen, parlour, sitting room, and so on. Had servants once lived in this basement? The house didn't seem to be all that large, certainly smaller than her house in Toronto. She wondered whether there were similar dumb waiters and bell call systems lurking behind the drywall of #2 Rose Park.

Charlotte felt uneasy thinking of the distance that lay between her and Leo as she climbed the stairs to the first floor. The tough persona she wore like a suit of armour was paper-thin, and the truth was she was frightened because she didn't krow what she was supposed to do to complete this Tower Room mission and failure was not an option.

The main floor was more chaotic, and Charlotte felt her anxiety begin to lessen. Books, magazines, scripts, notepads, pencils were scattered around a chair in the main room, and dust motes danced a merry quadrille in the air around her face. An empty teacup stained with lines of tannin was on the table by the chair, and pillows were scattered across divans, couches, and even the floor.

Charlotte picked her way carefully through the room. She gave the dining room, kitchen, and glass-enclosed conservatory a brief inspection and saw that these rooms also had a feeling of being very well lived in – not disorganized but in a constant state of transition from one activity to the next. A pot of soup simmered on the stove, a loaf of bread sat on a cutting board, crumbs scattered across the counter. Herbs, tied in bunches, dried in the rafters and, in the conservatory, basil and chives and rosemary grew in small pots.

The difference between these rooms and Gwendolyn's sky-high penthouse could not be more marked. Nothing was ever out of place in Gwendolyn's home, and every time Charlotte visited, Charlotte had a sense that Gwendolyn followed behind her with a broom and dustpan. Not that Gwendolyn would stoop to cleaning her own house, but she was a master at picking up tiny bits of dust, fluffing pillows, straightening lampshades, moving a chair a millimetre to the left or right the instant Charlotte stood up, spraying the air with an imported lavender spray, rearranging the marbles in her glass bowls.

At first it was fun to bother Gwendolyn, but after a few visits, Charlotte started to feel like she was locked in a prison made entirely of glass. Sometimes she dreamed that she jumped high and wide from Gwendolyn's mile long balcony and, swift as a soaring hawk, flew to her house right into the kitchen, where she landed on the hearth rug and beamed a smile at Leo:

"I'm home. I never want to leave again."

And yet she had left, not only her home but her country. There was that uneasiness again. She plucked a small sprig of rosemary and rubbed it between her fingers, the oily residue releasing a smell that gave her strength and energy.

She decided to leave the tour of the rest of the house for another day, principally because she felt she had invaded someone else's space without their permission. She would leave Ariel and Sarah with their privacy, or at the very least, inspect their quarters when she felt less headachy and tired.

She barely registered Henry and Jeremy's noisy arrival and ignored them as they played some elaborate mathematical game which required three pair of dice, two balls, six jacks and a timer. Charlotte knew she could win this game in the blink of an eye, but she simply wasn't interested. Instead, she retreated to the comfort of transcribing conversations and taking notes on all she had seen and done so far. She had been writing for more than an hour when she felt hot air near the corner of her ear which descended rapidly to cover her cheek and chin.

"Whatever are you writing?" Jeremy asked. "It looks like a maze of squiggles and dots and exclamation points. I can't make out one word."

"That is because I write in code," Charlotte said, returning her Hilroy to the waistband of her pants where it sat snugly against her skin, gently pulsing like something alive.

"This is top-secret information," she added, patting the Hilroy gently. "I have to be careful in case my notebook should fall into the hands of the enemy." She was trying to include all the conversations which had occurred in the sitting room and her brain was reeling from far too much data.

"Very wise," Jeremy agreed. "Even though no one will ever be able to make sense of it, the story is exceptional."

"And what is that supposed to mean?" Charlotte asked, too tired to put the usual 'who the hell do you think you are' tone in her voice.

"It's fantastical. You and Henry and that boy Lukas who is now a dog, dashing about in pre-World War II Toronto this past summer, locating the brooch in a teaming marketplace, finagling your way to London so you can avoid being in school. It's more than fantastical. I'd say it's brilliant. Smashing."

"Let's backtrack a minute," Charlotte said, stretching out on the floor and placing her hands beneath her neck. "You think I manufactured this whole chain of events, so I didn't have to be in school? There are easier methods like sticking your finger down your throat and pretending to be sick. Whose mind works like that?"

"Clearly yours does," Jeremy said, admiration coating every word. He took a seat beside her on the floor and crossed his legs.

"This course of events happens to be the truth, and nothing but the truth."

"I cast no aspersions," the boy said, staring at both Henry and Charlotte stretched out like a pair of miniature mastiffs across the rug. He could not remember ever being so happy.

Earlier, when he and Henry had explored the neighborhood and Henry told him about a "friend" he meant to visit, Jeremy, so used to being disposed of in favour of someone better, immediately reached into his pocket and took out the compass his grandfather had given him just the week before for his birthday.

"You should have this then," he'd said, offering the vintage compass in a solid gold case complete with floating dial. "In case you get lost."

And then the most curious thing happened. Henry looked at the compass, blinked, and smiled. "That looks like a very special piece. I thank you very much, but I wouldn't dream of borrowing it."

"It's yours," Jeremy corrected him.

"No," Henry said. "It's yours. I have my own," he added, patting his pocket. "But you can do me a favour if you don't mind. The friend I mentioned is really an old friend of my father's. I would rather visit him alone, without Charlotte. "

"Why? Is Charlotte dangerous?"

"Not dangerous. Just nosy. And she thinks everyone belongs just to her. I want to do one thing by myself. Do you think you could help me make sure this happens?"

Warmth flooded Jeremy's entire body, and if Henry had told him to lie down and die, he would have done it gladly. He had absolutely nothing against Charlotte, but if Henry wanted to have a London adventure without her, what could he do? And yet he knew intimately what it felt like to be the odd duck, and Charlotte was most certainly an odd duck, but did she deserve to be tossed aside because his new friend told him to do so?

Yes!

And no.

Jeremy had been brought up with no sense of right and wrong by parents he could barely remember, and luckily his damaged star and Oliver's stellar one joined up in a cold and dreary railroad station somewhere in northern Scotland. Jeremy, wild and feral, and cold to the marrow of his bones, had found safety in those muscular arms that picked him up and that stern mouth that breathed pipe tobacco all over his face. Oliver had taught him that there was only one thing that every person in the universe had in common, and that was the ability to be kind.

'This ability is what we are given, Jeremy. That is not to say everyone chooses to comply. Do you understand me?'

'Are you saying I might someday forgive my mother for leaving me behind? And my father for never having time for me?'

'Kindness is the goal, Jeremy. Those two delinquents may sort themselves out in time, but that is not our business. Foolishness is the obstruction you must bring down.'

"We can't do that to Charlotte," Jeremy had said, his empathy outstripping his desire for friendship. "I know what it feels like to be ditched."

"I understand," Henry had said thoughtfully. "But it is just this once. And we can make sure that she is engaged in something far more interesting. I never really get the chance to do anything on my own," he had explained. "Charlotte has complete charge of my life. She's my best friend but sometimes it just gets stultifying."

Jeremy, never having had a friend, let alone a best friend, had nodded wisely. "Just the one time. I could go along with that."

Henry, now asleep on the rug, was breathing adenoidally, his eyes darting beneath their lids. Jeremy, his mind still racing from the day, launched what he thought was an exceptionally subtle gambit and unintentionally spilled the beans to Charlotte.

"You wouldn't mind a solo tour with my grandfather for about an hour tomorrow afternoon?" he whispered so as not to wake Henry. He had no idea if Oliver would comply with such a request, but that could be sorted out later.

Charlotte grinned at the ceiling. "What does the sleeping prince have in mind?"

"Why should you mention Henry? This had zero to do with him." Which, in Jeremy's mind, was completely true.

He and Henry did not talk about setting up a private tour for Charlotte with Oliver, or even if such a thing was possible, given the fact that Mrs. MacFarlane-Fenton had to come first, and even if that was not a given, considering she footed the bill for Henry and Charlotte to come to London, Jeremy suspected that the sheer force of her personality would place her above all others. Hadn't Charlotte basically just said the same?

"It's just that he seems very tired," Jeremy explained, glancing at Henry whose mouth had fallen open. "And he might be happier staying in. You, on the other hand, do not resemble a person who needs a lot of sleep."

"Six hours on average but I can do four in a pinch. My metabolism," Charlotte stated proudly – for a moment, forgetting the point of this exchange. "It's extremely active and prevents me from wasting time in sleep. This condition makes things difficult for the people around me, but they simply must learn how to cope."

"Exactly," Jeremy exclaimed. "I knew that the minute I saw you."

Most likely troubled by some phantom Charlotte appearing in his dream world, Henry began to thrash about on the floor. The real flesh and blood Charlotte placed a stabilizing foot on his stomach and he groaned and subsided.

Interesting that, Jeremy noted. She had command over Henry even in sleep. He couldn't wait to discuss this with his grandfather and perhaps engage in a few experiments to see whether a person's control over another infiltrated into the realm of sleep. Of course, he had no way of knowing for certain if Henry was dreaming about Charlotte (he was) but there was no denying she was a forceful personality.

"Henry has spent our entire friendship trying to get away from me, so I knew he would follow suit even in a foreign land. Besides, I know where he is going and who he is meeting."

"You do?" Jeremy's eyebrows disappeared under his untidy fringe.

"People underestimate me; usually to their sorrow. Henry is completely transparent, and his hiding place for secret missions has been known to me forever. In honour of our friendship, I will not tell you the location."

"I agree with this. Friends should not betray friends, and yet I have this terrible feeling I have betrayed Henry. I don't know how to have a friend, I guess."

Jeremy looked like he was about to cry, which Charlotte simply did not have the energy to deal with.

"Look," she stated in a clear, sharp voice, "sometimes we cross a line, but it is never with the intention of being mean. It is more like offering a helping hand. To both of us. I won't have to feel disappointed if Henry goes on without me because I will already know this is going to happen, and my system will not go into shock."

"Right," Jeremy said, believing every word that Charlotte said.

He began to think she might be the smartest person he had ever met in his whole entire life. Except, of course, for his grandfather and Sarah, but they came first simply because they had been on the planet for decades longer than Charlotte. Jeremy couldn't even begin to imagine the powers Charlotte would possess if she should reach her ninetieth year.

"What's your story, Jeremy?" Charlotte asked, rolling over onto her stomach. "If your grandfather is Sarah's servant, then I am the Prime Minister of Canada. This has all been put on to annoy Gwendolyn. But why bother?"

"You've got it all backwards. My grandfather has been driving Sarah around for years, and he loves to cook, and Sarah doesn't, so it all fits together nicely, doesn't it?"

"Yes, but what does he owe her?" Charlotte asked simply.

After a few seconds during which Jeremy considered his options, he stated with undisguised emotion: "His life. He owes her his life."

And then, feeling it was time to play the one card he possessed, he asked: "Why are you here, really? Does it have something to do with that crumbling old journal I saw you reading when you thought no one was looking?"

For the first time in her life Charlotte was shocked into silence.

Jeremy, instead of being a limp dishrag type of boy, eager for approval, had metamorphosized into a formidable opponent – the kind that Charlotte had been looking for her entire life.

"Ah," she breathed. "Well, that is a very long story."

"I have all the time in the world," Jeremy told her, getting comfortable beside her on the floor.

Chapter Thirteen

Gwendolyn awoke slowly, carefully unclenched her stiff joints, opened her eyes, and stretched. Someone, clearly not Sarah, knew how to properly make a bed. The Frette sheets, as soft as baby down, and smelling of wildflowers, had made sleep in this foreign and slightly hostile land a pleasure and not an ordeal.

And as a bonus there were three different types of pillows: down, (yes) polyester (absolutely not) and foam (only in a pinch). But these foreign objects reminded her she was not at home and there was no one to see to her needs.

Was she to venture to the kitchen alone?

Why not?

She was the only one living in this cottage. It was hers to traverse at her leisure. How hard was it to plug in a kettle and make a cup of tea? Perhaps she would find a crust of bread, a wedge of cheese, a leftover raspberry from yesterday's overly rich luncheon, bring them all back to her bedroom and start thinking about whether she should fly home tomorrow instead of waiting out an entire week under Sarah's laughing accusatory eyes.

Gwendolyn almost felt like crying, but she never cried so this was not an option.

Demanding help was more to her taste.

She would march up to the front door of the main house, leave her finger on the bell until someone answered, and demand breakfast: immediately. Along with a typewritten itinerary of the day's events so that she could refuse to do them all.

Was that a scratch at the door?

Or a tentative knocking, like that of a frightened child.

She glanced at the watch that never left her wrist and squinted. It was 5:10 am.

She reached for her pale blue silk bed jacket and inched slowly to the door.

She placed her ear against the wood and listened. Definite scrabbling, faint tinkling and then a gentle knock that made her reel back as if someone saw her spying.

"Who is there?" she asked, pleased that her voice was steady.

"Your breakfast, Madam. Should I leave it outside the door, or would you like me to place it on a table inside?"

"Is that you, Oliver?" Gwendolyn asked, running her hands through her hair. She must look a fright. She considered telling him to leave the tray, but she didn't want to have to carry it to the table herself.

"It is, indeed, dear Madam."

"And why are you in such a good mood?" Gwendolyn said, opening the door and stepping back so Oliver could enter.

"My mood is never anything but," Oliver said, walking past her and depositing the tray on a table by the window. A whiff of honey, jam, and hot buttered toast swept by her, and Gwendolyn followed in its wake.

"The sun has not risen," Gwendolyn told him as she stood by watching him unveil a perfectly prepared breakfast, with a coddled egg instead of poached, but that was immaterial. The tray was polished sterling, and on it was a Wedgwood service of bread-and-butter plate, cup and saucer, jam, and honey pots.

"But it will as it does every day. I suspected you might sleep until midday as the time change is significant, but you strike me as a curious and robust woman who would eschew the comforts of bed in favour of a great unknown adventure that awaits in the world beyond the window."

Gwendolyn was certainly not robust, unless dominating worked as a synonym, and was never curious about her environment, only what resided within it, such as quality of bedlinen, lampshades, antiques. The outside world could stay outside as far as she was concerned, and if she were forced to take the air, she preferred being driven to walking. She had never owned a comfortable pair of shoes in her entire adult life.

She decided to ignore Oliver's statement or, better yet, pretend she didn't hear it.

"You retired so early, I calculated that, given an hour to prepare for bed, and eight hours asleep, that you may begin to stir around five."

"And if I hadn't?"

"Then I would have disposed of this and cooked another breakfast when the time was right," Oliver held the chair for Gwendolyn, unfolded the linen napkin with a flick of his wrist and placed it perfectly in her lap.

"Tea?" he asked, lifting the embroidered caddy and balancing the lip of the pot over her cup. The spicy smell of Earl Grey rose in cloudless puffs.

Charlotte's voice too wafted across her memory. '*That tea smells like Ivory soap to me...*' Gwendolyn repeated this ridiculous statement to Oliver. She was already angling to get Oliver on her side regarding Charlotte's many peccadillos.

"Strong and pungent," Oliver declared, smiling.

He, too, thought Earl Grey smelled like soap and only drank Tetley's, a tea for the working man, which he brewed stronger than most. Although Oliver did not have to be a working man, he was and always would be, and proud of his varied abilities.

Gwendolyn raised the cup to her lips, took a sip and caught the sigh before it escaped. Brewed perfectly. She looked up and bestowed a slight smile in Oliver's direction, a personal benediction she rarely offered.

The little charade Oliver was enacting on Gwendolyn's behalf pleased him immensely. He loved stubborn, willful, proud, and rude women and they had been his downfall because, given his countenance and general air of good-natured buffoon, none of these women had loved him back. He never took rejection personally. Life was far too short to wallow in self-pity, and thanks to Sarah's stalwart friendship, and that of others who saw life the way she did, Oliver found this a priceless balm for his self-confidence.

He had no use for his daughter, however; the only person he had banished from his life utterly. Her cavalier treatment of his only grandchild still caused his blood to boil.

"I thought I would go over the itinerary for the day, and you can say yea or nay. And, by the way, I have been instructed to deliver the box of Charlie's belongings so you may look through them at your leisure."

"How kind," Gwendolyn murmured, unscrewing the cap on her egg coddler. She tapped the top of the egg with her spoon, noting that the yolk was cooked but soft enough so she could dip the toast fingers inside – cholesterol be damned.

A very curious sensation began to attack her chest and spread through her arms and fingertips. A sensation that suggested, as it glided through her body, maybe it's time to bring a little rich, glistening fat, into her life. "Why do I care?" she asked herself. She had lived far too long as it was, but some perverseness of nature kept her moving ahead, one well-shod foot at a time.

Her feet now were swollen from being compressed for sitting too long on the plane. She was aware that her ankles were also swollen, and she tucked both feet beneath her chair so Oliver wouldn't notice.

Why was he lingering? Shouldn't he deliver her tray and be gone?

And what of her hair, her naked face, her sleep-wrinkled cheeks and hands that had not yet been adorned with their moisturizing crème?

But Oliver was a servant after all, trained to never comment on imperfection but assist in grooming and upkeep and nourishment.

And yet he hovered.

"And what is it you think you should care about but do not?" Oliver asked, pulling up a chair and sitting down.

"Have a seat, why don't you?" Gwendolyn replied sarcastically. "Perhaps you would like to share my breakfast?"

"Most kind, I am sure. My tray is at the top of the stairs." He stood quickly and squared his shoulders. "Give me a moment and I will return. I did not, of course, wish to impose, but your suggestion is gladly taken. I am most eager to help with your current dilemma."

Neither of Gwendolyn's husbands had ever dared disturb her morning ritual, and that ritual included breakfasting alone. Sometimes Gwendolyn thought she had gone through scores of husbands, but the actual number was a mere two. Back in the days when she had indulged the idea of friendship, she found that most of the women she played bridge with had been married far more often than she had…three, four, five times and carried the baggage of these attachments in the names which they reeled off with a kind of pride.

That was appalling, as was the idea of a game in which she was forced to play with a partner. Gwendolyn preferred doing everything solo, it was the only real way to win.

A nightingale sang outside her window.

She assumed it was nightingale because she was in England, but it could have been any number of birds. Songbirds did not normally appear on the balcony of her penthouse, and the particulars of nature and all their inhabitants did not hold her interest for long.

Something else did.

A desire to peel back the old carapace that had started to pinch at her skin and see if anything of the young and tender Gwendolyn remained. Looking through the box of Charlie's belongings before anyone was astir might unearth an ember.

The smell of bacon filled her room as Oliver marched forward carrying his tray of food; several rashers of bacon, sausages, fried eggs, toast dripping in fat.

Gwendolyn felt a pang of hunger that she first thought might be a kind of free-floating panic. Was she destined now to be breakfasting with strangers for the rest of her life? Would she be forced to make conversation?

"I don't believe I have tasted bacon for over thirty years."

"A travesty," Oliver said, folding a piece of sausage, a corner of toast, and an entire slice of bacon onto his fork, dipping it in egg yolk and bending low with an open mouth so as not to miss one morsel. "I am happy to share," he replied, chewing steadily.

It was time to regain the upper hand. "Oliver," she said. "How did you know when to make my breakfast?"

"I already explained. It's a mathematical equation. One can only sleep for so many hours before sleep becomes a symptom."

"A symptom?"

He shrugged while adding salt and pepper to the remains of his fodder. "Avoidance, which if left untended, leads to depression."

Gwendolyn was shocked although she forced her face to remain neutral. Sleep to her was a diversion, a hike across the bridge of doing to the land of dreaming where one merely had to lay back and watch a forever changing landscape and not feel obliged to interact in any way whatsoever. Sleep was a ritual, preceded by a carefully tended list of essential tasks which gave meaning and purpose to the daily toil, and recharged and regenerated the muscles so they might, if they wished, participate in daytime jobs. It took energy to pick up the phone and demand service of one kind or another and a precise and sharp brain to decide what was a reasonable cost and what was not. If the pattern of Gwendolyn's life shifted, she felt adrift, and sleep became her only salvation.

"Depression," she scoffed. "How is it that you are an expert?"

The smell of bacon was intoxicating. She looked down at her tray and saw Oliver had surreptitiously slipped a slice to rest beside her buttered toast fingers.

"I took one or two psychology courses during my time at Oxford." He did not add that being a "student of life" was far more enriching.

"Why is an Oxford-educated man working as a jack of all trades? Clearly you are a man of means. Your posture, your speech and bearing all prove my point. And yet you are masquerading as someone you are not?"

"As this Jack fellow," he repeated, lifting his busy eyebrows and grinning widely.

"And your teeth are well-tended," she added, noting the smile with evenly spaced cleanish looking teeth.

He bowed his head and agreed. "Once a year, I pay a visit to an old friend. We operate on the barter system."

"And yet you have money. More than me, I would wager. It is my belief you own this cottage and the main house. And yet you masquerade as a servant."

Oliver refused to indulge Gwendolyn's curiosity. "Why do you care?"

"You drive a limousine."

"As do many others."

"And you prepare meals."

"A man must look after his well-being, Madam," Oliver said modestly. "And if in doing so that same man might look after the well-being of others than it is all to the good."

Gwendolyn wiped her lips with her napkin. She'd eaten the bacon without thinking and it had immediately started a war with the memory of the more delicate morsels her stomach had received over the last many decades. It was clear who would win, but Gwendolyn didn't care.

"I care because I detest puzzles. I don't pretend to be anyone other than who I am. Most people find me unpleasant and annoying. There is little I care to do about this because I am comfortable in my being, and I will not ingratiate myself simply to be liked. I'm wondering if that is your problem. A compulsive and overwhelming need to be liked. I have seen this phenomenon before. It never works out well in the end."

Oliver sat back, laced his fingers across his stomach and appeared to listen intently to what Gwendolyn said. "Most astute observation and, based on your past experiences, a noble guess. But such is not the case. I am as indifferent as you to public accolades, and besides, it is impossible to be liked by everyone. How dreary that would be. A masquerade would most definitely be in play to have this outcome and then a man would lose himself utterly."

"You did not answer my question."

He shrugged eloquently. "Forgive me. I tried, and if you say I failed, then I must accept defeat."

Gwendolyn straightened her cutlery, brushed the crumbs from the tablecloth, transferred them from the cup of her hand into her napkin, folded the napkin into squares and suddenly, looking at the evenly folded piece of linen, remembered the fortune telling game she had been taught as a child – a game using nothing but a square piece of paper. The paper was folded into triangles, then in half, then in triangles going the opposite way and after making a crease in the middle it was possible to slide thumbs and forefingers underneath the flaps, opening and closing the paper with outcomes to every question revealed under eight little flaps.

"Fortune teller," Oliver said, watching Gwendolyn stare at the napkin.

"What?"

"It's called a fortune teller – or chatterbox, as Jeremy calls it. Every child knows how to make one. I assume you are remembering this experience?"

"How astute," she replied, impressed that Oliver had been able to discern her thoughts by watching her fold a napkin. What gave her away? She must remember to be more careful in what she showed on her face.

In the long-ago days when Gwendolyn made her own fortune-tellers, there were ones she used when she played with Lukas and Helen where bad outcomes were possible: 'You will slip on a banana peel' or 'You will be late home and sent to bed without dinner.' In the one she made for herself every outcome was the same: 'You will be rich, famous and loved by everyone.'

"I can only guess that your fortunes were uniformly excellent," Oliver stated, and Gwendolyn denied this at once, saying every fortune teller she made had both good and bad outcomes.

"Of course," Oliver agreed, nodding wisely.

A most annoying man, but one she was not quite ready to dismiss.

"And how is it you know Sarah? You have most probably been told many stories about me, untrue, or at the best, grossly prejudicial stories, but I am at a disadvantage. I know nothing of Sarah since she left Canada. I know nothing of you."

Oliver removed the napkin he had tucked into his shirt and sighed with satisfaction. "I shall endeavour to answer your questions in the order in which they were asked." He held aloft a cubby finger. "Who am I? That is a most interesting philosophical question because who are any of us, really? Are we simply this animated skeleton that is on view or are we something much greater? Do I dare mention the human soul?"

"This is not helpful," Gwendolyn pouted. And yet, there was an enlivening within her that she hadn't felt since her last argument with Charlotte. She had an overwhelming desire to best him, just as she needed to best Charlotte.

"What is your true profession?" she rephrased. "From where do you spring?"

As soon as the last question was released, Gwendolyn realized she had made a mistake, but it was too late to retract.

Oliver rubbed his hands together energetically, the abrasive sound of callouses intermingling, released far too many dirty particles into Gwendolyn's boudoir. "And now the inquiry deepens. Primordial mud? Our great creator? A single intrepid sperm? These are questions best debated over a bottle of cold Chablis, but if you wish I will tell you my personal theory of our presence on this…"

Young Jeremy came by his gift of gab honestly – from this old man who, replete after a good meal, was sitting back picking his teeth from behind the folds of his napkin.

Not knowing why, Gwendolyn tried again.

"Where do you and Jeremy live?"

A simple question elicited a simple answer.

"Currently we are camping in the nanny suite in the front house. And before you protest, I must tell you it is quite comfortable. Two cozy bedrooms, a sitting room with a large television equipped with one of those Nintendo devices, a decent bath, although there is no separate WC, and a kitchen that is more than adequate for preparing the evening cocoa. When you are not in residence we live here."

"And where does my niece live?" Gwendolyn could not remember her niece's name and with any luck she wouldn't have to meet this woman face to face because she was in Paris or Berlin or somewhere utterly foreign participating in a conference or some such nonsense.

"Ariel has a proper apartment in the main house, separate entrance, two top floors."

"She remains at home. How very curious. Why she must be at least..."

Gwendolyn's powers of mental arithmetic were not answering the request for information and Oliver stepped into the breech.

"Fifty-nine years old next week. We certainly hope you will stay for the festivities. Jeremy wants jugglers and a clown, but I favour a mummer. I teach a class in mime at the theatre school, and I would be very happy for you to join us. Mostly it is old age pensioners who have never been listened to during their lives and now find the solace they had never found before, in expressing themselves non-verbally. We do a lot of improvisational work, and you would be surprised to see..."

There was no way Gwendolyn would ever get one straight answer out of this man, certainly not at the ungodly hour of 6:15 am. She needed time to regroup, to investigate the front house, to have a chatty cup of tea with Sarah and then...

"After my bath, I would like to visit with Sarah. I assume you provide a breakfast tray for her?"

"She rarely rises before eleven am, so it is more like brunch."

Gwendolyn felt a surge of satisfaction. Sarah, the go-getter, the one who never stopped, the person who repeatedly told Gwendolyn when she was a mere child, that she had to pull up her socks and get on with it and lazing about in bed until eight am. on a Saturday morning was not to be tolerated if she expected to make something of herself. *That* Sarah, that lecturing,

146

dominating, irritating human being had become the very person she railed against, and Gwendolyn could not be more pleased.

"Sarah is getting on in years," Oliver explained, "And often she is at the theatre until past midnight and there are always discussions and plans with other actors that stretch until the wee small hours of the morning." Oliver waved a lazy hand in the air, a hand that indicated Sarah spent her time with dashing intellectuals and brilliant actors and Gwendolyn was almost an invisible speck on her radar. "She wishes for you to enjoy our outing and looks forward to meeting at the theatre in the late afternoon."

"Outing?" Gwendolyn asked. When she travelled, Gwendolyn ate, shopped, slept, and fidgeted, calculating exactly how many hours would have to be filled before she could return home. "I don't do outings."

Oliver ignored her. "The children and I will depart at ten which gives you ample time to see to your ablutions and perhaps examine the contents of the boxes in the garden, of course, where the air flows freely. The cats, in case you are wondering, have been temporarily relocated to another establishment, and the day promises to be cloudless, with no rain clouds on the horizon."

"I don't do outings," she repeated. "I am not interested in seeing the sights, whatever they may be, Oliver. Crowds distress me and there is nothing in this world worth waiting in line to see."

"Pity," Oliver murmured, interlacing his fingers. "I have scheduled a personal shopper to take you through Harrods from eleven thirty to one thirty, giving me time to see to the children, and then I booked us a table at Le Caprice for two. The children will not be attending as I have purchased tickets for them at Madame Tussauds, and they will dine on fish and chips after. You would have to endure their company in the limousine when we drive to the theatre, but I will instruct them to keep their voices down."

"Harrods?" Gwendolyn asked. "Not Asprey or Thomas Goode? And surely Selfridges is on the list?"

Oliver consulted a small notebook he removed from his breast pocket. "I will see what I can do while you attend to your bath." He had already noted several spots of interest for Jeremy, Charlotte, and Henry, such as the Horse Guards Parade, Nelson's Column, the Tower of London, Speakers' Corner, High Park, and Jack the Ripper Walk, believing these places might hold their attention for a quarter of an hour; certainly a few were ghoulish enough to spark interest. As a nod to Gwendolyn, he had also included Spencer House and St James's Palace, but he didn't realize she wanted to spend her entire time shopping. What could she need? The amount of luggage she had brought would be far too much if Oliver were travelling around the world – which he already had done, three or four times, once with nothing more than a backpack and a sleeping roll.

There were ways around Gwendolyn's preferences, but he was content to move slowly.

Sarah had spoken of the child she knew, and after their second phone conversation – the first had been an anomaly – Sarah had sighed. *'Gwendolyn is much the same, Oliver. Abrupt and terribly entitled. This should be fun, don't you think? Charlotte has been a great help and here is what I think we should do.'*

Oliver stood up, carried his tray to the landing, and returned for Gwendolyn's. He lifted the cozy and tested the warmth of the teapot before placing the pot and her cup on the table by her bed. "By the way," he added, a tiny taste of what was to come, "Charlotte has requested a tour of the Linley Sambourne House. Would you like to be included in that?"

Gwendolyn was immediately incensed. "How does that child know about the Sambourne House?"

She didn't, but that hardly mattered. Charlotte had already agreed, *post facto,* to go along with whatever ruse Oliver believed necessary to shake Gwendolyn out of her daily routine.

'I have a plan, too,' she'd told Oliver, when they met late the night before in the garden. *'This whole trip was my idea, after all. There is a lot of unfinished business to attend to before I can close the book and get on with other travels. If Gwendolyn won't change of her own accord, then she will have to be forced to do it.'* To which Oliver had felt obliged to ask, *'You are not suggesting anything dangerous, are you?'* He had been put in charge of everyone's safety, and it would not do if Gwendolyn met with an accident. Charlotte was indignant. *'Of course not. What do you think I am?'*

"Charlotte is familiar with Sambourne's cartoons," Oliver explained. "And since she is also an artist, she wants to see where a fellow traveller lived."

"An artist," Gwendolyn sniffed. "If she is an artist, I am the Queen of Sheba."

Oliver kept his face blank. By Gwendolyn's comparison Charlotte was an artist extraordinaire.

"There is a treasure trove of *Punch* magazines in the basement of Charlotte's home in Rose Park," he added. "It was one of the first things she asked me about."

Gwendolyn sniffed. "What isn't in that basement would be of more interest to me than what is."

"I assume you know the residence intimately since Leo is your gentleman friend."

"My *what*?"

For the first time since Oliver met Gwendolyn her expression was totally without artifice and her surprise was genuine.

"He is nothing of the sort. I am far too old to become entangled in that nonsense," she stated, leaving it wide open for Oliver to assume that Leo had pursued her with dogged determination, and she had resisted every overture.

"And yet here we are, entering the best decades of our lives. Speaking for myself, I say yes to everything that comes my way."

He took his tray to the hall, returned for Gwendolyn's, gave a brief salute, and was gone. The door closed so quietly Gwendolyn wondered if she had dreamed the entire encounter, but that was just jet lag, she decided. The misfiring of synapses in her brain that made her fuzzy and impressionable. Why else would Oliver have been able to hold her attention for so long?

From the Hilroy of Charlotte
Lisa Hansen

DAY: WEDNESDAY, SEPTEMBER 1, 1999
TIME: 10:00 AM or thereabouts. My watch now pretends it is London time, but I am in between here and elsewhere.
LOCATION: Behind a shrub on the side walkway – largely invisible
NOTES: misc. et.al.

I disturbed Gwendolyn in the garden. I ALWAYS disturb Gwendolyn even when she is expecting me to be present. She was clutching something to her chest. She ignored me, at first, and then, after circling around her and disturbing her air, she finally acknowledged my presence.

I asked her what she was holding, and she refused to answer. I told her that was okay because we all had secrets. I knew this would annoy her and it did.

She peeled the article from her chest and shoved it in my face.

A picture of the young Gwendolyn, nose lifted high, boater and Mary Janes firmly in place A historical artifact.

FUTURE SCHOLARS AND RESEARCHERS TAKE NOTE OF WHAT FOLLOWS

I asked her if Sarah had given her the photo (obvious) which got a frown and a no. I asked if she brought photo all the way across the Pacific, and she said she didn't and that it was the ATLANTIC we'd flown across which I knew. Duh! I was just testing her.

I told her I gave up. (Tedious) And she said she found the photo at the bottom of a box of Charlie's things under a pile of incontressential (sp?) papers.

She then said I understood nothing and crammed the picture so hard against her chest I thought it might disappear into her skin. Charlie had this photo among his things. Among his THINGS!! She said that about five times.

Okay. Yeah. Right.

Charlie had the picture. The picture went into a box. The box proves that Charlie had the picture that went into a box. Did he have other pictures, I asked, like maybe a picture of me? But she erased my question with the flick of her fingers.

Following dialogue almost exact:

"This alone, makes this trip worthwhile. It tells me that although he left me behind, he took me with him."

"That must have been pretty hard to do, the leaving behind and taking anyway, thing."

"To someone of your limited intelligence, that is true. Why are you hovering?"

"We're going out now and leaving you behind and not taking you anyway because you wouldn't want to come. Is that what you are getting at with the picture thing?"

"Inform Oliver he may return for me in an hour. And you will be elsewhere."

"Righty-o."

Which only caused her frown to deep dive across her face. As always, I won.

Chapter Fourteen

"We are nicely situated here, in Marylebone," Oliver explained to Henry and Charlotte, indicating with a wave of his hand the cul-de-sac they were leaving. "We could easily walk to our ultimate destination, but I think a short driving tour beforehand will be enjoyable."

"Grandfather loves to drive," Jeremy explained. "He thinks better when he drives."

"That I do," Oliver agreed.

The interior of the Rolls smelled like beeswax candles and the seats were as soft as what spun sugar might feel like if Charlotte could wrap that around her body and not immediately eat it. She loved riding backwards and staring at where she might have been if Oliver had decided to stop the limousine. Henry and Jeremy chose to sit together facing her and, as always, there was a territorial fight between where Henry was allowed to place his feet so they did not interfere where Charlotte wished to place hers, which was everywhere Henry put his. Jeremy solved the problem by changing seats, and Charlotte decided not to bully him since his grandfather was the chauffeur. She now wore yesterday's rose from the tiny glass vase beside the window in her hair and thoughtfully replaced it with a rust-coloured dahlia from the garden.

Regent's Park boasted a wealth of attractions, Oliver explained. There was boating, with a special tour, five days a week, that passed through the London Zoo, a zoo that boasted over six thousand species and held the distinction of being *the most pleasant zoo in the world.*

"How many in the Toronto Zoo?" Charlotte asked Henry, eager for a bit of competition.

"I have not the slightest idea," he responded. Often feeling caged himself, Henry had no interest in other species who had to spend their lives gazing through bars. He only hoped, that unlike him, these poor animals knew no other way to live.

"For stargazers there is the planetarium," Oliver suggested. "And the Royal College of Physicians for anyone thinking they might consider a career in medicine."

"No!" the children said at the same time.

"Perhaps a noonday concert at the Royal Academy of Music?"

"Only if we can listen while eating ice cream, Grandfather. There is this gelato truck that sometimes parks out front, and I recommend the chestnut flavour," Jeremy said. "In a cup."

"I like cones," Charlotte told him. "Sugar cones. Not those ones made from reconstructed paper that taste like chewed up Kleenex."

"Or a sugar cone," Jeremy added. As a host he was responsible for making certain his guests could choose what suited them best. He had a suspicion that Charlotte would always ask for the opposite of what was suggested.

"Shouldn't we show Henry and Charlotte King Edward VII's hospital so they can see where you recovered during the war?" Jeremy asked. "The hospital is overflowing with history," he explained when both Henry and Charlotte looked at him quizzically.

King Edward Hospital, in existence since 1899, located within the Harley Street medical district always, through ongoing donations and philanthropy, provided subsidized care to veterans. Although Oliver had not fit this requirement when he first spent time at the hospital, being only fourteen and not yet a veteran of anything save bad choices, he was treated with respect, kindness, and considerable medical expertise. The King Edward had benefitted greatly, in the years that followed, by Oliver's monetary contributions. It was, he told himself, the very least he could do. These contributions were made with equal amounts of gratitude and guilt, because giving away money was easier than sitting on the Board – which he steadfastly refused to do.

Jeremy was proud of both his grandfather's recovery and his sacred commitment to social democracy – a way of life in which the common man had a say in all government actions and there was unending help for those whose jobs fell short of an adequate salary. Basically, social democracy was an abstract concept that worked in theory but not necessarily in practice, Jeremy discovered, courtesy of the stratified society to which he was born. He tried, and failed, to explain this concept to his two friends.

"Leo, my grandfather has worked every day of his life," Charlotte explained proudly. "He told me to never expect a free handout from whatever idiot was currently running the government. Sounds like a better plan to me."

Oliver chuckled from the front seat. "I look forward to meeting Leo someday."

Jeremy wanted his new friends to see the building where his grandfather had been saved and continued describing it with a rush of passion. "I love it there," he said.

He walked by the hospital often and breathed in the imagined business inside, where sisters, matrons and doctors repaired broken bodies and tried their best to mend disturbed minds. Occasionally Jeremy paid a visit to the front desk and was treated with gentle kindness by the staff who all knew who he was and believed, by consensus, that he was a "bit touched."

'Here comes that boy again,' was a common refrain when the heavy wooden doors opened to admit Jeremy to a cathedral-like stillness. *'Oh dear, oh dear, you talk to him today, Gladys. You are so good with the damaged.'*

If Sarah hadn't driven the ambulance like a speedster angel to the doors of the battered King Edward Hospital and helped hoist the stretcher herself, Oliver would be dead and Jeremy wouldn't have had the chance to be born into a world that, up until yesterday, had treated him poorly.

"I'll go," Henry said. Henry had much experience with hospitals, the smell of disinfectant and apple sauce, the rush of white coats, the blinding fluorescent lights that turned everything a pale shade of green, and the metal chairs where he sat, endlessly waiting, and bidding farewell to a normal childhood.

"Me, too," Charlotte parried, not wanting to let Henry out of her sight. But if he did vanish, she knew where he would reappear and had every intention of showing up just to punish him.

Jeremy had a lot in common with Charlotte, he decided. Constant and chronic exclusion forced those who experienced it into believing they were better than everyone else or helplessly flawed. Even though they both experienced this condition, they related to it differently. He hadn't decided yet where Henry fit on this spectrum because Henry did have a friend, albeit one he said he didn't always want, and he was smart enough to stay quiet when others, including Jeremy, blabbered away non-stop.

"I have but only one thing left to offer," Oliver said sadly, steering the limousine around the outer circle of Regent's Park so the children could take in the trees, open fields, and birds without having to muddy their shoes.

"Camden Town?" Jeremy guessed.

"No."

"Westminster? St Pancras? Soho?"

"You aren't trying, Jeremy," Oliver replied, totally relaxed. Jeremy was right in saying Oliver loved to drive. Aimlessly motoring through the city, wasting time and petrol, was one of life's greatest joys. Nowhere to get to, nowhere to be, no one in your way. His brain went on cruise mode, and he felt like he was floating through the universe.

"Madame Tussauds!" Henry said. "Is that our final destination?"

Henry had the important bits of Baedeker's London Guide safely stashed in his memory bank and he paged through it quickly coming up with what he knew was the right answer. If pressed he could call up the map and tell Oliver exactly how to get there, but he didn't have to bother because Henry knew that, once they completed the Outer Ring, and if Oliver didn't take Prince Albert Road exit or Park Road Exit, he was merely waiting until they reached the southern point and a right turn on York Bridge.

"And Henry wins," Oliver said. "I have purchased tickets, and I thought fish and chips for an early tea. Jack and Sons," he added. "You remember how to get there?" he asked Jeremy.

"Two blocks to the south, one to the west. And I am not to call the owner Jack or enquire as to his sons since the establishment is now owned by a woman."

"Divorce," Oliver said sadly, though no one asked. "I believe Jack's wife keeps the name out of spite."

Charlotte added *spite* to her Hilroy. She knew what it meant but liked her alternate definition better. This definition meant that one part of a person's anatomy was spliced onto another person's anatomy. She had once seen a Vincent Price movie in which this occurred. She wondered if Jack's wife had suspiciously beefy hands and added this observation to her Hilroy before she noticed Jeremy sneaking a peak and quickly hid it beneath the waistband of her shorts.

She spent a fruitless three seconds wondering what Madame Tussauds and fish and chips had to do with the purpose of her trip to London, but her attention span was short, and she believed the spirits freed from their imprisonment in the Tower Room back home in Rose Park were looking around London for fun and entertainment before hunkering down to the job at hand.

A line had formed outside Madame Tussauds when Oliver eased the limousine to the curb. He handed Jeremy an envelope with their tickets and thirty pounds to pay for lunch and drinks. Oliver was very free with his money, having more than he knew what to do with, and Jeremy was punctilious about returning any unused cash back to the overstuffed coffers.

"Keep an eye on your guests," Oliver told Jeremy as Charlotte pulled Henry towards the entrance, ignoring the angry shouts from those who did not have the foresight to purchase their tickets in advance. "Charlotte likes to cut up a bit, Jeremy. Try and keep her on the straight and narrow."

"I will," Jeremy promised.

He wanted to say more, but he saw Oliver fix his gaze on the beggar Floyd who sat on the corner of Marylebone and Nottingham Place, his old tweed cap on the ground in front of his feet. Jeremy knew his grandfather was calculating exactly how much money would keep Floyd in food and lodging for the week and had already dismissed Jeremy and Charlotte and Henry from the forefront of his thoughts.

Jeremy was familiar with these distractions, and the musings that would accompany their wanderings throughout the city to help those who were unable to help themselves. Oliver never simply gave them money because he believed that this would lower their self-esteem, which was already seeping under the door of the WC, but either mental health or physical issues prevented them from accomplishing their goals. Instead, he offered cash for service: some were to keep a permanent eye on Jeremy if he was out on his own, others recorded the license numbers of cars that sped in residential neighborhoods, and others kept a watchful eye on the scam artists who preyed on tourists in Shepherd Market, St Pancras Station, Covent Gardens and near the Serpentine in Kensington Gardens to name but a few. Jeremy thought his grandfather had created a spy network to rival Sherlock Holmes' irregulars except that Oliver's spies were real, and the "irregulars" were fictional.

As he ran to join his friends, he felt a momentary twinge of guilt for what he was about to do to Charlotte. But he was not going to desert her, he promised silently, wishing the hot tingling of fear in his chest would dissipate. He would stay behind to keep her company and when Henry's absence was noticed, he would buy her an extra helping of chips and commiserate.

He longed to confess all this to Oliver, but deception was a necessary precursor to growing up and striking out on his own.

Whoever had told him this was both a liar and a fool.

Chapter Fifteen

For as long as she could remember, Sarah had disliked the mornings. Mornings were too bright, too loud, too crowded with people hurrying to work, distracted by a million tasks they needed to get done before returning home, exhausted, and putting their feet up – only to realize they had but a few remaining hours in the day to live the life they worked so hard to afford.

Her preferred schedule was to rise around eleven, slowly acclimatize to the day by taking a bath. While soaking in the hot water, she planned and plotted, arranging activities for her students, publicizing upcoming shows, and consulting with Ariel regarding the ups and downs of her business. Shopping, cleaning, and cooking (very little since Oliver and Jeremy had moved in permanently) were shoe-horned in as she felt necessary. She had always been an indifferent cook, and cleaning meant moving piles of manuscripts, books, envelopes, and papers from one flat surface to another so the table or desk could get a perfunctory swipe with a rag.

She had not always lived like this, this life of ease. Although, she steadfastly maintained that she would be right as rain living in a bedsit and slipping shillings into the heater while she argued a reduction in rent for the dilapidated building that housed her theatre and school. That she didn't have even a fraction of what was owed would be immaterial because things had a way of working out, they always did and – somehow – she would stay afloat.

It was only in the last three decades that she had been able to embrace a more relaxed lifestyle, which Oliver had been pushing her to do for years. Her work ethic had always been intact, and she'd had her first paying job at the age of ten, helping her uncle make costumes for Yiddish theatre companies in Toronto and undershirts for the 7th Parkside Police Division. In the summer, she sold the vegetables she grew in their tiny back garden. It seemed she had a green thumb when it came to growing tomatoes and peppers. Who would have known? *'The girl only has to look at a seed to make it grow.'*

When she went to Kingston to attend Queen's University, she worked three jobs as well as carrying a full course load. She brought her exceptional skills as a seamstress to the small town and almost immediately lined up a collection of clients, courtesy of some old woman whose name she no longer remembered.

And now I am that old woman, she thought often, when she put one of her students in line for a job or loaned money to a friend with more pressing problems than her own.

Back then, she'd worked in the diner, frying hamburgers at night and French toast in the morning, depending on when she was needed, and tutored drama students (mostly) who were falling behind in mathematics or history which they deemed irrelevant to their future careers. Sarah knew better. Basic geometry was essential if you wanted to build a set that resembled the seedy barroom called for in *The Time of Your Life*. If you didn't understand spatial relationships, how could you sew a gown for Lady Macbeth or pantaloons for Feste? And if you didn't study history, how could you know what was on the horizon for Canada and the rest of the free world in the late thirties?

But her most important job had been tutoring Gwendolyn, something she did as a favour for Charlie, whom she'd met in the theatre program at Queen's in Kingston. Gwendolyn was intelligent but devious, and she had no social skills. Sarah was to smooth her rough edges and make her softer. And that job was her most abject failure because Gwendolyn had not only been difficult – she was used to difficult students in the same way she was used to bored, dismissive, and rude students – but Gwendolyn MacFarlane had been steadfastly imperious and cruel. Even though Sarah knew the child only manifested these behaviours because of a difficult family situation, she had been unable to break through and touch the damaged soul within. That bit of nonsense about a damaged soul had petered out quickly when Sarah saw that Gwendolyn had no interest in anyone except herself.

She studied that specimen from her bedroom, looking out the window into the garden. Gwendolyn sat, back straight as a board, her teacup held at a precarious angle while she viewed the birds, chipmunks, and late blooming dahlias with a sense of superiority. And wouldn't you know, she had found her portrait in Charlie's box of belongings, and it now sat on her lap.

"Stop it," Sarah said aloud. "Aren't you far too old to bear these worn-out grudges?"

Yes. She was far too old, but that didn't matter. She knew Gwendolyn must have received the letters she sent, and now the adult Gwendolyn maintained she never saw one. She saw them alright, for about two seconds before she relegated them to the garbage bin.

She couldn't believe that all this nonsense and hard feelings were the result of a piece of jewellery. When Charlie gave her the Tree of Life brooch, all those many long years ago, she was flattered but also speechless. Her style had always leaned towards the bohemian (cheap, colourful, and casual) and the brooch was classical in design, best shown off against a black sweater or on the lapel of a stylish jacket which she did not have. And yet, it was the offering that was important, not the object. It was a pledge. *'This must go to our child. I don't know why, but I feel it is important. Will you promise?'*

And she had because she truly liked Charlie. *Liked* not loved. Such an important distinction. Sarah believed that friendship had a greater chance of surviving than romantic love.

Coward, she thought.

Outside, Gwendolyn ironed the pleats in her skirt with her hand.

A line from Shakespeare came to Sarah unbidden and she recited it to the glass. "Love is a smoke and is made with the fume of sighs."

They were similar, she and Gwendolyn. Sarah doubted that Gwendolyn could feel love. Love was too exclusionary; Sarah's conceit was she wished to embrace the entire world, whereas Gwendolyn wished to ignore the entire world. But their aloofness was what glued them together. However, she was also aware that she would never know nor fully understand another person. This is what gave her life energy, a gentle tug forward when she felt like sitting down, a shooting star appearing when she began to tire of looking at the sky.

She might not know, but she wouldn't give up trying.

She picked a prune from the plate on the tray that Oliver had prepared and slipped it into her mouth. A sluggish digestive system was only one of the many curses of old age, and she had grown to dislike the cloying sticky sweetness of prunes until Oliver, noticing the bowl came back full, started to simmer them with water, lemon juice, a touch of honey and a sprig of lavender. Lavender, she had asked, not even realizing the herb was edible. Now the prunes melted in her mouth, and she barely had to chew before swallowing.

Her reflections, always heightened by the presence of a new day, continued as she poured herself a cup of coffee. She breathed in the aroma of the Folgers – very hard to find in Britain, but Oliver had his sources. She took a sip and smiled with contentment. All was as well in her world as could possibly be, given the reality she could pass away at any second.

Passing away was one thing, but passing away without regrets was another thing altogether.

Had she been younger she might have finally relented and said yes, yes, yes to a contented life with a compatible partner. For a moment, a few months, a mere blip in the span of her years, Oliver might have been that person. They were unsuitable from the start: she twenty years his senior, stalwart friends who did not believe in mixing rapport with the fever of sexual longing, her beholden to him for everything – her comfortable accommodation, her theatre school, the education of her daughter and granddaughter. Why would she want to trade this for a simple sating of desire?

But neither she nor Oliver were practical people and rarely if ever considered the consequence of their actions. How did it happen? When he took her hand to help her across the street? When he showed up every night to clean the studio? When Ariel departed the family home vowing never to return? When she was beset with doubts and yearnings that had no name?

'Longing,' Oliver had mused. '*I know it well.*'

She remembered those words exactly but did not remember their first time together, nor their tenth or twentieth. Nothing in their relationship changed except Oliver's knock on her bedroom door or her knock on his – and then one day, almost by mutual consent, they stopped. She no longer remembered why. Had there been a cross word? Other lovers? To the best of her recollection neither had been the case. They had simply worn out their longing, or perhaps both began longing for something else equally inaccessible.

'*Do I take you for granted?*' she'd asked Oliver once and he had replied: '*Never.*' And she'd said: '*You will kill me if I do?*' And Oliver: '*In whatever manner you should wish.*'

She still had Oliver close by, and she had Jeremy, she had Ariel (whose departure lasted only twenty years), who, just like Sarah, had opted for the single life. The only one who had managed to escape was Celeste, who, by all accounts, was happily married and living on another continent.

Escape?

Why should that be the word to describe what Celeste had done?

All the better that she should be the one to possess the Tree of Life brooch since, clearly, she was the only one who understood its meaning.

And then it came to her, why she was standing still at the window, studying Gwendolyn.

Life's last gasp.

A chance to make a difference, a chance to do well by Charlie who would have been saddened (albeit briefly) by what Gwendolyn had become. After all Charlie could laugh. He could dance and play the piano better than anyone she had met since. And he had a spontaneous joy that bubbled up and overflowed when he spied a cat climbing up a newly hung wall of curtains, or when he sank down in a chair with a glass of scotch in his hand.

She no longer had anything to lose, and had everything to gain.

Gwendolyn's unexpected phone call and current presence in her garden called up more memories of Charlie than had emerged in half a century. And Charlotte, prattling on and on about their time together in Toronto in the summer of 1939, well that brought on, with the suddenness of a flash explosion, exactly what a tuna fish sandwich plate looked like at Diana Sweets on Yonge Street (slice of pinkish tomato with a sprig of parsley on limp leaf of iceberg lettuce). Suddenly Sarah could taste the soft doughy bread and salty greasy fish the minute Charlotte reminded her of the time they sat together at the counter. It was magic, pure and simple, helped along by the dream she'd had last night where she was dancing the Lindy Hop at Dilys Frank's cottage on the Island in Toronto and Charlie was prancing about with Charlotte sitting atop his shoulders. She could feel the heat in the room, the drumming pounding beneath her rib cage, she could see Dilys Frank's piercing blue eyes stare at her from across the room and she could hear her mouth the words: '*Remember this.*'

"Why?" she asked aloud.

Their last time together had been so brief. Charlie in a rush, a piece of toast in one hand, the clatter of keys in another, a quick kiss to her cheek, the smell of Old Spice and he was gone, out the door, vanishing from her life. For the longest time she couldn't bear the smell of toasted bread or the feel of it beneath her fingertips. It was too tactile, too abrasive, the way Charlie's cheek had felt beneath her fingertips in the morning before he shaved.

For a woman who prided herself on not being sentimental, the force of her emotions had come as a surprise, knocked her flat out before she took a breath and stood up for another round.

What was she missing?

What hadn't been done?

And then it came to her, the swift breath of memory.

How could she have forgotten her most important promise, the one she made to Charlie only a month before Ariel was born? Here she was trying to play with Gwendolyn when that wasn't what Charlie had wanted at all.

She went to her closet, flung open the double doors and began, with some discomfort from her back and aching knees, to find the old shoe box where she had stored remembrances; Charlie's Reverso watch with the leather strap given to him by Ian on his graduation from university. An elegant and expensive gift, Ian had the reverse side of the watch inscribed with Charlie's name and the message: fly high my son. Why did she have it when it belonged on Charlie's wrist? It took her a while to remember. '*I've been dumped into the water and the damn thing doesn't work anymore. Keep it for me and when the war is over, I'll have it fixed. Or buy a new one.*' Not verbatim perhaps but close enough. And there was a handkerchief, embossed with his initials, a navy blue tie with faint horizontal stripes almost the colour of the midnight sky, the keys to his flat. '*This way I always have to find you first, Sarah, otherwise I'll be breaking in through my own window.*

And letters filled with Charlie's errant thoughts when he couldn't sleep at night, lyrics to songs he meant to write, his sudden fear of clouds which he used to love.

> You are up there, soaring, looking and suddenly, out of
> a bank of clouds comes a score of Messerschmitt 109s
> using the clouds for cover. Makes me scared but angry
> too. I used to love to laze about on the grass in the
> summer and stare at the clouds. I don't think they'll ever
> look the same to me again.

She hadn't read the letters in decades. It was strange, but she had been able to read them over and over for a year after he died and then slowly, instead of getting easier to see his large loping script, it became more painful until she realized she might never look at them again. Ariel could deal with them after she was gone, or give them to Celeste, a memory of the grandfather she never knew. For a time, Ariel had worn Charlie's tie and clumped around their rooms above the theatre in Charlie's brown and white saddle shoes, shoes which now had come back into fashion. Where were they? Ariel would know, but did Sarah care to see them again? Ariel had had all Charlie's clothes cleaned and pressed and hung in the corner of her closet. For an unsentimental woman, this was indeed an anomaly, and Sarah had asked her to donate them to the theatre so they could be used in upcoming productions. *'Thank you, I think I won't,'* was all Ariel had said.

What was it she was looking for? She'd been distracted by long-ago memories, and her hand hung listless above the box, hovering. Her daughter, Celeste, Charlie?

'Give this to Gwendolyn. I can't put it in the mail. It may never get there and for all I know it won't be necessary.'

What did that mean?

'It's a worst-case scenario letter, Sarah. After a bad run or another death, I can hear the pens scratching across paper in the middle of the night. Not me. Too superstitious or too cocky? But then again...'

And there it was. The last item in the box, flattened into tissue paper thinness, GWEN peering up at her from the envelope, her watery eyes imaging exclamation points after the name.

She'd never mailed the letter to Gwendolyn. She'd never heard from her and suspected the child had destroyed all her letters before reading them. She might do the same with this, and that would never do. Sarah had always meant to deliver the letter in person, travel backwards in time to Toronto or find out somehow where Gwendolyn was living, but with one thing and another, the time never came.

The phone rang, and she turned away from the closet, letter in hand.

"I am late. Should be there in an hour," she heard Oliver say as she picked up the receiver, the harshness of horns blaring and the hiss of traffic reminding her that at least part of the city was getting down to business. "I didn't wake you?"

"I've been awake for a while now," she said. The dream had seen to that, the quickening within a body that was no longer young and nearly beyond being old.

"Have you spoken with her yet?"

"I'm building up to it. I found the letter."

"Ah," Oliver said, after a moment of silence. "Do not tarry, my dear. Don't you want her to have something to think about when she shops?"

Chapter Sixteen

Once inside Madame Tussauds, the air changed colour. This always happened when Charlotte entered a museum. The molecules, confined in rooms without windows, became denser, and the artificial light and forced air ventilation caused a refraction making what was invisible out of doors glimmer and become almost wave-like, inside of what Charlotte could best describe as a large, overly inhabited, and garishly decorated tomb. This passing sensation of not being able to breathe or see properly had been described to her as claustrophobia, the only condition Charlotte suffered from, and she had to steel herself from turning on her heel and leaving immediately.

She followed Henry and Jeremy and the steady locomotion helped steady her. Jeremy stopped in front of a display of four men lounging around a couch.

Jeremy introduced them as if they were alive and were his long-lost brothers.

"The Beatles," he announced proudly. "My kin."

Indeed, they all bore a striking resemblance to Jeremy: a bit nerdish, overeager, both proud and shy at the same time. One of the men looked vaguely familiar, and Charlotte knew she had seen him before, but she couldn't immediately place the time or location. The orange couch where they were lounging was similar in shape and colour to the one that sat in the inglenook in Charlotte's house back in Toronto. She felt a sudden wave of homesickness and took a step back, bumping into Henry, who didn't even bother to ask if she was alright.

Henry was awash with excitement. She could feel this heat spraying off his body, and she felt suddenly diminished for not sharing in the thrill of being on their own in a foreign city. By all rights she should be the one who was grinning and laughing and punching Jeremy on the shoulder and calling him mate and swaggering like a fool on the hill. In truth, Henry was doing none of these things, merely staring reverentially at Jeremy's waxy brothers, but Charlotte exaggerated his behaviour because she felt suddenly so unwell. Her head hurt and her skin felt clammy, but there was no way she would admit this in present company.

Jeremy, noticing her subtle retreat had the nerve to ask: "Not your métier?"

And there was nothing for it but to inscribe this remark as well as her impressions of the Beatles instantly in her Hilroy. She no longer tried to hide this activity from Jeremy, and Henry was immune to the sight of her black and white notebook. Charlotte saw herself as a reporter for an organization called the universe and made a big deal of licking her pencil, riffling through a few pages in her notebook and pausing for effect as if what she was about to write was the premiere definition for the meaning of life. When a person felt unwell it was a good idea to get busy with an activity, therefore giving the affliction no chance to gain ascendency. This had worked for Charlotte in the past, and it worked now.

Jeremy continued to talk – fast, loud, and supremely annoying – but Charlotte paid close attention. She learned that the Beatles had changed the course of contemporary music and were proudly British to the core. John, Paul, Ringo, and George were icons, having achieved a godlike status in just a few short years. One of the names triggered Charlotte's memory and she raised a victory fist.

"I knew I'd seen him before" Charlotte said, pointing at Ringo. "Wasn't he the conductor in *Thomas the Tank Engine*?"

Henry, Mr. All Grown Up with No Place to Go, appeared embarrassed by her inquiry – but Jeremy gave her a high five and said it was his favourite show of all time.

"Mine, too," Charlotte acknowledged, having spent many enjoyable afternoons lounging on the chesterfield with Leo while Ringo lifted her away on fictional adventures.

"Did you watch Thomas, too?" Jeremy asked Henry.

Henry had not been allowed to watch television until he became friends with Charlotte, which is why he spent so much time at her house. Charlotte decided she didn't need to embarrass Henry with this admission, because the restriction was not his fault and people should not be punished just because their jailers were cruel.

Henry passed over the question and asked for more information on the Beatles.

"They were so grand and important that they were given an audience with the queen which is very hard to get since Queen Elizabeth is so busy with public functions and her corgis."

"Corgis?" Charlotte asked. "Are they some sort of relative?"

"Dogs," Henry answered with a smirk.

"People obsessed about the length of their hair," Jeremy explained, hooking his thumbs in the waistband of his pants. "It almost became a scandal."

A scandal? Charlotte doubted that. Jeremy was now grandstanding for attention.

The man who drove the Crescent Road bus had hair twice as long, and Franklin Darice, a weirdo who taught Grade 3 at Rose Park public school, wore his hair in a ponytail. Very big deal, Charlotte thought when Jeremy continued his reportage on the "hair" scandal – ladies fainting and letters to the editor about moral decline. One might think that Jeremy had been standing by, microphone in hand, to get an 'as it happened' response, instead of not existing at all in the sixties unless the universe was playing a huge joke on everybody and people floated in and out of the nether at will. From Jeremy's encyclopedic knowledge of those he had never met, Charlotte learned that Ringo had been born in July of 1940 and was not even present on the planet while Charlotte and Henry were sequestered in a time travel adventure, circa May 1939. For a reason unknown, this made her feel somewhat superior to the famous quartet.

However, this thought quickly flipped on its side, and the pain behind Charlotte's eyeballs increased. She found a wooden bench where she could update her journal and keep a steady, if somewhat bleary, eye on Henry.

From her seat she saw Henry nodding wisely, his head bowed.

As if that blowturd, Henry, knows one bloody thing about the Beatles.

> And I will never ask him what metvay (sp?) means
> because he will lie. The entrails that make up Henry's
> brain have not yet digested the Spanish dictionary.

"French," Jeremy murmured reading over her shoulder and Charlotte slammed her Hilroy shut with a snap that was heard in the far corners of the room.

How could Jeremy decode her writing she wondered, and as the two boys leisurely strolled from the room in the direction of the "Chamber of Horrors" Charlotte took a quick look at the page she had just written.

It wasn't in her shorthand at all, but real words that *anybody* could read at will.

That was no good, no good at all, and she spent precious minutes ripping the page out of her journal and shredding it into confetti size pieces before relegating it to the trash can filled with purple cans of Ribena and Nestle's Lion Bar wrappers. A museum guard stared at her suspiciously, but Charlotte held up her notebook, mimed ripping out a page and then washed her hands of the gesture and the guard. It was time to push past the line of people waiting to get in to the "Chamber of Horrors" and meet a few more of Jeremy's *kin*.

Jeremy was on his way back when Charlotte bumped into him. He was leaving ostensibly in search of a water fountain and even though he was watching for her, Charlotte managed to step out in front of him without warning.

"Too much for you?" she asked.

He jumped slightly, making an odd hiccough noise before regaining his composure and finding a smile for her.

"Not at all," he said. "I've seen it before and although the wax figures are remarkably lifelike, one appreciates that these people are long dead and cannot continue their devilish behaviour."

He and Henry had spent the few private minutes they had finding an alternate exit that wouldn't set off an alarm. Although he hadn't murdered or dismembered anyone, Jeremy felt a sort of uncomfortable kinship with the monsters, masquerading as men and women, who appeared to watch everything he did. In his absence, he noticed that Charlotte had rearranged her hair – it was constrained in a messy topknot and with a pencil piercing the centre, a puckish fashion that Jeremy approved of.

"I rather like what you did with your hair. It's smashing," he told her, circling slowly so he could take it in from every angle.

Charlotte ignored him and accelerated straight to the point.

"And where is Henry?"

"Henry?" Jeremy asked, a confused expression crossing his face, confused and guilty simultaneously.

"Yes, Henry. A kid about your size, glasses, brown hair, vacant expression."

"Oh, Henry." Jeremy smiled. "He's using the facilities."

"The facilities are off the entrance, and unless Henry floated by me invisibly, that is not where he is." Charlotte pressed Jeremy up against the wall and heard a few well-bred British protests float by her ears. "You are lying."

Standing that close to Charlotte allowed Jeremy to appreciate the hay and lavender smell she exuded; an exotic perfume that made him dizzy. Plus, the force of her body against his was stimulating, in a perverse sort of way. If his arms were free, he might consider hugging her, but such a move was out of the question. If she succeeded in choking the breath out of him security guards would come running, and there would be explanations to make, and his grandfather would be called. He considered this option, an option that would give Henry a generous head start, for about a second and relented.

"I'm lying," Jeremy admitted. Henry would have to make do with the time he had because the intensity of Charlotte's stare unnerved him. At heart Jeremy was a bit of a coward, but a kindly one. "I'm sorry, Charlotte," he said. "He's made a run for it."

"I didn't think he'd act so fast," Charlotte said, removing her arm from his chest. "We've been here less than a day. Idiot."

"Me?" Jeremy asked meekly, holding his arms up in surrender.

"I'm the idiot," she said. "Henry is a sneaky devil. Do you think he hasn't done this to me before? But I caught him then, and I'll catch him now."

"I'm certain he will be fine," Jeremy said.

"Don't bet money on that, and if your grandfather knew, you would be toast."

"Toast?" Jeremy asked, not familiar with the expression.

"We better get moving," she said.

"Where?" he asked. "It's pretty early for lunch, but if you are hungry, we—"

"We need to go to Park Street near Borough Market. Do you know how to get there?"

"Not offhand," Jeremy prevaricated. Henry had not shared the address of his father's friends, but it was good to know he had not left the city. That was a relief.

"It's in Southwark," Charlotte explained. "I found Henry's note hidden in plain sight. He can't hide anything from me. Is Southwark a town or a village? Do we have to take a train?"

"No. It's a section of London. Rather near Guy's Hospital."

It wasn't a neighborhood Jeremy frequented, he explained, but he had, of course, been to London Bridge several times and Southwark Cathedral, the second oldest Gothic church in London. "Poets and other semi-notables are buried in crypts within the cathedral. Do you think they feel weird with tourists stomping about overhead?"

"I could care less. Is this what you spend time thinking about? Dead people in crypts?"

Jeremy scratched his head. "Sometimes. It's not like I want to. I can't seem to help it. The atmosphere presses in on me."

"Do you know for sure that Southwark is near this guy's hospital?"

Charlotte's intense stare began to cause Jeremy's eye sockets to overheat. This could not be a simple case of Charlotte missing her friend or feeling hard done by because Henry had gone somewhere without her. Was Henry journeying towards danger? And had Jeremy been complicit in allowing him to enter this frightening world? A world littered with clones of Buck Ruxton, George Chapman, Florence Maybrick, and their ilk, masquerading as street vendors, bobbies, and black cab hacks?

"Is Henry in danger?" he asked, heart palpitating.

"He's always in danger, don't you get it? I've been looking after him since the day I met him. He's completely innocent. Do you know what that means?" Charlotte had grown in stature and now appeared to tower over Jeremy.

"Guileless?"

"Well, yeah, he is gutless, but there is something about him that just screams out, 'take advantage of me,' and here he is in a city he knows nothing about."

"He has the entire Underground routes stored in his brain, remarkable achievement that, and he has street locations at his fingertips. I imagine you may be mistaken in—"

"I'm not," Charlotte insisted, grabbing Jeremy's hand. His palm was moist and sticky. "He's wandering the streets with a pile of money in his shoe."

"Oh, that's why he seems to be lame." Jeremy felt intense relief. "I thought he twisted his ankle yesterday when… how do you know this? If the money is hidden in his shoe, he couldn't possibly have told you."

Charlotte manhandled Jeremy out the door of Madame Tussauds and stopped, looking to the right and left, trying to get her bearings. "It's my business to know Henry's business. It's far too complicated to explain, but I got him in this mess to begin with and he is my responsibility."

"What mess? You mean the Tower Room and your otherworldly travels?"

Charlotte reached in her pocket, and pulled out the paper on which she had copied the address Henry had wrapped around a flat packet of British currency of various denominations. "This is where he's gone."

Jeremy looked at the paper, looked at Charlotte and looked at the paper again. "But I know exactly where this is. This is the place of residence of former business associates of my grandfather's." Jeremy felt a twinge of sadness that Henry had not trusted him enough to share the address. "They're slightly dodgy perhaps, but good people. I mean, my grandfather has said on occasion that a decent crook can be a better friend than a pious minister. All they did was create forgeries of very minor works of art, when they were young and knew no better."

Charlotte tapped her foot impatiently on the sidewalk as Jeremy went on. "And they had stopped doing this altogether when they became real artists. I met them once when I was with Grandfather at the National Portrait Gallery. They pointed out the ghostly silhouette in the Bronte sisters' portrait. All hush-hush, like it was a big secret. And told me most people didn't even see it. It's quite amazing. You see…"

"I don't *care* about portraits of sisters..." Charlotte tried to say, but there was no staunching the flow of words being directed her way.

"... they said it was a visitation, a permanent one, and we should all be alert to such in our lives. We are visited by ghosts constantly. Sometimes I wake up in the middle of the night and I feel like I'm not alone. Has that ever happened to you? Do you believe in ghosts?"

He stopped for breath then, and Charlotte narrowed her eyes at him.

"Jeremy, I *believe* you are deliberately holding me up here."

He dropped his gaze and studied the sidewalk. "I don't want Henry to be mad at me."

"I think you should worry more about me being mad at you. You've given him the best head start you can. Pat yourself on the back. From now on, the only thing I want to hear are directions to get us where we need to go. Got it?"

Jeremy nodded and grabbed her hand. "The Underground is two blocks away."

Chapter Seventeen

The Underground was truly a horrible place, Henry discovered. Quite aptly called "the Tube," the British system of belowground transportation was claustrophobic in a way that Toronto's was not. Granted, Toronto's subway system was an infant, a mere babe to London's elder statesman. Toronto's inaugural ride showcased in 1958. London had been operating this mode of transportation since 1863.

The first subterranean experience, or test case, took place between Paddington and Farringdon. Wooden carriages, lit by gas lamps, were dragged through dark and damp tunnels in the earth by steam locomotives no doubt thrilling for those brave enough to enlist as passengers.

But how did they get the steam locomotives into these tunnels? Were they dismantled and passed in pieces, hand over hand, to workers who painstakingly recreated them? Or did these hearty locomotives back slowly, belching furiously, into a narrow downward slanting pathway dug into the ground and reinforced by who knew what, commandeered by cheerful pipe smoking conductors? If these trains had to keep backing in and out all day, wasn't this rather counterproductive? Or maybe they careened carelessly through a roundabout, reminding Henry of a carnival ride he once had to endure when he was eight ('*Now, this is going to be fun,*' said Henry's Dad) ending in a trip to the emergency ward at Toronto General.

To Henry's way of thinking, not having the engineering design in his memory bank, this so-called Underground experience was ripe for disaster – fire, flood, landslide, and cave-ins were but a few of the obvious perils. Volunteering for this ride was akin to putting up your hand to stand on the rim of Mount Vesuvius, in Henry's humble estimation. Every one of his phobias kicked in as he contemplated the noisy, dank, and danger-ous experiment.

Henry knew the barebones history of the London Underground because he had ingested a lot of British trivia. Probably too much because, as his father once pointed out, '*No one likes a show-off, Henry. It's good to be smart but keep it under your hat.*'

His escape from Madame Tussauds had been cobbled together hur-riedly, resulting in some disorientation. As Henry had jogged down the street, he'd tried to get his bearings and figure out his route to freedom. He hadn't been able to do this the night before because he did not know what the plans of the coming day would be. He could just as easily have wound up outside the British Museum or watching the changing of the Guard at Buckingham Palace. Once he was a block away, he slowed his pace to a walk and paged through his memory bank, colliding with more than a few British citizens who were unfailingly polite when he walked straight into them.

It made sense to head to the Marylebone Station, and he would be on the Bakerloo line. Then it was a straight run to Elephant and Castle where he would only have to walk a few short blocks to arrive at his destination.

An unsettling fact alerted his nervous system, and he felt himself begin to tremble.

The Bakerloo line not only went underground, but it also went straight under the river Thames. Henry was certain that once he sensed water overhead, he would begin to scream and would not be able to stop no matter how many deep breaths he took. He had been taught this calming technique at Toronto General after he displayed overt panic when in the Aquarium room at the Toronto Zoo.

Henry took one breath and decided it was time to man up. His many monetary conquests at Camp Highland over the summer indicated he knew what he was about, and if he expected to make anything of himself, it was imperative that he conquer his fears and ride the Bakerloo line even if it took him to a place of fear.

> You gain strength, courage, and confidence by every
> experience where you stop to look fear in the face. You
> must do the thing which you think you cannot do.

Henry's mother had this quotation from Eleanor Roosevelt, printed in Century Gothic typeface and framed where it hung above the kitchen stove. Henry had always wondered if this was meant to inspire his mother to learn how to cook, but so far, the words had not been effective.

Courage was one thing, foolhardiness was another.

If he felt his nervous system could not stand the strain, he could always get off at Embankment, take a quick sideways glance at the famous Westminster Cathedral, should it be visible to the east, and walk across the Hungerford Bridge on foot. Or he could just flag down a taxi. He was tall enough to be seen and he could even wave a ten-pound note in the air. He had money. Scads of it.

Every second he remained indecisive was a boon to Charlotte, who he knew would be fast on his trail. He didn't think Jeremy would be able to hold her off for long because, even though Jeremy was now his best friend, he was a bit of a wuss, just like Henry himself was in danger of once again becoming.

He didn't mind being rescued once he reached his destination. It was only important that he get there first, thereby besting Charlotte in her forever game of "I win."

As he strode manfully down the stairs, filthy with the tread marks of a million pairs of boots, Henry decided expediency ruled. If he should feel unsettled, he would merely dip his head and examine the floor of the train and count to one hundred by tens in French, then Italian, and finish in German.

An active brain was a settled brain.

It almost worked.

Once the confusion of how to buy a ticket, an important item not stored in his memory bank, was solved and he stepped on board the foul-smelling train, he felt he had made the right decision.

When the doors opened at Embankment, he almost made a dash for it, but he was busy figuring out what to say to these supposed "great friends" of his father's and why he felt it necessary to pay Byron and Meggie a visit. It never occurred to him that they might not be at home, or any other permutation – arrested, dead etc.

As the train launched itself deeper into the earth's inner core, Henry could feel the great Thames pressing like an iron boot on his paper-thin skull, and his vision became wavy.

He knew things were getting bad when, reduced to his counting technique, he got to *funfzig* and found himself clutching the sleeve of a woman he stood beside.

"Here now," the lady said, placing her hand on Henry's shoulder. "Do you have a bit of a tummy?"

Henry looked at her glassy-eyed.

"A *seat*," she demanded, dragging Henry through the crush of commuters and yanking a teenager with an Apache cut off his seat. Henry felt himself manhandled into the slot and was aware that the seats on either side of him immediately became vacant.

"Now you put your head between your knees and breathe slowly through your mouth. Paper bag," she yelled and a bag smelling strongly of day-old fish was pressed between his hands.

The British Tube-riding population was extremely kind, Henry realized, feeling a bit of relief that if the worst happened, and the Thames won, he would be surrounded by caring souls.

"*Danke*," he whispered, his brain fixated on continuing a conversation in German although his vocabulary, other than numbers, was limited.

"You speak English?"

Henry nodded weakly.

His Nikes gave him away.

Did Germans wear Nikes?

"Here's what I think," his new friend told him, busy with a cloth bag that appeared to be sewn into her shoulder. "Always carry a biscuit with you."

At this she produced a miniature packet of McVitie's and broke the seal with her teeth. She pried a beige cookie out of its cellophane enclosure and placed it in Henry's hand.

"There's nothing like a real British digestive to set things straight. My name's Doreen, by the way. Tea?" She whisked a bullet-shaped silver thermos from her bag and unscrewed the lid.

The train veered dangerously but she didn't spill a drop. "Been riding this line five days a week, fifty weeks a year for twenty-eight years now, and I come prepared. If I told you all I seen, you wouldn't believe me, so best let those dogs lie."

"Henry," said Henry accepting the cup, spilling half on his trousers, and drinking the rest gratefully. It was warm, bracing and very sweet.

"It's nice to meet you, Henry. Nobody knows how to make a good cuppa anymore," she told him, watching in satisfaction as he drank every drop. "Steeping not stewing and warm the pot. How's that tummy?"

"Much better," Henry admitted. The Thames had receded into a harmless stream and the pressure he felt in his body had eased.

Henry's conditions were medically legitimate, up to a certain point. He did have irritant contact dermatitis mixed with allodynia, but the allodynia could not be neuropathically traced, and came with more pressure than pain, leaving the doctors to believe Henry suffered from what six percent of the world suffered from: an extreme sensitivity to every known external situation, whether it be animal, vegetable, or mineral.

Doreen was a bona fide office sanitation specialist and had been for thirty-five years, and not one of them fly-by-night immigrants. She worked evenings at an office tower, where, according to her, the associates lived like animals.

"Use the garbage cans for hoop practice, cigarettes ground into the carpet, fingerprints all over the window, and the loo… well, you don't want to know."

Henry actively shut down the part of his brain that began to imagine what went into her heavy-duty black garbage bag, because, firstly, it wasn't any of his business, and secondly, he couldn't imagine the grit and fortitude it would take to do such a job.

He was awash with admiration.

He watched her recap her thermos, screw it tight with a red, chapped hand, and deposit it back into her burlap bag. He felt quite at home with her. She resembled a large soft pillow with treasures like food and drink hidden inside the pillow slip.

"Take this," she told him, handing him a key fob that rattled when it made its way from her hand to his. A gold snake was coiled against a black background on one side and on the other a hieroglyphic figure that might be Japanese.

"Given to me many years ago at Charing Cross by a Japanese fellow who had lost his way. I had some time, so I took him to where he needed to go. Didn't think a thing about it, but he kept bowing, hands clasped and wouldn't let me go. Finally gave me this. Said he'd been waiting years to find the person it belonged to. You know what it means?"

Henry shook his head. Japanese was on his list of languages to study, but he had not had time to pursue the difficult task.

"It means *warrior*. A warrior never shirks when times are tough. A warrior is tough like a bear and sneaky like a fox. And a warrior always protects the underdog. You got that, Henry?"

"Yes. Thanks."

There was a comfortable silence while the train continued to rattle forward.

Both Henry and Doreen exited at the Elephant and Castle stop.

"On my way to what used to be my local before I moved. Nobody makes a better Scotch egg. You?" she asked. "What are you about?"

"I'm going to meet some business associates of my father's."

"And what business would that be?"

Henry shrugged.

"Nice of you to pay your respects, you from another country and all. You get into trouble, I'll be here," she said, stopping in front of a pub bearing the name the Jolly Wanderer. "Good part of the next two hours, this being my day off."

Henry said goodbye with a sense of regret. He thought about asking Doreen to stay with him, but what excuse could he give? It wasn't as if he were frightened. He wasn't. He just liked the absoluteness and nowness of her presence. He lingered for just a second and she smiled.

"Get on with you then. We both got business to see to."

Chapter Eighteen

Gwendolyn dismissed her personal shopper within minutes of entering Harrods. The very idea that a stranger, and a badly-dressed one at that, knew what Gwendolyn needed and wanted was ludicrous. She disliked any kind of tour guide, whether it be a museum docent or real estate agent. They all had their own interests in the foreground: the former pretending, for his own sense of personal importance, that he knew more than he did about what life was like in Rome under Nero, and the latter, her eye on the prize of a five percent commission, failing to point out the hidden pitfalls of a given penthouse in the sky such as neighbours and a concierge who kept track of her every coming and going.

Gwendolyn preferred living in a bubble of her own construction, and once the personal shopper said that Burberry had a Macintosh that "Madam would love" Gwendolyn showed her the door. Or, more accurately, pointed her in the direction of Oliver who paid her for her time and offered the apologies that Gwendolyn was unable to offer herself. Had she honestly agreed to this travesty?

To steady her nerves and banish the sound of that pompous voice from her mind, Gwendolyn strolled the perimeter of the perfume counter and sprayed her wrists and décolletage with Chanel No. 5. For a brief period (ten years to be exact) Gwendolyn had used Chanel No. 22, but it lacked the elusive yet tantalizing aroma of the original and there was something a bit pedestrian about No. 22 – it began to remind her of a long-ago summer day, but not the good kind (if there was such). More like the humid, oppressive and deadly boring kind of summer day, the type she endured for years when she was a prisoner in the Great Canadian Prairies. Gwendolyn was sick of long ago because long ago had done nothing for her except tie her down to people who had never loved her and never would. As she had poured her last bottle of No. 22 down the kitchen drain, adding a cup of bleach to purify the air, she had smiled in satisfaction. She deserved a fragrance that stated quite clearly that she was in the room and had no intention of going anywhere.

She turned the bottle she held in her hand upside down so she could read the price.

"Ridiculous."

Although she didn't know or care what the conversion rate was, she knew Harrods was overcharging because that was their sole purpose. When a patron left the store carrying a bag with Harrods stamped on it, a bag that cost more to manufacture than what it would cost to feed a family of four a nourishing dinner, it stated clearly that the proud possessor of this bag and whatever was inside had arrived in some upper echelon of society filled with people as boring as themselves.

Gwendolyn acknowledged she was in a bad mood – the unopened letter from Charlie the primary culprit – but that was fine because it increased her air of haughtiness. But it was not fine that she had muttered some of her thoughts aloud.

"I sorry, I'm afraid I don't understand, Madam."

The shopgirl, too tall without the added height of an unfortunate beehive hair arrangement, had the gall to whisk the bottle from Gwendolyn's hand and replace it on a silver tray, polishing it with a handkerchief she whisked from the cuff of her shirt.

The tone, rather condescending, was not to Gwendolyn's liking, and she placed her hand, the hand with the sapphire and diamond ring she bought herself on her sixtieth birthday prominently on display. She tapped the counter with her fingernails.

"You perfume is overpriced," she repeated.

She had no idea if this was true, but prudence dictated, and she had to complain of something since the shopgirl had rudely removed the bottle from her hand.

For a moment Gwendolyn wished she was back in the garden talking with Sarah even though the conversation had created a river of anger.

For a woman who had just turned ninety, Sarah looked and acted like she could be Gwendolyn's age. Yes, her hands were liver-spotted, and her fingers were crooked. Yes, her face was wrinkled and marked with sun freckles. Yes, her toenails had yellowed and thickened, but she clearly didn't care that Gwendolyn noted all these imperfections with a quick flick of her eyes, down and up and then straight ahead, unwavering, to give her a moment to digest these faults. Who wore open-toed mules at Sarah's age? Gwendolyn had tossed hers when she turned fifty.

And who used their crippled hands to embellish her dialogues – Sarah didn't speak so much as emote. Who spread her fingers, lifted her hands to the sky, smiled freely which only exaggerated her wrinkles and displayed teeth that needed a dentist's attention and not Gwendolyn's brief piercing stare? And who appeared in public wearing a costume of navy and white striped sailor pants with a bright red bolero jacket that was ripped at the right shoulder and smelled faintly of mothballs?

But worse, who radiated a complete ease that could never be purchased, even with all Gwendolyn's money, at Harrods?

The brief discussion about Charlie, her dearly loved older brother had irritated, confused, and hurt Gwendolyn more than she wished to admit.

"Charlie was already a pilot when we arrived in London in October of 1939. Because of his British citizenship he—"

"His what? Charlie was not British. He was Canadian."

"Actually," Sarah had said gently, "Charlie was born in England."

Oh, yes. A rather major historical fact that no one bothered to tell Gwendolyn at the time. The tale of the man who had abandoned Gwendolyn's dear mother and his unborn child in one fell swoop. But not before leaving the Tree of Life brooch for his child. A brooch worth a great deal of money. Was this absconder a lord, a member of the tired old British aristocracy, or just filthy rich? Had he been killed before he could drag Eliza to the altar? Was he married? Oh, yes. That was the answer Gwendolyn liked the most. Had Charlie even bothered to find out his true parentage? If this indignity had been foisted on Gwendolyn, she would have used all her money to hunt down the defector and, if he happened to be dead, stomp on his grave and then search for any remaining family so she could tell them exactly how she felt.

"What do you mean he was *already* a pilot? Driving around at top speed in his motor car hardly qualifies." The truth, which she chose to ignore, poked a hole in this statement allowing her anger to once again course through her body. She *knew* Charlie had been taking flying lessons and had been incensed that he refused to tell her because, if he admitted it, he would be forced to offer her a chance to come to the airfield and watch. Yet another indignity forced upon her by a family who did not care for her in the slightest.

Sarah had corrected her kindly, not knowing she was lancing an unhealed wound. "He started taking flying lessons when he was in Kingston at Queens University, and completed his course in Toronto at the Eglinton Hunt Club, which, I believe, was the primary training school of the Royal Canadian Air Force. It was such a long time ago, and all I can say for certain is that Charlie had this strong desire to be up in the sky. Your father indulged him. This was Ian and Charlie's little secret. I do remember how Charlie fretted and paced about the flat while I quizzed him on mathematical equations far beyond my grasp. He was so certain he would fail the test." Sarah shrugged with a grin. "Quite naturally, a man of his talent and expertise was accepted into the RAF at once. Just as I predicted. Consequently…"

Sarah had kept speaking but Gwendolyn was not listening. She was too angry to speak. The gall of the two of them, Ian and Charlie, keeping this an open secret from her simply because she was a girl and didn't deserve to know anything even though she was smarter than the two of them put together.

"… entire squadron had to rise at dawn, fly two to three patrols a day and then back to base to sleep before rising to do it all again. Was it a Hurricane he flew? I can't remember. He loved it at first."

Bully for Charlie. Bully for her brother who had abandoned her without a word. Gwendolyn's roving eye had rested on a plant skirting the western side of Sarah's garden. She hated all kinds of vegetation because plants were messy and infected with bugs and slugs and required care, which she firmly believed was a pointless waste of time.

"That changed as the bombing intensified over London. He was still carefree when he visited and, believe it or not, we went dancing every night. I remember we managed to get tickets to the New Faces Revue in London when 'A Nightingale Sang in Berkeley Square' was premiered. It became his favourite song, and when we went to clubs and he sat in with the band he always played this piece first. Do you know it?" Sarah began to hum.

Gwendolyn had swatted the air thinking a wasp was hovering. But she'd kept her eye on the wayfaring tree. It was viburnum. The only plant she could identify with certainty. Such an innocent little meandering plant, so cheerfully green and lively, so fresh and vibrant. In fact, it was nothing but a pretender, an evil pretender, the sort that had dogged Gwendolyn's footsteps her entire life. All its cheerful green gaiety masked a deadly secret.

"Charlie started having headaches, piddly at first, but later they developed into migraines. He became distant, preoccupied. His friend Reggie had been killed. Reggie was such a wonderful cut up, so funny and optimistic. His death hit Charlie hard, and he kept saying over and over, *'They just come out of the clouds. Lines and lines of enemy planes.'* You remember how lively Charlie was, how much fun he was to be with?"

"I never really knew my brother," Gwendolyn had said shortly. "Certainly not like you did."

She'd rubbed the palm of her hand back and forth to dull a distant ache. This ache was the fault of the viburnum, her lifelong enemy who waved at her when the wind rustled its leaves. Viburnum grew a very special kind of dust, deadly dust. Embedded in each particle of dust were razor-sharp spikes so that the innocent (Gwendolyn as a child while reaching out to run her hands across the verdant, curled leaves) had their skin cut in thin red ribbons. She looked at her hand now and fancied she could still feel the stinging cuts, each laceration racing straight to her heart and leaving a permanent wound.

She barely listened when Sarah explained how Charlie had died.

"… the Channel, off the coast of France. Or the Ruhr Valley," she had mused. "I am ashamed that I can't remember. I could look it up for you while you are here."

Gwendolyn had no idea where the Ruhr Valley was and had no interest in knowing. As a young girl she had assumed Charlie had been lost at sea; a romantic, if somewhat horrific fairy tale, invented courtesy of her imagination because Ian, her father, her *real* father and not some pretender, had been too distraught to tell her the details. But she had known this, with a finality that brought tears to her eyes: The Tree of Life brooch was now lost forever, and she was adrift in that sea where she imagined her brother had perished.

Her roving eye had returned to the viburnum. Perhaps she could kill the plant at night when everyone was asleep. Pour ammonia into the soil or hack it to bits with a steak knife.

"… gun panel detached and became lodged in the fin, or so I was told. Search and rescue found bits of his plane but no sign of Charlie. I just can't remember all the details. I was within days of giving birth, and I couldn't afford to collapse although I seemed to have entered a fugue state where nothing seemed real. I wrote to you, Gwendolyn, after Ian was informed, but I never had an answer. That's why I couldn't risk sending you the letter Charlie left behind. I didn't want it to disappear. I wanted to make sure you had it. I grew to believe I would never have the opportunity."

"Charlie wrote me a letter?" Gwendolyn had asked, her eyes finally resting on Sarah's face.

"I saved it for you, Gwendolyn. I have it right here."

"Is Madam alright?"

"What?" Gwendolyn asked, coming back to herself, and not liking the feeling.

"You've turned very pale. Are you feeling unwell?"

"I am perfectly fine, thank you very much."

"Might I show Madam a body lotion or soap instead of perfume? These products are all reasonably priced."

An array of boxes and bottles appeared on the counter before Gwendolyn, and as she feigned interest she felt the weight of the letter Sarah had passed to her in the garden. Sarah had stroked the envelope lovingly with withered old fingers, almost as if the paper was alive and in need of comfort, before pushing it gently across the table. Gwendolyn could not bring herself to open it, certainly not in Sarah's presence, and had hidden it away immediately in her purse. She did notice that the seal was unbroken. Sarah had not invaded her privacy. If the situation were reversed, she wondered if she would have acted the same.

"I like the body lotion." The salesgirl prattled on, pretending the body lotion had miraculous healing qualities. "It is light but has excellent hydration."

What if Charlie told her she was a spoiled brat (which she was) and was glad to be free of her? What if he gloated about giving the Tree of Life brooch to Sarah? What if he said a million more terrible things? Wouldn't it be better to burn the letter and never read it? Or place it in her safety deposit box once she returned to Toronto and forget about it entirely? It could be sold at auction along with all her belongings and some poor sap could read it and say: "*This guy really didn't like his sister. Wonder what she did.*"

"You will find that the soap lasts for months. Most soaps dissolve within a few weeks but not Chanel."

Of course, there was no way to protect the letter from Charlotte's prying eyes. The letter, her letter, her private message from her long dead brother, would be copied word for word into that dreadful Hilroy of Charlotte's, and then when Gwendolyn was long dead, some two-bit archaeologist, lobbying for a grant, would discover these appalling Hilroys in the bottom of a fossilized waste bin and he would publish his findings under the title *Privilege: The Curse of the Twentieth Century* or *No Longer Taking Up Space on the Planet*.

"Madam is breathing very heavily. May I offer a chair?"

Gwendolyn did not like the way the attendant was assessing and evaluating her. It was too smug.

"The smells are overpowering," she stated, taking a step back from the counter.

This superior attitude reminded Gwendolyn of her own behaviour an hour earlier in the garden.

What had Sarah said when Oliver appeared at the gate, his hat in his hand?

'*And you will come, I hope, to the theatre at four so I can show you around? You'll want to stay and watch the children. They are all uniquely talented and boastful, a pleasure really. In a way, their attitude reminds me of you, Gwendolyn, when you were their age. It's a compliment, please understand. I was always a bit cowed by you. In a way you were my first real teacher.*'

What did *that* mean?

Oliver whisked her away so fast she did not have a chance to answer.

The woman/girl/attendant (in essence merely a poorly paid employee) looked over Gwendolyn's shoulder and her attitude dissolved as if it had been a mirage. Her chin lowered, her eyes widened, a true sky-blue Gwendolyn noticed, innocent and warm, and her lips broke open into a welcoming smile.

"Oliver," she cried, leaving Gwendolyn to stand alone, her fingers continuing their drumming pattern on the counter. "I haven't seen you for months. Where have you been?"

Oliver pocketed his monstrous cellular phone and gave the woman his complete attention. "Taken up with the youngster and matters of trade. I have not had the time to breathe in the heady aroma of Harrods although I missed it."

"How is Jeremy?"

"Better now that true friends have arrived across the Atlantic. He'd been feeling a bit pinched until yesterday. I see you have already met one such friend."

Gwendolyn watched this exchange with the air of one who had stumbled across a reunion between a foreign dignitary and a street urchin, although she wasn't altogether certain who was who.

"Sophie, I am certain that you have been taking very good care of my dear friend, Mrs. MacFarlane."

Dear friend? Who was Oliver kidding? Or was this how people talked when they were out in public? No matter how polite the words, they were spoken with an inflection that stated quite clearly the speaker was put out or annoyed. She had noticed this immediately upon setting foot on British soil, this tiny negative shake of the head, the impatient tone.

"I believe she is browsing, but I am eager to assist."

And there it was again, the stress on *believe*, almost as if Gwendolyn were a burglar who had come on a reconnaissance mission which would, under cover of darkness, turn into an outright assault.

"Harrods inflates their prices," Gwendolyn stated clearly. She was a woman of wealth and standing and refused to be cowed. "I read that in an article in *Forbes*."

She did not have Henry, the human calculator at her side, but she assumed this was true and brought Forbes into the conversation as padding.

"One pays for the *experience* more than the product," Sophie explained, leaning across the counter in a confidential manner, suggesting, once again, by inflection that Gwendolyn should know this. "He is the one," she said, pointing to Oliver, "who told me that when I first started working here. I simply could not *believe* how expensive everything is. Ridiculous, really. I can tell you where to get all the Chanel products for two thirds of what we charge."

"Rather a case of falling off the back of a truck. Literally," Oliver stated and both he and Sophie broke down into a fit of giggles.

Gwendolyn was shocked.

People simply did not behave like this in high-end stores. High-end stores possessed the hush and sanctitude of being in a cathedral, and no one ever laughed in such a raucous fashion. This behaviour belonged in a rowdy pub. And yet, for a moment, the sound of laughter was invigorating, and Gwendolyn smiled beneath the hand which covered her mouth.

"One of Sarah's drama students," Oliver told Gwendolyn. "Resting at the moment, but a fine actress as I am certain you noticed."

Sophie nodded, confirming Oliver's evaluation of her talents. "I'm *far* too young to play Lady Augusta Bracknell, but I try for her imperious upper-class Victorian respectability. Most of my ladies like it, but I'm not sure about her," she concluded, pointing a thumb at Gwendolyn.

"And how did she do, Gwendolyn?" Oliver asked.

"No." Sophie gasped and covered her mouth. "You did a near perfect Gwendolen, and you even have the *same* name. In the *Importance of Being Earnest* Gwendolen is all about style. She is not sincere and has absolutely no idea what it means to be genuine. But you know that. I think you performed admirably, Mrs. MacFarlane. Are you a professional yourself?"

Sophie had summed her up, rather smugly, Gwendolyn thought, but the youngster did radiate a certain sincerity.

"I wasn't aware I was acting in a play," Gwendolyn stated, quite honestly. "I was shopping."

"Oh, but we are always acting, aren't we, Oliver? That's what Sarah taught us right from the start."

Gwendolyn straightened her back in disbelief.

Acting belonged on the stage, not at the perfume counter of Harrods. Gwendolyn was proud to think she had found no reason to pretend she was anything other than herself. It was not her fault that most people she met were woefully inadequate and, knowing this, were forced to put on a show. This was not a tragedy; it was a farce, and one she saw through effortlessly. If she showed her disdain, this was not acting, this was a matter of seeing reality without distorting it into unrecognizable form.

She was about to clear up this matter once and for all when Oliver's large cellular phone rang once again, a bright, brittle sound like a tree branch breaking. He unearthed it from a deep pocket in his jacket and punched a button.

Gwendolyn did not carry a cell phone or a pager or a beeper. There was no one to whom she wished to communicate, and if she should happen to experience a heart attack or a bout of food poisoning after enduring yet another meal at the Windsor Arms, there were paid employees on site to see to her well-being or, should her health betray her with absolute finality, arrange for an ambulance to cart away her remains. People who carried cell phones needed to have jobs, so she allowed Oliver this conceit. Others who carried this radioactive object merely to seem important would one day regret their decision, most probably around the time when the skin around their ear began to peel away and expose their skull.

Oliver held up a finger and pressed the receiver close to his ear, and after a minute his lips thinned, and eyebrows drew in slightly.

"I will meet you there in fifteen minutes. Do nothing until I arrive."

Gwendolyn and Sophie exchanged a look of honest concern.

"What is it?" Gwendolyn asked before Sophie could jump in with an inappropriately emotional series of dramatically panicked words.

"Your boy, Henry, seems to have gotten himself into a pickle."

"He's not my boy," Gwendolyn said and then remembered that he was, de facto, her responsibility and she wondered whether she had signed some document attesting to this before Henry was released from the parental grip.

"We must go," he said taking her by the arm. When she resisted, he spoke quite simply and with complete authority.

"Now, Gwendolyn."

And that put an end to the matter.

Chapter Nineteen

Henry quickly scanned both sides of the street to see if Charlotte had caught up with him. She hadn't (unless she was descending by parachute). He looked up at a dirty blue cloudless sky. He then glanced around the neighborhood where he found himself and had to quickly realign his opinion of elegant downtown living.

Henry had spent most of his life cloistered and cut off from the *normal*. This wasn't his fault; he was a pampered victim of his environment, namely, stately Rose Park with its elegant tree-lined winding streets and boulevards, gas streetlamps, and enormous houses with fountains and stone-carved lions securing driveways that were closed off by metal gates. Charlotte's house was a bit of an anomaly, as the exterior gave the impression of an edifice that had seen better times.

In the section of London where Henry now found himself, there were few trees, no gardens, no flowers, and nothing but a wide expanse of concrete with fast-moving cars and sidewalks with fast-moving pedestrians. Calling up his map of London, Henry stood still as a lamppost until he acclimatized to being above ground. His lips moved soundlessly while he consulted the map, his eyes straightening and then crossing. His stomach itched and he scratched mechanically.

Eyes crossed, muttering, scratching. While these might be common occurrences in people seven times Henry's age, a young boy manifesting symptoms of abnormality caused the pedestrians to give him a wide berth, until a shape solidified before him, and he heard:

"You, there, boy, you alright?"

Henry came to immediately, the map tucked away neatly in the proper file folder in his brain. He grinned mindlessly, like a black Labrador emerging from a lake and shook his shoulders with a canine, care-free energy.

"Perfectly," he responded. "But thank you for your inquiry." He had survived the Tube, extricated himself from Charlotte, and was on his way to track down his father's friend. Just being in the open, unencumbered and expectant, changed his posture from a forlorn waif into a youngster of determination and purpose.

"Looked like you might be having some type of seizure." The concerned citizen, swarthy and short, seemed reluctant to believe Henry. His skin emitted a tantalizing spicy smell that made Henry realize he was a bit peckish.

"I was thinking," Henry replied mechanically. "Getting my bearings."

"Ah." The man continued to study Henry for a few seconds and then let him go with a warning to do his thinking in a more private place, and not where he might be run down by pedestrians or automobiles.

Just to be agreeable Henry said he understood, but he didn't understand because in truth he was thinking all the time and privacy was not always an option.

He took a right at the corner, walked two blocks south and took a left. He then entered what was supposed to be a laneway (not at all like the laneways in Sarah's neighborhood) more like a darkening alley with a large metal gate at the end.

Henry scanned for predators. There *was* an old man urinating on the wall about halfway down the alley, but he didn't look particularly trouble-some, and Henry's skin had not started to prickle, an automatic warning of danger.

The man tipped his hat as Henry walked by, and Henry presented a steely countenance, pretending he didn't see the gesture.

Never make eye contact with vagrants – this had been repeated to him so often it had become a mantra. Still and all, he'd never been given a chance to follow these instructions before as he was escorted everywhere under the vigilant eye of his nanny, Lena. Besides, looking directly at anyone was not Henry's forte. His crossed eyes and mag-nified lenses in his glasses gave the impression he was examining the nose on his face and nothing else.

Hearing the steady stream of pee caused Henry's stomach acid to swell. He would prefer to have his bladder explode rather than expose himself and piss all over a wall.

Another very valid reason for not wanting to become an adult.

"Help you out there, boy?" the man called out as Henry tried to blend into the shadows. "You got a dead end coming up case you don't see so well."

A slur about his glasses!

From a man who was wiping his hands on his trousers and had not fully zipped up!

"26a Dartley Way?" Henry mumbled, examining his note, not his memory bank which had fled in horror, leaving him alone and undefended. He quickly replaced the note in his pocket as the man reached forward a hand.

This address caused a certain amount of amusement as the man hissed and popped like an exploding can of severely shaken soda – a trick that Charlotte did occasionally when Henry wasn't paying close attention to what she was saying.

He wished Charlotte was here.

"You could back up, go through the Indian Grill, on Hester, make your way through the kitchen if there's room." He paused for a minute in thought. "Should be. Food was delivered about an hour ago although, depending on staff availability, it has been known to sit around for a while before it gets put in the refrigerator."

"Perishables?" Henry gasped.

"Oh, pish posh, a heavy dose of spice will neutralize any lingering bacteria. Naabhi knows what he's about. Most of us today will throw away perfectly good fare simply because it has gone past the so-called best before date. Trust your eyes and nose, I say. I tell you, lad, we are all controlled by the invisible man, that voice that tells us we have no right to trust our instincts."

Curiously, this man appeared to have an upper-class accent, although Henry, having seen but a few British movies with both Cockneys and Toffs, was hardly an expert.

"Like peeing on the side of a building?" Henry couldn't help himself. A few rules did exist for the common good, or so his father told him – 'Not many, but enough to keep you on your toes.'

"Got a bit of a problem with the old prostrate," the man told him, apologetically. "I'm getting on in years. Didn't mean to offend the sensibilities, but in my defence, not many wander this way. Off-putting is the best way to describe this laneway."

Henry gave an inch and forgave the man, not totally understanding the purpose of the prostrate – his memory bank remained inaccessible due to the dark and dank circumstance in which he found himself, and he felt it was time to move on or Charlotte might reach the destination before he did.

"You come here again, you go through the restaurant, there's a good lad. Once you're out of the kitchen you take a left in the courtyard. Building on the east side. Courtyard's a treat it is, a magnolia and a few dogwoods, a stone bench, even a water feature when it's working. Safer than using the laneway here. Naabhi can be a bit of a trial, as he doesn't take to strangers wandering through his kitchen, but you tell him that George sent you, and you'll be fine."

George had a mouth crowded with crooked teeth and a bit of a lisp. His wispy hair was plastered to his skull, but he was clean shaven and only smelled if Henry got too close. George also carried a leather briefcase so Henry could not decide whether he was a vagabond on his way up, or a financer on his way down.

"Here, now, you just carry on until the end of the alley. Doorway at the end behind the trash cans. Can't see it til you come up against the fence. Protected address this is," he added, giving a thumbs up followed by the victory sign. "Three flights, take a left and there you be, all of a piece."

"Are there rats?" Henry asked, fear causing his shoulders to hunch.

He hated rats, particularly the long slimy tails.

"I'll rattle those cans for your first, lad, don't you worry, but garbage pickup was earlier in the day. You shouldn't have a problem. Known Meggie and Byron for a while, have you?

"They are friends of my father's."

"Well, you're in for a surprise, I don't mind telling you for free."

Henry thanked him politely and carried on, staying out of the way until each garbage can had been kicked with a resounding thump. Nothing appeared so he pushed open the door and entered a stairway that was remarkably clean and smelled faintly of the same astringent that lingered in hospital corridors. The railing was black metal, recently painted and free of rust. Nevertheless, Henry ascended keeping his hands in his pockets.

Artwork adorned the walls as he climbed higher: a series of carved wooden dolls, dressed in pale pastel twirling summer skirts, holding hands and smiling grandly with oversized wide eyes. When Henry reached the first landing, wheezing faintly, he saw the dolls now wore hats, toques, beanies, berets, bowlers, checkered, lined, plaid and plain. And sunglasses, glasses with sharp pointed corners, pink, red, green, and orange. On the second floor landing the line changed once again and the dolls wore top hats, carried canes in the crook of their elbow and sported moustaches. Although there was absolutely nothing creepy or menacing about these carved dolls (the moustaches *were* a bit odd) Henry felt a tingling of fear and his wheezing kicked into high gear.

Why was he not enjoying himself at Madame Tussauds? Why did he feel compelled to track and find long-ago friends of his father's?

He arrived at his destination, walked to the window at the end of the hallway, and took a seat on the ledge.

He needed to get his breathing under control.

First, he cleaned his hands with an antiseptic wet wipe. Henry always carried three or four individually wrapped wipes in his pocket in case he was far removed from running water and real soap. He scrubbed between his fingers, his wrists, palms and back of his hands and instantly felt cleansed. He placed the soiled wipe in a Ziploc bag and put it in the side zipper compartment of his backpack.

He then removed his Bricanyl Turbuhaler from the other side pocket, unscrewed the cap and inhaled deeply. His heart immediately began to race, but that was normal, and within a minute or two his airways felt less obstructed.

He combed his hair with his tortoiseshell comb, slicked down his cowlick, cleaned the lenses of his glasses, and tucked his T-shirt neatly into his pants. By the time he finished these simple tasks, the Bricanyl had fully kicked in, and the wheezing was gone.

He marched purposefully to the door in the centre of the hallway and closely examined his surroundings. What he saw was a hallway swept clean, the wooden floor polished and the passage well-lit with facsimile gas lamps flickering at both the north and south corners. He examined the miniature compass he carried on his keyring and discovered that George's instructions were clearly wrong. The building he now stood in could not be in the eastern side of the courtyard, a quite presentable place Henry saw during his sojourn on the window ledge, but on the southern. These were the kind of details that never failed to get Henry in trouble as he was known to put up his hand repeatedly in class and say: "I believe you might be wrong," to whatever teacher was dispensing information.

Henry suddenly felt strong and invincible, a common side effect of the Bricanyl, and supercharged with nervous energy – another side effect.

The door before him had a brass knocker and handle. There was a black mat that said Welcome and a large pot of marigolds. He touched one and it sprang back. It was alive, not a plastic replica – yet how did this plant survive without natural light? And then Henry looked up. A skylight rose to a peak in the rafters and although the glass panes were dirty, enough light came through to fuel the marigold which, according to his limited knowledge of plants, appeared to be doing well.

After carefully wiping the wooden door with the sleeve of his shirt he leaned his ear against the panel and listened.

There was scuffling inside. And the faint cheerful whistle of a teakettle. The scuffling came closer to the door and paused. Henry pulled back as the door was flung open dramatically.

A woman with orange hair piled on top of her head regarded him quizzically. It was impossible to tell how old she was, but Henry put her approximately in the same region as his mother – fifty and fading. She was squat and compact, and attractive in a gamin type of way, with a big smile and rosy cheeks. She examined Henry closely.

"I thought you were Jonesy," she said, looking him up and down. She wore the same sharp pointed eyeglasses that adorned the faces of the dolls on the first landing, her frames bright pink and set with rhinestones. "It's not Jonesy," she shouted over her shoulder.

"I'm here for Aaron Jacobs. I'm Aaron Jacobs's son," Henry said all in a rush, the words colliding with one another into an incohesive whole – another unfortunate Bricanyl side effect.

"Collecting for charity," she added, braiding a multi-colour scarf she wore between her fingers. "A disease," she added parenthetically. "Arronjacobson."

It was unclear as to whom these announcements were directed, as the room behind her was empty.

"Congenital eye disorder?" she asked, staring intently at Henry's face. "You've got pluck, out and about without a cane or dog. I'll donate a pound if I can find my purse, but it's been missing for the last three hours. Need a receipt of course." She rocked back on her heels and smiled widely, her red painted lips forming a Cupid's bow. "Frankly, I don't know how you managed. People who can *see* cannot find this location, so you get a bonus for perseverance, dear."

"I'm not blind," Henry told her. "I'm Aaron Jacob's son. Requesting a minute of your time." He peered past her into a room with floor-to-ceiling windows, the floor scattered with oriental rugs and large soft bean bag type chairs. Painted canvases adorned almost every square inch of the brick walls, an explosion of vivid colours depicting animals or monsters, Henry couldn't be certain. But their energy was palpable. A profusion of tall tassel shaded lamps lit the room. It was a different universe, plain and simple.

"Byron, find me my purse," she shouted into the cavernous silence.

There was no response.

"I can give you five minutes dear, for your pitch, although promise not to quiz me after. I'm simply no good at remembering symptoms even when I have them myself. There are so many new diseases nowadays. And yours is a mouthful. Lyme's Disease is so much easier to say. One thinks of a gin and tonic with a splash of lime. Or Diabetes although I've always thought there were too many syllables, and I haven't yet come up with an association."

"No," said Henry, a little shaken. "I, well, you don't understand. You see—"

"Oh, for crying out loud. She's just pulling your leg. At least I think she is."

Henry leapt because, as usual, Charlotte had appeared behind him with the stealth of a panther.

"His name is Henry," said Charlotte, "and he is not a disease."

He sighed audibly but then realized he was glad she had come. He had gotten as far as he could on his own and was beginning to feel a bit other-worldly, as if he were both in his body and not. He had been mistaken for a disease and did not know how to extract himself from this misconception. He had used up his quota of bravery for the day and explanations eluded him. He realized that annoyed as he was, he was glad to see Charlotte.

"It's you," he said, and slid a bit closer to her so he could feel the heat of her arm against his own. "Why am I not surprised?"

Chapter Twenty

"Two are always better than one," Meggie announced leaning on the door jam. "The neighborhood is perfectly safe, safer than most of the posh areas in this city, but the alleyway is a bit iffy. Did you come through the back?"

Henry nodded.

Charlotte immediately butted in. "I came through the restaurant, and the owner was particularly rude to my friend Jeremy. Who is still down there, by the by," she said giving Henry the evil eye as if a stranger's bad manners were his fault. "Jeremy's trying to get out of paying 50 p for a samosa that got knocked to the floor by accident. I told him to run, but he wouldn't do it," Charlotte explained to Meggie whose eyes suddenly darkened.

"Byron," she shouted. "Get a move on, dear, and call down to the restaurant. Naabhi is holding a young boy captive."

"I like your glasses," Charlotte announced moving closer to Meggie. "And the dolls are totally weird in a good, weird way. I haven't seen anything like them before even though I am in and out of galleries daily. Clever," she added, taking on the role of art connoisseur.

"Byron will be so pleased, dear. He's an artist. Byron, the children love the dolls," she called out, not at all concerned that no one had answered any of her remarks.

"What are you doing here?" Henry whispered. "But thank you for coming."

"I am duty bound to protect you. End of story," Charlotte hissed. In her normal voice she dismissed Henry with the shrug of her shoulder and said: "I have a pair of aviators myself, but I left them in Toronto. And rimless, metals, tortoise shells and an ancient pince-nez I found in the garbage."

The last had the ring of truth. Charlotte routinely went through the street garbage in Rose Park because people routinely threw out brand new items of clothing, shoes and now, he learned, glasses, 'pinch nest' according to her pronunciation.

Once again Henry was relegated to second chair as Charlotte dominated the conversation. She knew more about frames than he did, and he'd worn glasses since he was three. He'd barely had forty-five minutes in the outer world before the great invisible lasso descended on his shoulders and held him tight.

"Just a minute, dear. Did you say Toronto? Do you mean Toronto, Canada?"

"Yes. Toronto. Absolutely." Henry breathed a sigh of relief.

Meggie swung her head away from the door, cupped her mouth and issued a directive: "We have guests from abroad. Aaron's child if you can believe it." And to Henry and Charlotte she added: "Forgive my confusion, dear," she added, patting Henry on the head. "Byron will be thrilled if I can drag him out of his studio. He's been trying to summon the muse all morning, and the groaning! One day he's going to eat through his tie, and then what?"

Henry had a sudden vision of a man bound and gagged in one of the back rooms, relentlessly chewing through his restraints. He and Charlotte locked eyes for one second, and it was decided, telepathically, that they would not run for cover.

"I know he'd like to meet you, dear," Meggie said, focusing on Henry. "You are the spitting image of your father. Minus the glasses, of course, but everything else, yes." She sighed and smiled and opened the door wide. "Where are my manners? Keeping you standing in the hall for ages," she asked the air above her head. "Come," she said, sweeping her arms to the side. "'Tis a humble abode, but our own."

The humble abode was even more cavernous and grand than what Henry had been able to glimpse from the door. Given the alleyway, the hidden, graffiti-filled steel door, the deserted staircase (wooden dolls excluded), Henry expected a tenement, more on the lines of the meagre quarters inhabited by Charles Dickens' protagonists the Cratchits, and their six children.

Henry knew *A Christmas Carol* by heart – he had first read it as a means of understanding his own position in the world and then, as he paged through the book in his memory bank from time to time, he gained a greater understanding of the real message of the novel.

Don't be surprised if, from time to time, you are visited by a ghost.

Nothing he had seen since he had arrived in London was as Henry believed it would be.

His freedom was dependent on the kindness of others – witness his rescue by the staunch Doreen on the Tube – an event that now appeared to be part of his very distant past. He was currently wandering into a vast sitting room perched on top of a building that was more likely to hold a rabbit warren of cramped rooms and screaming babies, this expectation a natural result of the hours he had spent watching forbidden television shows at Charlotte's house.

What did he know about real life? He'd hardly had a second to experience it, and now it was swirling around him, showing off its treasures like a pretty girl showing off her legs. Legs and pretty girls had never been on Henry's radar until his father told him one day this would be all he wanted to see. When Henry had asked why he would be interested in something so currently unappealing his father had replied: '*Life, Henry, my son. It changes us daily with a bushel of surprises.*'

Life with surprises galore.

Like friends appearing the minute he stepped off the plane.

Friends like Jeremy.

Where was Jeremy?

Henry spun on his heel, became dizzy (Bricanyl) and leaned against the wall. "I must return to the restaurant," he explained. "I have to find Jeremy."

Before he could set his body in motion, he heard a frantic pounding at the door. Charlotte reached it one second before he did.

Jeremy, red faced and indignant announced: "He wanted me to eat the samosa. He said, 'You throw good food in garbage? I take money, you eat food.' I barely escaped with my life."

"Did you pay?" Charlotte asked.

"Of course. A gentleman always pays even if it is not his fault." He pushed his way past Charlotte and shook Henry's hand. "I'm sorry but I decided at the last minute I couldn't let you go alone. What if you had come to harm? I could never live with myself."

"*You* decided?" Charlotte scoffed.

Jeremy took a minute to look around. "How did you get in? Are you here alone?"

Meggie had vanished, leaving a trail of sandalwood perfume in her wake. In the distance a murmuring conversation could be heard but recognizable words did not make their way over the divide.

Charlotte, reclining comfortably on a forest green ottoman raised her hand. "Could we come to an agreement?" she asked.

Jeremy flashed a thumbs up, but Henry remained silent. It was never good to say yes until you knew what you were agreeing to. And with Charlotte that could be anything from *let's make a pact for one solid day to only eat what we find growing in the park...* to *let's promise to pool our money for the greater good.*

A brief silence.

"Right," she said. "Let's agree to not strike out on our own, okay? That goes for me, too. I won't desert you and you won't desert me. It's not an inferiority type thing. I just don't want anything to happen to you, Henry. Whatever this is, we are in it together, and I don't think we'll be able to go back home until we sort it out."

Her face radiated intensity, and for once Henry believed she might be speaking the truth.

"I don't think I want to go home," Henry said, failing to do the pinky grip necessary to seal the deal.

Charlotte sighed audibly. "Not that again, Henry. You don't have to stretch your brain very far to remember how that did *not* work out before."

"What's she talking about?" Jeremy asked, sinking into a bean bag across from Charlotte.

The children had taken over the room effortlessly, perhaps seeing it as a playroom devised specifically for their comfort. Gone were fears and worries because whatever "this" was, they were now in it together.

Henry lowered himself into another beanbag, wishing there was a chair in the room with a back. He wasn't used to lounging and preferred to be uncomfortable.

"I didn't want to come back from the summer of 1939," he explained to Jeremy, leaning forward to clasp his hands around his knees. "And I had it all figured out, too. After I put together a plan, I enlisted Charlie's help."

"And he agreed?"

Charlotte remained silent. It was hard work, but she was learning to listen and not just jump right in with her own opinions, even if her opinions were the right ones. Her great-great-uncle, Gus Frank, shared this admirable characteristic, and he often used what he heard to his advantage. *'Trap a man with his own words and you got him good.'* When she told Henry this, just the night before he'd said, *'Maybe not so admirable after all.'*

Charlotte knew some of what Henry had been up to during their week-long adventure in 1939, she had never been privy to it all. He had been reluctant to discuss exactly what happened on their last day, mostly because he was locked in the grip of a time travel–induced nervous breakdown.

And, of course, he blamed her.

But she had to save Henry. It was her role in life. Whether he appreciated it or not.

As the world stilled and froze around her, while the crowd of thousands waited in Hart House Circle to see King George and Queen Elizabeth, Charlotte, with superhuman strength and determination, was able to prevent Henry leaving her for good by grabbing onto his shoe and refusing to let go.

However, what she didn't know was Charlie's duplicity. This hurt in a way she had rarely experienced, considering the great gift she had left behind for Charlie and the note, inscribed with her mark.

Henry's next words made her feel marginally better.

"Charlie said he would give me some space. Every person in the universe is entitled to space. What I did with that space was not his business. And then he shook my hand." Henry's eyes began to tear, and he sniffed audibly. That he missed a man who had ceased to exist long before Henry had been born was a conundrum his brain refused to accommodate but this did not dissuade his tears.

"Get a grip, Henry," said Charlotte (and strangely enough that seemed to do the trick).

Purposeful footsteps echoed in the distance, accompanied by vigorous throat clearing and the sound of hands slapping together.

The master of the house arrived centre stage, placed his hand on his heart, bowed from the waist.

"Byron Oakes. At your service." He then allowed the children time to acclimatize to his sudden presence.

Byron was a man in his seventies and wore ratty cotton pants that had, no doubt, been old when Charlotte and Henry were born, likewise a white collarless tunic and a tie of many colours knotted around his bare fleshy neck. The tie was stained with paint, smeared with glue, and stained with coffee, egg yolk, tea, and mustard so it was impossible to see what it might have looked like when it was new and not under the control of a whimsical sprite, or muse, as Meggie had said. Byron was a solid man, with thick hands, sculptor's hands, and a smooth face, saved from the lines and crevasses of advancing age by a generous layer of fatty deposits which filled in his cheeks and chin and piggy backed on the grey pouches beneath his eyes.

Balding, of course. The mark of a man who needs his skull to be fully exposed to inspiration, he explained on many occasions and then had to listen to the cheek of his detractors ask why the tie was, therefore, necessary? His belly fat was clearly visible under the almost transparent white painter's smock. He still carried the air of the chubby neighborhood boy who was first in line when treats were handed out, his cheeks perpetually stretched by the jawbreakers he sucked, his fingers stained with licorice and smeared with chocolate. His nature was beneficent and kindly, though he could easily become an *enfant terrible* should a critic demean his work (which was done on a routine basis). He enjoyed interruptions because they allowed the creative in him time to stew and simmer and bring forth unexpected flavour when he returned to his studio. He was smart, determined, and at times, when he felt it warranted, vindictive.

He liked children, although he never wanted his own, and could often be found sitting in the park, sketching the rough and tumble of children at play. He believed children to be the most truthful of the human species and yet, conversely, also the most duplicitous. Children were skilled at getting what they wanted and generally impervious to insult. They were natural explorers, not yet hindered by wanton desire or greed.

The only unfortunate thing about children, according to Byron, is that one day they were forced to grow up. He had spent a lifetime defying the inevitable.

"Henry, dear boy."

Henry blinked and saw that Byron was standing in front of Jeremy, rubbing his hands together with glee.

"Made in your father's image," Byron added. "Deeply moved you made the effort to visit." He pressed both his hands against his chest and coughed deeply.

"My name is Jeremy, sir," Jeremy said, springing from the ottoman and standing to attention. "I apologize for lounging about. That's Henry," he said, pointing to his friend.

"Henry, my boy," Byron said, performing a delicate pirouette. He had extremely dainty feet for a man of his girth, and he wore the same black Chinese slippers that Charlotte favoured. "Now I see it, of course. The glasses put me off. As I recall, your father has excellent vision as does your mother – but foolish of me to assume the same of an offspring." He observed Henry closely and added: "Your stare is deeply penetrating."

Henry shook Byron's hand, heartily he hoped, although the answering press was a bit limp. "And you grace me doubly by bringing friends," he added, including Jeremy and Charlotte in his welcoming smile.

Henry made the introductions and added that he had hoped to come alone but he was a stranger to London and thought it best that he not travel solo.

"And yet you did arrive on your own," Byron said, correcting him immediately. "George rang and told me you were a bit turned about in the laneway."

"George?" Henry asked. "The urinator?" The words escaped his lips before he had time to erect a blockade.

"Oh, George." Byron shook his head sadly. "I told him to use the loo before he left. Meggie was doing her hair, but she wouldn't have minded. George is shy," he added, as if this excused the man's behaviour. "Never wants to be a bother. I have told him time and time again that this shirking from what is necessary will be the death of him."

"The laneway was deserted so I suppose he thought he had some privacy. I'm sorry if I insulted your friend."

"You are forgiven, my boy," Byron waved a generous hand absolving Henry of all his sins. "I will have a private chat with George, don't you worry. This transgression will not happen again. George is our accountant and visits on a routine basis. You see, the thing is, Henry, our entire space here is, in fact, not only a home *extraordinaire* but also a private gallery." He studied a canvas that depicted a large white rabbit peering through a cover of Hawthorn bushes. "Marvellous, is it not?" he asked, admiring his own work.

The children nodded enthusiastically. The rabbit had piercing blue eyes and appeared to take the adoration in its stride.

"It would not do at all for the visitors to our establishment to come upon George doing his business. It's a quaint idiosyncrasy, but I'm afraid the world at large finds it off-putting."

"The man in the alley is an accountant?" Henry was not able to hide his surprise, but, as he had earlier noted, the man did carry a briefcase.

"Thirty years if not more. Made me more money than I made myself. I see that you are a recorder of life's daily pageant," he said, pointing to Charlotte. "The pencil behind the ear is a dead giveaway. Where is the scroll?"

Charlotte patted her stomach.

"Clever," Byron said, bowing. "We artists are always on call, are we not?"

"My father gave me your address in secret," Henry told Byron, but quickly saw he did not have the great man's full attention. Charlotte had taken the floor and was lecturing on what was wrong with the world as she saw it.

Her voice cut through Henry's effortlessly. "It's like everyone is in a tearing hurry, can't even stop to listen to the sounds around them…"

"Too true," Byron mused, lowering his bulk to the floor and arranging his legs in lotus position. "Rush, rush, rush."

"… a secret," Henry repeated raising his voice even more. "And my mother couldn't know. Mustn't know, I think he said, but my father can sometimes be very dramatic."

"Listening is essential, truly a forgotten skill," Byron said, picking at his teeth and removing a piece of masticated toast which he investigated closely. "But the sad truth is people daily walk the streets with their ears closed. What they don't hear…

"Could fill a book," Charlotte said happily. She pointed a thumb at Henry and said: "He's the reason we are here. I suppose it is only fair to find out why."

"Thank you," Henry said, clearing his voice. He decided to start from the beginning. "My father said…"

"Dear boy," Byron added, adjusting his lotus posture so he could see Henry and pat his hand. "I heard every word that you uttered. I was merely processing the content before moving on to the confirmation. Forgive me for being derelict. I have had a difficult morning."

"I'm sorry," Henry said. "I don't wish to add to your troubles. Perhaps we could come back another day?"

"And disappoint Meggie who is, at this very moment, preparing crumpets and tea with homemade orange marmalade and Devon cream?" He patted his stomach which rested on his upturned knees. "A British treat to welcome our foreign visitors – although, bangers and mash might be more appropriate. Just between friends, that is my preferred meal although daily I languish awaiting its arrival. To hell with dreams," he shouted, waving his hands in dismissal. "And welcome new friends instead. You will stay and, Henry, when I feel the time is right, I will have a quiet word with Meggie. The story is hers to share, not mine – but I must warn you, Meggie can be a bit difficult regarding secrets. Shall we join her?" he asked, rising slowly to standing position by crouching, pressing, and rearranging his creaking and protesting joints.

The small parade, with Byron assuming the role of the Pied Piper, stopped in the hallway as voices were heard arguing outside the door.

"I will not return to the car. And I would like to wash my hands immediately, Oliver. The air feels much thicker and dirtier in this part of town."

"Friends?" Byron enquired, raising a busy eyebrow.

"I called Grandfather," Jeremy admitted, hanging his head in apology. "We are supposed to be at Madame Tussauds."

"Very wise that you abandoned that establishment. The wax figures are a bit too realistic for my liking and what is this technicolour nonsense? Has all subtlety fled?"

"Pease stop offering me baby wipes. I want my hands to be clean, not sticky with chemical residue."

Gwendolyn's voice was clearly recognizable, her mood predictable.

"And would that be grandmother?" Byron asked. "She sounds a formidable sort. Shall we refuse entry?"

"She's nobody's grandmother." Charlotte said, grabbing Byron's arm and preventing him from immediately opening the door. "Her name is Gwendolyn MacFarlane, and she is the reason Henry and me are in London right at this very second," she explained. "You see, we met her in 1939 when she was eleven years old, and just a week ago, we found the missing brooch that she insisted was hers even though it wasn't. Although, to be fair, Peabody found it first. But who cares? Because the brooch reappeared, we located Gwendolyn's missing family who are mostly living in London. And voila! We stand before you. "

"I can hear you, Charlotte," Gwendolyn hissed through the door. *"Let us in at once."*

Jeremy piped up assuring Byron that Gwendolyn was a respectable and decent person. "She is extremely courteous and very well-travelled. And," he added, parenthetically, "I believe she wants to use the loo."

"The deciding factor," Byron allowed, shaking off Charlotte's arm and throwing wide the door.

"Did you come through the kitchen?" Charlotte asked as Gwendolyn swept into the room. A line of sweat dotted her brow.

"I did not see a kitchen in the courtyard but as it was cluttered with too many trees and benches it was difficult to get clarity. Have you never heard of elevators?" she asked Byron without introducing herself.

Byron was immediately charmed. He enjoyed sparring with dominant women, as they so steadfastly refused to give ground. "Rather hard to squeeze one into these old buildings. Exercise is very good for the heart," he explained, smacking his chest twice.

"I can see it has done nothing for your girth."

Byron patted his stomach. "The mark of a man who embraces all of life. Never trust the whippets, they are too busy snarling and miss all the joy that surrounds them."

Oliver apologized on behalf of Gwendolyn and introduced himself and his stalwart companion. "We have met," he added, "Many years ago at Randolph's."

"Randolph's?" Byron asked suspiciously. "You can't possibly mean that time when..."

"Yes," Oliver said without elaborating. "That time."

"But the man I dealt with was covered in scarves and I could barely hear a voice let alone see a face. I recall a broken-down lory and an air of clandestine busyness. You were merely picking up a canvas."

"Yes, but it was a *special* canvas, was it not?"

"Ah," Byron said, his mouth dropping open in delight. "The Modigliani."

Oliver coughed once. "As you say. It was bitterly cold, and we were rushed. You were very particular regarding the handling and there was always a chance we were being watched."

For some reason that the children could not understand, Byron appeared embarrassed. "The olden days," he said with a wave of his hand. "Very far behind now. But your face," Byron exclaimed, lifting his hands to indicate that it might be the most engaging, the most expressive and certainly the most dramatic he had seen in a fortnight. "Your face is remarkable," he added. He snapped his fingers. "We met again. The National Portrait Gallery. How could I have forgotten? My most abject apologies, dear sir."

"Told you," Jeremy said, nudging Charlotte in the ribs.

"Please don't apologize," Oliver said, extending his hand. "A wartime injury that still receives the occasional glance."

"But we were just this moment talking about the year of our Lord 1939, and then you appear. How extraordinary."

"Not really," Oliver protested modestly. "I was merely following up on a phone call from my grandson."

Byron circled Oliver then cocked his head from the right to the left.

"Would you ever consider sitting? It would be my greatest pleasure to create a bust. A few days of your time, my good man. Meggie reading aloud from the book of your choice, lunch and dinner breaks unless we decide to do a plaster of Paris cast, but then the drying time is almost negligible."

"Oh, say yes, Grandfather, please," Jeremy said, grabbing Oliver's hand. "We could all come and watch and help decide which sketch you like the best."

"That arrangement does not suit me," Gwendolyn stated, staring at Charlotte as if this might be all her fault. "Oliver is our guide for the week we are in London, and because I will never be coming here again, I see no reason to give over the few precious days we have so that you can dabble in clay," she said to Byron who smiled and nodded throughout the chastisement.

"Dabbling. Such an emotive word. There is no rush, no rush at all. We are likely to be alive for at least a few more weeks, wouldn't you say?" he asked, looking at Oliver.

"More than that, I hope."

"There you are," he said, taking Gwendolyn's arm. "Your guided tour through our illustrious city will in no way be compromised."

Gwendolyn ignored the remark. She was not through fighting and began to chastise Charlotte. "I assumed you would take charge, Charlotte, as taking charge is what you are all about, so I am curious as to why you wandered so far afield? Do you wish to lose all your freedom and be walked around London wearing a baby harness?"

"It was my fault," Henry explained.

Gwendolyn had no choice but to accept this as an apology and warning to criticize the one who deserved it.

"I expected better of you, Henry. You have been properly brought up and know how dangerous it is to wander off by yourself."

"You call this alone?" Charlotte asked and her smile became a laugh.

"I see nothing humorous in this flagrant breaking of the rules." And then remembering she was in a stranger's house Gwendolyn elaborated. "The children arriving here unannounced is inexcusable. I apologize on their behalf, and we will go at once."

She indicated the door which everyone ignored.

"I thought you wanted to wash your hands," Charlotte said. And then asked Byron: "Is that alright?"

"My dear," Byron said, stepping forward and bowing slightly from the waist. "Or may I be allowed to use the familiar and call you Gwendolyn?"

"Since we are of an age, you may."

"I notice the children address you similarly with the exception of the gallant Jeremy."

"Charlotte won't be told," Gwendolyn said. "It is a waste of time to try and get her to be respectful."

"There are few things more nourishing than a large plateful of wasted time," Oliver responded. "Yet, we are strangers here, and we can find an abundance of wasted time in the outer world. We will leave once Gwendolyn cleans her hands."

As Henry watched Gwendolyn disappear down the long hallway his eyes clouded, and he had what he would later describe to Charlotte as a vision.

A perfectly rendered vision ripe with messages for the future.

With startling clarity Henry could see the *Treasury Reader*, the Grade 5 tome of literary greats, laying on the double sized wooden desk he shared with Lukas in the ancient not-so-long-ago classroom of 1939, and the poem he chose to memorize because in the past memorization was the key that led to higher learning. Henry quickly decided to siphon into his memory bank "Lost Time" by Frida Wolf, because the language was simpler and did not include sacrifices, servants, covenants, or any words ending in "est" or "eth". Within seconds it was safely stored in the spongy material that made up Henry's brain and that might have been the end of it but something in the poem called out to him in a plaintive voice, a voice he'd been shocked to realize closely resembled his own.

> Timothy took his time to school,
> Plenty of time he took.
>
> But some he lost in the tadpole pool,
> And some in the stickleback brook…

And he recalled the short essay he had written after his reflection:

> Is losing time simply taking the time to look at what is happening around you? If so by adding the negative 'losing time' and the positive 'taking time' the result is zero, or neutral. This means, therefore, that taking time to explore the world is neither good nor bad. It invites the intriguing possibility that by looking around a person may gain an awareness that is pivotal and could lead to great scientific advancements.
>
> I would love to swing on a garden gate, or watch a tadpole, or see a stickleback streak by or hold a water boatman in my hand. Charlotte is an expert at wasting time, and she often leads me to the brink of a land filled with nothing but wasted time, and there have been

occasions when I have passed through those flimsy
gates and watched her run away and wish ever so much
that I had the courage to follow and leave everything
else behind.

And behold, by not following the proscribed plan for the day it was
Henry, his actual self, who brought everyone to this very spot.

Maybe it wasn't so much wasting time as creating something entirely
new, an off-the-cuff adventure that valiant and purposeful people experienced every single day.

His scalp itched.

His hair started to rise on its own and his eyes widened.

How could he have known the importance of the message he so cava-
lierly tucked inside his memory bank?

"Can we stay for tea?" he asked Oliver. "We've been invited. It would be
rude to leave so abruptly," he added.

"Can we, Grandfather?" Jeremy added.

The impromptu was Oliver's métier, but there was the problem of
Gwendolyn. And yet when opportunities arrive only a fool looks the
other way.

Oliver stroked his lip and reviewed the pros and cons. "I would like to
say yes."

He also felt it was necessary to highlight the problem.

"Gwendolyn will protest."

"Oh, I can fix that," Charlotte said with assurance. "I'll tell her that I
want to leave, and she will insist we stay."

"It can't possibly be as simple as that," Oliver said, looking at
her suspiciously.

"Prepare to be surprised."

Chapter Twenty-One

After a late lunch at *The Spiced Café*, with an apologetic Naabhi preparing his finest and most elaborate dishes, Oliver decided, in keeping with his promise to Sarah, that it was time to tour the theatre. Doreen had joined them for the feast, and Henry had wanted her to tag along, but there was no room in the Rolls.

"Get on with you," Doreen told Henry when he pouted. "You give me that address, and I'll be there if you put on a show, Henry, don't you worry." She pressed Henry's hand and tried to hug Gwendolyn who quickly stepped aside and almost twisted her ankle.

"A pleasure," Gwendolyn mumbled, clearly indicating by her frosty smile that listening to Doreen had been no such thing.

She climbed into the limousine and slid closer to Oliver to make room for Meggie. Wasn't it enough that she had been forced to endure a lunch with three people she did not know? Did they have to completely take over her life as well?

Henry was behaving strangely, she concluded. Picking up old women in the Tube, ferreting out disreputable friends of his father's. Gwendolyn had no facts to confirm her suspicion of disreputability, as Byron and Meggie's place of residence was presentable if one eliminated all the rooms except for the decently-kept kitchen. They did have Earl Grey tea on offer, and Meggie had enough sense to warm the teapot. Plus, the china was acceptable (only one cup was chipped, and Meggie took that one for herself) and she offered cloth napkins instead of paper.

But both these strangers were too large for Gwendolyn's taste. Byron's frame and behaviour confirmed the definition of overload and Meggie, although much smaller and cleaner (Gwendolyn noticed that Byron smelled like he had been dipped in turpentine), wore harlequin glasses and long ragged skirts just like Sarah's. When one was no longer a child one put away childish things. Gwendolyn would have a private word with Meggie because, at heart, Gwendolyn believed she was a kind person, and a kind person tried to prevent people from making blunders and presenting themselves to all and sundry as fools.

But this Doreen person was another matter altogether. Henry simply had to rush to the pub on the corner, where Gwendolyn was certain children were not allowed admittance, because he needed to introduce the woman who had *saved his life* to all his friends.

Saved his life?

Had Henry been under attack by a band of masked gunmen?

No, he had not. He had simply taken the Tube, which Gwendolyn would never consider using even if she was a youngster and heavily armed. This drama on the part of a well-brought-up boy was not to Gwendolyn's liking. It was all a misguided attempt to best Charlotte, and while Gwendolyn would agree, in principle, that this was the correct thing to do, she quickly backtracked when a charwoman arrived, clearly intoxicated, and took over the entire conversation – leaving Gwendolyn, once again, ignored and cast aside.

Was it her fault that she had decided early on in life that picking up strays was not proper behaviour? To give herself credit, she had very little adult instruction in her early years about how to be, whether she wanted to be at all. She had amassed, all on her own, a list of 'instructions to self' that would rival Emily Post. It was a pity she had never published her proclamations and become the best known 'agony aunt' that Canada had ever produced, but she was far too busy divesting herself of husbands and finding fault with wherever she found herself and these occupations demanded all her time.

It was quickly decided, once everyone had eaten far too much food and praised the proprietor far too much, that Byron and Meggie would make the journey to Sarah's theatre school to keep Oliver company.

Byron, squeezed in the back of the limousine with the children, immediately took centre stage and proclaimed that he would teach the children how to play an intricate version of cat's cradle that included knots that could only be broken by the proper positioning of overlapping fingers.

His peculiar odour perfumed the interior of the limousine and began to seep into Gwendolyn's pores.

She was deeply torn. She wanted to insist in an imperious manner that she be taken home, but she also did not want to miss the opportunity to examine, with a microscope, the workings of Sarah's life and livelihood and once and for all get to the bottom of why her brother Charlie, who she barely remembered, had chosen this woman above all to award the sacred Tree of Life brooch.

And yet, when she had seen this brooch again, on the shoulder of Celeste's dress, she had been shocked at how small and insignificant it was. It had always loomed much larger in her mind, a polished masterpiece, two beautiful carved ivory doves lifting their beaks to heaven, the entire piece flashing rubies and emeralds and opals and gold.

Yes, it had been that for certain.

But, somehow, so much less than what Gwendolyn had always pinned her own hopes upon.

This, alone, was the reason she had chosen to make this trip. To come to terms, once and for all, with all the people who had destroyed her life.

Byron droned on, stinking up the car, the children quarrelled, and Gwendolyn remained as still and beautifully carved as a Henry Moore sculpture, although not as voluptuous.

Meggie prattled on, mindlessly, about her career in the theatre.

The theatre. Gwendolyn scoffed silently, drawing the word out so that it had four syllables instead of the correct three. She would have liked to close her eyes and sink into the comfortable leather seat, but Meggie demanded her attention.

She explained to Gwendolyn that she had spent many years working in stage and costume design and was eager to see whether she could be of assistance to Sarah in upcoming productions.

"Are there such?" Gwendolyn asked Oliver.

"Always," he answered.

"I thought Sarah ran a school for children."

"An addendum. To keep busy. Sarah likes to keep busy. And give back to the community."

"Why? She's ninety years old. Isn't it time to rest? The community can look after itself."

Oliver smiled kindly. "Sarah has always believed in the betterment of society through cultural exchange and dialogue. Most of her young students attend for free."

"Why, isn't that marvellous?" Meggie crooned. "Such selflessness."

Nothing was free; that was an absolute. Someone was footing the bill. And Gwendolyn knew that person was Oliver, masquerading for some unknown reason as a chauffeur. Perhaps Oliver, like Dragos, had started with nothing and built a small empire through the judicious purchase of polished limousines. Dragos, who had arrived in Toronto with nothing and started his career picking worms, was moderately well-off. Perhaps this accumulation of currency had to do with the *work ethic*, a term bandied about by politicians and social workers. Gwendolyn did not have to concern herself with such nonsense, as she had inherited all her money and just stood back and watched it grow. It took nerves of steel to make certain nothing happened to that pot of gold and Gwendolyn believed that doing so was akin to working a full-time job.

"I simply cannot wait to meet her. Sarah will be there, won't she?"

Oliver checked his time piece, a cheap skeleton mechanical watch that had so many gears and wheels and tiny pins rotating sluggishly in one direction or another that it hurt Gwendolyn's eyes to look at it.

"She usually arrives at four and works in her office until the children arrive."

If Gwendolyn were Sarah, she would hide in the office and not emerge until every dirty little ragamuffin had left. Charlotte, case in point, was arguing in the back about the proper way to wrap her pointer fingers around her thumb, questioning Byron's technique.

"You're wrong," Charlotte said. "Try it my way."

Gwendolyn closed her eyes briefly. Her stomach churned.

"There's nothing like the thrill of seeing a set come to life," Meggie said, rummaging happily through her carpetbag, an item masquerading as a purse. Her glasses had slipped down to the tip of her nose, and Gwendolyn fingers flexed as a reminder to keep her hands to herself. If Meggie lost her glasses, and the ridiculous harlequin frames became damaged in the fall, she had only herself to blame.

"Hammering, sawing, painting. It is all so visceral. When I assisted with *Ivanov,* I barely slept there was so much to do – a ballroom, a wedding, a funeral, all warring with one another and that was just the scenes, not us workers who could agree on virtually nothing. The blueprint we were given by the director made no sense, but then, he was hardly there as he had his business to run. He was a mechanic."

Gwendolyn remembered reading an article in the *New York Times* about this play and looked at her seatmate with sudden interest.

"You worked on the Ralph Fiennes production? I must say I find him a most distinguished actor."

Surely the director on that project did not spend his time seeing to leaking carburetors. But then, there was no money to be made in the theatre. Gwendolyn knew that.

"Oh, no." Meggie laughed with great amusement. "Our show took place in the Midlands in a theatre about the size of Naabhi's with no hot water, sporadic lighting, and bats. It was my greatest challenge, and I don't mind telling you I spent all my time scrounging every treasure I could find in attics and cellars. Some of those cellars in the houses I visited were nothing more than mud holes."

Gwendolyn shuddered.

"Came down with the most dreadful cough, but it was worth it in the end. The play was sold out for the run of the show."

"And how long might that have been?"

"A week," Meggie said proudly. "One of the longest running shows in my career."

"Oliver, is this Westminster Bridge we are crossing?" Byron asked.

"It is indeed."

"I have scarcely set foot out of my own neighborhood now for a decade," he announced.

"More like days, dear, although you tend to walk north and not southwest."

"Girl is more a birddog than a person. Put her anywhere and she can pinpoint a direction better than a compass. As a boy I walked all of London, I never knew where I was, never cared. Henry, get a grip on yourself. You are not in danger of losing a finger. Charlotte, release Henry's digit, if you please."

"Henry, stop squirming. Just give me your hand and I will untie the knot," Charlotte instructed, spoiling Gwendolyn's chance to ask why Meggie bothered to do such unrewarding work. "If you keep squeezing your fingers they will swell and turn purple."

"They already look purple," Jeremy commented. "Do you have a knife, Grandfather?"

"In the tool chest in the boot. I'll pull over."

"Don't you bother," Meggie said, upending the carpet bag once again on her lap. She extracted a pair of scissors about the shape of a quarter, pulled the miniature handles and two blades unfolded. "Best scissors I have ever owned." She handed them to Byron and Charlotte chirped excitedly at the sight of them.

"I have the exact same pair that I bought in China Town for a dollar. One day they simply disappeared. I always thought you took them, Henry."

"Why would I do that?" Henry asked. "You're not going to cut my skin, are you?" he asked, a worried note in his voice.

"Probably not."

"Did he double twist around his thumb?" Meggie asked. "Like I did the first time?"

"Exactly," Byron said. "Why don't you show Gwendolyn?"

Meggie found a small ball of grey knitting yarn and cut a piece with her teeth, the famous scissors working diligently in the back seat.

"No, thank you," Gwendolyn said, hiding her hands beneath her shawl.

These people were simply outrageous. No better than the children, who, by comparison, seemed decades older. And yet, there was a quickening Gwendolyn felt, and then repressed. Perhaps it was because they were impossible to catalogue. They fit no social norm that Gwendolyn had ever seen, and, by her own observation, both felt perfectly at ease with themselves.

Which was odd. Wasn't it?

Oliver sped south along Victoria Embankment following the line of the River Thames, oblivious to all except the road ahead. For all his misshapen facial features, curious mannerisms, and reluctance to wear anything but uniforms (Sarah was to blame for this, clearly, as people in the theatre were always everything except who they really were) Gwendolyn had decided Oliver was an attractive man.

"You are enjoying the drive?" Oliver asked, not turning his head.

"Very pleasant," Gwendolyn said. "The river Thames is an excellent feature. I believe all cities should have rivers running through them. It helps dispel the monotony of concrete."

"Aren't we close to that National Trust estate, Grandfather? You know, the one that is owned by the Wilmingham family who is related—"

"That's enough, Jeremy," Oliver counselled. "No one is interested in long-ago history."

"Most things in London are based upon long-ago history," Meggie said. "It's unfortunate that you can't stay for a month, Gwendolyn. Oh, there is so very much to see and do here."

"I have pressing business in Toronto, or I would consider it," Gwendolyn lied.

"What pressing business?" Charlotte asked. "You don't do anything. You barely leave your penthouse."

"But Grandfather, I'm sure we could gain admittance to the estate on another day and maybe even drive over to see the gardens—"

"Another time, Jeremy. Henry deserves your full concentration now."

"That's Charlotte's hand, Byron, not Henry's," Jeremy said, dropping the topic as he turned his attention to the malpractice occurring.

"Are your fingers permanently fused, child?" Byron asked.

"I have the strength of a bear. Just try pulling my fingers apart."

"Another time, perhaps. Henry? Your hand please."

Surgical procedures continued apace in the back seat of the limousine, with Henry whining, Jeremy offering reassurance and Charlotte demanding that she cut the string as Byron clearly could not see what he was doing.

Gwendolyn heard only Jeremy's remarks and deduced that Oliver, descended from a titled family, was clearly a man of means. Most people put on airs, they didn't take them off, and she wondered why he was so reticent to be viewed as a man of substance and worth.

"The theatre is undergoing a bit of renovation at the moment," Oliver warned his guests, tapping his horn lightly as a stray dog shot across the road. The roadway had seamlessly changed names and was now Grosvenor. "A refit of some pipes in the bowels beneath the corridor behind the stage. It is advised that everyone respect the barriers in place."

"Did you hear that, Charlotte?" Gwendolyn asked, raising her voice.

"Hear what?" the child demanded. She was trying to convince Henry that it was normal for his fingers to turn white before they regained their usual uninspired beige.

"The theatre is under renovation. You will abide by the rules."

"How come you're only telling me?"

"She's telling everyone dear," Meggie said kindly. She nudged Gwendolyn and whispered: "Go easy on the girl. Criticism creates conflict."

"Perhaps for you," Gwendolyn muttered, but she did swivel her head to look at Charlotte. She saw what she always saw. An overbearing, pig-headed child who believed she was always right and refused to compromise. Not only that, but the child was also wearing, if Gwendolyn was not mistaken, the same clothes she wore when they departed Toronto which seemed a lifetime ago. Was it Gwendolyn's responsibility to make sure that Charlotte bathed every day, changed her outer and under wear, and washed that tangled mass of wild black hair now made more unpresentable with her bangs tied upwards with the errant string? The only people Gwendolyn had ever had this authority over were her husbands, who, mercifully, thought too much of their good looks to let themselves go completely to seed.

Charlotte was manhandling Henry as usual while Byron sat by unconcerned, sketching the entire charade. Jeremy was talking non-stop, and when Gwendolyn unplugged her ears, she heard: "If you consider our veins and arteries, and then factor in the heart rate and obstructions such as the compression of string against..."

And just as quickly, she tuned him out again.

Charlotte, sensing a foreign object, looked up to meet Gwendolyn's eyes.

"What?" she asked. "What am I doing wrong now?"

Was that sadness she saw or the marshalling of the usual combatants advancing with clubs and bayonets. A flash of afternoon sun cast Charlotte in a ghostly amber glow, and Gwendolyn felt a prickling of interest. Perhaps there was something salvageable in the child after all. She had good bone structure and straight teeth and large luminous eyes that sucked in everything surrounding them.

For a moment Gwendolyn felt faint.

Was she being unnecessarily cruel with all her criticism?

"I want you to be the absolute best you can be, Charlotte," she said, surprising herself by the neutrality of her tone. "And that means you are on your best behaviour when we reach the theatre. That goes for you, too, Henry," she added when Charlotte's lips tightened. "Can you flex your fingers?"

Henry showed her a fist and then a five-pointed star.

"Continue doing that," she instructed. "Honestly, Byron, you could be of greater assistance than what I've seen."

"Ah, but then I wouldn't be able to capture this moment so perfectly."

He flipped his sketchbook and instead of seeing a mishmash of lines and spaces approximating the lines and spaces that constituted the children, she saw a portrait of herself. Incomplete, yes, but remarkable in its intensity. It was a profile like Gwendolyn noticed when, on the rare occasion, a Canadian nickel crossed her line of vision. Queen Elizabeth was imprinted on the worthless coinage and Gwendolyn noticed in Byron's attempt that she, herself, looked far more regal than the queen – more determined, absolute, and, to her great astonishment, so darkly beautiful that the image of the queen faded into insignificance.

"Man, that's good," Charlotte breathed wrestling the sketchbook from Byron's hand.

"Telling," Jeremy confirmed, leaning across Byron to get a better look.

"Is that the queen?" Henry asked, confirming Gwendolyn's own assessment.

"It's Gwendolyn, you idiot," Charlotte told him. "Do me next," she demanded, showing Byron her profile.

"I will do you many times, that I promise, but my hand is now tired. This is a gift for you, dear Gwendolyn, if you should accept such a humble offering."

Gwendolyn accepted with a gracious tilt of her head and frowned briefly when she saw marks of Charlotte's sticky fingerprints embedded on the outer edges of the paper. No matter. She would trim those away with her nail scissors later in the evening and place the portrait between two sheets of wax paper, the way she did so long ago as a child when she gathered the falling leaves of autumn and pressed them to preserve their beauty.

"Well done, my dear," Meggie said, congratulating her husband with a vigorous nod of her head.

"I am eager to know what you will see when you do your preliminaries of me, Byron," Oliver announced, taking his eyes from the road to briefly glance at the portrait Gwendolyn had placed on her lap.

"I doubt either of us will be displeased."

"I'm rarely displeased with anything these days," Oliver said. "The unexpected company, the sustaining meal. And behold, we are now close to our destination." The limousine had turned away from the river and was cruising down a laneway that barely accommodated its girth. The laneway opened to small park surrounded by a wrought iron fence. He parked across the street and turned off the engine. "Button up your overcoats."

"What overcoats?" Charlotte asked.

"It's a metaphor," Jeremy explained. "A theatre is a place of disguises, and we must respect the tradition even if it is just in our minds."

Chapter Twenty-Two

The Sackville Theatre was on Kilmer, kitty-corner to the park. Predominantly limestone and built in the classical design, it had an imposing front door flanked with two columns and topped with a pediment, rectangular windows, and Dentil mouldings. Because of its symmetry and proportions, it was easy on the eye. The building, straight and strong and on the thinnish side, perhaps no more than fifty feet across, resembled a tower and boasted battlements on the roof.

"There is a summer garden on top," Jeremy said, pointing upwards, "and tables where guests can take their tea or drinks during intervals. During the summer, our fencing and boxing instructor, Arthur, trained us on the roof. It was very exciting because it felt like we were up in the sky."

"Another tower," Charlotte shouted. "Look, Henry, it's almost like we've come home. I wish Leo could see this," Charlotte prattled as if this one building was worthy of a transatlantic voyage. She had a beatific expression on her face, most unlike what usually was on display. She tried to grab Gwendolyn's hand in her excitement, but Gwendolyn ushered her aside and turned to Oliver, asking:

"Intervals? What intervals?"

"For fifty some years," Oliver told her, helping Byron extract himself from the back seat, "the Sackville has been the best Fringe Theatre in London and the longest-lasting."

"We've been here, Byron. How serendipitous." The excitement pouring off Meggie was palpable, and Gwendolyn had to take a step away. "Surely you remember *Artist Descending a Staircase?*"

"As I do every day," Byron said, scratching his head. "But I'm afraid I don't remember the particulars." In a sotto voice to Oliver he said: "In the early days I loved the bottle a bit too much."

"There was another one, what was it?" Meggie clicked her fingers. "*It was a Dark and Stormy Night.* There was this girl, a minor character, and you waylaid her saying she had the most dangerous eyes you'd ever seen."

"Red hair, curly, a Putney accent?"

"Yes. That's the one."

"She slapped my face?"

"You *do* remember." Meggie clapped her hands.

"I used her as a model if I am not mistaken."

"What an amazing coincidence. If it wasn't for Henry showing up at our door, we might have permanently misplaced this whole section of our lives, Byron, and been the poorer for it. If only had I been more forthright at the time I would have approached Sarah and most possibly secured a lifetime appointment."

The way people rewrote their lives with 'what if' and 'if only' and 'I might have been' was a constant source of annoyance to Gwendolyn. Things were what they were. Full stop. She turned to Oliver and asked:

"Sarah has been in charge the entire time?"

Oliver tapped his upper lip and pondered. "There was a brief break when she was in hospital some years back, but other than that, the theatre has been under her leadership."

"Surely this theatre is not self-supporting?"

"Sarah has many patrons. There will always be those among us who believe it is important to support the arts."

Gwendolyn felt a momentary sadness, so sharp and painful she had to force herself to stand still and take stock of herself. It had happened to her before, this longing for something intangible, and in general, she had been quickly dismissive of something so elusive and had distracted herself immediately by rearranging the furniture in her house or buying a new dress she did not need. She had filled herself with more, more, more, and it worked well enough. This 'feeling', this 'disease', always passed, but now she wondered if, perpetually unsatisfied, this foe (because what else could she call it?) retired quietly and lurked in the background of her psyche, ready and able to ambush her for no reason whatsoever.

She could not understand these sudden longings that refused to crystalize into clear and attainable form and found their presence most unwelcome. It felt like homesickness, which Gwendolyn experienced often as a child (most notably when she had been at home) but clearly, she could not be homesick for a city in which she had never lived and where everything was foreign, no matter that a kind of English was spoken. But these longings attacked her from time to time in Toronto, she admitted, or in Auckland, or in Berlin, or Paris, or the wilds of Winnipeg because, no matter where she was now, she felt homesick for what she had missed or was currently missing and longed to be anywhere but where she was.

Everywhere she had ever lived had felt foreign, alien, unknown, and for a terrible moment she saw herself as a young girl, walking down the street at twilight, drawn to the windows where the burning logs in a fireplace exuded warmth and comfort and a standing lamp cast a glow across a navy blue chesterfield with scrunched pillows and an old patchwork quilt.

Someone is happy there, she would think. Someone is content. Someone is loved, and it doesn't matter that the couch is old, and the pillows disarranged. Someone is safe.

And then she would ask herself what it even meant to be safe.

Safe from what?

Gwendolyn was shocked with the sudden introspective direction her thoughts were taking her. What had she seen or heard that hit her heart with the suddenness of a sucker punch?

Was it the word *leadership*?

She rejected that as unsubstantial. Leaders were often people who desired attention, an audience, a platform from which to present themselves. Gwendolyn had always preferred the shadows, where she could tilt her nose upwards and think of how much better she could do whatever was on display if she only believed in something, which for most of her life, she hadn't.

Victories were so fleeting.

Was it Meggie and Byron reminiscing? Leaning on one another and conferring? Was it the partnership with another that she missed?

Certainly not.

Gwendolyn was privileged in that she enjoyed her own company above all others and followed a routine which gave balance and clarity to her life. It would be impossible to have balance and clarity if she had to share a space with another who would drop crumbs on the floor and put his feet on the coffee table or allow himself to appear in public dressed the way Byron was dressed.

Did this sadness, which had turned hot and sticky, have to do with Sarah and what might have been had Gwendolyn answered any of the letters she sent? Would her life have taken an entirely different direction?

And just as fast Gwendolyn remembered her autocratic tutor and rejected this foolish notion. Sarah hadn't changed, not that Gwendolyn could see. And she would have tried to micromanage Gwendolyn's life, shrink it into a size Sarah could carry around in the palm of her hand.

That left Charlotte and the words the child had spoken when she had stood in front of the building and looked upwards. What was it she had said, and why did these words have the power to bother her this intensely? Everything that Charlotte saw or participated in was the very best of the best. She was not shy in her pronouncements, but they were childish and egocentric – as if the world revolved around Charlotte and Charlotte alone. There was nothing there, nothing at all.

Could it be Jeremy and his simple adoration of Oliver? Or the way the sun seemed poised to set or her shoes pinching her toes, the unwelcome havoc the Indian spices placed on her stomach? Or was Gwendolyn simply, absolutely, and completely *tired* from travelling, from being forced to talk to strangers, from pretending to be part of a group when she was without question, all unto herself, never asking for help from others and standing, albeit somewhat precariously from time to time, on her own two feet?

On second glance, the building, this 'remarkable' theatre which elicited such 'ooohs' and 'aaahs', was a bit shabby. She noticed that someone had left a used candy wrapper on the top step. The windows were streaked with dirt and exhaust, and the brass door handle needed polishing. There were cracks in the stone steps and faint whiff of fish and chips drifted past her nostrils.

Nothing was as good as it seemed.

Everything was an illusion.

With a quiet sigh of satisfaction, Gwendolyn was able to take the arm that Oliver offered, pick her way carefully to the top of the staircase, and calm the erratic beating of her confused and overtired heart.

Gwendolyn strolled the perimeter of the theatre, taking her time to inspect the carpet (dirty), the red velvet seats (ancient), the sconces (in need of polishing), and the mahogany ceiling (stunning, although a fire hazard). The feeling of displacement which had overcome her as she stood outside was gone, and she felt comforted in her usual role of inspector general. She was no longer used to open spaces, she concluded, remembering her feeling of discomposure at both Pearson International and Heathrow. Wide open spaces had no beginnings, no endings, were cluttered with too many people and reduced her status and importance to that of a gnat. "Not very large," she commented. "How many seats are there?"

"One hundred," Oliver told her. "Many years back there was some discussion about building a theatre in the round. Very relevant at the time but antithetical to the design of the building."

"Nonsensical, in keeping with most fads. Very wise of Sarah not to go in that direction."

Gwendolyn ran her hand along the corner of the stage. She had once seen a play, the title long forgotten, in a theatre which was experimenting with equal views for everyone, no matter the cost of the ticket. It had been both confusing and exasperating to see the actors make their entrances and exits through the seating area, exciting the audience and causing far too many heads to swivel.

As she continued her slow walk below the edge of the stage, she came to a sudden stop. "Oliver, surely my eyes deceive me. This cannot be an orchestral pit?"

"They do musicals from time to time," Oliver replied. "A few years ago, there was enough money to install a lift which expands the length of the stage. The pit is cordoned off due to renovation and repair. The floor needs reinforcing. Additional access is in the wings and cordoned. Quite safe as the men are working below."

"I hear nothing," Gwendolyn said, tilting her head towards the ropes.

Oliver checked his watch. "It's after five."

"And?"

"They've finished for the day." He paused, placed a finger on his lip, and added: "There might be a minor labour dispute as well. Perhaps that is why it is so quiet."

Charlotte appeared beside Gwendolyn and placed her hand on the surrounding rope. "Can we see the pit? How many musicians can fit inside? Is there room for the conductor? How is sound dispersed? Dispersed is a new word I learned last week."

"Please do not sneak up on a person, Charlotte," Gwendolyn said. "Sarah will be able to answer all your questions, I'm certain, once we find her."

Oliver climbed the stairs on the side of the stage and beckoned with his hand. "Come and see the crossover, Charlotte. Jeremy, bring Henry."

"It's a hidden hallway that connects both sides of the stage," Jeremy explained, pulling Henry from his seat and manhandling him down the aisle. "You find this often in old houses behind the dining room and the kitchen. A seamless and invisible passage for the servants to bring food to the table and clear plates."

"We have one in my house," Charlotte announced, taking a bow centre stage. "Hey, Henry, do you remember when we were re-enacting the battle of Queenston Heights, and all the lights went out?"

As she said these words, she shuddered involuntarily, and in her mind, she saw vividly and in slow motion, a stalwart brown spotted palomino pony fall with an arrow in its chest. This brought sudden tears to her eyes.

"Steady on," came from Byron who immediately noticed Charlotte's distress.

"Surely it was only a game," from Meggie. "No need to worry yourself now."

"A decisive battle that went against the Americans," from Oliver. "Those are righteous tears of relief."

"Charlotte," said Gwendolyn, "Stop making a scene."

The image passed so quickly Charlotte could not contain or save it, and she shook her head, wondering what had just happened. And then she remembered her story.

"Right. Anyway, there was a complete power outage and with no windows in the hallway it was black like coal. I had a clip-on flashlight attached to the top of my pants, and we pretended we were tunnelling beneath a mountain. You remember how you held onto my ankle, Henry, and we both crawled on our stomachs?"

"No," Henry answered perfunctorily.

He did remember, however, and was ashamed by how frightened he had felt. Charlotte, naturally, had taken it all in stride and had come equipped for any disaster. She'd unclipped the flashlight from her pants, flicked the switch, and within minutes they were back in a shadowy daylit sitting room. For Charlotte it had been a lark; for him, an ordeal.

Henry entered the hallway behind the stage with Jeremy, leaving his many failures of courage behind, and was slightly disappointed to see that it was only a hallway and not some mysterious interior cavern with twisting turns littered with stalagmites and stalactites. It smelled faintly of old socks and Lysol. Dust bunnies tickled his nose, and it was cold, a permanent wintry late afternoon.

"This gets a lot of use during performances," Jeremy told him.

"Have you been in many shows?" Henry asked, eager to wash his hands. His fingers had touched the wall which felt both oily and sticky.

"Not even one. I was referring to what goes on in class, but you'll see for yourself."

Chapter Twenty-Three

Sarah's office was on the first floor, which is to say the *second* floor in Canadian terms. Gwendolyn did not trust the elevator – an antiquated version of the contemporary model, replete with an ornately carved metal door that had to be closed manually. When Oliver began to crank the elevator into life, a protruding handle that took the place of easily read buttons reflecting floor allocations, Gwendolyn said she'd rather walk.

The elevator was so small that she had difficulty making certain the delicate fabric of her shawl did not touch the walls (festooned as they were with ancient playbills and letters of congratulations from minor British stars). Not exactly minor, she was forced to admit when she saw pictures of Wendy Hiller, Joan Greenwood and Christopher Lee amongst many others.

The framed letters were a bit too effusive for her taste and she couldn't help but think they had been scripted.

Marvellous... inspired... thoughtful... invigorating... brilliant... were but a sampling of the adjectives used to describe the plays in which these actors had a role, and Gwendolyn wondered if they were merely self-congratulatory missives rather than a comprehensive analysis of the theatre in general.

The wall running up the staircase was similarly adorned, and Oliver stopped to pay homage to a few stars who had passed on to greater celestial heights. Except for Sarah, whose name Gwendolyn saw stamped across so many playbills that she stopped counting. She felt pressed in by the ochre-coloured walls, the vibrant multi-coloured woollen carpet runner, the old, polished mahogany banister, but worse, she was feeling diminished by witnessing the lifetime achievement of her oldest enemy.

She banished this claustrophobia by taking a deep breath and then she sniffed, imperiously. There was dust everywhere and some of the frames were hanging crooked. She longed to clear the walls of all this clutter and exchange the garish ochre for a soothing clean and pure pale blue, which would tone beautifully with the carpet, but this was not her business. None of this was her business.

"Are you certain that Sarah is here, Oliver? There is little point visiting her office if she is not in attendance."

"We arranged to meet at five, and Sarah is usually quite punctual. She asked to see you when you arrived, and then I can take you home if you wish. The improvisational classes are a bit rambunctious and, unless you are participating, can be trying. It is an excellent way for children to let off steam."

Gwendolyn had made no decisions about where she wanted to be in an hour. Home, as Oliver called it, had its benefits but with it would come a declaration of both her age and her solitude, neither of which she wished to broadcast, since Sarah was a good eighteen years her senior and seemingly had no problem with so-called rambunctious behaviour.

"A cup of tea would be most welcome," Gwendolyn stated. Having reached the upper level, she felt a bit breathless. The high ceilings on ground level added many more stairs than she was used to climbing.

"Is that you, Oliver?" a voice called out.

"Yes," he called back. "We have arrived."

Taking Gwendolyn by the arm, he led her down a hallway lined with blood red carpet.

"This is the commissary," he said, pausing at the doorway of a room filled with chesterfields, plush armchairs, and a makeshift kitchen with a stove, sink, and large refrigerator. "Costumes is next and where the seamstresses ply their magic."

This room had a collection of old Singer sewing machines and tables filled with bolts of brightly coloured fabric, boxes of thread and wool, and half-clad dressmaker dummies. The built-in shelves which stretched the length of one wall were filled with wigs and hats, each resting on Styrofoam heads. Someone had decorated the heads with long black eyelashes, dots of rouge and blood red lipstick. The male heads had goatees or moustaches or both. Gwendolyn decided Meggie and Byron would feel quite comfortable in this room, as it clearly mimicked the dreadful dolls adorning the walls of their staircase.

"Sarah is often to be found here, designing and creating. We receive donations of used clothing from patrons, and last year's models from several shops. Nothing is wasted, and during breaks hats, booties, rompers, and buntings are run up and delivered to shelters." Oliver entered the room and held up a bunting bag made from sky blue fabric adorned with white felt clouds.

The sheer industry and usefulness inherent in the very air of this chamber made Gwendolyn weak with fatigue. She did not know how to work a sewing machine and had difficulty fixing a loose button. That is why tailors existed. At least she kept people employed and at times, felt she alone sustained the economy.

"Oliver?"

The annoying voice was scratchy and loud, and it rang out more persistently than before.

Oliver accelerated the pace and Gwendolyn was whisked by a rabbit warren of smaller rooms and hallways ending in darkness until they arrived at their destination.

Sarah's office occupied the entire front of the building and was larger than the two rooms Gwendolyn had already inspected. This room had a gas fireplace with a small but beautifully ornate carved mantel, two old sagging armchairs and a long wooden table from which, it could only be assumed, Sarah held meetings with staff and donors. The table was littered with piles of playbills, notebooks, scripts, bills, ashtrays, to-do lists, and empty cracker boxes. A Turkish carpet covered the floor, a carpet sweeper abandoned in the middle, and Sarah lounged on an old red velvet chesterfield, half-reclining, an empty cigarette holder clamped to the side of her mouth.

"Gwendolyn, how marvellous. Have you enjoyed the day?"

For a brief second Gwendolyn felt a strong desire to boast and tell Sarah about the two new friends she had made (neither of whom she liked) and the Indian meal she had sampled (disruptive to her digestive system) and the courtesy and intelligence of Oliver (the only truth, but since he was Sarah's man, the remark seemed redundant).

She confined herself to a tight smile and a nod of her head.

"Have you been sweeping?" Oliver asked, disposing of the carpet sweeper in a closet behind Sarah's desk.

"An attempt was made."

"Where is Cranston?"

"She's ill."

Sarah motioned with her hand for Gwendolyn to take a seat in the slipper chair at the foot of the chesterfield. A butler's table sat alongside complete with tea service, cozy, and plate of biscuits.

The room had two floor-to-ceiling windows overlooking the street, and the late afternoon light flowed through the room illuminating millions of dust motes lazily drifting. Gwendolyn strolled to the window, ignoring, for the moment, the offer of a seat, and saw a group of children gathered around the limousine, polishing the fenders with chamises.

"Oliver, there are children disturbing your car," she said urgently. "Almost a gang."

"Students," he explained, peering out the window. "They perform this service weekly for a small fee."

"They think polishing the fenders, indeed the whole car, brings them luck," Sarah explained. "And Oliver often drives them home."

"They enjoy giving instructions while I drive, and I have to pretend I am lost," Oliver said, unbuttoning his jacket and placing it on one of the chairs in front of the fireplace. "It's quite warm in here," he stated.

"Is it? These old bones are always a bit chilled but turn down the flame if you wish."

Gwendolyn saw that Jeremy, Henry, and Charlotte had joined the throng outside and introductions were being made. She was intrigued to see that Charlotte stood back and let Henry have centre stage. Instead of insinuating herself into the midst of the group, she reached beneath her shirt and extracted her Hilroy, liberating the pencil that was stuck in her ridiculous topknot.

How similar and yet how different they were, she and Charlotte. Observers, outsiders, loners. Why should the fact of this recognition cause her to bristle?

"I'll have one sugar in my tea, Oliver," she said, moving the chair away from the foot of the chesterfield and placing it at an angle that would make

Sarah have to turn her head to have a conversation. She began to iron the pleats in her skirt, recognized the loaded silence that accompanied this action, and stopped.

"There are two people in the theatre right now, Sarah," Gwendolyn began. "And one is clamouring for membership." She explained the odd twists and turns that had taken her and Oliver to the home of Meggie and Byron and added: "She is a set designer and costume maker. Or at least she was."

Sarah flashed a smile at Oliver. "Very timely, wouldn't you say?"

"I would."

Gwendolyn asked what was so very timely about two people resting their weary bones on two well-worn theatre seats.

"Having a neutral pair of eyes and ready hands to help put together a set seems to be just the ticket."

"I would suggest those ready hands may be a bit grasping."

Sarah pushed this aside. "It's not the manpower that is important. We have that. It's the fresh take on an old endeavour. I've been waiting for this," she said with some excitement. "I thought it might come from Charlotte, but it was Henry. Or," she added, narrowing her eyes, "was it you, Oliver, keeping silent because you knew how it would please me as a surprise?"

Oliver placed his hand on his heart. "I knew nothing of this. Henry was acting out of character by deserting his friends and journeying across London to meet old friends of his father's."

"And how wonderful is this, Oliver? I am eager to meet them. And check to see that Arthur has arrived. He will lead a fencing warm-up before the improvisations start."

Gwendolyn studied Sarah who was enjoying a biscuit and dropping crumbs on her lap. She looked so smug and sure of herself, basking in Oliver's warm, appreciative smile, queen of this ramshackle theatrical establishment she ran and never prey to the voices Gwendolyn always heard which repeated the same mantra over and over: *And what, may I ask, have you accomplished today, Gwendolyn?*

"I took fencing lessons in my youth," she said, surprising herself that she would reveal any part of her past that was not a misery. "It's been many years, and I am interested to see a master swordsman at work."

Oliver and Sarah exploded with laughter.

"A master swordsman Arthur is not. Boxing is more his arena, so to speak," Oliver explained once he had wiped his eyes and tidied his expression, so he no longer resembled a basset hound choking on a golf ball.

"But the boxing got a bit out of hand. One of the students got injured a while back," Sarah explained. She began the laborious process of putting what she needed in her carpet bag – and to Gwendolyn's closely watching eye, it appeared that Sarah needed far too much.

"A loose tooth, a black eye. It was an accident, but Arthur could not control the outcome if the students did not pay attention to his direction. Why are you taking the tea cozy, my dear?" Oliver inquired.

"To keep my hands warm if I feel a chill. I forgot my muff at home."

After the pandering (both vocal and tactile) when Byron and Meggie were introduced to Sarah, and the repetition of the same theatrical stories Gwendolyn had heard during the drive through London, broadcast loudly enough to reach the ears of the students pretending to kill one another with plastic swords on stage, silence prevailed, and seats were taken.

"Truly a beautiful space," Meggie whispered, patting Sarah's hand.

"Thank you, dear. We do try," Sarah responded.

Gwendolyn hid her frown behind her hand. What exactly had Sarah done, besides taking five minutes to arrange herself in a chair, to deserve such praise?

And the misshapen gnome posturing on stage. Who was he?

"Arthur," Sarah told Gwendolyn as though answering her obvious concern. "We couldn't get by without him."

Gwendolyn lifted her eyebrows but remained silent.

It was immediately clear that Arthur knew the fundamentals of fencing, but he was lackadaisical about rules, and from what Gwendolyn could see, the children merely danced around the stage, wielding their plastic swords above their heads and pretending to charge one another. Charlotte was naturally in her element, bashing Henry around the shoulders while Jeremy tried to defend his friend.

"Adorable," Meggie cooed. "They look like modern day warriors."

"They look like children who do not know what they are doing," Gwendolyn countered.

"Stellar," Byron added, crossing his arms across his abdomen and belching. "It is always refreshing to see a joust."

Gwendolyn shook her head in disgust. This was not a lesson; this was a free for all and she protested in a loud and imperious voice. Arthur, a rather dishevelled elderly gentlemen who looked like he would be more comfortable lounging on a bar stool was happy to give the stage to her after she announced that she was well versed in the art of fencing. Before waving her up he arranged the children in two opposing rows facing centre stage.

"Have you taught the lunge, the parry?" she asked, as they swept by one another, her climbing up, Arthur on his way down.

"We touched upon it," he said. "The children prefer to pretend they are dressed in suits of armour and mounted on a destrier. The spectators are screaming, and a joust is about to begin."

"Hear, hear," Byron bellowed loudly.

Gwendolyn only frowned. "I have no idea as to what these strange remarks refer."

"Make-believe," Arthur explained. "Imagination. Knights fighting duels. That staple of every child I know."

"And what does that have to do with fencing?"

"Not a hell of a lot," Arthur admitted. "But if I can sneak in a rule or two every time, I consider it a job well done."

Twenty minutes later, the children had learned the basic fencing stance, the shuffle (as Charlotte insisted it be called) and the correct way to hold the sword and position the other arm. Sarah directed from her front row centre chair and the two lines formed a figure eight with the children moving forward through the full eight and then backwards to where they started. Legs were not kept bent, the front foot was not always pointing straight forward, the sword arm did not maintain a consistent forty-five-degree angle, but the overall impression gleaned from the audience was positive.

"It's beautifully choreographed," Meggie said.

"A breakaway to the two remaining fencers who meet at the point of the eight. The rest fall back and continue the sequence in bisecting lines. What do you see as the backdrop?" Oliver asked Sarah.

"Nothing too distracting, but nothing modern either. A field? A forest? A village?"

"It reminds me of your play, Gwendolyn," Charlotte said suddenly, allowing the hard-done-by lady to feel less disabused (since no one was asking her opinion on anything and she, alone, had trained these poor performers into doing something quite spectacular). "Henry? You know what I mean?"

"*The Three Questions*," he answered at once.

"You are a playwright?" Byron bellowed. "Renowned? Do I know your work?"

Gwendolyn ignored Byron's question and turned to Sarah. "You were there," she said frowning. "You were directing *my* play. Quite naturally you took over what was mine."

"Yes, I was there, Gwendolyn, so many long years ago. But I'm certain you were the director."

"And Charlie's gang of drunken friends who laughed and cheered at the antics of some stand-in for Lukas who was *supposed* to be the king."

"That would be me," Charlotte said modestly. "I remember it perfectly. You were the director, and Sarah looked after wardrobe and hair. I was the king. I can still remember most of the lines I didn't say if you are interested."

"I am not," Gwendolyn said, bristling, unwilling to even look at her. This long-ago meeting, which she had steadfastly denied, was beginning to crowd her and demand her acceptance.

Gwendolyn looked pained just then, almost vulnerable. But she rallied, and her features hardened. "Soon after the play, Charlie disappeared from my life completely. You spirited him away and told me nothing."

Sarah shook her head. "Although we might have left Canada at the same time, I had no part in spiriting him away. Charlie was always his own man. He took instruction from no one and always did what he felt was right. You will remember, Gwendolyn, that Canada was at war in September of 1939, and Charlie was doing his bit."

"I remember it quite differently, thank you," she said, her face stony. In fact, she remembered very little except Charlie's sudden departure, her father's long and intractable depression, and the disappearance of the Tree of Life brooch.

"Thank you, Gwendolyn. You have opened a world of possibilities," Sarah said, rising from her chair and walking slowly towards the stairs. "Please don't go anywhere. We are about to start the improvisations."

"I have no interest in participating in—"

"Arthur will bring you a chair. You don't have to participate. You can watch or help me direct, and we will all be the best of friends. Arthur, collect the swords, please, and everyone else pick a partner. I think we can build on this idea Gwendolyn presented and see where it leads."

"What idea?' Gwendolyn asked. "Fencing is not an idea."

"No. But where it leads us is."

From the Hilroy of Charlotte Lisa Hansen

DAY: WEDNESDAY, SEPTEMBER 1, 1999
TIME: 9:00 PM London, England. TIME: 4:00 PM Toronto, Canada. Still can't wrap head round such
LOCATION: window ledge of MY bedroom in Sarah's house.

In my call moments ago, Leo said that it was wonderful (his word) that Gwendolyn participated in so many events today and told me I should be proud of myself.

I couldn't figure out why and then I thought, okay, well, maybe I can take credit for a few things.

By saying I wanted to leave the Byron and Meggie establishment, Gwendolyn was duty bound to insist that we stay. By refusing to eat Indian food, Gwendolyn would have nothing else. So what? This is hardly news. This is the nature of my relationship with Gwendolyn. She dislikes me for reasons unknown and is always out to best me, which is an ugly trait for an elder such as herself.

Fencing and improvisational exercises at Sarah's great and good theatrical school and my own incredible abilities in both fields I recognize as a given, but maybe because I did not goad or push Gwendolyn she acted out of character and participated. This goes against aforementioned ugly trait so perhaps progress is being made.

Fencing: Watching Gwendolyn throw off her shoes and slide around on stage courtesy of her slippery stockings was cool, even though part of me was watching intently to see if she would fall. (She didn't). Even cooler, she

238

appeared to know what she was doing. Not one of Sarah's students knew what to make of her, so they watched, listened, and learned the basic moves:

Lunge – a great attacking technique.

Parry – what a person does when the lunge is coming their way.

Riposte – (thank you, Jeremy for spelling it for me even though I didn't ask you how to spell it) my favourite move because it is the counterattack when blocked with a parry

I have practised these moves ten times and am now an expert.

Improvisation exercise:

A non-starter. I have spent my life improvising from one moment to the next and pretending it is an activity that needs to be developed is weird. We had to imagine we were something we were not, and others had to guess what that was. I chose to be a lion, a tree, and a hot air balloon and no one could guess the hot air balloon even though I kept rising on my toes and pretending to vanish into the ether. Once again Leo congratulated me, because Gwendolyn ended up being my partner. This was only because no one wanted to be **her** partner, and she had the nerve to tell me she felt sorry for me because no one wanted to be **my** partner, and this started a fight, and we were both banished from the stage for refusing to apologize to one another and I would like to know how this is fair or how this even qualifies as improvisation. I was so put out I didn't watch the rest of the activity, but Henry said it was "Great Fun" and I said, "Get stuffed!" and things were very icy in the limousine as we drove home.

DAY: WEDNESDAY, SEPTEMBER 1 (Continued)
TIME: 11:00 PM London, England – Toronto eating dinner
NOTES: Organization of detritus-essentials for future archivers
LOCATION: On floor of same said room reclining on pillow – sleep late to arrive

It is important to always carry a primo first aid kit because one never knows when a person such as myself will be called upon to save a life. I have emptied my navy blue zippered pouch to classify and rearrange all the necessities. Future scholars and historians: PLEASE, for your own good, take note of the following:

a spray bottle of hydrogen peroxide, BAND-AID metal box filled with guess what? plastic waterproofs, bandage compresses, triangulars, safety pins and what not. Also, scissors, tweezers, disposable gloves, wound closures, a flare, a space blanket and several individually wrapped packages of Krispy Chews, Chez Whiz treats, gator aid, and an OFFICIAL St. John's Ambulance card (manufactured by self).

Articles of archaeological significance to be catalogued alphabetical later
- Dinner menu from Naabhi's café – stained with a bit of biryani with goat that I insisted on ordering when we all took over the café. Goat is a bit greasy but A-OKAY if followed by lots of water. Note to self: memorize items to eat and think up lots of complimentary adjectives so I can become an expert in this cuisine and start writing restaurant reviews once I return to the land of Toronto.
For now, all I know is this: dosa is not served with maple syrup. Henry embarrassed himself by asking for this condiment, thereby saving me from the same humiliation.
- Entrance ticket to Madame Tussauds
- Underground ticket picked up off floor of station
- Theatre playbill called "Let it All Fly" peeled from wall at Sarah's
- Gold hair clip from dressing room (broken)

Final most important piece of information
to be kept to self and not broadcast or shared with anyone:

This slipping in and out of my current reality is disorienting. It happened while I stood on the stage this afternoon at Sarah's theatrical school, and I could see a palomino pony fall with an arrow though its chest and I lost control of my emotions. I have never had a pony, nor have I ridden a pony (to be rectified post haste once I return to the place called Toronto). I put it down to being in an airplane compression chamber far too long, which disarranged and disorganized my inward cells and caused them to scream in panic.

Additional note to self: In my momentary disorganization, I become fearful, a state to which I am largely immune. It's almost like the ground on which I stand or the chair on which I sit is resting on nothing but empty space and the only thing I can compare it to is being hurled, willy-nilly through space at a breakneck speed which happened when Henry and me became disgorged from our current reality and wound up in 1939.

And here is where it gets interesting because, in Gus Frank's journal, he wrote about this condition when he was a prisoner of some chain gang that was building the great Canadian railroad through vast mountain ranges in Western Canada.

What I have so far been able to translate from Gus's scribbles are illuminating if accurate and totally ridiculous if not.

"he adds two vincers to axe heaves nix outing Art hurt Art to hell kink Arthur"

At first glance this is what the words look like but after a careful decoding this is what they really were:

"head split in two by invisible axe...heaving...voice shouts Arthur... Arthur...where is King Arthur"

Ergo, a solid reason for my head hurting. It's got to hurt badly if it is split in two by an axe.

Still and all, neither version makes the slightest bit of sense considering Gus was in Western Canada and not in Great Britain where Henry told me King Arthur sleeps on and on and on...

OOOOOOOHHHHHH!!!

I am in England which is part of Great Britain – I'm not sure what the other parts are but it matters not. Henry told me that Arthur was a mythic king (not real) who defeated the Saxons (no idea) in the 5th or 6th century and is largely regarded as a good luck charm, someone to call upon when times are tough.

Lukas and Henry went mad about a book that had just been published in 1939 called The Once and Future King which was all about King Arthur fighting battles with Excalibur, his sword pulled out of a large stone. As fairy tales go this one isn't bad. I simply have not had the time to read the book and must rely on Henry's conclusions.

Axes, swords, who cares? They are both weapons. And King Arthur had his Knights of the Round Table, just like I now have Henry, Jeremy, Oliver, Sarah, Meggie, Byron, Arthur and Gwendolyn.

And Ariel.

Who is arriving in the morning.

My conclusions:

1. Headaches are common to those of us who are in service to others across the spectrum of time.
2. Knights, kings, lancers, and swords appear out of nowhere when they are needed.

Note to self: As soon as I realized such existed in the universal, I felt that weird dizziness again, the room tilted and then stabilized. If somebody had been standing right beside me, they wouldn't have noticed a thing. But I noticed and added another tick to the back page of you, dear Hilroy, where I have been keeping a running tally. 5 ticks since arriving in London.

Additional note to self: Investigate side effects of long-distance plane travel.

Chapter Twenty-Four

"Look at her," Henry insisted, nudging Jeremy. He pointed at Charlotte, who was busy dissecting a flaky buttermilk biscuit and spreading it with butter and jam. "She was awake when we went to sleep, demanding cocoa from Oliver. And she was up creeping around at five this morning."

Charlotte looked up then, her lips smeared with blood red strawberry jam.

"And don't deny it," Henry said, "because I heard you. I'd like to know how you manage to get along with no sleep."

"I sleep," Charlotte said indignant.

Because she did.

The curious thing was she never stopped writing even when her eyes were closed, and her mind was shut off. Something inside her, a part of her – but also not – was desperate to get every word she heard recorded on the blank pages of her Hilroy. This was a new phenomenon, and it had begun the minute she got off the plane at Heathrow. Both mornings she had awoken to find her fingers still grasping her pencil and more pages of the Hilroy covered with marks and scratches and hieroglyphics that took her several minutes to decipher, primarily because she didn't remember writing them. Her writing had begun to resemble that of Gus Frank's, as if she were being directed by a ghost.

This knowledge of wheels turning without her guidance was curiously abnormal.

"I have enough energy to run around the block ten times and not even breathe hard. Just like Archworthy," she said, defiant.

"Archworthy?" Sarah asked. "Who is that?"

"A horse that won the Queen's plate back in 1939 and came in at 4 to 1. I had enough money to make a bet and then buy a ticket on the Queen of Australia. This is exactly what would have happened had I been allowed to stay in 1939 instead of being whisked back to my own time. I would then have been able to live with you and Charlie and arrange for Leo and Henry to join us."

"Charlotte," Gwendolyn sighed. "I happen to know you and Henry spent a lot of time in the Reference library. Your grandfather told me. You are making up these stories simply to annoy me."

"Amn't," Charlotte said smugly, her lips oozing blood red jam.

"After breakfast, you and I are going to have a private chat," Gwendolyn concluded.

"I have a better idea," Sarah announced to the table at large. She was up much earlier than normal getting things ready her daughter's return. Oliver had left at eight for the pickup at Heathrow. "A few days ago, I came across an ancient script that caught my attention. This script was in one of boxes of treasures from my past. I looked through it when I knew you were coming, Gwendolyn."

"If I recall, Sarah, you left Canada on a ship. Don't tell me you took steamer trunks full of old papers with you."

Breaking with tradition, Gwendolyn was sharing a second breakfast with company. She was unusually alert and almost in a good mood. The fencing exercise the night before had rejuvenated her, the choreographed techniques of the sport, both elegant and potentially dangerous, a combination of qualities that suited her just fine.

Sarah took a sip of tea and frowned as she examined the rim of the cup. "I took very little, probably enough to last me for a month or so, for I was not going to stay in London."

"And?" Gwendolyn asked with the arched tone of an empress dowager. Although her routine of breakfasting alone had been broken, she refused to appear at the table wearing her nightdress and was wearing a black suit, her makeup perfectly applied.

Unlike Sarah who was dressed like a hobo.

"When the war was over, and I decided to stay, I wrote to my friend who was storing all my boxes in the basement of his family home. He

244

shipped them to me." She shrugged and her shawl drifted to the floor. "Isn't that what people do when they relocate? You've relocated many times, haven't you?"

Gwendolyn nodded. "And it was my great pleasure to leave everything behind and start from scratch." Gwendolyn long ago realized it was impossible to truly start from scratch because she was steadfastly accompanied by her hefty collection of grievances.

"I couldn't do that, could you?" Jeremy asked Henry. "I need to have all my treasures around me at all times, so I feel safe."

"I get by without too much baggage," Henry countered, pushing his plate aside. "I took very little when I was shipped off to Camp Highland last summer."

Charlotte snorted. "And yet, look how much you brought to London for just a week. How many pairs of socks and pyjamas and shoes and T-shirts and—"

"My *parents* insisted," said Henry. "It was for their comfort, not mine. At camp we are expected to be dirty and dishevelled. It is a different story when you are a houseguest."

Sarah waited patiently until the children stopped arguing and then continued her conversation with Gwendolyn. "I have lost more boxes than I can count over the years, but remarkably, the older boxes have remained intact. And you will never guess what I have found."

Jeremy asked: "A play you wrote yourself when you were my age?"

Sarah smiled. "What I found was a play written by Gwendolyn. When *she* was your age. It was mentioned last night."

Gwendolyn went very still. She stopped ironing the pleats in her skirt, stopped fiddling with her teacup and spoon and stopped scrapping breadcrumbs off the table.

Jeremy, Henry, and Charlotte all placed their elbows on the table simultaneously and leaned forward. For a moment the steady drip of a leaking faucet was the only sound.

"My enterprise project," Gwendolyn finally acknowledged.

"Gwendolyn took Leo Tolstoy's short story 'The Three Questions' and turned it into a play," Sarah explained to the children. "Although, Charlotte and Henry, you both know that. Gwendolyn refused all advice from me, and I think you were right to do so because I read the script last night. It's an excellent adaptation, and I'd like your permission to have my students, along with Henry and Charlotte, perform it while you are still here. You can direct, Gwendolyn. Would that interest you? We can add the fencing routine you began last night as one interlude and others will come. Perhaps a soliloquy or two on the nature of existence. There is always much from which to choose."

There was a long silence.

Gratifyingly – to Sarah, at least – both Charlotte and Henry, better placed to remember this special dramatic piece, were grinning and performing a thumbs up routine.

"I would need to see the script before I can answer that question. The whole story might be dated and no longer significant. The three questions, for instance. What are they? I have forgotten."

"I remember," Charlotte said. "I know the whole story backwards, forwards, and sideways."

"I'm the one who told you the story," Henry said, interrupting with uncharacteristic insistence. "You were too lazy to read the script."

"Tell me," Jeremy insisted. "I haven't read Tolstoy. I'm not sure I know who he is."

"Russian," Henry said shortly. "No longer alive. The story is this: a king has been given three questions to answer and he wants to know the correct answer to each because if he does, he will live a successful life."

"I would say an *honest* life." Sarah glanced at Gwendolyn as she said this, but the woman was staring out the kitchen window, lost in her own reflections. "Alive to the moment in which he lives."

"Maybe," Henry agreed after giving the remark a bit of thought.

"What are the three questions?" Jeremy insisted. "How long do I have to live? Will my grandfather always be here to guide me? Questions like that?"

"Those are important, to be sure," Sarah said with deep appreciation. "Even though they are not the questions asked. But think about that if you choose to direct, Gwendolyn. Think about the importance of what Jeremy just said."

"I simply cannot believe you have that script, Sarah," Gwendolyn said, stuck in the past. "Do you have others that I wrote?"

"We'll look together later. Now, Henry, tell us. What are the questions?"

Henry closed his eyes. "'When is the right time to begin a project or start to work?' That's the first question the king asks."

Charlotte jumped in with the second. "What kind of people are the most essential is question two." She raised her voice just as Henry cleared his throat. "And what is the one thing to do that is more important than any other thing?"

Gwendolyn crumbled a piece of toast and stared at the mess she had made on her plate. "As I said last night, there was this *person* who disrupted the performance and turned it into a farce." She was having difficulty pretending that Charlotte had not mysteriously appeared in her life as a child, disrupting everything and everyone around her. Whatever witch-like skill that Charlotte possessed, Gwendolyn was positive she did not want its essence polluting her life now.

Charlotte watched as Gwendolyn swept crumbs of toasted biscuit into a neat pile with the edge of her knife.

"I turned your play into a masterpiece."

"Whoever this person was," Gwendolyn continued, doggedly refusing to give Charlotte the confirmation she required, "she played to the audience for no other reason than to get a laugh. Any fool can do that. This person disregarded the solemn qualities a king possesses, a regal sense of duty, an obligation to discover the facts and pass them on to others."

"I don't remember the particulars," Sarah said when Henry turned to her for support. "It was so long ago."

"You have to understand," Henry explained to the table at large. "I was not present for the performance. I was helping Charlie with the music. I played selections from Schumann's *Kinderszenen* as a backdrop to the actions going on outside. When the king first appeared, I had to play *Wichtige Begebenheit*." After seeing Jeremy's confused expression, he translated. "An Important Event. Everything is an important event if a king is present."

"More to the point I think everything is an important event if anyone is present," Sarah said. "Wouldn't you agree, Gwendolyn?"

Gwendolyn thought for a moment and said: "No. I would not."

"I was in the living room," Henry said, "and the French doors were open. I heard a lot of screaming and shouting and laughing, that's true. But most of the audience had been drinking all afternoon and my father gets like that if he has a couple of beers."

"Nothing is good in excess," Gwendolyn pronounced. "If there is one lesson to be learned in life that is to practice moderation."

Silence was not agreement, she reminded herself when she looked across the table and caught Charlotte's eye. What had she ever done to attract the attention of these children? She didn't even like children. They were far too immature and loud for her taste. And yet, they had inserted themselves into her life for no reason save aggravation.

"Moderation," she repeated. "That above all else."

Charlotte guffawed.

"You have something to add, Charlotte?"

"Nothing," she said, reaching across the table for another biscuit.

Henry leaned forward, his fingers tapping the surface of the table as if it were an imaginary keyboard. "There was this fantastic piano at your house, Gwendolyn," he said, remembering the touch and quality of sound that piano produced. The resonance alone made him feel he was ten times the player he was. "A Bösendorfer grand, isn't that right? What happened to it, was it sold?"

Gwendolyn stared off into space. "I have no idea. I assume it was destroyed in the fire."

"A fire? In the house? How awful." Jeremy sat back in shock.

"I suppose it was," Gwendolyn admitted.

"How old were you?" he asked.

"Twelve. Thirteen? One forgets."

Jeremy's face paled. "How horrible for you. I would expire, I believe. Seeing everything I love devoured by flames."

Gwendolyn patted his hand. "I never think about it. Never," she repeated as if trying to convince herself this was true. "I am amazed you still have my play, Sarah. I have literally nothing from that period of my life."

"I was the king," Charlotte told Jeremy swinging the conversation around to where it belonged. "I was chosen by Sarah, for the role," she added, pointing across the table. "Lukas was sick, there was no understudy, and I was asked to step into his shoes. You remember Lukas?" Charlotte asked Gwendolyn.

"A sad little boy," Gwendolyn acknowledged after deciding there was no way to stop Charlotte's intrusion into her past. "I did all I could for him because he was my friend. Not yours," she added. "Never yours."

"I think he liked me well enough, but Henry was his chosen mate," she said. "They were this thick," she told Jeremy, linking the fingers of both hands. "Henry really isn't cut out for travel through the decades," she explained. "When we were forced to come back to our time, he wouldn't leave his room for weeks. He couldn't cope."

"Is that true?" Jeremy asked.

Henry nodded. "True enough. It's terrible to lose people. Even people you've only known for a week."

"Love and loss move hand in hand," Sarah mused softly. "The cost of being human."

"You make it sound horrible," Jeremy said, his eyes downcast. "Like we are trapped no matter what we do."

"A trap is an illusion," Sarah said to the table at large. "They exist only in your mind. You know, I am considering a trip to Toronto. It's been on my mind for months. I would like to be present for the birth of my great-grandchildren and see how much the city has changed in my absence. Oliver is looking into renting a house for a year."

"Nonsense," Gwendolyn said. "You will stay with me."

"She's staying with us," Charlotte insisted. "And that's all there is to it. Leo will cook the best food ever, and there is more than enough room in our house for Oliver and you, Jeremy."

"Let's not fight," Sarah suggested. "I could move from place to place, travelling within travelling, and everyone will be happy. Or not," she corrected. "Because I am an old woman and require quite a bit of care and—"

Sarah braced herself on the palms of her hands and slowly stood up, her eyes bright with expectation. "Ariel has arrived," she stated.

She alone had heard the clank of the sewer lid as the Rolls arrived in the cul-de-sac, the quiet drone of the engine, more a vibration than a sound and she turned towards the sitting room and the front door.

Gwendolyn bit back a rude remark. One would think Sarah had not seen her daughter for a century or more. And what near sixty-year-old woman still lived with her mother? One, no doubt, who had been cowed and bullied into submission. Gwendolyn felt a fleeting pity for Sarah's daughter, who had clearly had not been allowed to have a life of her own.

She missed Charlotte's piercing stare, intent as she was on refreshing her lipstick and studying her reflection in the polished surface of the tea-spoon she had buffed to a shine with her napkin.

And then, not wishing to be left behind, she followed the parade and seated herself in the chair by the fireplace where she was prominently in view.

Chapter Twenty-Five

"I'm fine, of course I am. The flight was forty minutes."

Sarah murmured a few words that Gwendolyn could not make out.

"Charlotte, it's very nice to meet you. My mother speaks highly of you."

Naturally, Charlotte had pushed her way forward and was busy interrogating Ariel as Jeremy, always eager for notice, told her what they had been doing during the time she was away. There was not a sound from Henry.

Gwendolyn folded her hands in her lap, plucked an errant cat hair from her skirt, and studied the ceiling of the sitting room. The ceiling had been recently painted, all the *fleur-de-lis* picked out in pale gold. That was a nice touch, understated, elegant. Gwendolyn considered having a similar decoration put on her living room ceiling, with an elegant, intricately carved bowl in the middle to hold the chandelier. And a more flamboyant rug, Turkish or Iranian, one with a brilliant mix of bright colours. The wall-to-wall beige, real wool, she had insisted on for sound maintenance was far too traditional. She would see to these changes the minute she arrived back in Toronto and check herself into the Windsor Arms Hotel until the room had been returned to perfect order.

But she had invited Sarah to stay with her.

If the woman came.

So deep was Gwendolyn in her reflections that she failed to notice the light had dimmed and people had gathered around her chair.

Charlotte tugged on her hand.

"Say hell-o to Ariel," she insisted, insinuating that Gwendolyn was being rude.

Gwendolyn lowered her eyes and tried to control her breathing. She did not like to be crowded and felt pressed by the presence of the children.

"Please move back," Gwendolyn insisted and then corrected her statement. "Not you, Ariel. You can stay."

"How kind of you," was the curt reply.

The very same lifting of the right corner of the mouth, not a sneer exactly, but the beginning – or perhaps the end – of a smile, referencing a joke that had not been stated aloud.

Charlie's expression.

Charlie's highbrow and patrician nose and coal black hair, although on Ariel, the black strands (cut fashionably short) were woven with shades of grey. No artifice, although the understated elegance of one who was indifferent to what people thought of her.

Not a clone of Sarah at all, but someone entirely different.

Gwendolyn offered her hand but didn't stand. She felt weak, her breathing shallow. She did not want anyone in the room to notice her sudden discombobulation.

Ariel stared at Gwendolyn with an irritating half-smile as if she were sizing her up and finding the specimen somewhat lacking in substance.

"Are you enjoying your visit?" she asked. "Mother says yes, but she is not always to be trusted. Her assessments often err on the side of what she would like to be rather than what is."

"Oh, now, Ariel," Sarah protested.

"It is very comfortable here," Gwendolyn said, returning Ariel's stare. She folded her hands in her lap to contain the trembling that coursed through her body. If she hadn't remembered her brother for fifty years, she saw him now, different shape, different sex, but the same penetrating eyes that seemed to peer straight through her skin and bones and pierce her heart. "I have been treated well. And the food is excellent."

"Compliment accepted," Oliver interrupted, his arms carrying packages which he placed on the table in front of Sarah.

"Presents for us?" Charlotte asked.

Ariel grinned. "Cheeky, aren't you?"

Charlotte agreed.

"When I go to gift shows, I order what appeals to me, but the ones I am not sure of I bring back to show Mother. She has an instinct for what people might like."

"I never would have guessed," Gwendolyn said politely. "And how is it that you came by this instinct?"

"You're either born with it or you are not," Charlotte answered, taking a seat beside Sarah on the chesterfield.

Gwendolyn had taken over the special chair that Jeremy said was reserved for Sarah but curiously, Sarah did not order her to move as Charlotte would have done.

"For instance," said Charlotte, "Sarah knew, without knowing, that Eaton's second basement was the place where I would find, for next to nothing, all the clothes I could ever want or need. We even found the perfect dress for you, because, by accident I managed to tear the one you loaned me."

"Accident?" Gwendolyn lifted an elegant eyebrow. "Please continue. I remember none of this."

"Back in 1939, girls had to wear dresses to school," Charlotte told Ariel. "Can you imagine? And I didn't have one, I don't have one now. Gwendolyn gave me one of hers, and I ripped it by accident when I was on the banks of the Don River waiting for water boatmen to come my way."

"School sounds very exciting in those days. Classes held by the river, water boatmen arriving to ferry you across to the other side," Ariel said, winking at her mother.

"Learning was rigidly controlled," Henry said, asserting himself into the conversation. "The classrooms were stark and filled with wooden desks, and we learned penmanship and were asked detailed questions about the characters in *Gulliver's Travels*."

"And yet the Don River?" Ariel asked. "How does that factor in? A fieldtrip?" She watched her mother unwrap one of the objects she had brought – a brilliant red thermos, rectangular in shape and looking like an oversized flask.

"Yes," Sarah said, nodding her head. "People like to travel with water these days. Even if they are only walking around the block. And this is useful and small enough to be slipped inside a purse or a briefcase."

"No one carried water bottles in 1939," Henry continued. "The only water on hand was in fountains, and we had to line up to get a drink. The basins were stained brown, and the water tasted like rusty metal."

Jeremy hung on every word. "Is The Learning Academy rigidly controlled? I like a bit of order myself."

"There are no desks at all," Charlotte said happily, unwrapping another package which contained a furry change purse with the words 'Kiss Me Once' stitched in black yarn. Without consulting anyone she put it in the reject pile, a pile which would later make its way upstairs to her bedroom and inside her Hello Kitty backpack.

"There are pods. Learning pods. And we can wander around at will and work on our very own projects," she explained, eyeing a package shaped like a baseball and wrapped in yellow tissue paper.

"Oh," Jeremy said. His shoulders slumped.

"It's not that bad," Henry said. He attempted to narrow his eyes as he had seen others do when they didn't like what they heard. "You can have a desk if you want, and you don't have to participate in groups if groups make you uncomfortable and you can read one hundred books if you are so inclined and report on them to the people in class who don't believe reading is important." He gazed pointedly at Charlotte who held up a blue squishy ball with a bas relief of a not to scale globe.

"What is this?" she asked, ignoring Henry.

"You squeeze it if you feel anxious," Ariel described. "I like it and it might be useful. I've noticed that more and more of my friends are prescribed pills for various nervous disorders. Squeezing a ball gives all those emotions a place to go and, as a bonus, builds up strength in fingers and wrists."

Charlotte tossed the ball to Henry, who missed the catch. "For when you want to punch someone, but they are too far away."

"My interview at the Academy was a bit of a joke," Henry explained. "I had a place, guaranteed, because of my test results, but I wouldn't have minded having one of those balls with me as a distraction."

"You think it works, then?" Ariel asked Henry.

"Yes. I do. It's restful," he said, realizing he had been squeezing it nonstop. "It will sell."

"You look like my brother," Gwendolyn told Ariel. She was back in charge of herself, her breathing normal, her body calm. "Quite a bit, actually." Charlie had been a handsome young man. Even Gwendolyn had to acknowledge that.

"Greg Peck," Charlotte shouted. "Charlie looked exactly like Greg Peck."

"Who?" Ariel asked blankly.

"Gregory Peck," Sarah corrected quietly, giving the actor his full name.

Ariel nodded in recognition and a bemused expression crossed her face.

"How on earth do you know about him?" she asked.

"*The Guns of Navarone*," Charlotte answered immediately. "We watch war movies on Friday nights with Leo once we returned from the past. Leo thought we should know what happened after we left Gwendolyn's house. Greg is the kind of person who you want to know if you are in trouble. Leo says, when Greg gets mad, it is righteous anger. Just like Charlie when he saw those nasty signs on the Island. They were all over Germany …what were the words?" she asked Henry.

"*Keine Juden erlaubt.*"

The words were whispered and Henry immediately cleared the air around his head, waving frantically, afraid their toxic quality would poison the atmosphere.

Charlotte's eyes became distant as she went into a trance.

"That means, if you are Jewish, you can't go in, you can't order food or buy a loaf of bread. Your children can't go to school, and all kinds of people can't do their work, even doctors are forbidden to practice, and soon you won't be able to have money in the bank or pictures on your walls or dogs or cats or birds because all these animals will be polluted. That was back in 1939 and Henry and me knew the world would be a bad place for a very long time."

"Why, Charlotte," Sarah said softly. "I remember that. I remember you warning me."

"I had to tell you what was going to happen even if there was no way I could have known," Charlotte added, coming back to herself.

"And you and Henry tried to warn me," Sarah added. "You *can't* cross the ocean," she recited, her voice becoming child-like and intense. "The waters are not safe."

"Must we?" Gwendolyn asked, smoothing non-existent wrinkles in her skirt. "The past is a place I would rather not visit."

"The past?" Ariel asked blankly. "The Island?"

"It's a long, complicated story," Gwendolyn answered. "I'm certain Charlotte will fill you in, but I advise you to keep an open mind."

"And yet, from the pictures I've seen, my father did resemble Gregory Peck."

Sarah smiled. Peck was an apt comparison in terms of colouring but not physique. Dirk Bogarde was a closer match. She said this and watched Charlotte turn to Henry.

"Have we seen him?"

"*A Bridge Too Far*," he answered after a few seconds.

"Oh, yeah," Charlotte said, agreeing. "Skinnier, a panther, more like Charlie on the move. A bit darker, too, personality wise. I get a lot of my facts from fiction," she explained. "I have to because I wasn't alive during the war, and I need the fictional facts to make sense of my reality."

"A perfect way to describe yourself, Charlotte," Gwendolyn said. "Fiction being the operative word."

"I have all of my father's old clothes," Ariel said, turning to face the children and ignoring Gwendolyn who kept tapping her foot on the floor. "Would you and Henry be interested in seeing them later?"

"Am I to be included in this?" Gwendolyn asked. She did not know if she wanted to see Charlie's clothes but she refused to be left behind.

"Of course," Ariel said with less enthusiasm. "But only if you are truly interested."

Oliver arrived with a tray holding bowls of strawberries and blackberries and handed out small plates decorated with the Union Jack and four tiny crowns, one in each corner. "We sold these out in two days last year," Ariel told Gwendolyn, accepting a plate from Oliver and helping herself to the berries on offer.

"A fool is born every minute, or so they say." Gwendolyn suggested, trying to return the plate to Oliver who was busy dispensing fruit to the children. Instead, she examined the plate closely and placed it, empty, on her lap. She scanned the room and noticed that all eyes were on her.

"An observation?" Oliver asked. "Or a criticism? But it is just a plate, after all, with no feelings and certainly no ability to create a schism amongst friends. What say you, Ariel?"

"I say yay," she answered.

Ariel wasn't certain what to do about her aunt. If she had been an acquaintance, and not a relative, she would have lost interest in her acerbic and insulting remarks within seconds and not given her the consideration of a reply. But her mother had some nonsensical plan afoot to "domesticate" Gwendolyn, whatever that meant, and she had promised not to walk out of the room at the first sign of an insult.

Originally, Ariel had no interest in meeting Gwendolyn, and when Sarah informed her of the chance meeting with Celeste and the upcoming trip, she was relieved that she would be away for part of the visit. Family was her mother, Celeste, Oliver, and Jeremy, and that was more than enough to keep her entertained and amused.

And yet, there was a quality Gwendolyn possessed that was compelling. Anybody could be rude, but Gwendolyn did it with style. Perfectly dressed, her makeup excellently applied, wealth winking from the display of precious jewels on her fingers, she might have cut an impressive figure if not for rigidity of her posture, her nervous mannerisms, and, most interestingly, her sudden fear when she noted the close resemblance between Ariel and her father. This resemblance was not news to Ariel, she had been told this by her mother her entire life. Was there bad blood there? Charlie and Gwendolyn were half-siblings, almost a decade apart in age, and Charlie had been dead for almost six decades. There was nothing to fear here at all, and yet Ariel had caught the sudden shrinking that Gwendolyn had tried and failed to control. Added to all this was Gwendolyn's obvious dislike of Charlotte whom, by all accounts, was the reason Gwendolyn had managed to reconnect with Sarah.

Charlotte reminded Ariel of herself as a child, and the one word that leapfrogged over every other was: self-contained. The girl was alert and aware of every slur passed her way and yet was totally unaffected. Oliver had explained during the drive from the airport that Jeremy had blossomed over the past two days.

"Make no mistake, Charlotte gets under your skin, but it is awfully difficult to disagree with what she says or refuse her command. Stretch your mind, if you will," Oliver had instructed, and instead of her mind, it had been easier and more relaxing for Ariel to stretch her arms over her head and touch the top of the limousine. "You know the story the children tell of journeying to the past and meeting Gwendolyn, as a child, and your father,

Ariel. You want to know about Charlie, you would be better off speaking to Charlotte."

"How did she come by her information? I know the family had wealth and influence in Toronto and were part of a pictorial history of Rose Park that was published a decade ago. I've read it myself and there is some history of my grandfather, but little on Charlie and Gwendolyn is hardly mentioned. Can one imagine a life, imagine a person merely by looking at a few old photographs?"

Oliver had thought of all the times he had imagined himself to be other than who he was and how those displacements had helped him manage his pain, his fragmentation. He had done his job so well that often he awoke wondering who he would that day without benefit of photographs or stories but through a sheer act of will. 'Surprise me,' he often said aloud, and the universe, with a laugh, conceded. And yet, none of this fit with Charlotte's and Henry's insistence that they had experienced a complete transposition of time and returned relatively unscathed. But to what purpose?

"Are you thinking, Oliver?" Ariel had asked gently, as she watched him concentrate on the road ahead.

"I am. But to no avail because there is no answer we will ever know." He'd smiled. "I would like to speak with Charlotte's grandfather, who manages to take all this travelling in his stride."

"Perhaps you will meet face to face," Ariel had laughed. "Mother's plan to domesticate Gwendolyn will now stretch to another continent if she is serious about wanting to be close by when Celeste gives birth. I hope there is room for me in the house you plan to rent."

"Your mother is not capable of keeping a secret."

"Just so," Ariel agreed.

The question was why Sarah would be interested in Gwendolyn, after all these years? Ariel knew her mother collected strays with abandon, but Gwendolyn had the look of a sleek greyhound who had wandered into the sitting room by mistake and refused to leave until she had whipped all the mongrels into shape. Ariel, master of her own fate, would not be one, she determined – and winked at her mother to seal the contract.

"These plates would do well in Toronto," Gwendolyn said, staring at the dish in her lap and outlining the crown with the tip of her finger. "My fellow countrymen are quite enamoured of the Royals. Their movements are scrutinized, their behaviour dissected, their affairs broadcast as if these rather pedestrian events were more important than scientific discoveries. In that regard, there might be a modest living to be made, stocking anything that carries their picture or titillates with a few pictures of crowns."

"Titillates?" Charlotte asked. "Nobody is naked on this plate."

"If you think you are being funny, Charlotte, that is not the case. If you don't know what the word means, ask."

"I know exactly what it means. Duh! Naked. Like I said. But I'm tired of hearing you run everything down."

"Perhaps you misunderstand me, Charlotte. Royalty, particularly British royalty, tends to give the average citizen hope," Gwendolyn said. "Charlie took me to see King George and Queen Elizabeth at Hart House Circle in the summer of 1939. I remember it like it was yesterday."

"I was there, too," Sarah remarked.

"You were?" Gwendolyn crinkled her brow. "I didn't notice because of the crush of people. Thousands of people filling the circle, lining the streets and sidewalks. Charlie held my hand and even put me up on his shoulders so I could see my subjects, he said."

Charlotte decided not to correct Gwendolyn's misreading of the past. It was, admittedly, sixty years ago and quite possible she had forgotten the details of what really happened. It was Charlotte who had ridden on Charlie's shoulders, until she'd noticed Henry was trying to escape.

"I remember the Circle very well," Sarah said, studying Charlotte and wondering at her change of expression. "Your father, Gwendolyn, lunched in the Great Hall. He was one of three hundred or so honoured guests."

"A man of means," Ariel murmured. "Like you, Oliver."

"I would more likely have been working in the kitchen. A lad carrying trays."

"I have more stories of Charlie that I would be happy to share," Gwendolyn said. "Do we have plans for the day?"

"I have been assigned the task of recruiting both Meggie and Byron to assist with the production of *The Three Questions*. Time is of the essence, and everyone will be asked to help. Am I right, Sarah?"

"Absolutely. You may need to call upon your street people as well."

"Street people?" Gwendolyn asked with a gasp.

"Who are Byron and Meggie?" Ariel asked. "I have not heard them mentioned before."

"Friends of Henry's who just so happen to be skilled artists," Sarah answered, smiling at Henry. "I predict this will be a wonderful experience for us all. Have you decided whether you wish to direct the play Gwendolyn, or do you wish me to do so?"

The question elicited a reaction which was both uncharacteristic and abrupt. Gwendolyn answered immediately so she could not change her mind.

"It will be me, of course. And I will need approval over these 'street people.'"

"They have been vetted," Oliver said, a hint of steel in his voice. "And they are my friends."

"Friends?" Gwendolyn asked. "I find that…"

"They are my friends, too," Jeremy piped up. And Henry and Charlotte, who had not yet met any of these folk, added their voices to the alliance.

Gwendolyn knew she was outnumbered, and acquiesced with a slight tilting of her chin. Oliver could hob-nob with as many derelicts as he wanted but she did not have to follow suit. As for Henry and Charlotte, she knew they were lying but decided not to call them out. "Very well," she said. She smiled insincerely and glanced at Ariel. "I will need new clothes. I wonder if you would take me shopping, dear. The children are taken care of and Sarah has my script to prepare and copy. I assume we will have a meeting this afternoon?"

"You agree?" Sarah was not surprised by Gwendolyn's decision, merely by her desire for more clothes.

"With one or two reservations, I do. And I need suitable attire. Ariel?"

"I don't frequent the kind of stores you do, Gwendolyn." Ariel indicated with her hand Gwendolyn's designer suit and jewels.

"All to the better. I'd like to visit the out-of-the-way places. I am looking for clothes that make a statement. Shall we say noon?"

From the Hilroy of Charlotte
Lisa Hansen

DAY: THURSDAY, SEPTEMBER 2
TIME: 11:47 AM London time although watch going crazy and saying 5:47
EVEN though Henry says he fixed it. (Liar)
PLACE: Bedroom floor as usual

Hilroy, am I going to have a starring role in "The Three Questions?"

Sarah said her lips were sealed.

And Gwendolyn!

When I told her a mere hour ago that I considered it vital to stay on in London for at least two more weeks, because of the rush to produce a play and more importantly because the universal insisted, and I would feel awful deserting my mission, she outright laughed in my face.

She said something like this: "I am the universal Charlotte. And what I say, goes."

Right!

I did manage to make her angry by getting a private viewing of Charlie's clothes, and the long-term loan of his brown Fedora hat, which almost fits me perfectly.

"That hat looks ridiculous on your head."

Gwendolyn. Who else?

Because I knew I looked fantastic, I said nothing. I told her that Ariel and me talked for at least an hour and she totally believes that I spent time with her father. In fact she listened to me the way few people do. She asked me so many questions and almost, Hilroy, I am not kidding, she looked like she was under some enchantment spell, and I was the enchantment. Very, extremely, cool.

"She is humouring you, child."

The arrogance!

Then she told me that Ariel was taking her clothes shopping because even though she brought fifty outfits with her none were right for her new position as director of stage and queen of the universe. There was a smugness to this remark that irritated me greatly.

I told her I couldn't wait to see what a stage director wore, and she frowned. Or at least tried to frown. Her face appears to be frozen in some unlined concrete slab that is kind of frightening to look at for too long.

Maybe Gwendolyn is right about one thing.

She has no problem being Queen Bee and doesn't seem to need my help with anything.

It's time to take charge of me. It's time to get rid of these headaches and dizzy spells and realize I am not a saviour but simply me, Charlotte.

UNIQUE and IRREPLACEABLE!!!!

I took inventory of my supplies in my Hello Kitty backpack and cross checked them with the list I had written last night when I couldn't sleep – with explanations for my future biographer. When this person drifts into my universe, I wish them to have all necessary facts on hand so my life can be documented exactly as I lived it.

- Red thermos stored in the freezer. (There are no ice cubes to be had in London and I hate lukewarm water.)
- One peanut butter and red currant jelly (not marmalade) sandwich, one meatloaf sandwich (without hot mustard), two peeled carrots, a banana, five McVitie's and a bag of gummy bears.
- My CN tower sunglasses, which are necessary for show as I recently discovered that shop owners were struck speechless by the sudden vision of me wearing aforementioned.

Wait until I add the Fedora.

Watch out!

- Two sharpened pencils

- The stress ball that Ariel decided I could have when I refused to give it back
- A bottle of black ink should a disguise be necessary
- A map of the London Underground
- St. John's Ambulance First Aid Box with additionals

And, my Hilroy, because now (thank you) very much, I have a rash on my stomach

Chapter Twenty-Six

Given Sarah's suggestion that the theatre class select Gwendolyn's 'masterful' adaptation of Tolstoy's short story "The Three Questions" and Gwendolyn's quick acceptance of resurrecting her sixty-year-old enterprise project, the green light was given to all and sundry that a production must be cast, rehearsed, designed, and presented in a record breaking four-day time frame. Because *The Three Questions* was approximately forty minutes in length, it wasn't an impossible project. Soon after Gwendolyn departed with Ariel, Sarah and Oliver made a flurry of telephone calls to the parents of the students in the class. They called Arthur the pugilist and contacted Byron and Meggie letting them know to stand by for set construction and costume design. Finally, Sarah reached out to a few of her most loyal patrons, inviting them to attend with the promise of champagne and pastries all free of charge.

Henry, Charlotte, and Jeremy were dispatched to Byron and Meggie's where a hurried consultation resulted in an impossible list of essential items Byron needed to create backdrops. The list was whittled down, laboriously by Oliver who stated quite clearly that there was not enough time to create a set to rival the one Chagall had created for *Aleko*, Pushkin's great dramatic poem.

"I see a total fusion of music, dance, and art against a backdrop of great spiritual illness." Byron paced the room, throwing up his hands with each pronouncement. "This will not be some meagre attempt to throw paint on plywood boards but a daring work utilizing sculpture, collage, fingerpaints, aerosols, graffiti—"

"You have three days." Oliver interjected mildly.

"Three days? Ridiculous. I need a year, perhaps two."

264

"And a plethora of assistants eager to help in every way possible."

"These assistants? Are they skilled tradesmen?"

"Of a sort," Oliver said, twiddling his thumbs.

Byron stopped pacing and stood in front of Oliver, his gaze directed upwards.

"I envision angels floating towards heaven in a sea of blue or perhaps more in the line of the great man's design for *Firebird*. Deep purple and reds, these colours will predominate, with birds and prehistoric monsters rising from the depths." Byron began to pace, throwing out one nonsensical idea after the other. He held his tie, looped around his fingers, and kissed it repeatedly.

"I suggest it may be a good idea to read the script first," Oliver suggested. "We are not dealing with angels or birds or prehistoric monsters here, and I think that Tolstoy might rise up and disagree strenuously with such a suggestion."

Byron turned a scornful eye in Oliver's direction. "I have no time to read scripts. I must think. And Tolstoy does not factor into my considerations since he is long departed."

"I'll read the script," Meggie told Oliver. "He will come around once he knows what the story is. This is just his way of marshalling his creative energy." She dumped a large art book on the ottoman and Byron pounced on it, almost ripping the pages to get to what he wanted.

Oliver sat back unperturbed, and while Charlotte and Jeremy were swept up by Byron's manic enthusiasm, Meggie discreetly caught Henry's attention and motioned him to follow her to the kitchen. At the ottoman, Byron chirped and cooed every few pages and threw out suggestions which grew progressively more fanciful (and less possible). Oliver just let him be. Caught up in the flickering heat of possibilities, Byron was almost incandescent.

"I like the method," Charlotte volunteered. "It's always good to roar through a lot of totally senseless proclamations before arriving at the only conclusion possible given the situation at hand."

"A complete waste of time," Henry muttered.

"What's that?" Jeremy asked sotto voce.

"I'll tell you later."

Henry had just returned from a very confusing conversation with Meggie where he was told that the reason Henry's mother didn't like her was because Henry's father *did*. After all his fantasies about gangsters and thievery and possibly even abductions, the answer he had sought was unintelligible and boring. Although, he admitted later, forgery did play a small role.

"I was just a girl when I met Byron," Meggie had said nostalgically, forcing Henry to eat another day-old scone which was rock hard and caught in his throat. "He tried to sell my father a Gainsborough, a miniature of his famous *Wooded Landscape with Peasant Resting*. A fake, of course. My father ran a very famous gallery in Soho, and he was no fool. That said, the brush strokes were magnificent," she reflected, gazing out the window. "They were perfectly rendered and the colours magnificent. You could feel the breeze, smell the scent of leaves beginning to decay." She shrugged her shoulders. "We both knew it was a forgery, but such a magnificent counterfeit that my father bought it as a curiosity, and not," she assured Henry, "for the fantastical sum Byron wished."

Henry gagged trying to swallow the scone and Meggie thumped him on the back.

"With *your* father, of course, it was not a Gainsborough but a Richard Dadd, if I recall. And so, yes, Byron *might* have sold your father a *facsimile* Dadd," she said preferring that word over forgery. "Your father knew, but your mother did not. Byron did like Dadd back in the day, all those fairies and such. And Byron's brushstrokes... ah well, this is just between the two of us, dear. It is not meant to go further."

"A fairy with long red curly hair?" Henry asked, slowly coming to after his choking incident. "Dressed in a multicoloured robe and leaning forward with a painted box in her hand?"

"I believe that is the one," Meggie said, reflectively. "Byron painted so many in the old days before he found his true voice."

"It's in our living room," Henry said. "Above the fireplace. My mother thinks it is worth a fortune."

"As it is," Meggie agreed. "Unless she tries to sell it. She was against the purchase initially, but Aaron talked her into it. She thinks I seduced him into doing so, which is not my way at all."

"Seduced?" Henry asked, his eyes widening. The word had sinister overtones.

"By our friendship, dear. The two of us cut up quite a bit, mostly on the dance floor. Your mother does not like to dance."

"But she wanted to be a ballerina," Henry stuttered, confused.

"There's dancing for fun and there is dancing for work, and never the twain shall meet. It meant nothing that your Aaron and I took walks together and talked. That is what friends do, Henry, although I am woman of the world enough to know that I might have overstepped the invisible boundaries. I tried to explain this to your mother, but she remained firm that I was a bad influence. That is all there is to it," she said, tweaking Henry on the nose. She insisted he finish the scone and drink a cup of milky tea before he was dismissed and allowed to re-enter the studio.

"Most people are idiots," Charlotte said. "They just do what everyone else does and have no artistic vision." Artistic vision was an expression Byron had used at least ten times, and Charlotte decided it was worth adding to her repertoire.

"I agree," Jeremy said. "In principle."

He loved watching Byron skip and dance around the studio like he was a circus clown, and if this gave the man artistic inspiration, that was okay with him. And Charlotte's behaviour was also a treat. He was fixated on the change in her manner of speaking. He heard her call Henry an 'idiot' about five times since they arrived in London, but this morning she pronounced it 'idiawt' the way his schoolmates did when they made a similar pronouncement about him. Was she fast becoming British?

"I will need at least a dozen assistants, Oliver. Take note. Perhaps two dozen."

Oliver pondered. "It is possible I could round up that number, but you must treat each and every one with respect."

"I am not an animal. I know how to muster a crowd." Byron shut his eyes and quickly opened them when a new thought occurred to him. "As for my salary I believe..."

"If you sign on, you will work for free," Oliver said, accepting a cup of tea from Meggie with a cursory nod of his head.

"For free? Out of the question."

267

"There will be daily meals and beer and pastries on the evening of production."

"Well…" Byron dithered, running his finger along his upper lip. "What kind of meals?"

"A fry up in the morning, bubble and squeak for lunch, bangers and mash for dinner, the usual fare offered to technicians on site. Unlimited pots of tea and McVitie's."

"A private office where I will be undisturbed during my moments of reflection? A comfortable bed so I do not have to make the tedious journey home. A straight edge and several wardrobe changes, perhaps a man to see to my needs?"

"You will have the old chesterfield in the common room to yourself and the school desk in the corner for your own personal use. As for a man, you will be stuck with me."

Byron perked up. "The limousine will be at my disposal."

"You will share it with Gwendolyn, Sarah, and the children."

"Supplies?"

"Already being ordered. Sarah has been on the phone all morning."

"And that woman? The unpleasant one who keeps turning her nose up at Meggie and myself?"

"Gwendolyn," Oliver answered at once. "What about her?"

"I assume she has a role in this production."

"She wrote the script and will direct."

"Blast. The woman does not approve of me. We might come to blows."

Charlotte smiled and nodded her head.

"She is in charge nominally," Oliver said. "Sarah will oversee, of course, as she always does."

"I do not know Sarah," Byron said. "She is time-tested, like a great work of art, that much is clear. And polite. But is she a steady sort, quiet yet decisive? Accommodating to great genius? Tolerant… but resolute in doing what is right?"

Oh, I have no worries that those qualities you insist upon and many others are well within Sarah's repertoire," Oliver said airily.

Chapter Twenty-Seven

Gwendolyn's entrance into the makeshift boardroom at the Motley Theatre came just as Sarah was handing out parts for *The Three Questions,* ensuring that everyone had a speaking role, and insisting that no role was more important than another.

"I want you all to be at your best because I am listening carefully and will not make my final decision until the script is read in its entirety."

Gwendolyn paused at the door for recognition. "I will be making the final decisions, Sarah. I am the director."

A hush, rather like the silence created by a first snowfall, blanketed the room. No one said a word because they were too busy examining the woman who stood before them. The students had met Gwendolyn the night before and although their privately spoken words to define her were different, they all had the same uniform meaning.

"Tosser...

"Rude...

"Old bag...

"Cretin."

Todd Reynolds came up with the word that stuck: "mummy." Because, as he explained, sharing his bag of licorice with the others, "she looks like she's been wrapped up in a black cloth and buried in the earth for about ten thousand years."

The change from mummy to *harridan* was apparent to all whose eyes skittered away from Sarah to Gwendolyn, remained steady as she made her pronouncement and then quickly skittered back to Sarah. The children were too polite, and too scared of Sarah, to show what they felt.

Gwendolyn's transformation from black and white to colour was startling and not altogether unattractive. She wore a red velvet director's jacket with a white silk blouse and purple trousers, the first pants she had worn in over three decades. She was stunned at how comfortable they were and bought a pair in forest green, navy blue and a russet gold that reminded her of oak leaves in the fall. All the colours went beautifully with the red velvet director's jacket, but she bought the jacket in black as well, mostly because black was black, and she couldn't get away from it entirely. She wore a pale lavender toque, hand knit in soft wool, which emphasized the colour of her eyes and softened the lines of her cheekbones.

The most astonishing change to her wardrobe was a pair of running shoes, Nike Waffle Racing Flat Moon running shoes, circa 1972 which she found in a charity shop Ariel insisted on visiting. So enamoured was she of these shoes that she set Ariel the task of finding as many pairs of used Nikes as she could and damn the cost. *'These are three pounds six,'* Ariel had told her. *'The pants you just bought cost thirty times that.'* To which Gwendolyn had replied *'I thought that was the size. I am a 36 European, 7 Canadian. I can feel my toes in these shoes. Remarkable.'*

Isabel Thompkins, who couldn't help being rude and was a young Gwendolyn in training asked aloud: "How come you are walking on your toes?"

Several decades of wearing high heels had shortened Gwendolyn's Achilles tendons, and it felt quite natural to be balanced on the balls of her feet. The stiffness she felt as she elevatored downwards was sharp and painful. She ignored the question and turned her attention to Sarah.

"I would like consultation rights on the final cast decisions, Sarah. I wrote this drama, and I hope you will agree that I know it best."

"Tolstoy wrote it, you adapted it," Sarah said.

The correction was not well received. Gwendolyn removed a large notebook from the new leather satchel she now carried and made a note. "After the first run through, which I assume is now, we will talk, Sarah. I wrote this down just in case."

"In case you *forget*?" Sam Teadsdale asked.

Sam Teadsdale, also known as Samantha, Tattie, and Mess – the school name she was christened for always being able to wind a fairly simple situation into a complicated knot – leaned her arms across the table and stared at Gwendolyn.

"How can you forget? We're here to remind you, and if all of us forget, which is unlikely, we can always start this scene from the start, where you walk in the door and tell Sarah you are in charge. If that doesn't work—"

"That's enough, Sam." Sarah said sharply.

Instead of the remarks annoying Gwendolyn, she lifted her eyebrows and made another note on her pad.

"Your name?" she asked, pointing at Sam.

Sam told her and added all her nicknames as well so that Gwendolyn would not be confused. "She would make a decent counsellor. The one who says that warriors are the most essential people."

"I agree," said Sarah, and Sam held up her script, her lines already marked with a yellow highlighter. "I haven't read the entire script yet, but who is more important in the universe than a warrior?"

"Read it and you'll see," Henry told her.

Charlotte added nothing to the discussion but wrote continuously in her Hilroy.

"I have a part in mind for you, Charlotte, but you may also act as my assistant. I feel I can count on you for not letting things get out of hand."

"Check," Charlotte said, without looking up. She liked Sam Teadsdale, but so did Henry, made obvious by his rude remark.

"Your input is essential, Gwendolyn," Sarah said. "And now that you are here," she added, glancing pointedly at her watch, "I think we can begin."

There were ten characters in *The Three Questions*, and because there were twelve at the table, the understudy role for the king and for the hermit were counted as essential roles. Usually, the read-throughs were casual affairs, the students reading various roles whenever Sarah pointed at them but this time, she had ideas about who should play each part, and she asked that each stick with what they were assigned.

"We will read the script twice, understudies reading second time around. There will be a half hour break for lunch. Mark your calendars, performers. Today is Thursday and we have three days to pull this production together. For those unable to attend Friday night and all through the weekend, you will find your role forfeit to one of the understudies. We must be ready to perform on Sunday. Any questions? Is there anyone who is not in agreement with this timetable?" Sarah spoke with the assurance and authority of more than half a century, and not one pair of eyes left her face.

"I know that you haven't had time to read the script as you have just received it, so I would like Charlotte to give us a breakdown of the actions that will take place to simplify your understanding."

"Righty-o," Charlotte said, snapping shut her Hilroy. She stood up and went to the end of the table facing Sarah and began speaking quite clearly and simply.

"There is a king who is quite confused because he needs to know the answer to three simple questions before he can govern properly. It is important for him to govern properly because he believes that his subjects are important, and he does not cast himself as a know-it-all who exists merely to please himself."

"He is modest and wants to be kind," Henry added.

"Thank you, Henry. Continue, Charlotte," Gwendolyn said, assuming with force her role as director.

"This is what he wants to know so that he will never fail in any job that he undertakes. First off, he needs to know when it is the right time to start work, whether that be the second he wakes up in the morning, after breakfast, after a walk or maybe after he sits around for a while thinking about nothing."

"We can do without the add-ons, Charlotte. If you do this again, you will be replaced."

"Cheers," Charlotte said brightly. "Not one unnecessary word will be spoken henceforth."

"I'll believe that when I see it," Henry whispered to Jeremy.

"Question One: When is the most important time to start a job. Question two: who can help the most."

"You mean advisors and such?" Jeremy asked.

"If you wish," Charlotte answered grandly. "And the third question, what is the most essential thing to do. To recap: "Time, people, job to do. These are the three questions."

"Sarah?" Gwendolyn asked. "I believe that to block this out on stage, we can have the king pace his throne room and ask these questions aloud so the audience will know what is in store. Who is designing the sets?"

"Byron."

"Byron?" Gwendolyn's voice went up an octave. "That fat, garish man who calls himself an artist?"

"The time is now, Gwendolyn, we don't have a second to waste. Byron is available, and he has a wealth of experience, and we need to have the backdrops ready by Saturday."

"Is that why I hear hammering below? It is quite distracting."

"You'll get used to it. You may continue, please, Charlotte."

Charlotte cleared her throat and thumped her chest after getting a thumbs up signal from Mess. "Word is sent out across the kingdom that the person who can answer these questions correctly will receive a massive reward. Out of the woodwork come all these counsellors and they all believe they know the answers. The first counsellor says that the king must keep a daily calendar and in the daily calendar he must write down everything he has to do that day and check it off. Days, weeks, months, years, it all must be scribed…"

"*In*scribed," Jeremy said.

"Noted," Mess argued. "Noted is better."

"Whatever. The point is that once the calendar is filled to overflowing with all jobs and events and wars and what not, the king will have to comply with what is written and will be powerless to change even one small thing."

"My mother does that," Phyllis Landsdowne said. "It drives my father crazy."

"I'm told to keep a list," another young actor added. "And I am forced to write it all out for the week, but I rarely see it through. Writing down what I am supposed to do makes me feel like I have already done it without the bother of doing anything."

"Sarah, is this feedback necessary?" Gwendolyn adjusted her beret and frowned.

"It's your call, but I find it helpful to let the actors breathe their way into their roles."

"There's a lot more breathing than necessary in my opinion. Carry on, Charlotte." Gwendolyn licked the tip of her pencil and steadied her hand above her notebook. The licking of her pencil was so out of character that her eyes widened at exactly the moment Charlotte's did.

"The next counsellor argued the first point, naturally, and said that no one could be prepared for every possible situation, so it was best to not spend even a second in idleness but always be alert for what was happening around you. Ergo, what you see you must participate in. Toss the list and rely on your eyes."

"Well, that will never work," Jeremy said dismissively, lounging in his chair. "We have to sleep, which might be considered an idle occupation, and what about necessary visits to the WC? Hard to keep an eye on what is going on around you when you are closeted in a small room with only a toilet as company."

"Sarah?" Gwendolyn asked, lifting an eyebrow.

"Thank you, Jeremy. I think we will agree that no further interruptions will be allowed until we reach the end of the story. Any questions or statements will then be considered before we commence with the reading."

Charlotte took a deep breath, refreshed her memory by glancing at the script. It had only been four months since she and Henry had stood in Gwendolyn MacFarlane's back garden, utterly and completely lost in time. The original script, an enterprise project that Gwendolyn took on because she was far too smart to merely do what every other fifth grader had to do, was treated like it was written on golden pages spun by Rapunzel and the amount of screaming that ensued when Charlotte touched the original still gave her a headache. However, the benefit of this strange transposition in time meant that she and Henry had little time separating them from the original production, whereas Sarah and Gwendolyn had sixty years. Charlotte's experience was fresher, more vivid, and she knew that was why Sarah chose her as the spokesperson. Henry's eidetic memory could top her own flawed recall, but he was too wooden to present the material with the visceral anguish it required.

"Counsellor Three argues that one man alone cannot decide what needs to be done at any given point in time and must have a council to direct his actions. The next suggestion, personally my favourite because it makes the most sense is this: a council would be as inadequate as a solo practitioner because, facing facts, who are these people but mere mortal men?"

"And women," an older teenager announced perfunctorily. "Speaking for myself I think this outdated notion that only men decide what is important to do is repulsive. If you consider all the work that is done by women, menial work, I might add, and with no recognition, whatsoever…"

"Thank you, Shirley. This is exactly why some of the counsellors and the hermit will be women."

"Wait for it," Charlotte said, holding up her hand. "You will like this one. Counsellor Four suggests that before any action is taken one must consult with a magician. A magician is the only person alive who knows beforehand what is going to happen, so the suggestion is logical in a skewered type of way. The only problem here is the king must find a reputable magician, one who isn't a sham."

"David Copperfield? He's not a sham. He's the real thing. Do you think he would do it? Could we get him, Sarah, to agree to star in the production as a publicity stunt?"

"Highly unlikely. Can we hurry this along now, Charlotte, please?" Sarah consulted her watch. "Best not fall behind or dinner will end up being late."

A low moan erupted across the table, and it was agreed there would be no further outbursts.

As for the second question, who are the right people to listen to, the list included doctors, priests, warriors, and others of high standing in the community. And as for the third question, the most important occupation, the answer fell into predictable lines, mostly reaffirming those who should always be listened to and revered: doctors, scientists, priests, and warriors.

"No artists, I notice," Gwendolyn said. "Or musicians or scholars." She picked up the script and studied it as if seeing it for the first time. "A curious omission."

In a spurt of uncharacteristic behaviour Charlotte gave over her role as speaker to Henry, saying she had to rest her voice. In truth, her headache had returned, and she felt top heavy. She sat down and gave a weak smile to her friend who reluctantly took up the charge.

Henry analysis of the king's disappointment and voyage into discovery was succinct and modest. He wasted not a word taking the king from his council room into the forest where he went to find a hermit who he had been told was wise beyond all others.

"Byron understands we will need a set change for this part of the play? He will need to create a forest primeval. I see long branches, twisted tree trunks, crows and ravens, perhaps a fox or two."

"He has his instructions. Whether he will follow them is another matter."

"Grandfather will see to it," Jeremy volunteered. "Grandfather has Bryon wrapped around his finger."

"Plus, he has us," Charlotte added. "I can sleep here if necessary and will work my fingers to the bones."

"Always the martyr," Gwendolyn murmured and received a kick in her shin from Sarah.

Sarah had cast Charlotte as the hermit, the man the king was about to meet, and she pondered her choice as Henry described the king, who was forced to leave his crown and royal robes behind because the hermit would see none but the common man. Charlotte was a peculiar choice for the role and one of the older boys would be more suitable. The hermit was old and weak, and Charlotte was neither, but there was a fragility underneath all that hard-won bravado and a somewhat twisted but perceptive ability to cut through all the dross and get to the essential. Gwendolyn would fight her on this choice, but she remained determined to keep Charlotte in play. She caught Charlotte's eye and winked as Henry described the king leaving his bodyguards behind and venturing into the forest on his own.

Equally, Sarah's choice of Henry as the king was open to question. Henry projected neither strength nor determination, but there was a quality of persistence and a desire to truly interact with everyone he met. Sarah had heard all about Doreen, and made a note to invite her to the performance. And if it wasn't for Henry, defying everyone and setting out on his own through the twisting laneways of London, Byron and Meggie would not now be arguing one floor below them. It took courage and stamina to go against orders, and Henry had shown himself both willing and able. Sarah added a mental check to Henry's name and as she listened to him talk, she knew she had made the right choice. His deadpan expression and slightly hunched shoulders clearly illustrated a king at odds with both himself and his kingdom.

"He finds the hermit digging in front of his hut with a spade. The man is weak and frail and breathing heavily, but that does not stop him from his

276

work, nor does it stop the king from approaching him. Without wasting a second, the king asks the hermit the three questions.

"Certainly, the hermit listens, because his eyes never leave the king's face," Henry continued, his own eyes, magnified by his thick lenses, stared straight ahead at nothing. "But the hermit doesn't answer. He simply spits on his hand and continues to work the ground with his spade."

"We will need a hut as well," Gwendolyn interjected, making another note on her pad. "Part of the forest can be two-sided, and as the king nears his destination the panel can be turned. It's possible to have the hermit turn the panel himself as if both appearing out of nowhere. I assume you have decent stage lights?"

"Not decent. Brilliant," Jeremy told her. "Grandfather and Arthur set up an entirely new system just a year ago, and we also have a turntable built into the floor at centre backstage so the forest panel can be placed on this, and it will turn effortlessly as if appearing all by itself in the depths of the forest."

"I thought Arthur was a swordsman and a boxer? How did it happen that he knows about lighting?"

"Arthur is a trained electrician," Jeremy answered at once. "Once he became too old to box professionally, he learned a trade. He never really liked the lights in the boxing arenas. He said they blinded him. He knew he could do better."

"Perhaps you would like to direct this play, Jeremy?" Gwendolyn asked sweetly. "You are far more knowledgeable about mechanics than I am."

Jeremy sat back quickly, stung by the retort. "Not at all. I didn't write the play. I have no knowledge of the interior workings of the characters, nor do I have a particular vision. I just had information I thought you would like to have."

Murmurs of dissent against Gwendolyn began to grow in volume, and she thought it politic to apologize. "I meant no offence, Jeremy, and if you thought I did, I am sorry. In my defence I can only say I am unused to the enthusiasm I see in the faces before me."

These remarks did little to change the frowns to beaming smiles, but the whispering stopped, and Henry continued.

"The king saw that the hermit was tired and offered to dig the flower beds. He took the spade and worked while the hermit sat on a log and watched him."

"The holes in the earth might present a problem," Gwendolyn said.

"This is *theatre,* Gwendolyn. We ask people to stretch their minds. Illusion is manufactured by gesture, by nuance, all concepts you fully understand, I'm sure."

Gwendolyn nodded. She would get that disreputable old man to manufacture a realistic set, the *theatre* be damned. Gwendolyn did not believe people were able to pretend to see something they did not.

Henry stared blankly at a swirl of dust motes that had gathered directly east of his right eye and began, mechanically, to count how long it took them to disperse. He knew that Sarah had cast him as king because she'd had a private discussion with him before the group met in her office. Before this conversation, he considered himself to be one of these random dust motes floating effortlessly through the universe, touching down, now and again, on new people, new cities, new bedding and new staircases, resting briefly before a flurry of activity around him demanded he once again join the jet stream and continue to flow who knew where.

Being a king in *The Three Questions* did not jibe with Henry's idea of being a free-floating dust mote.

Part of Henry didn't believe that he deserved the starring role in this production. He was an indifferent actor, believing that theatrics were in essence 'much ado about nothing', a Shakespearean play he had photographed with the click of his eidetic memory while standing in the MacFarlane study a lifetime ago. He'd failed to get a good grasp on either the plot or the characters, and he'd found the language tedious.

He had tried, earlier, to explain his position to Sarah.

"I am one of those people who go through life as an observer."

"Nonsense, Henry. You are too young to have these fixed notions."

"I have absolutely zero presence. Most people don't even know I am in the room when I am standing right in front of them." His eyes had crossed as he sorted through pages in his eidetic memory. "*Let me be that I am and seek not to alter me,*" he had finally replied, pleased that such a succinct statement be found in the aforementioned play – one that fit his current situation like a second skin.

Sarah's eyes had widened and she'd studied him intently. "*'Why, what's the matter? That you have such a February face? So full of frost, of storm and cloudiness.'*"

She'd led him into her office and sat him down on the chesterfield. "That you can effortlessly quote from *Much Ado About Nothing*, Henry, proves that you have more theatrical blood flowing through your veins than you believe."

Henry had examined his arm; he saw the same network of pasty skin and pale blue veins and arteries he always saw when he periodically inspected his body for signs of hives or other allergic disruptions.

"What am I to do?" he'd asked Sarah.

"You are to take the role, Henry, and run with it."

"I don't think the king runs, does he? He mostly paces and digs holes in the hermit's garden and ministers to the wounded man."

"It's a figure of speech, Henry."

"Oh." Henry's file on figures of speech was largely empty, save one that his father used constantly: *'Mark my words, Henry, this is the beginning of the end.'*

Henry had wondered if that was really two figures of speech since it was near impossible, unless one was writing down every word that every person said (and not everyone was Charlotte!) to mark anyone's words because words disappeared as soon as they were spoken. Words had no substance at all. This analysis, quick and concise, had lifted Henry's spirits. If he made a complete ass of himself on stage, no one would blame him because words were ephemeral, rather like the dust motes he was studying.

"Henry," Gwendolyn demanded, banging the table with the flat of her hand. "Can you get a move on, please? We are fast becoming tired and hungry."

Henry apologized which was not graciously received. Clearly it was time to utilize his theatrical blood and stop being such a namby-pamby apologist.

"Take everything you are feeling right now, boredom, hunger, exasperation, irritation and throw that right back on the king because that is exactly what he feels times ten," he stated forcefully. He took a deep breath and saw a few pairs of eyes regard him with curiosity. "He's come all this way, dug flower beds for the hermit, asked his three questions twice and received no answer." Henry pronouncement had bearing and dignity that caused many eyebrows to lift high, including Charlotte's – which caused him a pang of pleasure. "This is beyond pointless, the king decides. No one knows the answers. His whole adventure has been nothing more than a fool's journey. Right at the very second, he's ready to pack it in, the hermit says: 'A man is approaching. We must see who it is.'"

Henry held up his hands, in a stop sign gesture, one that had been used on him repeatedly by most of his classmates at Rose Park Public School. He used this gesture to give himself time to page through Gwendolyn's old script which was stored in a file called: Miscellaneous Rubbish. The script appeared as if by magic, tattered and torn and stained with the imprint of Charlotte's chocolate covered fingerprints.

"The man is wounded, his hands clutching his bleeding stomach, and the stranger falls at the king's feet." Henry paused once again for dramatic purpose and was pleased to note his audience was attentive. "The king, a seasoned warrior, acting on impulse alone, tries with vigour to stem the bleeding. He uses his own garment, tears the sleeve of his robe to shreds and baths the wound again and again. He rips his other sleeve from the shoulder," Henry said, demonstrating by ripping the sleeve from his own shirt (much easier than he thought it would be) and using it to make a bandage on Jeremy's stomach, who was instructed by a few succinct hand gestures to lie on the table and pretend he was dying.

The audience was hushed and respectful, all leaning forward on their forearms to watch Henry manhandle Jeremy into submission.

"With the hermit's help, the wounded man is carried into the shack and immediately falls asleep. The king is exhausted by his efforts and makes a bed across the threshold. In the morning, the wounded man is staring at him."

Henry allowed his eyes to move slowly around the table, closely examining everyone who sat very still, staring at him. The magnification created by his thick lenses gave the impression of an owl who had come across a tasty vole and was about to pounce.

"'Forgive me,' the wounded man begs the king. And the king, still groggy from sleep, moves to his side. 'I don't know you,' the king says kindly. 'You have done me no harm and do not have to ask for my forgiveness.'

"'But I know **you**. You killed my brother and I vowed to avenge his death. I saw you leave the castle and I followed.'"

"Wait a minute here," Sam Teasdale interrupted. "How can this wounded man even talk if he is so badly injured? Wouldn't he be in a coma? Or at the very least, gasping for breath, or wincing in pain? I'm sorry. It just doesn't track."

"The night air has restored me and although I am in pain, yes, terrible and swift, yet I am desperate to tell the king my story," Jeremy replied, improvising on the spot.

Jeremy was flat out across the table, his hands pressing an imaginary wound in his abdomen, his adoring eyes never leaving Henry's face. Sarah felt privileged to be able to witness such an intimate exchange of trust and friendship. Once again, her instincts had proven correct. Jeremy, as the wounded man, was perfectly cast. Was he not a wounded child that needed to be saved?

"Well, then, get on with it," Sam stated. "Your stomach might be sliced open but mine is empty and is demanding food."

Sarah sat back and listened as Henry picked up the narrative.

"The wounded man explains himself in an impassioned flow of words, explaining how he set out that morning to kill me because I had executed his brother and taken his land," Henry explained, gesturing with his hands. "He followed me into the forest, knowing that it must be my intention to visit the hermit – so he hid and vowed that he would murder me on his way home. But I never emerged from the forest primeval, and the wounded man had no patience to wait any longer."

"He was filled with righteous anger, so no kidding," one of the students interjected. "I'm surprised he waited for more than a minute. You killed his brother."

"He managed to put in a good couple of hours," Henry said, agreeing with the remark. "Because this is a parable and time doesn't really exist except as a marker. But it is possible," he said, swatting at a fly, "That people were more patient in the olden days. Perhaps it was because they didn't have our current distractions. The mission was everything. To continue," he said, seeing Sarah's hand begin to rise. "For whatever reason, he finally decided it was time to move. Unfortunately, the king's bodyguard recognized the wounded man when he crept out from beneath the bushes, the wounded man who wasn't wounded yet, and stabbed him in the stomach. Ergo, he arrives at the hermit's cottage near death."

"Is the hermit's cottage located close to the small town of Death?" Geoffrey, one of the older students asked. "That bucolic country hamlet a few kilometres past mid-Life and before the one called End of the Road?"

"What?" Henry asked, instantly confused.

"Sod off," Charlotte said, snapping to attention.

"It was a grammatical mistake," Geoffrey added mildly.

"Oh, well, then," Charlotte countered. "Sod off times two."

"Gwendolyn?" Sarah inquired. "You are the director."

Gwendolyn sighed deeply. Childish spats were generally fuelled by low blood sugar and the overwhelming desire to poke fun at someone simply because their intelligence was inferior. Gwendolyn had deep familiarity with the second component and the only way to still the rebellion was to deliver a mandate coated with honey.

"We're almost done," she said. "And then we will take a break. I'm asking that you save all your comments for now unless they relate directly to the material at hand."

Geoffrey saluted Gwendolyn and apologized to Henry. "Sorry, mate. My English teacher is always doing that to us, and it slipped past my internal monitor. It's only gratifying for about a second. Hardly worth the effort."

"I can't even remember what I said," Henry added, accepting the apology and nodding at Charlotte. "She's my defender."

"Smashing," Geoffrey said. "We all need defenders."

"Let me finish this," Charlotte said, standing up and motioning Henry back to his seat. "Is that alright?" she asked Gwendolyn.

The director lifted her hands, palms pointing to the sky and then dropped them back to the table. "You have five minutes."

Charlotte nodded and her eyes swept the table. "The wounded man explains that he wished to kill the king to avenge his brother, but instead the king saved his life by tending to his wounds. 'I am profoundly moved by your kindness,' he says. 'I will serve you the rest of my days if only you can find it in your heart to forgive me.' The king knew a good thing when he saw it and agreed. I mean, he would be stupid not to, am I right?"

"Charlotte," Gwendolyn warned. "No editorializing."

Charlotte shrugged her shoulders eloquently and continued. "The king returned to the wounded man all the property he stole, and said he would send his own physician to care for the man until he was fully recovered. Still and all, the king was mightily confused, because he had come all this way and instead of finding the answers to the questions, answers he desperately needed to know, he had been sidetracked into this small drama. He confronts the hermit and asks one last time for the answers he wants."

Henry added his voice from the sidelines. "The hermit is amused, but being a hermit, he doesn't show it. He explains to me that I already have my answers, which confuses me even more."

"Thank you, Henry," Charlotte said, bowing from the waist.

"Cracker jack," Geoffrey murmured. "Now I get it. Very clever."

"Well, I don't get it," Phyllis Landsdowne complained.

"Me either." A chorus of protests emerged.

"Patience," Charlotte pronounced. "Here's the deal and it is amazingly simple. And the hermit lays it out by example. He says: 'If you had not pitied me for my weakness and stopped to help me dig flower beds, you would have gone on and been attacked in the forest, possibly killed. The most important time to begin a project was when you saw I needed help. The most important person was me and the most important thing to do was to help me.' Push this forward, my good man," Charlotte said, making her voice frail and weak, "And you will see that when the wounded man rushed out of the forest, it was time to help, he was the most important person, and to tend to him your most important job. If you had not done that, he would never have made his peace with you.'"

"Oh," Henry pronounced, lifting his arms high. "How could I have failed to see this? The most important time is Now! Period, exclamation point."

"Because that is all there is. No past, no future, just now," Charlotte added. "Now, now, now. The most important person is the one standing beside you, or in front of you or behind you, because that person might be the last person you ever see. And what must you do, king? What is the most *important* thing to do? The *only* thing?"

There was dead silence. The transformation in Charlotte's voice had altered her appearance and she appeared frail and old yet cast in gold by the dying afternoon light flowing in from the windows. Jeremy looked at her with admiration and began to cheer and the other students started to pound the table drowning out the hermit's final proclamation.

Gwendolyn was transfixed. In that moment, the second the final question was asked, she realized a universal truth – but as soon as it registered in her brain, it disappeared and no matter how hard she chased after it, it was gone. As were the goosebumps that had briefly lifted the hair on her arms. She saw Charlotte's spotlight of a smile and was annoyed that her nemesis had once again stolen the show.

From the Hilroy of Charlotte
Lisa Hansen

DAY: FRIDAY, SEPTEMBER 3
TIME: THE WITCHING HOUR – 1 AM
RECAP OF PHONE CONVERSATION WITH LEO
LOCATION: On bed in my room at Sarah's, where else?

Leo couldn't believe that Gwendolyn now wore trousers. He didn't think that the word trousers had a place in her vocabulary or on her body.

Leo was dead keen to hear about the play, and I filled him in with all the savoury details at my disposal.

- 4 fights between Byron and Gwendolyn one in which they almost came to blows.
- Gwendolyn reducing Meggie to tears.
- Gwendolyn complaining about the city excavators who had manufactured a large drop hole off to the side of the stage.

The latter mystified him, and I had to provide more details.

I don't understand it either, Hilroy. No one does. But the great thing is the excavators have stopped work entirely due to some labour dispute.

Leo wanted to know if it was safe for us to be on stage, and I told him what the deal was, or at least how I understand it.

There are orange and yellow sawhorse barricades around a hole the size of the average manhole you might find on any city street. Point of fact number one.

Gwendolyn says that a backstage is hardly a street – point of fact number two and mainly to be ignored.

Meggie decorated the enclosure with fabulous drapes of deep purple brocade to remind us all to stay away. Refer to Gwendolyn reducing Meggie to tears for wasting good fabric.

While everyone else was busy I examined said hole with my trusty flashlight. It appears to be an enormous cavern, ten or twenty time larger than the average crawl space. There are rusty rungs hammered into 2000-year-old stones and those rungs lead down, down, down into a dank and smelly dungeon. Big old black pipes weave in and out of holes blasted into stone and there are a few tools lying around and drop clothes and wooden planks and who knows what else because I did not have time to investigate thoroughly as I heard my name being called.

I told Leo it was perfectly safe and far less dangerous than our ginormous water heater which hisses at me whenever I try to touch it.

I explained to Leo that, after a near mutiny amongst the boy students about my being cast as the hermit, Gwendolyn made a rather unusual pronouncement. She approved the selection and said that I was a master of not answering questions asked and pretending to know more than anyone else.

Insulting!

Gwendolyn does not like the hermit wig that Meggie is creating for me. She keeps screaming for it to be greyer and insists that the beard is revolting.

The beard, a few strands of curly horsehair, is BRILLIANT. It makes me look like I am at least 200 years old.

Leo wanted to know if I was trying to get along with Gwendolyn, and I told him I was and that we all stayed until 10:30 working our hearts out.

"And your headaches?" he wanted to know.

Not wanting him to worry, I told him there were largely gone which they largely are. I had a sharp pain in my head before I went to sleep last night, as you know, Hilroy, but it passed as soon as it arrived. It came when I was trying to remember what I forgot. It was like playing a game of hide and seek with the wind and being thrown up against a tree for my efforts.

Anyway, Leo got stern and wanted me to promise to stop what I am doing and rest if I get another headache. I agreed but did not promise. Agreements can be broken, promises cannot.

Leo said he has found the perfect house for Oliver and Company to rent, only one block away from our own.

They will be living in my pocket! Leo laughed. There is nothing better than making someone laugh. I learned that a long time ago.

I told Leo the first run through is today, starting at five. Everybody needs to show up right after school or they will be sacked. I plan on peppering the city with notices about the production and Henry and Jeremy will be my assistants.

"Break a leg, Charlotte!"

When I heard that I screamed in protest, mostly because our time for talking had come to an end. I have absolutely no intention of breaking anything!

Chapter Twenty-Eight

Byron had surpassed even his most lofty pronouncements and in record time had built and painted two sets. The grunt work had been done by scores of minions, Oliver's "irregulars", who he treated with the utmost respect because they all steadfastly referred to him as "Guv" and thought he was "smashing." The kingly chambers and the forest primeval were easily exchanged as they were slotted into wheels and merely reversed as the story line indicated. For the third set a cottage front was wheeled on and set at an angle to the forest, this put in place as the lights dimmed to indicate the king deep in thought and despondent, feeling he might never find the hermit and therefore, never get the answers he wanted.

Byron was a colourist, his sets vivid and bold. The king's chambers were largely purple and orange. Two painted tapestries were placed either side of the throne giving the chamber the illusion of warmth and fire. Byron wanted hand-sewn replicas of the Unicorn in Captivity Tapestries, but even he had to admit there was no time to forge these masterpieces. He settled for hastily painted hunting scenes involving boars and lurchers, with a suitable amount of blood spilled across the lower quadrants of the facsimile tapestries.

Gwendolyn loved the chamber, although she would never say it out loud. For her entire life, she had lived by the standard that one could never go wrong with black – black shoes, black dresses, black coats, black sweaters, black mood. Black spoke of good breeding, restraint, and class, that irrefutable state of being that one was born possessing and which could not be imitated by those who were inferior. Having dispensed with all the clothes she brought with her to London and replaced them with items she would have dismissed as "common" not a week before, she felt she was on

the verge on some tremendous transformation – although her tempera-
ment, exacting and dismissive, was largely unchanged.

The theatre was her milieu, even though she had inhabited it only
briefly, sixty years in her past. She was born to direct and command, and
there were no social norms she must adhere to. One minute she might raise
her voice in an argument with Byron, and in another, consult with Sarah
as to a change of wording in her original script. All she had to do was snap
her fingers and a pot of tea was produced, a reading lamp, a plate full of
cucumber and cream cheese sandwiches, and once, out of spite with herself
and no one else, an order of fish and chips inside a greasy newspaper.

"What?" she asked Charlotte who had suddenly materialized at her side.

"I just never thought I'd see the day."

"A person must be willing to try everything, Charlotte, if a person wants
to live fully."

"What person?" Charlotte asked, taking a seat beside Gwendolyn, and
helping herself to a chip.

"Any person, Charlotte," Gwendolyn answered with a hint of annoyance.

"Even you?" Charlotte persisted.

Gwendolyn consulted her watch. It was six thirty. The children had been
fed, and it was time to start to work. They had less than two days to pull
together a fantastic show. Impossible? Not a word in Gwendolyn's vocabulary. "You have exactly one minute to place yourself in position beside your
hut, or I will consider turning your role over to the understudy."

Gwendolyn had words with Meggie as well.

"Why is the king's robe pale blue?"

"Because that is his state of mind, dear."

"I don't understand."

"Surely you know the lyrics to that famous Elvis Presley standard?"

"Who?"

"He's a singer, dear. He immortalized the song 'Blue Christmas'. You
know it, surely. 'I'll have a blue Christmas without you...'"

"What does that have to do with anything? This drama does not take
place at Christmas."

"Blue in this context means sad. Our poor king is depressed because he
can't find the answers to the questions he so needs."

"I don't like it," Gwendolyn said shortly.

"I suppose I could add buttons in contrasting colours, or perhaps a large ornate golden brooch at his shoulder. Or," she added, becoming excited by her own thoughts, "a lining of florid purple illustrating how his own nature has become subdued by his condition."

"What are you doing standing here talking? See to it at once."

Gwendolyn made no friends in her current role, but friendship was not what she wanted. She required drama, an essential ingredient that had long been missing from her own life. Here, in this rundown theatre, she could be anyone she wanted to be, and the freedom was intoxicating.

"The actors are complaining that you don't have anything good to say about their performances, Gwendolyn," Sarah told her, easing herself into the seat recently vacated by Charlotte, and stretching her legs. She commandeered the chair beside her to store her paraphernalia – purse, notebook, sweater, cane. Then with painstaking precision she slid her arthritic hands into a pair of fingerless gloves and flexed her fingers as best she could. "They are just children, and they require a lot of encouragement."

"Nonsense," Gwendolyn retorted, hypnotized by the tedious rituals that accompanied old age. Would she, too, be a slave to their demands? She examined her pantaloons and saw three cat hairs that had journeyed with her to the theatre. She removed these interlopers with a flick of her finger. "I received no encouragement from anyone as a child and look how well I turned out."

Sarah was silent as she fitted a cigarette into her cigarette holder.

"If you light that within fifty feet of me, I will scream."

"I have no intention of lighting it, Gwendolyn. It is a prop. Sometimes props make people feel more secure. Words can act as props. Kind words can make people feel confident and more eager to surpass themselves simply for the pleasure of receiving another kind word."

Gwendolyn drummed her fingers on her knee. "This works?"

Deep within the depths of her own heart, fortified into near petrification, she felt a curious ping, almost like a minor electrical shock. A distant memory surfaced – Charlotte's face as she chauffeured Gwendolyn across the island on the much-loved bicycle Gwendolyn once owned, a bicycle that had a side car and many secret compartments. Once again, the loud and omnipresent child had won some competition that Gwendolyn did not know she was competing in and had secured the driver's seat on the bicycle.

"Did it ever occur to you to thank Charlotte?" Sarah asked, as if reading her mind.

"Thank her for what? She should be thanking me. If I hadn't paid for her and Henry to accompany me to London, they wouldn't be here. Leo can't afford the airfare, and Henry's parents think only of themselves."

That the children were here at all, starring in her theatrical accomplishment, spoke loudly to her largesse. And to give Henry credit, he had freely shared some timely information on a mining stock that he had in his own portfolio and Gwendolyn had purchased shares which saw a profit of more than $478 in three days, more than making up for the meagre amount she paid him. That Henry had a stock portfolio at age eleven was an accomplishment and reflected his frugality and common sense.

Charlotte, on the other hand, relentlessly asked for favours, to borrow money to buy presents for people Gwendolyn did not want to buy presents for and to contribute to the food that Oliver was preparing for the students daily. Such extravagance was not within Gwendolyn's purview. She knew Oliver was rich and that he owned the Rolls that ferried her to and from the theatre and owned the house where Sarah lived, because instead of sneaking around like Charlotte was forever doing and spying on people who did not want to be spied on, Gwendolyn had asked Oliver and he had replied in the affirmative. 'Sarah is very fortunate to have met you, Oliver,' she had told him, and he had said, 'No. I am the fortunate one. She saved my life. For such a selfless act I am forever in her debt.'

"I have performed many selfless acts in my life," Gwendolyn said, continuing the conversation she was having with herself out loud. It was important for Sarah to know that she had not lived a life of complete disregard for other, but why did she care? Was she still trying to impress her distant and sarcastic tutor, the skinny young woman who flounced around Gwendolyn's house in a cloud of cigarette smoke, radiating a self-confidence that most semi-employed people would be frightened to exhibit?

"Charlotte likes you more than she likes me," Gwendolyn acknowledged. "You are more approachable, and possibly warmer, although I can't attest to that. It might be to your advantage to stop trying to change me. I am who I am."

"As fixed as the planets?"

"Exactly. Now let's get down to business and discuss the last scene before we call the actors back. I am not at all happy with the final scene between the hermit and the king. It must be…" She tried to find the word she wanted and failed.

"Different?" Sarah suggested.

"Exactly. It's the king's moment. He is the one who is experiencing an awakening, and Charlotte is pushing herself forward a bit too much. She must remain in the background, rather like an annoying fly that won't go away."

Ariel appeared suddenly, storming down the aisle and waving a piece of paper.

"I was just given these instructions by Oliver," she said, coming to a stop alongside Gwendolyn's seat. "You want me to find five floppy hats, seven metres of grosgrain ribbon in various colours and more fake fur. Wait a minute," she said consulting the paper she held in her hand. "Preferably fox? What is all this about?"

"I don't like the counsellors' costumes," Gwendolyn said simply. Surely that was implicit in her request. "They need to be more decorative, and Meggie insists that she has no more ribbon."

"Mother?" Ariel asked. "Really? You have enough supplies in that room to make a hundred costumes. Can't we use what we have?"

Sarah shrugged. "It's her decision," she said, pointing to Gwendolyn.

"If you would be so kind?" Gwendolyn asked. "I would do it myself, but I am quite tied up here with obligations, and I do not have your knowledge of the city. Get Oliver to drive you."

"He's busy helping Byron."

Gwendolyn reached inside her satchel and extracted a wad of bills. "Take a taxi. And buy yourself something for your troubles."

"Honestly," Ariel said, fanning her face with her hand. "I already had to waste an hour buying you a megaphone which no one will ever use again. It's just so unnecessary. And wasteful," she added, frowning at Gwendolyn.

"I love my new shoes," Gwendolyn replied ignoring Ariel's temper tantrum. "Have you been able—"

"No. I have not had time to find you more. One pair lasts a normal person for years."

"But I never pretended to be normal," Gwendolyn stated, smiling gently. She liked Ariel. The woman had spunk and was not afraid to spar.

Ariel flounced off but not before throwing a disgusted glance at her mother.

"My, she has a temper, doesn't she?"

Sarah bristled. No one was allowed to criticize Ariel, particularly someone as selfish as Gwendolyn. She took a deep breath, composed herself and replied.

"Ariel is very particular and hates to waste anything. She is a conservationist, Gwendolyn. A trait you might like to consider embracing."

Gwendolyn focused on the words and ignored the tone. She would not allow Sarah to become the judgemental tutor she had been so many long years ago and now had the skills to parry such a thrust. Words were easy to deflect.

"Admirable, I'm sure. That quality would come from you, Sarah, as Charlie did not consider conservation a primary concern."

"And yet, what might Charlie have become?" Sarah answered...

Would he have become a stodgy old man, set in his ways and churlish if his afternoon tea did not arrive on time? Or a jazz pianist, playing until two in the morning and keeping the same hours as Sarah did? Would they have met once or twice a week in her sitting room, discussing their thoughts on art and music? Or would they have a gigantic family? A score of children and grandchildren and constant music? They hadn't married. There was no time, and Sarah did not believe in marriage. Charlie had known she was pregnant but did not push to give the coming child his name. There would be time for that once the war was over. Or not. But he did give her the Tree of Life brooch. A pledge to always be there in some capacity. More to the point, would Charlie have liked Gwendolyn or decided he had no use for her and corresponded, with irritation, only once or twice a year? The dead were frozen in place, a snapshot of who they had been and no future pictures to show what they had become.

Gwendolyn was silent. At least the dead no longer had to endure lectures on how and why they should change. She was considering parrying the blow, but Sarah side-stepped to a new issue.

"I don't know if you are aware of this, Gwendolyn, but earlier today Charlotte sold fifty tickets to the show. She gave me over two hundred pounds, and she's determined to sell more in the morning."

"Two hundred pounds? That can't be right. You said she sold fifty tickets?" Gwendolyn's shock caused her body to stiffen.

"Yes, she did."

Gwendolyn picked up her megaphone, pressed a button, and her voice filled the theatre. "Henry Jacobs, wherever you are, this is your director speaking. Come see me at once. I am sitting in the front row."

Twenty seconds later Henry appeared. He stared at Gwendolyn and thrust his hands in his pockets.

"What?" he asked. "You didn't need to use the megaphone. I was sitting on the corner of the stage."

Gwendolyn fluttered her fingers and dismissed his remark. "How much is a pound worth in Canadian dollars?"

"Approximately $2.48," he answered immediately.

"If a person sold fifty tickets and received two hundred pounds how much was each ticket selling for?"

"Four pounds," he said, "or about ten dollars. Is this a break for math exercises or what?"

"You don't need to be rude, Henry. I am shocked, deeply shocked to hear that the tickets for our production tomorrow night are selling for a pittance."

Henry's face brightened immediately. "You should have seen Charlotte working the crowds. She unloaded those tickets in less than an hour. You know how she did it?"

"I cannot imagine," Gwendolyn said.

"She went to one of those places where you can buy cut-rate tickets for West End shows near Paddington station, but they were all selling for about forty pounds a ticket. To be honest I thought she might sell a few tickets to tourists who felt sorry for her. But she put on her CN tower sunglasses and Charlie's brown fedora, and no one felt sorry for her as far as I could tell. She had them eating out of her hand."

Gwendolyn sighed. "Naturally."

"Jeremy and me sold our tickets, too, or rather Charlotte sold them for us. Free food and drink were a real draw."

"I don't think you can offer free food unless there will be free food," Henry had whispered, as Charlotte sold eight tickets on the spot with this enticement.

"Oliver will provide," she'd whispered. "And if he doesn't, so what?"

"It's lying," Henry had insisted.

"The theatre is a lie, isn't it? It's all make-believe. I am just keeping with what is."

Henry had sighed mightily and then grabbed Jeremy's arm when he saw two policemen approach. "We have to make tracks," he insisted, trying to move Charlotte out of harm's way.

"Coward. Watch me go into performance mode."

And she had. First there had been a brief exchange of hats and then a long fascinating story (mostly lies) about how they had come to be in London and the history of Sarah's theatre (partly true) and the importance of *The Three Questions* as a morality tale.

"An order of fish and chips costs the same as a night at the theatre, roof-top entertainment during the intervals, food, drink, and a chance to schmooze with the director. Everybody who is anybody will be there, and this is a one-time offer, two tickets for the price of one."

"Schmooze?" The bobbies were unfamiliar with the word.

Henry smiled a distant smile, which annoyed Gwendolyn because he refused to explain from whence it had come.

"Charlotte was on the verge of getting arrested seconds before the last ticket was sold," he said, "because apparently, we were trespassing and selling goods without a license to sell goods but catch this: she managed to sell the two bobbies who came to arrest us tickets, too, which she made up on the spot with three by five index cards she carried in her backpack. They get a free tour of the backstage and a private audience with the director. I think there was a mention of a free dinner after the show as well, but I can't be certain. You'll have to ask Charlotte."

In the history of Henry's life on earth, he had never spoken these many words without being pushed aside, ridiculed, or told to be quiet. He added to this feeling of liberation by grabbing Gwendolyn's megaphone and issuing an order that Charlotte present herself front and centre pronto.

"Jeremy thinks Charlotte is the coolest person he has ever met," Henry continued.

"I never said I would grant an interview with anyone," Gwendolyn said. "Charlotte will just have to retract that statement. I did not give permission."

Henry rolled his eyes. "They'll probably just want to say hello, so you don't have to worry about being put on the spot. Or arrested," he added, as an afterthought. "But I saved the best for last."

"There's more?" Gwendolyn asked, sinking back into her chair. Henry's commanding presence made her feel like she was being attacked.

"The commotion that Charlotte created with her illicit sales attracted the attention of a BBC reporter who was waiting in line to buy a ticket for *I Love You, You're Perfect, Don't Change*. The reporter confessed that the show was his wife's idea, and he didn't really want to go so he's coming here instead, and he is bringing a crew. A crew!"

In fact, what had happened was a bit different. The arrival of the bobbies and their interest in the children had caused a disruption in the line of tourists and a few had broken from the herd to watch, and record, if necessary, the sight of two strapping young officers harassing derelict children. This had caught the attention of a BBC producer who had just joined the line and in search of a story he had wandered over to see if there was anything newsworthy.

"Once Charlotte caught sight of his name tag, a tag he had worn to try and get preferential treatment since a series of telephone calls had elicited no results, she was on him like a lion on a wildebeest. And he is bringing a crew," Henry repeated reverentially. "A crew! You are going to be famous."

Gwendolyn's stomach rumbled, an embarrassment she tried to mask by coughing. Did she want a BBC crew in the audience? Could she handle reviews that were less than stellar?

"This is a major human-interest story, or at the very least, a page ten version of a major human-interest story. Hugh Williams, the BBC producer, sees the production of *The Three Questions* as a 'cross cultural tour de force' although, besides the accent, there isn't a whole lot of difference between Canada and England except for things like maple syrup and geographic dimension. But it's the time travel idea that hooked him."

"The time travel dimension?" Gwendolyn could feel her face turn pale. It was almost as if the blood in her body refused to travel beyond her neck.

"You'll probably be interviewed by the BBC," Henry added as an aside. "You, too," he said, thoughtfully including Sarah.

Sarah had not interrupted Henry's story once because she was enthralled. Charlotte had behaved in the same fashion she herself embraced throughout her career. Getting noticed when you were a goldfish in a sea of whales was near impossible unless you played the kind of game Charlotte did, and while Henry might see it as lying, Sarah saw it as being colourfully inventive. She prided herself on thinking her audience had never been disappointed. They might hate a production or love it or be somewhere in between, but she made sure that her audience was always as fully engaged as her players. What difference was there between the two? None that she could see.

"It's been a year at least since the BBC has been here," Sarah said. "They consider us an anomaly, content with where we are and not wishing for greater acclaim. They are always respectful," she added, concerned that Gwendolyn was sinking deeper into her chair. "I promise they will treat you with courtesy," she said, patting Gwendolyn on the knee.

Gwendolyn fought off the impulse to brush the aged hand aside. Like a dam breaking, the blood pooled at the base of her neck flushed to her checks.

"It's just so embarrassing," she admitted, rubbing her face. She adjusted her beret and sighed deeply. "This time travel nonsense. If I say it is a fiction, there will be no story, but if I say I do believe it, what kind of fool does that make me?" Her innate snobbishness won the battle between truth and fiction, although she had time to decide how she would spin the story. "Nevertheless, an interview by the BBC is quite a coup."

"A thank you would be nice, Gwendolyn." Charlotte added, appearing as if by magic beside Henry. "Make room," she said, sinking into the chair.

"Must you always sneak up on a person, Charlotte?" Gwendolyn placed her hand on her chest. "You startled me."

"Probably the idea of the BBC thrusting a camera in your face startled you more."

"I sincerely hope you informed this reporter that we will have had but two days to rehearse."

"He loves it," Charlotte said, getting comfortable in the chair and kicking off her shoes. "He's heard of Byron, and he's going to do a piece on him, too. He likes the idea of time compressed – and expanded," she added with a laugh.

"It would be welcome if time did expand because we do not have enough of it," Gwendolyn said, turning to Sarah. "I would like to do another run through after dinner. Could you note any shortcomings or changes you think we should make? Hopefully everyone has memorized their lines. Tomorrow will be the first dress. A disaster in the making."

"Lines are memorized," Charlotte said. "We were running lines before you bellowed with the bull horn. Oliver is coaching the advisors, and Arthur is teaching Jeremy how to run when he is supposed to be wounded. Arthur has had a lot of experience running while wounded," she added. "And by the by, the wheels for the set changes are parked in the wing to the left so Byron has space to spread the canvas of grass and twigs he and the "irregulars" created last night. He hasn't slept in over forty-eight hours," she said, her eyes widening. "That beats me by over twenty although I think he's lying. Still and all, he hasn't gotten enough, that's for sure. He keeps getting me mixed up with Jeremy. I suppose it's because I cut my hair."

Gwendolyn finally looked at Charlotte without eyes clouded by mistrust. How could she have failed to notice she was looking at an entirely different child? This one was handsome in a way that the 'old' Charlotte was not. The old Charlotte resembled a coyote that was covered in mange, feral and ready to attack at any second. This new Charlotte was cool and composed, more like a baby panther with grey eyebrows.

"What have you done to your eyebrows?"

"It's makeup, Gwendolyn. I'm easing into my part."

"Who cut your hair?" she asked. It looked like someone had inverted a bowl on Charlotte's head and cut round the rim, a Buster Brown haircut that looked frighteningly familiar. Back in May, Charlotte had been prancing about with the same haircut, but in the intervening months, abnormal hair growth and lack of hygiene had turned her hair into a squirrel's nest, replete with real twigs and bits of grass and leaves.

"I did," Sarah answered, raising her arm. "About an hour ago. And then we washed it in the bathroom sink. Didn't we, Charlotte?"

"And dusted my neck with baby powder. The wig itches," she explained to Gwendolyn. "It will be better if I don't have so much hair to stuff inside it. Also, the beard itches and it makes my nose run which complicates my vision in a way I don't quite understand. But it's authentic and makes me feel old, like the hermit. So I am completely in character. Meggie is adding a hem of dirty looking fabric to my tunic because I don't think the hermit washes his clothes all that often. You're going to like it when you see it in the dress."

No mention of a canvas for the stage floor had been approved by Gwendolyn, and Arthur, that derelict compatriot of Oliver's, had not been given permission to coach Jeremy.

"I am going to have to do a quick costume change as I am one of the fencers. I have the lunge, the parry, and the riposte down pat, and Arthur says I have an instinct for fencing. My stance needs work because I keep forgetting to keep my free arm behind my back. I prefer the high outside attack because it is my nature to be bigger than life."

"Charlotte..." Gwendolyn tried to interrupt but failed to get the child's attention.

"The low outside and the low inside are just not much fun. It's hard to keep the sword close to my body with those moves because it is very heavy."

"Extremely," Henry agreed.

"And the stance is a challenge what with trying to remember which foot moves first and I find..."

"Silence," Gwendolyn pronounced, lifting the megaphone to her lips and dismissing Charlotte with a wave of her hand. "Everyone on stage in five minutes. That includes stagehands, costumers and set designers and fencers. No excuses will be tolerated for tardiness."

"Wait until she sees Henry's costume," Charlotte whispered to Sarah.

"You don't think she'll like it?" Sarah whispered back.

"Only if she designed it herself, but she'll figure out a way to have it look like she did."

Chapter Twenty-Nine

"It's dangerous, Byron," Gwendolyn repeated, standing on the corner of the stage, her megaphone dangling from her fingers. "You can't drape a piece of canvas across the floor and not expect people to fall."

The stage, now the home of the hermit and his garden, not only resembled the floor of a forest but embodied its smell as well; mud and damp leaves all manufactured by Byron and his tireless team of assistants. The only thing that was missing was a trio of ravens, perched high in a papier mâché tree observing the idiosyncratic behaviour of humans.

"The boy fell," Byron explained patiently, "because he has been dreadfully injured by a sabre."

"Actually, it was a sword," Jeremy said, continuing his crawl across the facsimile forest floor gasping realistically for breath.

"I don't care if it was a kitchen knife sticking out of his back," Gwendolyn retorted. "The actors are now using this covering as a skating rink in case you haven't noticed."

Three of the counsellors to the king were enacting a game of running and sliding across the canvas to see who could end the furthest from the starting point. Nervous energy needed an outlet, and the children were reaching a point somewhere between boredom (from Gwendolyn's constant interruptions) and hysteria (ditto).

"Noticed? I see everything, my good woman, and I assure you that children have far better reflexes than we do." Byron's face was grey with fatigue, but his voice was strong and resonant. He grabbed one of the counsellors by the scruff of his tunic and removed him from the floor covering before continuing his monologue. "On my last hike through a nature preserve somewhere in the northern outreaches of London, I tripped on a tree root and sprained my ankle. Now I guarantee," he said, stressing the point by raising his voice, "that if any of the actors you currently see on stage had been with me none of them would have fallen, and even if they had, they would have leapt to their feet and carried on."

After climbing slowly to the stage, Sarah weighed in on the debate. She put her hand on Byron's arm and said kindly: "It's all an illusion, Byron. We have the hermit's cottage, all these shrubs and trees, the magnificent papier mâché rocks and boulders and that is enough. We don't need facsimile grass and mud."

"Yet another work of art relegated to the garbage heap," he sighed in disgust. "What is more, I observe there are no such restrictions put on the costume designer. The king's robe is far too elaborate, and it clashes with the tapestries behind the throne. Now if this was a Cézanne production..."

"Which it is not, Byron. And even Cézanne did not decorate the floor. One must stop somewhere."

"Ah, but if you knew the time that went into this, the endless instruction I was forced to give..."

"He got that right," counsellor number three stated rubbing his neck. "It was like... 'you, there, boy, that colour is wrong, too starkly brown. Where is the subtlety, the dance of shades that nature wears as her cloak? Where is your vision?'"

"The canvas goes, Byron. We have enough to contend with as it is." Sarah spoke firmly and Byron hung his head in defeat.

"Blast! Dispense with it then. Throw it in the bin. Destroy another great work of art. See if I care. Oliver, I need a drink," he added. "A real drink, mind, not one of your endless cups of tea."

"At your service," Oliver replied, removing a flask from the pocket of his jacket.

Byron stormed off in a huff, the flask in hand, and the counsellors got busy rolling up the forest floor. Charlotte and Henry rearranged the boulders and shrubs beside the hermit's cottage. Jeremy huddled with Arthur and began to practise crawling in a more realistically painful way. The pugilist watched his progress and barked out a series of commands.

"Boy, feel this experience fully," he insisted. "You fought bravely with your sword, you thrust and parried, and you were pierced by a low inside. You are lucky your heart was not cut in two. But still, you must feel the wound, you feel the basic animal instinct to survive at all costs." Arthur cleared his throat and continued. "It's a primal emotion, pressing and powerful, but understated. Use your elbows and envision a haven. Many a time in my life I have found myself in difficult situations and…"

Gwendolyn tuned out this nonsense and turned her attention to Charlotte.

"What is that you have on?" she asked looking down her nose at the ragamuffin who stood in front of her.

"It's my hermit outfit," Charlotte explained proudly. "All wrinkly and smeared with dirt. The hermit is poor and doesn't have running water so he can't wash his shroud daily like some people I know."

"Meggie!" Gwendolyn screamed, the megaphone at her lips. "Stage. Immediately."

"At your service, Gwendolyn, dear." Meggie arrived, flushed and out of breath, and her realistic attitude of distress caught Gwendolyn's attention.

"Look here, Jeremy," she said, interrupting the coaching in dying that Jeremy was receiving from Arthur. "You see how Meggie is short of breath, how her eyes are glassy, her attitude supplicating. This is what I would like to see in your character."

"What the hell does that mean?" Arthur asked, picking his teeth with a toothpick. "Supplanting?"

"Are my eyes glassy?" Meggie said, turning to Charlotte for confirmation.

"No. They are normal eyes."

"Meggie, I want the hermit's robe fixed. And not in an hour. Right now. I don't want the robe dragging on the floor. Make a belt. Out of rope if you can't find anything else."

"Yes, dear. It is on the rooster. Ariel delivered these hats, which I am told must take precedence. I'm just finishing sewing the fur on the Counsellors' robes and the hermit is next on my list."

"I can't wear belts," Charlotte complained. "They cut off my circulation and make me dizzy."

"Nonsense. You are an actor, and you will wear what I say. You're lucky you are not dressed in a bear costume or the hind end of a donkey. I want a blouson effect," Gwendolyn added. "And do something to hide those bony ankles. Paint or socks will do."

"I hate to correct you, dear," Meggie replied, calm and complacent. "But a real hermit would have bony ankles. The hermit, poor man, lives on what he plants in his garden, he is old, his skin has thinned and unless he suffers from gout, which is highly unlikely, the fatty deposits covering his ankles would be non-existent. And this is the theatre, after all. We are asking the audience to come with their imaginations in place, are we not?"

Gwendolyn wished her pantaloons were longer because she saw Meggie staring at her very own ankles, as if to say: 'You may not be a hermit, but you are old.' "But, of course, I will do as you say. You are the director."

"First the robe is too long, next it is too short, next it has to be long again to cover my ankles" Charlotte stated clearly. "Make up your mind or leave me in limbo but if you do that, I might spoil the show. Is that what you want?"

Gwendolyn experienced a sudden recollection, fragile, and covered with a dusty film. This memory, brief and telling, informed her that some misshapen child – she would never acknowledge publicly that this child had been Charlotte – had long ago reduced her only theatrical production to a vaudevillian clown show. And now, this bold as brass warning, issuing from the mouth of the same misshapen child, a warning that stilled everyone within hearing distance, literally begged to be taken seriously. There was no limit to the amount of trouble Charlotte could cause if she put her mind to it, and with the BBC in attendance, Gwendolyn could not risk the unknown.

"I agree," Gwendolyn said, after pretending to give the problem of Charlotte's ankles considerable thought. Apart from Henry, and possibly Jeremy, Charlotte was no more irritating than all the other children who crowded the stage and refused to take Gwendolyn seriously.

But this was her time.

And she was ready to meet it head on.

"The belt stays," she added, and was pleased to see the smile vanish from Charlotte's face.

Sarah crossed her ankles, sat back in her chair, and waited. It had been a terribly long day though it was only now six o'clock. No production she had ever mounted had taken shape in such a short period of time, and Sarah put it down to scores of eager assistants, Byron's genius with canvas and wood, and Meggie's with cloth. The number of assistants Oliver had managed to find – mostly grabbed off street corners – had helped Byron admirably, as had all but four of the actors who had called in sick to school. Time compressed into two-hour intervals where with an abundance of swearing, shouting, sawing, and painting, backdrops appeared as if they had been dropped from the heavens.

The king's chambers were magnificent swirls of colour with fiery-eyed beasts and blood dripping in the corners. The forest, almost claustrophobic with towering trees that appeared to bend from being touched by an unseen wind, was a natural counterpoint to the king's regal chambers. It was all stunningly realistic, including the hermit's cottage, with its thatched roof and tiny windows. Paint cans had emptied as soon as the lids were pried open, boards cut to size in minutes, not hours, trees, rocks, and sky appearing almost with the snap of Byron's fingers. Each time she descended in the rickety elevator from her office another illusion had been created.

It was magic, pure and simple, brought about by the presence of Charlotte and Henry and a journey into the past which would lead to a future unknown.

Something splendid was about to happen. Sarah could feel it in her bones.

Meggie's band of seamstresses had outdone themselves, and yet from where had they come? Oliver, of course. Oliver, who knew more people than Sarah had met in her life. He had called in favours, demanded, cajoled, and the hoards had arrived. The air positively bristled, and Sarah loved every minute of it. There was simply not enough room for this amount of activity, but the theatre itself had seemed to expand to accommodate it all.

Physics be damned.

Enchantment was at play.

However, the noise, the dust, the tears, and threats had begun to wear on her nerves, and although she didn't want to admit it, she was tired. Charlotte was dragging her feet, unusual for a child who had unlimited energy. She put it down to Gwendolyn's constant criticism, but there was little she could do. She knew in her heart, a place that acknowledged the impossible, that Charlotte had played the king in this production so many long decades ago. Although she had not followed the script that Gwendolyn had written, she had stolen the show and instead of making a mockery of Tolstoy's moral, had illuminated it.

The actors were gathered in a semicircle on the stage in full costume and makeup, awaiting a *moxie*, a term that Sarah had borrowed for pre-show huddles in which she tried to pump adrenaline into her cast.

"Some people say acting is a game for fools. Now why would they say this?"

"You can't make a living being an actor, according to my father. A lorry driver does much better. Maybe you can pick up a few tips on how to behave if you are a politician or a businessman, but that's all it's good for."

"Interesting," Sarah replied, biting her lower lip.

"Stage makeup is bad for your skin. It makes my face and eyes itch."

"An irritation to be sure," Sarah said, agreeing. "But if you wash your face afterwards, carefully and completely, there will be no problems."

"Everything about the theatre is an illusion. Costumes only look good from a distance. Up close they resemble a pile of shite."

"Why Jackson, how can you say such a thing?" Meggie asked. "Do you not like your hat?"

"Okay," Sarah said as she watched Gwendolyn bring the megaphone up to her lips. "That's a good start. Always important to get the negative out of the way first. Are there any other thoughts?"

"In Shakespeare the fool is a clown," Jeremy volunteered. "The fool cries when he should laugh, he insults the king or queen, he makes a mockery of everything that should be taken seriously."

"How come there aren't any female fools?" Charlotte asked. "How come they are always men? Girls are pushed out of the way."

"I agree completely with Charlotte," Gwendolyn stated sans megaphone. "Which is why this play has been cast against gender."

"First of all, there aren't any women in the story. Not one," Henry said. "You have to cast against gender, or half the kids here wouldn't get a part."

"Now listen closely," Sarah instructed. "You must begin to feel your character long before you step into costume and put on your makeup. How would a counsellor to the king behave? How would he stand? If he rode the Underground, what would he experience? The same goes for you, Henry, as king. You climb into his very being."

"But how?" Mess asked.

"By exchange," Sarah answered simply. "You've all felt hungry. You call up that feeling and notice what it does to your body. Do your hands tremble in expectation, do your shoulders hunch, does your mouth begin to water?"

"I dance in circles."

"I slam open the cabinet doors."

"I whine," Mess said. "Like this. Feed me, I'm hungry," and her voice changed, became higher pitched and clipped.

"Next you must decide who your character is and what qualities you want to portray. If you exchange this quality for one you have felt in your own life your character suddenly becomes more genuine. You have given this fictional creation life."

Henry corrected his posture and Jeremy squeezed his hand. "You can no longer think the way you would think or talk with the same inflection. Some people need complete quiet in which to prepare but most of us do not have that luxury. You must create the stillness within yourself, rather like being the eye of the tornado."

The cast went very still, all shuffling and mumbling coming to a halt.

And then Mess spoke:

"It's akin to magic," she said. "Watching someone take on a role when you know that isn't who they really are. And yet, they really are who they pretend to be. Like you, Charlotte. There's no way any of us thought you could pull off being this hunched over old man who lives in the forest and eats worms when all you do is write in that notebook of yours, paint your eyebrows coal black, and take off on your own to sell tickets. Why didn't you ask me? I would have come. We all would have come. We'd follow you anywhere."

Charlotte didn't know what to say. It never occurred to her that her compatriots would have swarmed the cut-rate theatre ticket pavilion and sold as many tickets as she did herself. She was a loner, not a joiner, and certainly not a group captain, but the warmth of Mess's words enlivened her and she nodded her thanks. Perhaps, then, what she should really do was share the force of the hermit's very being with the other cast members, pushing them to become the character they were not and make this production stellar.

"It's nothing to do with me, you understand," she said gruffly, putting on her hermit's voice and adopting his shrunken posture. "It's only about what I force you to see."

It was seven thirty before the rehearsal got underway. Sandwiches took the place of bangers and mash because everyone was in full costume and Meggie did not want food spilled down the fronts of shirts and jackets that she and her crew would have to clean. Not everyone had their lines perfectly memorized, and those who didn't were chastised by Gwendolyn. The placements weren't exact, the costumes were in their last stages of stitching and fixing, and the stagehands mixed up the sets, but the atmosphere was charged, and that magic that Mess had mentioned was clearly pleasant if only in a grand and glorious muddle with gold glittering at the edges. Gwendolyn insisted on resetting the scene with the king entering stage right for his final conversation with the hermit. The actors had obliged but Charlotte was dragging her feet and was muttering to herself. Sarah thought she heard her say, "It's not right..." but she couldn't be sure.

The lights dimmed, the backdrop of the hermit's hut was moved a metre and Byron started to swear before he was subdued by Arthur. There was the sound of giggling backstage and then silence as the hermit took his place and stood silently, his right ear cocked to the sky.

"Look down, please," Gwendolyn bellowed through the megaphone.

Charlotte did not comply, but when the king entered, she altered the slope of her shoulders and seemed to both rise and shrink simultaneously. She didn't look at the king and did not acknowledge his presence even when he came to stand in front of her.

"I like that," Gwendolyn shouted. "Remember it for tomorrow."

Henry, keeping with the dialogue of the script, asked the hermit for the last time to give him the answer to the three questions. There was a certain desperation in Henry's voice that seemed real enough and a look, that could be fear, when he gazed at the hermit.

Fear was not in the script. Anger and impatience, yes but the king had no reason to be frightened of the hermit. Sarah swiveled her head and tried to see what Henry was seeing and then realized she was gazing at a stranger.

The child known as Charlotte, the endearing, irritating, sometimes abrasive, sometimes sweet person who had taken over Sarah's house and reclaimed her heart simply wasn't there anymore. Sarah saw an old, tired man who was sick of being bothered and desirous of solitude. But she also saw a man who no longer had the patience to be ignored.

"You refuse to see it because it is too simple. You need other people to tell you the answer to your *all-important questions*, so you don't have to take responsibility if life doesn't work out the way you want it to. Stepping up takes courage. Why should I make your life easier for you? Haven't you figured out that we are all the same? We are *energy*, that's all we are. All your distinctions between wise men, counsellors, priests? You think *they* have the answers? You know. You've *always* known. It is just *fear* that keeps you separate from yourself."

The speech was brief but during the delivery Charlotte's voice changed in register and volume, soaring, dipping, first a bellow and then a piercing whisper. The actors who were waiting backstage crept closer and squatted, resembling frogs and rabbits and other forest dwelling animals. Sarah was in favour of altering the script, so this exchange happened before the hermit, understanding of the king's dismay, gave him the answers he requested. In a way these words were more honest and what Charlotte said the truth: it's so simple. Act in accordance with what is before you at this very moment.

And then Sarah noticed Gwendolyn.

She was thumbing the script vigorously, her glasses anchored across the bridge of her nose. Her face did not radiate interest or acceptance, only impatience and anger. This was typical of a director, who desperately short of time, needed everyone to adhere to the script. The luxury of exploring character and alternate dialogue was not available and Sarah understood this as well. She intertwined her fingers and waited. She would not interfere.

"These are not your lines, Charlotte. Improvise during the dress and you'll be replaced."

"What did I say?" she asked in confusion.

She thought she had spoken the lines from the script, but clearly, she had not. She didn't mean to cause a scene, but the minute the king had looked at her something else had taken over and had spoken through her. She figured this was not the correct thing to say to Gwendolyn and instead of arguing she raised her hands in defeat.

"I'm sorry. I got confused. It won't happen again."

"It better not," Gwendolyn advised.

"Righty-o," Charlotte answered, her eyes never leaving Henry's face. She shook her body, like a dog emerging from the lake after a swim, stood on her mark and took note of every move Gwendolyn wanted her to make during the dress rehearsal. "Count on me," she said, giving a thumbs up.

Much to Gwendolyn's chagrin Mess offered another compliment.

"No offence to anyone, including me, but I think that if it wasn't for Charlotte, this show wouldn't be all that good. If she can't use her own words during the dress, okay, but I hope she uses whatever it was she put in her body because she looked like a tired out old man who was sick of dealing with idiots."

"Idiuts," Charlotte echoed with a smile. "It sounds so much better with a British accent."

"Ta, mate," Mess said, waving aside the tribute. "Because you can be whoever you choose to be without compromising who you really are, that helps us be better, and if that isn't magic I don't know what is."

Perfect stillness followed this remark. The children neither fussed nor moved nor raised a voice to argue and instead turned inwards, picking at the laces on their shoes, gazing at their fingers, or stealing a glance at Charlotte. Life returned in a series of momentary flashes: the distant noise of hammering and sawing, as Byron and his crew put the final touches on the scenery sets, the squeaking joints of a ladder, the hum of a fan, the gentle lifting and falling of the fabric covering the hole in the stage at the corner of the wings, the creaking of the floorboards the smell of sandwiches and chips, greasy and rich, drifting through the air as the doors of the ancient elevator creaked open and platters of food began to arrive.

Dinner was terribly late, but the children stirred as if woken from a brief nap, bleary eyed but expectant.

"I could not say it better," Sarah said, accepting a plate of food from Oliver. "The only way that meaning comes through is if you are totally honest in the character you have been assigned, or," she added, a light flashing across her eyes, "the character you choose to be in this moment of time."

From the Hilroy of Charlotte
Lisa Hansen

DAY: FRIDAY, SEPTEMBER 3
TIME: Late. Maybe 8:00 or 9:00 PM? Maybe later. Watch says 2:00 PM. Useless bloody thing.
NOTES: Tired, tired, tired. Rehearsal pending… oh boy!
LOCATION: Broom closet in theatre. Only place to update without interruption.

The final placement of players on stage, lighting modifications, set changes and swordplay interludes went by without a glitch until, for some reason known to something other than self, I veered off script and mouthed a few unholy words to the king. I have no recollection of what I said, but the other actors thought it was powerful. Henry says he can't remember what I said either. (He's lying. Henry forgets nothing.)

Here is the thing. My vision becomes cloudy when I step into the hermit robe and the wig and beard are placed upon me. I don't know if that means I have become the hermit or if I am undergoing some sort of physical changes my brain refuses to register.

And then, Hilroy, WHAM! All went dark, and I felt a piercing blow around my right cheek which hurt a hundred times more than the paper cuts I constantly get, and then, fast like the wind, I experienced the soothing touch of a warm cloth and a soft voice saying: "It's alright. I found some herbs in the forest, and later I will make a poultice with honey."

But then images and words passed and disappeared into the rafters. And no one noticed I had disappeared. What was that?!

I went and found Sarah in her office, resting on the old chesterfield, and told her what happened to me and asked her advice.

Sarah said I had an AURA, which happens frequently to actors who are forced to stand under hot stage lamps. These AURAS often trigger head-aches, but I didn't have a headache much to Sarah's relief and, more the mystery, the stage lamps were off.

And then it came to me.

It's not about AURAS. It's about FISSURES, which is something com-pletely unscientific that happens to those of us who journey inside and outside the Tower Room. I remember reading about them in Gus's journal. I will find the exact passage when I get back to Sarah's house tonight, but what he talked about was sometimes seeing people who were not in his studio through the lens of his camera (that's what the Tower Room was originally, a photography studio). He described them like they had stepped through a "rip in the universe," and it reminded him of sudden cracks in the mountains that workers opened with drilling and blasting when he was in the Rockies building a railroad on his first Tower Room trip.

A fissure. People and places who aren't there and me the only one who can see or hear them.

In conclusion, Hilroy, I will just have to stick to knowing what I don't know and rely on the universal for support. I suspect that I can now, in less than an hour, play the hermit with complete confidence and a bit of that hottie disdain which annoys Gwendolyn so much. Sarah said she liked the 'irritatingly obtuse' dimension I had added to the character right before Oliver filled up my plate with sandwiches and chips.

Side note: She couldn't quite remember what I said either.

I have no idea what hottie disdain or irritatingly obtuse mean but for once, I am too tired to care.

Chapter Thirty

It was late Friday. The cast and crew were tired and edgy but excited too. The first full rehearsal had been a disaster, of course, which both pleased and upset Sarah equally – it certainly hadn't surprised her. Except for Charlotte, that is.

Charlotte had proven something of a revelation as the hermit, though she'd gone off script in an inspired improvisation that had sent Gwendolyn around the bend. Sarah was a little worried about Charlotte. The girl needed some sleep, and was possibly dehydrated, but maybe it was more than that. She'd come to see Sarah in her office with a tale Sarah might have been written off as a flight of fancy coming from anyone else.

As for the rest of what had transpired – the counsellor robe mix-up was disaster number one. There were no dressers, and the actors had to fend for themselves. A hurried tussle exchanging robes had the second counsellor arrive, off point, and deliver his answer to the king's question while arranging the folds of his garment. A note was passed to Oliver who passed it to Arthur, putting him in charge of all costume changes. And then Meggie had to find secure places to hang the robes, which necessitated a hasty construction of a neat little rack in the tiny dressing rooms with the appropriate labels.

Because of the speed with which the production was launched, these details were not unexpected, and Sarah took them in her stride. She calmed Gwendolyn and all was well until the hermit's cottage was tardy arriving on stage because the joint of one wheel was jammed. The musical and swordplay interlude had to go on a bit longer than one wanted while an investigation was launched into the recalcitrant wheel. A piece of fabric was found lodged in the casing, and Meggie was chewed out by Gwendolyn.

It wasn't her fault, as all the children had too many roles to perform, and when not on stage as the counsellors the actors became stagehands, and a bit of the fake fox fell off one of the collars and caused a commotion because Mess screamed and kicked at it, thinking it was a rat that had crawled up from the hole in the wings left by the city crew.

"It's come from below," she bellowed, loud enough to raise the hair on the back of Ariel's neck.

"I told you," Ariel said succinctly, making sure that Gwendolyn was close enough to hear. "That hole should be closed off completely."

"It is," Oliver thundered. "Do you think I am a fool, girl?" Oliver, for reasons not known to many of the cast and crew, had a natural mistrust and fear of open holes no matter where they were placed, and had elected himself safety marshal.

"I'm sorry, I'm sorry, I'm sorry," Mess repeated, all in a rush. "Rodents make my spine turn to water."

Like a sudden summer storm, a sprinkling of laughter filled the auditorium.

"I want no one close to the safety cones, do you hear me?" Oliver stated clearly, his voice filling the theatre.

"They are children, mate," Arthur suggested. "Go easy."

"Don't care. They must follow instructions. Full stop."

A chorus or meek and apologetic voices called out in the affirmative. Ariel collected cloaks and hats and disappeared backstage to hang them on the correct hooks. Sarah consulted with Byron on how to fix the wheel so it would move properly on opening night, and Arthur collected the swords which the actors had not placed in the appropriate box in the wings.

"You alright, Gov?" Arthur asked, coming across Oliver who was pacing behind stage.

"Need a break," he answered, more to himself than to Arthur. He was distracted and aloof. As for Arthur, his body was already at the Spotted Fox, his favourite New Castle Brown in his hand.

As the children gathered their belongings to depart for the night, Charlotte retrieved her Hello Kitty backpack from the change room and returned to the stage. She wanted one souvenir of the set, a memento for her Toronto

314

dresser drawer of treasures. There wasn't much to choose from. The rocks and boulders were not real, the trees were painted, but they did lend a disturbing three-dimensional effect as the cleanup crew moved them, one by one off stage. What could she take that would be a significant reminder, but one that no one would notice? Byron was issuing orders and holding a can of paint in his hand, Meggie fluttered back and forth from the wings, picking up bits and pieces of costumes that had been abandoned and there was no internal indicator, that flash of 'this is it' to move her feet and ready her hands.

"I can take this for you and put it in the car if you want," Henry said, indicating her backpack. "I've already loaded up my stuff. Oliver would like to get going as soon as possible."

"No, it's okay," Charlotte told him, swinging the backpack across her shoulders. The pack felt unnaturally heavy and her back ached. Why couldn't she make up her mind, and what did it matter anyway? Wouldn't a program from opening (and closing) night be good enough?

"Do you have anything in the dressing room?"

"I can't remember," she answered, staring straight ahead. "I'm going to check in a minute, but I want to help clear the stage first." She put her hand against one of the remaining trees and was amazed at how real it felt. "Feel this, Henry," she said.

He rolled his eyes.

"No, honestly, it feels real, scratchy and cool."

"Byron is a genius," he repeated by rote, merely echoing the great man's assessment of himself. "Charlotte," he added, hesitantly, in a deferential tone he never used.

This got her attention.

"What?"

"You nailed the hermit. And you nailed me, too, as king. I thought I understood this fable on an intellectual level, but it went deeper tonight. I can't explain it."

Charlotte accepted the compliment but didn't feel she deserved special praise. All she had done was stick to the script, change the quality of her voice, and refuse to be bullied by the king. It was all very simple. All that was needed was an appreciation of the here and now and to hell with the future. She'd read this time and time again in Gus Frank's journal, and it was – unsurprisingly now that she thought about it – a sentiment that Leo had preached for as long as she could remember.

"It's pretty simple," she replied, starting to roll the tree towards the wings.

"Charlotte, I would like to speak with you," Gwendolyn called out from her front row seat. She had completed her list of jobs to be done before the performance, a roster that would take days to complete, not hours, and snapped her notebook shut.

"Ten minutes, please," Sarah called, appearing at stage left. "Jeremy, help Henry and Charlotte clear and then I'll shut down the lights. The car will be waiting in the alley. You, too, Gwendolyn," she said, spotting the older woman seated comfortably in her chair. "I have a meeting with some donors at the house in under an hour."

Gwendolyn scoffed but nodded her head, nonetheless.

"Go hurry this along, please, Jeremy," she said as the boy appeared beside her carrying a rubbish bag.

"Anything for the trash?" he asked.

"On the floor at my feet. Now get on with you, Jeremy, and tell Charlotte I would like a private word."

"Smashing job. I really thought she was an old man, didn't you?"

"Perhaps more than I believed you to be wounded."

"Was I that bad?" he asked brightly. "You know, we have all day tomorrow to practise and practise some more before the performance on Sunday."

"The first and *only* show, so it must be superb," Gwendolyn reminded him. "Now go."

There was one tree left on stage, and Charlotte and Henry appeared in tandem to remove it. Gwendolyn noticed that Charlotte had started to limp and wondered if she had failed to realize she was no longer an elderly hermit. A bid for attention, no doubt, as Jeremy took her place at one side of the tree (the facsimile pine could not weight more than a few pounds) and Charlotte, unencumbered, directed the removal.

Just as she picked up her scarf and wrapped it around her neck Gwendolyn spotted something grey trailing along behind Charlotte. This grey matter looked suspiciously like a snake that attached itself around Charlotte's middle and wrapped its other end around the base of the tree.

She rifled through her bag for her glasses, her usual neat and tidy purse a jumble now that she had less time to attend to minutia.

The entourage was moving outside Gwendolyn's range of vision once she located her distance glasses and put them on.

It wasn't a snake, but the hermit's belt which anchored Charlotte to the tree; a disaster waiting to happen, as the girl was now limping badly, unseen by both Henry and Jeremy who were tussling and pretending to be lumberjacks.

Why did children always think that life was a game? Gwendolyn had never believed that, even when she lingered briefly in that heady domain. Life was a series of mostly tiresome events to parse, press into shape, and dispense with. When a job needed to be done, it needed to be done properly, under the authority of a person who knew what was expected of them.

"Untie that belt," Gwendolyn shouted just as the procession edged closer to the wing and the pylons beyond, protecting the hole in the floor.

"It's easier this way," Henry said. "The trees are heavy. It's okay with Charlotte."

How could they be heavy? They were made from plywood or Bristol board or some other flimsy material. And where were the older boys whose job it was to see to this nonsense? And all the street people Oliver had corralled to help Byron? Gwendolyn was merely one person, she couldn't manage everything, could she? She felt her anger rise and stick in her throat.

"Now," she shouted, lifting her megaphone to her lips. Her voice, unusually tense, alerted the trio of elders, Sarah, Oliver, and Arthur, who appeared stage left, staring myopically into the distance. Ariel, carrying the king's crown, crowded in beside them.

"Stop screaming," Charlotte called out, bad tempered and curt. The crackling from the megaphone and the tension in Gwendolyn's voice made her dizzy. Lightheaded and giddy, she fell against the barricade, stumbled, and tried to get her balance. The backpack shifted and fell above her shoulders, pulling her towards the edge.

"Charlotte," Henry shouted. "Be careful."

"Shut-up," she stated, exasperated.

She turned, and her feet became tangled in the rope. She was suddenly hobbled, her knees buckling, her right hip bending to the side. Completely off balance she tripped against one of the pylons and fell on top of the purple brocade. Like frosting in a pastry tube, she shot down the hole and disappeared.

"*Charlotte!*" Gwendolyn's chest clenched. "Help. Someone quick…"

The spruce came next, skidding towards the hole with Henry and Jeremy holding on and trying to pull it back. Henry, hanging on to the underside of the tree, could not get free.

"Henry!"

For a moment he dangled above the gaping hole until the tree snapped in two and he was gone.

"Henry… Charlotte… someone help, someone help them!"

There was a naked panicked quality to Gwendolyn's voice that was immediately unsettling.

"Jeremy," Oliver shouted. "Stand back."

Ariel, sprinting across the stage, grabbed Jeremy around the waist just as he was prepared to shimmy down the hole after Henry.

"I'll get them, Grandfather," he shouted, panicked. "Let me go," he insisted, and wriggled free of Ariel's grip, pushing her hard so she fell over backwards.

As Arthur careened across the stage, Jeremy levered the base of the tree upwards until there was enough room for him to ease over the edge and swung around beneath it. The tree shifted back precariously, and Arthur dropped to his chest sliding forward, his arm outstretched.

"Dammit, Jeremy," he called. "Stay there."

But Jeremy wasn't listening. He heard the murmur of voices beneath him, Henry's steady drone and Charlotte's answer. They were alive but confused and disoriented. They spoke in a language that Jeremy didn't quite comprehend or else the words had become distorted because of an echoing effect.

"They're okay," he called back. "I'm going down."

Arthur cursed under his breath, got to his knees, and grabbed at the remains of the tree to keep it from toppling down on the children below. By then Oliver was there too, his eyes wild with equal parts anger and terror. He looked over the edge and shuddered, grabbing the prop tree and helping Arthur pull it clear of the hole.

He was about to say something when Arthur cut him off.

"I wouldn't," he said, "some of them rungs are older than you. Sarah said the workers were using an extension ladder. I wonder if they took it with them."

"I don't know," he said. "You stay here, I'm going to see what I can find and get some bloody light on this hole."

Jeremy, meanwhile, had found the first iron rung – it felt mushier than it ought to, like a loose tooth – and was climbing down and deliberately *not* looking back up at his grandfather. He felt bad for disobeying everyone, but he couldn't stay, not while his friends were in danger.

"Hallooo," he shouted, and heard an uncertain *hallooo* echoed back at him from below.

"I'm coming," he called, and then climbed into the darkness.

Chapter Thirty-One

Months before, when Henry was dumped on the floor of a summer house, out of breath and disoriented, he had felt nothing but a curious blankness when he first opened his eyes. The same disassociation occurred in the present when the breath left his body and he found himself in an all-encompassing darkness that was laden with a pungent, rusty odour. His left hand was wedged beneath his back, and when he was able to roll to his side and free it a sharp pain radiated upwards to his shoulder. He flexed his fingers and felt them all move, one at a time. The pain was liquid and hot, and his eyes began to tear. His eidetic memory kicked in and gave him a bit of welcome guidance: If you feel pain, it is most likely a sprain. If you feel numbness or tingling in the immediate aftermath it is most likely a fracture. Another indicator, Henry's overactive brain informed him was the 'sound' the body made when the injury occurred but try as he might he could remember no loud crackling or popping, just the muted sound of soft moveable tissue hitting hard immovable floor. Another saving grace was the brocaded fabric and the tarp that had been left by the workers on the floor, not much in the way of softening but something.

He was alive, stunned, sore, but still functioning.

At least he could now breathe, shallow but no longer gasping. He moved his hand inside his pocket, found his Bricanyl and inhaled the medicine as best he could.

"Jackson?"

A voice whispered in the darkness and caused the hair on Henry's body to stand to attention.

And then a series of incompressible syllables followed this inquiry, spoken in a language Henry, to his amazement, was not only able to understand but able to speak as well.

The question: Are you here? Find my backpack.

Henry's answer: I am. My name is not Jackson. I have the backpack.

"Henry?" a frightened voice uttered. This voice was bearing down on him from above, and he could just make out a shadowy figure clinging to the side of the hole, a giant spider come to devour him.

"Don't bite me," he cried.

"It's me, mate. Jeremy. There are metal steps on the sides. We'll be able to get out. But we need a flashlight."

In response an explosion of sound in an unrecognizable language.

"What is that?" Jeremy asked, frightened. The voice sounded like the gurgling of a goblin and Jeremy's body shrank closer to Henry's for comfort.

Henry wanted to say it was Lily because he knew he recognized both the voice and the person, but the reasonable no-nonsense portion of his brain informed him immediately that this was complete and utter bosh, brought on by his fear of confined, dark, and odious smelling underground places. "It's Charlotte," he told Jeremy. "I can hear her, but I can't see her. She has supplies in the backpack. A mini flashlight," he said, in sudden inspiration. "That's what she said. Get the flashlight."

Jeremy peered at Henry through the gloom. "I think she might be speaking in Welsh. Brythonic or Goidelic, one of the insular Celtic languages. I didn't know Charlotte knew this dialect."

"It's not Welsh." Henry was certain of that. He also knew it was a made-up language known only to two young children. He was one of those children and he and Charlotte must have invented this once when they were playing in the tree house in her backyard.

Jeremy began to explore the hole, cautiously, his hands out in front should he stumble and fall. "Grandfather speaks one of the dialects. He's good at languages. Henry is getting the flashlight Charlotte. We'll find you in less than a minute. I promise. *Rwy'n Addo*," he added in a tone or reassurance.

"Who is Ryan?" Charlotte asked in her normal speaking voice. "There are two containers of applesauce in the backpack that I took out of the fridge this morning. We need sugar. And Gatorade for energy but I don't have any Gatorade."

"My applesauce?" Jeremy paused and wondered if the lump he could just make out, spread across the floor against the furthest wall, was Charlotte. "I wondered what became of that," he blabbered, extremely nervous. "I always start the day with applesauce, and I said to Grandfather..."

"I've got it," Henry said, breaking into Jeremy's monologue. The flashlight was only slightly larger than the AA batteries it held. He pressed the button at the base, and it sent out intermittent beams of yellow light. Charlotte was illuminated during one of bursts, pressed against the corner, her hands folded over her chest. "Three dashes, three dots, three dashes. Someone will find us." And then she added as an afterthought: "My head hurts."

Before Henry could start with the requested dots and dashes, as if in peremptory response to his distress call, a spotlight was directed to the mouth of the hole above. It could not be directed straight down to where they were, but the area was at least now dimly lit if somewhat indirectly.

"Are you sure that's not Welsh?" Jeremy whispered for Charlotte had once again lapsed into the foreign dialect.

"Did you hit your head? Can you move? Perhaps you shouldn't try to move." Henry answered in kind and was now seated alongside Charlotte. He pressed her hand, and it was cold to the touch.

He tried to remove his sweater but was stopped by the pain in his shoulder. He bent his neck, reached his good arm around to his back, and shrugged himself free of the garment, laying it across Charlotte and rubbing her hands.

Charlotte said in a calm and happy voice: "Peachy. We've always looked after one another. Now, before, and after forever."

"What?" Henry removed his hand and studied Charlotte's face while Jeremy held the flashlight from above. There was a thin trickle of blood running from her right eye down her cheek and he reached inside the backpack, laying out on the floor all the first aid equipment that Charlotte carried with her daily. She had a disaster-prone consciousness – bad things always happened to *other* people, and she must have the means to assist. She was also a pack rat. Henry now understood that preparing for a cataclysmic event was not the worst way to live. Since everyone within his own personal sphere, parents, grandparents, and nanny had always feared for Henry's safety, and treated him like he was far too delicate to engage in day-to-day activities, he had developed the stoic attitude of the chronic watcher even after his friendship with Charlotte. He did not want to be blamed for encouraging the injuries or kidnappings that his close circle of hysterics had feared and the break away from this behaviour, which began in Camp Highland and escalated in London had felt liberating and heady. But now that he was a participant in the more nitty, gritty messiness of life, he felt woefully inadequate.

He awkwardly bathed Charlotte's face with the alcohol wipes she had swiped from the doctor's office and spread a layer of sweet-smelling gooey substance from a plastic vial marked: "Antibacterial cleanser."

"That smells like honey," Jeremy noted.

Henry tasted his finger. "It is," he said, clearly mystified.

Charlotte smiled, enigmatically.

"I can get back up, using those rungs, and bring down some sort of stretcher," Jeremy suggested. "Then we can hoist her up. We must support her neck in case of a spinal injury."

"My head hurts a little, but it's not bad," Charlotte replied with a giddy smile. "I'm tired though. Hardly slept since arriving in London."

"You must stay awake in case it's a concussion. Follow my finger," he advised, beaming the flashlight in Charlotte's face, and directing her gaze to the right and left." He nodded his head encouragingly. "That's good, Charlotte. Your eyes are tracking. Now keep talking. Talk to Henry while I try to get help. I need to alert everyone that we are alive. They can't come down here. They are all too old. It's dangerous." Oliver's face swam before Jeremy, and he felt an urgency to get to surface and reassure his grandfather.

"Hank," Charlotte murmured drowsily.

"Stop calling me Hank," Henry said, trying for an offhand affection. He failed miserably. Why was she referring to him as Hank and Jackson, and a minute ago as Harold and Dorothy.

Dorothy?

"Are you sure she's not concussed?" he asked Jeremy after consulting with his eidetic memory for symptoms of head trauma. His eidetic memory wasn't cooperating the way it had in the past. It was becoming increasingly difficult to access the necessary information and the lack of blank spaces. In this hole in the ground, a space where he could project the data he found and skim through it quickly was non-existent. The flashlight was a bonus, to be sure, but the radiance created an aura around Charlotte, leaving the rest of the hole in shadow. There was a steady drip of water, and Henry realized he was counting the seconds between the drips. The count was eight and if he didn't concentrate on something else quickly, the noise would inch its way under his skin and render him useless as a consultant and helpmate.

"I'm not sure of anything," Jeremy replied.

"Can we strap her onto one of those planks?" he asked Jeremy. "If you get a pulley system going from above, she can be hoisted up once we secure her."

"We'll need rope and lots of blankets. Can I leave you alone? Will you be alright?"

"I'm fine," Henry lied. All his phobias were waking up, yawning, and sniffing the air. His fear of confined spaces, rats, darkness, spiders, rancid smells, bone-chilling damp. If Charlotte were not so fragile, her beatific grin unnerving, she would bully him, pressure him, punch him, separately or all at the same time, to get his defensive juices flowing. Charlotte never minded putting herself in front of Henry's wrath if it got him moving and focused on his strengths as opposed to his weakness.

'You have two legs, don't you, Henry?' she'd once asked when he stalled climbing the rock wall at Mountain Equipment Coop. *'Yes,'* he'd whispered, petrified. *'Then use them or I will step on your hand.'*

And when they were lost in the ravine, late at night, breaking all rules of curfew and promises to never venture that far afield after dark, Charlotte – while an expert at most spy craft except for the ability to orient herself in space, had said: *'If you want to curl up and play dead that's fine with me. But the coywolf will get you for sure. A tasty little morsel like you? Is that him I hear coming?'*

These remarks had been cruel and cutting, totally lacking in warmth and understanding. But they had not been meant to coddle, they had been meant to propel, to push Henry to try new and sometimes dangerous things and to survive. And survive he did, because fear was a temporary condition if a person simply accepted its presence and asked it to make room for positive action.

"You are going to be fine. Do you hear me?" Henry said, his voice clear and resonant.

"Righty-o, Gaffer," Charlotte replied grinning, her eyelids drifting lower.

"This is the best plank I can find," Jeremy said, returning to Henry's side with the flashlight. "Do not try and move her yourself."

"I won't," Henry promised. He gazed at the plank. It was streaked with mud and clay and Henry could already feel the splinters he would get if he touched the board.

"We can spend the night in the cave and venture out in the morning," Charlotte proclaimed, her eyelids springing open. "What do you say?"

"I'd better get going," Jeremy said worriedly, pressing Henry's shoulders. "They are starting to scream up there."

"Righty-o," Charlotte whispered.

"Keep her talking. Even if it is nonsense."

"I promise."

Henry took the flashlight and aimed the beam behind him and upwards so Jeremy could begin his climb. He felt his stomach sink as Jeremy's right foot disappeared and somewhere high above, muffled but frantic came the repetition of his name, Jeremy's, Charlotte's.

"I'm here," Henry said, turning back to the patient and bending close to her face. The pain in his shoulder was subsiding but he still felt tears slip down his cheeks.

"It won't be long now. We'll be out of here soon."

"Lie low," Charlotte whispered, grabbing Henry's hand. "Do not let them see you coming."

"Who?" Henry asked, massaging her hand.

Charlotte did not reply to the question and said instead: "Ta, mate. You're always saving my life."

Chapter Thirty-Two

"The emergency services have been called, yes, of course, Jeremy, but we can't wait," Oliver explained. "There are blankets from the office. I'm going down."

"I have fabric," Meggie said, hurrying forward, her arms full of brightly coloured cotton strips. "I ripped it all so that they can be used as ties."

"Oliver, what can I do?" Sarah asked, standing dead still in the centre of the stage. Her face was pale, her eyes frightened. Oliver had never seen Sarah scared, believing that she had no use for this emotion. He was wrong. He also knew that he was as panicked as she was, but he did not want her to see that.

"Nothing, my dear. I want you to sit down. We have this in hand."

"Are they badly hurt?" she asked Jeremy, her voice trembling. Sarah suddenly looked all her years, her trembling illustrating a fragility that few had ever seen.

"No, no, not at all," Jeremy replied, leading her to a chair. "Charlotte might have hit her head and Henry has hurt his shoulder, but they are okay, and he is keeping her talking."

Sarah wouldn't let go of his hand and he had to pry her fingers loose and pat her hand assuredly, just the way Oliver always did when Jeremy feared things he could not see.

"Where are those paramedics?" Gwendolyn shouted, storming down the aisle. "I've called three times and demanded to talk to a superior and I was told to calm down and stop being rude."

"They can take up to thirty minutes if it is a busy night," Ariel said, carrying a portable phone in her hand. "I'm calling every two minutes. Mother, you are not to worry. We have this in hand. I promise."

"Tomorrow, we launch two suits, one against the city for negligence on site and the other against the city for failure to comply," Gwendolyn stated clearly, the only elder who was truly in charge.

"Let her talk," Oliver whispered, counselling Jeremy to keep his mouth shut. "Perhaps if you scan the street once again, Gwendolyn?" he suggested, wanting her out of the way. Her demands for immediate attention, her scathing remarks on the efficiency of public employees was starting to grate on him. What she said next surprised him.

"I'm going down. Oliver, you are to stay above and marshal the troops. Clearly you would be useless below. Your hands are trembling, and your face is white with shock."

"I'll come with you," Arthur volunteered.

"And me," Ariel said.

"You stay here and deal with the paramedics, Ariel. And Arthur, you are to assist with Sarah. Make her tea with lots of sugar and make sure she is warm. And now, please get out of my way," she said, pushing him aside. "You climbed up, Jeremy?"

"Yes, but it's slippery. Lots of the rungs are loose. And it's dark." He had a terrible feeling he knew what was coming because of the look of determination in Mrs. MacFarlane-Fenton's eyes, the same look she'd had when she'd said to him: *'Enough of this Mrs. MacFarlane-Fenton routine, Jeremy. Manners are one thing, but I've given you permission twice to call me Gwendolyn. Do I have to smack you on the side of your head?'*

"Sarah," Gwendolyn said firmly, and with a kindness in her voice that no one had heard to date: "I'm going to take care of this. Once I am below, I will sort this all out. I'm belligerent and arrogant and impossible, as you have said many times, and more than up to the task." She smiled, and Sarah nodded her head. "Drink your tea like a good girl, and I will be back with the children before you know it."

"You will do no such thing," Oliver said. "You might fall."

"Oliver, look at me," Gwendolyn insisted. "Do you think I would let that happen? Charlotte means to best me. I've known it my entire life. Do you think for one second, I am going to let her leave before me?"

"Gwendolyn, I don't understand," Oliver said as he watched her grab the material from Meggie and toss it down the hole.

"Where are those blankets?"

"Here," Byron said, carrying several grey woollen blankets he had found backstage.

Gwendolyn gathered the blankets in her arms and let them drop through the hole.

"Gwendolyn," Oliver protested, trying to take her arm. "You are in shock. I will not allow you to do this."

"Stand aside," she said, removing a can of pepper spray from her pocket. She had transferred this object from her purse to the pocket of her pantaloons when she went out on the street to wait for the emergency workers. She trusted no one and had read of too many old women attacked on the street as they tried to wend their way home, pushing their shopping trolleys before them. That Gwendolyn rarely walked on any city street and was driven everywhere was immaterial. She hadn't been without the pepper spray for thirty years and didn't even know if it would work anymore, although she did once experiment with a few blasts on a pink poinsettia she had received, in honour of the festive season, from the management office at her condominium. The leaves on the poinsettia shrivelled but the plant survived, diminished in grandeur, and had met its death on the balcony where it was placed, in the snow, so Gwendolyn could admire it from afar.

"If I can't stop you, please, pay attention. The rungs are loose."

"Don't pull on them," Jeremy added. "Step lightly and be as quick as you can. We'll beam the flashlight, and there are some handholds on the side should you get in trouble."

"I'll be fine," Gwendolyn promised, easing herself over the opening. "And don't just stand there looking stupid, call the emergency services again."

Below ground, Henry was struggling to continue a conversation with Charlotte. The various names which she used to refer to him were disorienting, as was the hermit beard and wig that shrouded her face. Her garment was ripped and her ankles, those bony protuberances that so annoyed Gwendolyn, were sad reminders of the fragility of this small body lying defenseless and injured. If anything, Charlotte now resembled more an ancient wanderer than a young girl, a sexless primordial being who had seen everything the world had to offer and was fully immune to its vicissitudes and challenges.

"Righty-o," she murmured, fast followed by: "Idiut." The British pronunciation had slipped, but Henry felt the sting of the insult nonetheless, because he did not understand her ramblings.

"We've always been here," she stated in a moment of surprising lucidity. "Together."

"Of course," he agreed, taking her hand and pressing her fingers. Human contact, touching, hugging, kissing, all existed in some nether region, a roped off zone where Henry rarely ventured. But now it was imperative that he show Charlotte he cared. "If what you say is true, I'm not going to be able to make it without you. If we have always been together then you can't leave me in this hole while you go and cause trouble elsewhere. You are the constant everything, good and bad, so you're going to have to stay or take me with you. Do you understand?"

Henry could not believe he was saying these words. But he continued, hoping that previously unexpressed feelings, from a person who up until the present moment barely felt anything, would shock Charlotte into a wakeful and avid consciousness, giving her ammunition for years to come.

"Who am I without your constantly irritating presence? Who do I think about before I go to sleep, relieved to finally be alone and peaceful? Whose face assaults me the moment I open my eyes, and what is my first thought? It is this – I wonder what trouble Charlotte will get me into today. Do you understand how boring and utterly meaningless my life would be without you?"

But Charlotte was elsewhere in her mind, muttering in some foreign language to which Henry instantly, and without conscious thought, replied. She was his sister, and they were running a scam on the Americans who were currently in charge of Fort George.

"What?" he asked aloud. How could he remember so clearly something that had never happened? And yet he knew they had just silently rowed across the Niagara River and were pilfering supplies from the sleeping American soldiers. She had a pair of boots, a blanket and a knife, and he held a can of cooking oil and a belt. They were creeping back towards their boat, her silent and cunning, him a bit clumsy and unfailingly good-natured.

Who were these people?

This was followed in rapid succession by a nightmarish witnessing to a facial surgery in long-ago Buffalo, an explosion in a mountain where an old man was screaming and running, carrying a young Chinese girl with Henry fast in pursuit. There were other images, a bakery in the Middle East, a jungle in the Amazon… and in each one, there was Henry, father, son, husband, mother, *compadre,* and Charlotte, grandmother, priest, vagabond, friend.

His head hurt terribly, and he realized with a start of cloudy awareness, that he, too, had landed with more stress to his cranium then was good for the generalized safe and reliable regulation of brain tissue. Either that or the force of the unknown being who lay before him was imparting some strange hypnotic message that his eidetic memory was warring with by reciting:

"What are you telling me, Charlotte?" he asked, leaning close to her face. "It's me, Henry. Your friend."

"Son, listen to me. If you don't cover the dough with a damp cloth, you might as well toss it in the trash. Haven't I told you this time and time again?" A brusque voice issued from the hermit's lips.

"I forgot," he said honestly.

In the last few minutes Charlotte had referred to him as son, daughter, father, brother, sister, and in a confusing sequence (which first seemed to take place in Ancient Rome) husband, and (next in the Highlands of Scotland) wife.

Henry felt a whoosh of air and the thud of a delivery arriving down the hole. He prayed that it would not be another person who he would have to take care of. He shined the flashlight behind him and saw a mess of blankets and scraps of fabric and briefly wondered if he and Charlotte were meant to spend the night in this hole. He stood up, and shuffled towards the offerings, plucking a tattered grey blanket from the heap and using it to cover Charlotte. His right shoulder protested every movement he made but at least his arm was not dangling, useless.

"Cozy," the hermit muttered, and Henry dearly wished he could remove the beard from her face. But when he tried, she brushed his hand away. "Remember the paper airplanes?" she asked next in her own voice.

And thankfully, Henry did. Charlotte's attempt at communication as the Daimler, with Leo at the wheel, drove sedately down the street. For weeks, whenever Lena took him for a walk (like a docile dog) these paper airplanes arrived at his feet, and he caught a glimpse of a girl, tussled black hair and fiery eyes gazing at him in recognition before the Daimler passed him and turned right at the corner. "I wanted you to notice me."

Even though Charlotte was feeling lightheaded and dizzy she knew that Henry was in trouble. She always knew when he was in trouble because his eyes became rigidly fixed, and he started to breathe through his mouth in a loud adenoidal way. Her reaction was to displace his fear by bullying him into moving or distracting him with stories, some true, some invented. The story idea felt right because her body had no interest in moving.

Stories flew through her head in a rapid, disjointed way – snippets from Gus Frank's journal, her own tireless scribbles in her Hilroy, reminiscences from Leo regarding Dilys Frank who had left Leo her house and the legacy of the Tower Room. She travelled, courtesy of her World Books, through foreign countries and long-ago historical times, and felt her body swell and shrink with every transposition. Charlotte's power of invention was one of her strongest traits and it did not desert her.

Therefore, without any conscious intention, this time below ground simply became an interlude, rather like the choreographed swordplay, allowing the set to change as the king journeyed from his palace to the forest. It was right and proper that she was called upon to be the wise fool, to enliven the audience and distract them from whatever problems existed in their own lives. Made-up languages, real languages, and curious dialects sprang from her lips, and she didn't know if she was a character from one of Gus Frank's journals or an actor of her own making, scripts she would write when sleep was elusive. What she spoke aloud was a fraction of what poured through her head, but she sensed that Henry's fear had been replaced with utter confusion.

"Crackerjack," Charlotte said as Henry tucked the blanket beneath her body.

Henry was struggling with the concept that no matter how hard he tried he would never be free of Charlotte in this lifetime. But more overwhelming, it seemed he had never been free of her through all eternity. But worse was the overwhelming desire to never be free of her at all. Her irritating, disruptive, cloying presence was all he longed for, and he knew he was not capable of putting any of these feelings into words.

His eidetic memory, his staunch companion through the vicissitudes of his life, was powerless to help him when it came to emotional uncertainties. Also, unfortunate but true, his memory had not imprinted enough articles on concussions to allow him to make a safe assessment of Charlotte's condition. Of course, she could say whatever she wanted and make up a whopper, she was famous for doing this when she stood on her own two feet, fists belligerently placed on her hips before saying: *'Now listen to me, Henry.'*

But this was different. How could he answer her in all these languages he did not know? Or had he just parroted the sounds she made and returned them to her, like a weird echo that caused his voice to change in tone and timbre?

The cave became more claustrophobic with the passing of each minute, the walls pressed in on him, the air became dense with the smell of oil and refuse, and his body itched and ached simultaneously. An hour of scrubbing under a hot shower would not remove the layer of grime that attached itself to his skin, and the floor was wet, the damp seeping through his pants and chilling his flesh.

Charlotte, or the hermit, or whoever this was laying on the floor before him was a powerful presence, no matter what her situation, but she was also fragile and temporal. Not the all-powerful Thor or Hera of his imagination, but a flesh and blood child, just like himself, vulnerable to all things, even death.

"You are my best friend," Henry told her. His voice cracked, and he started to cry.

"Smashing," she answered, winking.

"Someone's coming," Henry said, lifting his head. He could hear voices, Gwendolyn's predominant. Surely she wasn't descending into this darkness? Gwendolyn would never actively help anyone. She was much better at giving orders.

"My nemesis," Charlotte whispered. "We must brace ourselves to face the enemy." She closed her eyes and appeared to doze, her almond shaped eyelids resembling a cat, a cat who needed to conserve energy.

Gwendolyn's hands were scratched and bleeding, but she was supercharged with energy and barely felt the discomfort. Her Nikes had not let her down and rested, only briefly, on each wobbling rung. She felt as light as a cotton ball, and acknowledged that 'something' unknown was taking the weight of her body, but she put it down to the burst of adrenaline, the white-hot flame of fear, that displaced the ounces and pounds of her being and willed the rungs to hold her weight or else they would feel the complete wrath of her displeasure.

She knelt before Henry and placed her hand on his head. "Look at me," she ordered, but her voice was kind. "Are you alright? No broken bones, no shattered sternum?"

"A bit bruised but okay," he answered, noting an intensity in Gwendolyn's gaze that gave him strength. "Charlotte needs help. Please help her."

"That is why I am here, Henry."

"She stopped talking a moment ago and, I can't rouse her." He crawled over to Charlotte and tugged at her arm. "Speak to me," he begged, but she slept on, a peaceful expression on her face.

"Move aside," Gwendolyn commanded and knelt at Charlotte's side. She took her pulse, a procedure she knew very well since she was always practising on herself. "Tacky," she said aloud. "Weak but steady."

"Charlotte," she stated imperiously, poking the quilt in the region of Charlotte's chest. She shook her shoulders and tried to pry open her eyes. "Now you listen to me. You are not going to win this one."

Henry started to cry, soft whimpers like an animal in distress.

"Stop that at once, Henry. The child needs encouragement, not a defeatist attitude. Get over here and rub her feet. I will do her hands."

Henry obeyed, his tears now flowing silently so as not to disturb Gwendolyn.

"You are needed here, Charlotte. You are my responsibility, and I have never shirked from duty." Gwendolyn pressed one of Charlotte's hands and interlaced her fingers with the hermit.

Charlotte dreamed on, her bearded face calm in repose.

"I see right through that silly beard and wig," Gwendolyn said, sitting cross-legged on the floor. Later, she would reflect that she barely felt her body as she contorted it into positions she had not used for decades. She felt young, invincible, and all-powerful. She had enough energy to return

Charlotte to perfect health. "You've always been in disguise, but I know who you are. You are not escaping, because I will continue to say this until you open your eyes. You did this. You did all of it. I wouldn't be here if it wasn't for you. You were sent to annoy me and harass me…"

"Gwendolyn," Henry said, his anger finally overcoming his distress. "This isn't helping. Hang on for a few minutes, Charlotte. The emergency crew has arrived. They are here."

Bright light radiated down the shaft and new voices were heard giving command.

Gwendolyn ignored it all. She had a purpose and would not be deflected from it. "That's what I meant to say when I called out to you, when the dress was finished but you wouldn't come over." Her voice dropped to a whisper. "Why? Were you afraid I had only words of criticism? Or did you think it was your job alone to clear the stage? Don't you understand there's something I forgot to tell you?"

Henry lifted his head and stared blindly at his friend. Gwendolyn was almost on top of her, and it was difficult to see where one ended and the other began.

"You bested me as a child and stole the brooch for Charlie, but if you hadn't done that, where would I be? You will not best me now. You can't save someone and then just nod your head in understanding and disappear over the horizon. If you go, I will have to go, too, and I am not ready. There is far too much to do, and I have wasted almost an entire lifetime."

"The only place anyone is going is up and out of here," one of the paramedics said, dragging a plank across the floor.

"She's unresponsive," Henry reported, clutching a uniformed arm. "But only in the last minute. She was talking before that."

"Step aside, Madam," the second paramedic insisted, and when Gwendolyn refused to move, he forced his way between her and Charlotte.

"Gentler, my good man," Gwendolyn said, criticizing both the technique and the way she had been brushed aside. "This is a child, not an oil drum."

She watched, lips pressed tight, as Charlotte was carefully lifted and placed on the board, her head immobilized between two attached cushions. Once the third strap was secure, the medics carefully lifted the board.

Gwendolyn, erect and quiet, her hands joined in front of her body, stepped aside to let the paramedics carry the plank to the base of the hole. A sturdy ladder was now in place and the business of hoisting Charlotte to safety was difficult but not impossible.

"One moment, if you please," she said softly.

She leaned close and touched Charlotte's cheek with fingers she had wiped clean on her handkerchief. Her beret was askew, her pantaloons ripped, but she looked and acted every inch the great lady she had always been.

"Charlotte, thank you. Once you recover, which you will, I will say thank you again. You have witnesses."

"Whatever you are thanking her for can wait, Madam."

A shadow of a smile crossed Charlotte's face. As the paramedics readied the board into position and began their careful ascent Charlotte's eyes snapped open and regarded Gwendolyn with a penetrating clarity.

In a voice determined to take command of the room, she stated clearly and without hesitation:

"What took you so long?"

Chapter Thirty-Three

Charlotte fully regained consciousness in the ambulance. She started talking, and no one could stop her.

"I am one of the principal players in *The Three Questions* and should not have been removing trees from the stage, but I had to dig in and help because that's what a good person does. Am I right?"

"Trees?" a paramedic inquired, monitoring Charlotte's blood pressure.

"Birch mostly but fir trees, too. All manufactured within twenty-four hours and honestly, if you touch them, they feel real. Look. I even have a splinter," she said proudly waving her hand in the air. "But it's no great mystery. I tripped over my belt, lost my balance, and fell. I was briefly disoriented, but the universal protected me and now I am fine."

"Take a deep breath," the paramedic ordered seeing a spike on the monitor. "Try not to talk."

"You have no idea how much I have left to do. Time is short." After this pronouncement Charlotte closed her eyes and dosed.

"Is she mental?" the paramedic asked, lifting his eyes to the heavens. Then he watched as the sleeping Charlotte grinned. *Almost like a demon,* he thought, but wisely kept the remark to himself.

An orderly who helped wheel the stretcher into the hospital became flustered when he saw Charlotte's face.

"What is this?" he said pointing to the hermit's beard and bushy grey eyebrows. "Is this a lad or an ancient?"

"I am in costume, my good man," Charlotte replied, her eyes snapping open, her voice and tone reflecting too much time spent with Gwendolyn. "I need food," she added. "Anything will do, but perhaps a bag of Skittles to start?"

The orderly shook his head – and then, feeling pity for the beseeching look in the child/elder's eye, hurried off to find a vending machine.

No one could find anything wrong with Charlotte. Her vision was clear, she was not slurring her words. There were bumps and bruises, which was expected, but nothing that required stitches or compression bandages. The hospital staff, enamoured instantly by Charlotte's *stiff upper lip*, coddled her with a tenderness rarely seen in the professionals who were overburdened. They loved the way Charlotte spoke with her flat Canadian accent and how she giggled when she was x-rayed, palpitated, and inspected. In fact, everyone liked her so much that she managed to sell fifteen more tickets to the staff within three hours of arriving at the hospital and, according to Sarah, who alternated between keeping watch on Charlotte and talking non-stop on Ariel's cellular phone, the production would move ahead as planned. Either with Charlotte playing the hermit, or the role taken by her understudy. Sarah had called in favours from some of her more prestigious past performers, and the evening would be nicely filled out with swordplay, Shakespearean monologues, and an old-style music hall tap dance and magic show.

"It will be standing room only now," she announced, making the calculation quickly in her head.

Gwendolyn had called in a favour, too, from a neurologist she had known many decades ago, who owed her and was not altogether happy when she called him at home past midnight and demanded that he examine the brain scans that had been done on Charlotte (that were causing a bit of consternation from the young intern).

The scene took place in Charlotte's hospital room, with Gwendolyn in attendance.

"What day is it?" the intern asked Charlotte.

"What time is it?" Charlotte countered.

Flustered, the intern looked at his watch. "Eleven fifteen."

"Then it is still Friday, September third, 1999. In forty-five, or maybe forty-four minutes it will be tomorrow." She smiled serenely, pleased with her answer. "And then it will be Saturday."

There was more perusing of the film images, and a gentle exploration of Charlotte's skull which she said tickled. "Either brush my hair or remove your fingers, asap," she stated clearly.

"Nausea?" he asked.

"I don't see a nose, do you?"

"Very humorous," he said without cracking a smile. "Can you tell me what city you are in?"

"At the moment, that would be London, England. But moments change rather rapidly if you catch my drift as do places. I was in a hole in the Motley Theatre, and now I am in bed at a hospital. I liked the ambulance," she added. "I wouldn't mind another ride."

"She doesn't seem to have a concussion. There is no sign of hematomas or contusions in the brain," the intern assured Gwendolyn in the hallway. He was flicking through the films in his hand in the manner of one playing with a cartoon flip book.

"What is it?" Gwendolyn demanded.

He met her stare and stated matter-of-factly. "A small section of her brain is animated. And pulsing, I would say. Tiny inhalations and exhalations. You understand this is impossible with a static image but nevertheless."

"And?"

He shrugged his shoulders.

Gwendolyn got busy on the phone, and an hour later she was none the wiser.

"Charlotte is in tip-top shape," Dr. Stuart Bramwell, the neurologist, confirmed. "The tests show no abnormalities, no bleeding or injuries." Without hesitation, Gwendolyn had paid out of pocket for an MRI, a magnetoencephalographic image, and an electroencephalogram – all which Charlotte had enjoyed immensely, according to the various technicians. She had promised to lie as still as a corpse and told the attendants she "had a lot of experience doing just that."

"No damage?"

"None that I can see."

"Then I can report such to her grandfather?"

"You may," he said and then paused as he studied the films. "And yet, I must say, I've never seen anything quite like this before." He pointed to a mass of grey, black, and white brain matter full of shadows, totally meaningless to Gwendolyn. The neurologist seemed nervous which was not to the great lady's liking.

"Explain," she said.

"It's the right side," he said. "This small area, right here," he continued, pointing to a section of Charlotte's scan. "It's…"

"What?" Gwendolyn demanded. "Don't prevaricate, Stuart. Tell me what it is." She feared a brain tumour, a malignant growth.

"It's scientifically unsound and open to interpretation but, well, it's almost like it's pulsing," he finally admitted. "On this printout there is what looks like a motion blur, while all around it is crisply in focus. The thing is, I was watching the scan as it happened, and I'll be damned if it didn't seem to twitch. The follow-up scan looks perfectly normal. Now I was admittedly very tired and perhaps my eyes were playing tricks on me, but that wouldn't explain this first image. Furthermore—"

"Don't be absurd," Gwendolyn stated. "As you say the second image looks perfectly normal."

"True enough, but—"

"What is that section of the brain? What does it do?"

Dr. Bramwell was silent. Gwendolyn tapped her foot impatiently and repeated her question.

"I cannot say with absolute certainty. Speculation mostly, although there has been an uptake in research and some intriguing preliminary findings."

"You're babbling, Stuart. Get on with it. I should be at the child's bedside."

"The child is not in bed, as you well know." Bramwell turned away from the films and moved to the window, a still form against the black night sky. "Since Charlotte must stay awake, she has been making the most of her time. She's at the nursing station selling tickets to some production she is starring in. I'm not altogether sure that's a good idea," he continued and then shrugged. "But I will be in the audience so I can keep an eye on her."

"She sold you a ticket?" Gwendolyn's eyebrows lifted high.

"Four. I'll bring my grandchildren."

"Get on with it, Stuart. I don't have all night. I must call Charlotte's grandfather."

"I've already spoken with him and assured him that Charlotte is doing fine."

"When?" Gwendolyn was outraged. Nothing was under her control. She was the one who should be speaking with Leo. Not Stuart Bramwell. Since

339

she had called him in, he was under **her** authority. And she had footed the bill for everything. Why would no one appreciate that?

"An hour ago. Charlotte was speaking with him when I visited her room. Now, if you are interested, I will tell you what I saw. Or what I think I saw. Or see."

The good doctor appeared confused, and Gwendolyn watched him shake his head as if to remind himself this was a serious consultation and not idle, meaningless chitchat.

"If you are who I remember you to be, you probably won't like what I am about to say."

"Who else would I be?" Gwendolyn asked rudely. "Are you trying to tell me Charlotte is somehow different than the rest of the billions of us who also have brains?"

"No," Bramwell answered slowly. "There would be others. Monks, nuns...."

"Oh, please," Gwendolyn said, lifting her hand and dismissing these observations. "This is a child, not someone who has joined a monastery. She is a noisy, opinionated, clever child who is quite adept at getting her own way."

"Interesting," Bramwell stated, twirling his thumbs. "If what you say is true then I expect to see more activity in the left side of her brain, but this was not the case. In fact, even though she was conscious and chatty before the scans, the results were quite different."

"I can't wait," Gwendolyn said sarcastically, but she shivered and wrapped her arms more tightly around her chest.

"It was the right side that was animated."

"So?"

"It's the right side that connects us with all humanity and the consciousness that exists that has no name. I see that smirk, Gwendolyn, but you could do me the service of hearing me out. You had no problem waking me in the middle of the night so now it's my turn."

"Fine. Carry on."

"This consciousness is what we had before we were born. In most of us it remains dormant until we die when we enter that consciousness again. Most of us have forgotten how to access that part of our brain. Except," he said after a long pause in which his face underwent peculiar transformations, shedding years like a cat shedding its winter coat. His eyes became animated, and he appeared young again, excited, expectant. "Except," he repeated, "for the very few who never lost their connection to all humanity and the cosmic forces that exist, past, present and future."

There was much Gwendolyn could say, sarcastic, caustic, and unfriendly statements that would remind Dr. Bramwell that he was a doctor and a scientist, not a two-bit mystic orating from a soap box in Speaker's Corner at Hyde Park. But Gwendolyn held her tongue. Already she could see that momentary animation drain from Stuart's face and the elder man return. He became quite businesslike in his summation, and later Gwendolyn would wonder if he regretted sharing this silly analysis.

"You are familiar with *the universal*?"

Gwendolyn could not repress the jerk of her body, the blink of her eyes. *The universal* was a term bandied about by Charlotte all the time. Gwendolyn had been introduced to the term back in 1939, when Charlotte had been boasting about being in touch with the universal, which gave her supreme powers. And in London, the word had been repeated, many times – the universal this, the universal that. Gwendolyn informed Charlotte that she was not using the word properly, that universal was primarily an adjective and if she wanted to use it as a noun, she must look up the proper meaning, but Charlotte would not be told: *'It's okay if you don't understand what I'm saying,'* she'd insisted. *'Most people don't.'*

"It's a very rare aspect, the universal, and there are very few neurologists who accept its legitimacy, but it is a term, used for the moment, to describe exactly what I just stated. A person, experiencing this illumination, shall we say, has managed to access the primal force..."

"Please, Stuart. Spiritualism has never interested me. And fairy tales even less."

Bramwell lifted his shoulders in resignation. He understood that very few people shared his enthusiasm for this discovery. He meant to keep in touch with Charlotte, who had agreed to visit him from time to time should he wish *'to foot the bill for her travels'* and promised, with a wink of her eye, to let him in on some very unusual travel that took place in some Tower back in Toronto.

"This is not new information I am reporting, Gwendolyn. There has been research into right- and left-brain activity for decades. Stroke patients have been studied, and there is currently a doctor right here in London, associated with Guy's, who has amassed a great deal of data…"

"I'm not interested in studies and data. I want to know Charlotte's prognosis. Full stop."

"Good. Her prognosis is good." Bramwell sat back and folded his hands across his stomach. He took off his glasses and placed them on the desk. "I advise rest for a few days and certainly you should delay your flight home by a week. She refuses bed rest and says she can get by on three to four hours of sleep a night." He smiled. "She's quite engaging. With an extraordinary imagination."

Gwendolyn agreed and sighed in relief. Her main concern had been eased. Charlotte's injuries were not life-threatening and indeed, seemed not to exist at all. By comparison Henry's body was covered in more bruises than Charlotte's.

When Gwendolyn had questioned Charlotte, the child had replied that she didn't remember hitting the floor at all and had insisted she had drifted downwards on top of a cloud that transported her to the corner of the hole and then entertained her with countless stories before evaporating into the nether.

"A cloud?" Gwendolyn had repeated.

"A cloud," Charlotte had confirmed. "Rather like this huge cotton ball that wrapped around me as I floated downwards. Henry wasn't so lucky. He hit the floor harder than I did but," she added, "He did not break anything, so something was looking after him, too."

"Something?"

"The universal."

Gwendolyn had paused for a moment, deciding whether she should betray Henry's confidence. He'd told her that Charlotte was speaking in 'tongues' and that he understood every word she said.

"Perhaps you imagined it," Gwendolyn had said kindly when Henry told her about the peculiar conversations.

"Yeah. But no," Henry replied. "I know what I heard. And Jeremy can confirm."

"I thought it might be Welsh, a particular dialect that my grandfather speaks," Jeremy said, immediately taking Henry's side. "He'd been there, too, and remembered everything he heard. "But Charlotte is a pretty good mimic, and maybe she was just confused and remembered a few expressions that she had been taught."

"When?" Henry asked belligerently.

"When what?" Jeremy asked, confused.

The entire conversation had taken place in the corridor of the hospital as Henry lay on a stretcher waiting be examined. The fluorescent lighting was ghastly and hot, and Gwendolyn fanned herself with her beret.

"When did Oliver teach Charlotte to speak Welsh?"

Jeremy shrugged. "I don't know. We can ask him."

"Where is Oliver?" Gwendolyn asked looking around. The corridor was deserted.

"With Ariel and Sarah in the waiting room. Arthur is bringing over the percolator from the theatre because it will be a long night. Sarah needs her Folgers."

Gwendolyn examined her hands. What she needed was a wash. Her hands were filthy, her nails coated with dirt and her rings dull. She began to polish her emerald when she saw Jeremy and Henry exchange a glance. "Excuse me," she said. "I need the Ladies."

She washed her hands thoroughly and studied her face in the mirror. She looked tired, haggard: small wonder after what she had been put through, both good and bad. Travel, a long-lost family, a new interest, a new wardrobe and then disaster, screaming, crying, the wail of an ambulance, two children injured. And not one of these events would have occurred without Charlotte, nosing her way through Gwendolyn's life, dogging her footsteps, insulting her, challenging her.

It was a script she couldn't have written had she tried.

Why had Charlotte continued to torment her after their brief visit to Gwendolyn's past? She refused to acknowledge this transposition publicly because it was absurd, her mind playing tricks on her, and the more Charlotte insisted, the more Gwendolyn resisted. It was a game, a game between two adversaries, and she had no intention of letting Charlotte win. Gwendolyn knew herself very well. What else had she had to do during her seventy-one years of existence but hone the characteristics she was born with, polish them to a brilliant shine as she did with her rings? She knew all the adjectives applied to her and agreed with every single one. She was a selfish, opinionated, autocratic, and unpleasant person to be around at the best of times, and yet Charlotte continued to appear at her penthouse door routinely, badgering, lifting her eyebrows, examining the containers in her refrigerator, scoffing at the neat and orderly existence Gwendolyn insisted upon.

Therefore, it came down to this, she thought, studying her face in the mirror. Why was she, Gwendolyn MacFarlane, totally undeserving, given this second chance? There were millions, if not billions of souls, tormented, yearning, impoverished, who deserved this more than she did. She stared at her reflection, demanding an explanation, but a tired woman returned the stare and shook her head.

"It wasn't up to me," Charlotte said, when Gwendolyn asked her why she had kept coming to the penthouse when it was clear Gwendolyn did not want her company. She even went so far as to hold the child's hand and hold her gaze with what she felt was true affection.

"I didn't deserve this attention," Gwendolyn said, using her polite, quiet voice.

"I know," Charlotte said, and Gwendolyn released her hand, realizing she did not want an agreement but an argument, a staunch acknowledgement of how important Gwendolyn was. "But I couldn't let it go," Charlotte told her, fluffing her black hair with her fingers and then scratching her scalp. "I had no choice. It was the universal. The universal kept pushing and it was a whole lot stronger than me."

"The *what*?" Gwendolyn asked.

After a long silence during which Charlotte's stare turned inward, her eyes flickering back and forth, accessing, accessing, accessing. Gwendolyn was reminded of Henry until Charlotte began to laugh. Henry never laughed.

"I suppose the universal is everything you can't see but all there really is. As to why it chose you, I couldn't say."

Gwendolyn did not share these remarks with Dr. Bramwell, because obviously he had been tricked by Charlotte into believing the animation truly existed whereas Gwendolyn knew better. Life was nothing more than chance and coincidence, good choices and bad choices, genes and heredity, spunk, and determination. Nevertheless, the child's laugh had been slightly unnerving, not at all like Charlotte's usual hysterical giggling, but resonant, deep, an Old Man River type of laugh that knew far more than Gwendolyn ever would. She left the hospital room both relieved and irritated, because she had once again been bested by Charlotte but didn't know how it had happened.

From the Hilroy of Charlotte Lisa Hansen

DAY: Saturday, SEPTEMBER 10 1999
TIME: Teatime (that's afternoon current, but basically any time at all here in London)
LOCATION; Conservatoire in Sarah's house, wicker chair with extra soft pillow
NOTES: Where to start?

I know I have been absent, Hilroy, since the accident, but I have had a hard time putting pencil to paper. Readers will not even know what I mean by ACCIDENT because I haven't written about it, have I? No time for that now. Maybe later, on the plane.

I am not promising anything.

The IMPORTANT thing is I survived and so did Henry, and "The Three Questions" came off without a hitch and to rave reviews. Just one show. "Leave them wanting more," as Oliver pointed out.

So much to write... where to begin?

Luckily Henry started his own journal the day after the accident when he noticed I wasn't writing in mine. He didn't even ask me, CHEEKY BUGGER. Just got Jeremy to get Oliver to get him a journal ASAP, this very, very fancy journal called a Moleskin. Jeremy says Henry is "a dab hand at chronicling." He is a lot more organized than me, that's for sure, and lets anyone who wants to read the journal (so far just Jeremy and me) look whenever we want. No codes or ciphers or shorthand.

Examples:

"I spoke at length with the BBC crew after the show and every single person said they like my glasses."

Liar.

And: "Charlotte won the 'best of show'. Not all that unexpected since she personally knew 75% of the audience, having sold them tickets. Nevertheless, her performance was close to spectacular."

CLOSE TO? Come on.

If you are paying attention, you noticed I mentioned the plane. Yes, we are still in London. After the ACCIDENT (see JOURNAL of HENRY JACOBS #1 – prepare to be bored), the Doc suggested we delay the flight home by a week. Okay by me. More time in London with Sarah and Jeremy and Oliver.

Henry and I have missed four days of school, but we're not too worried. Though Henry's mother "pitched a fit" according to Henry. Leo is smoothing things over. It'll be good to see Leo again.

It's strange but since the ACCIDENT (see JoHJ #1 – boring, etc. et. al.), I can tell that whatever was supposed to happen for Gwendolyn has happened. I can't even say for sure what it was. But it's left me feeling unwound and relaxed and sleepy so sleepy. After the show I slept eight hours.

Gwendolyn has been… different. But in most ways the same. It's hard to explain.

We fly back to Toronto on Sunday. It'll be hard to go but Sarah has promised that she and Oliver and Jeremy will be arriving within a month. And Jeremy will stay on to attend "The Learning Academy" (soon to be renamed "The Academy") with us.

Anyway Hilroy, and future readers, the main reason I am writing now is that in my last entry I brought up a passage in Gus Frank's journal. I found it today and thought I'd sign off with Gus's exact words, although his writing is perhaps not as clear as my own. Here is what Gus wrote in his journal decades or centuries ago. Unlike moi, he dates nothing.

> I'll be damned if nother worlds don't show up when I
> look threw the lens of my camera. Off-putting but hardly
> lasts. Squiggled lines in the air, people I ain't never seen
> in my whole damn life and me, standing in the middle
> of this mess, looking straite back at me looking through

the lens. It's a god-damn rip in the universe, one of them fizures like happened out west when the drilling cracked the mountain of rock souse a person might, if they was so inclined, look straight inside. And god damn if it don't look like a jagged part in a man's hair. Dilys, blast her to pieces, says I need glasses. I lifted a finger, swung it around in her face and said: Daughter, wait til it happens to you and then we talk.

Charlotte Lisa Hanson (September 10, 1999)
London, England

Chapter Thirty-Four

It was on the flight home to Toronto that Gwendolyn decided to read the letter Charlie had left for her, a letter that Sarah had kept for almost six decades. She couldn't read the letter when she was in London. In the beginning she had been too distracted by the oddity of having a family, and then when Sarah had made her suggestion regarding *The Three Questions* she had been far too busy.

But, in truth, she was scared to read this last message from a long-ago brother. So now, high in the sky, soaring soundlessly atop a bank of clouds, she decided that glancing at a few words and assessing the tone of the letter was all she could do. Would she see: *"I'm sorry?"* Or: *"I miss you?"* Or possibly: *"I treated you terribly"*? The Charlie Gwendolyn remembered would never admit to these feelings and yet, conversely, she couldn't bear the thought that Charlie might have wanted to atone when there was no way she could nod her head and say: *"Thank you. For acknowledging me."* She had no idea who her brother really was, and maybe she didn't want to find out. And yet the pull of not knowing kept her fingers returning to her satchel, the beautiful multifaceted soft black leather briefcase she had purchased when she decided her purse was woefully inadequate to house the trappings of her newfound trade. The letter now rested in one of the zipper compartments, and it radiated an intense heat that caused her fingers to vibrate when she reached for a pencil, her eyeglasses, her notepad, a tissue.

Could she simply ignore these sensations for the rest of her life, or give in to curiosity? The ambiguity bothered her. And yet, she was frightened that the letter would produce a long-repressed sadness that would be unshakeable.

Once she had eaten and visited with Henry and Charlotte and ascertained they were fast asleep – particularly Charlotte, who was such a sneak that Gwendolyn could almost feel the child reading over her shoulder – she considered her options. She *could* read the letter when she was sitting outside on her balcony, a cup of tea by her side, the glow of the city lights illuminating the night sky. Or right before sleep, her three pillows in perfect order behind her head, or at breakfast when the sun was bright, or maybe in the afternoon when she was feeling a bit out of sorts – except she didn't feel out of sorts anymore. She was filled with a new sense of purpose and an excitement unknown during her long decades wandering, drifting from one place to the next, wondering what had become of the person she might have been.

Sarah had not sent her the letter after Charlie died. A wise choice, in retrospect, because the child Gwendolyn had been would have destroyed it, just as she destroyed all the letters Sarah wrote and then when the letters stopped, nursed a deep grudge that had lasted her a lifetime. *"Nobody cares. I'm alone."* Her personal mantra.

"Just do it," she told herself when the lights dimmed in first class and the slippery grumbling sound of people nestling into their seats was all she heard. Wasn't it right and proper that she should read this letter when she was flying through the clouds, a fitting tribute to Charlie, who sacrificed his life so she could enjoy this pleasure?

She moved quickly, removed the letter, put it in her lap and stared at the envelope. Too much thinking was not productive.

Her name was on the front: GWEN, in capital letters and there was a smudge of soot on the right hand corner. She wanted to remove the smudge and wet her finger but stopped as her finger hovered above the corner. Whatever this was, whatever it had been, whatever moment in time created this dark imperfection, the swirl must remain.

The envelope was pale yellow, the paper thin as tissue. She wondered if Charlie had begged the stationery from Sarah. It had a feminine look to it. The Charlie she remembered would have been happy to write her a note on the back of a match book or a menu swiped from a restaurant. This presentation looked like he had given thought to what he wanted to say, a nod to the proper child Gwendolyn had always been, a child who would have not appreciated a torn piece of newsprint or a series of match book covers.

How dreadfully serious she had been as a child. How critical as an adult. She was still the same person, but she had softened, her body relaxing into a slightly different version of Gwendolyn the matriarch, Gwendolyn the vastly superior elder whose head was always tilted slightly to the side, all the better to be able to look down the elegant slope of her nose and pass judgement. But she had not evolved enough to render her cloying and unrecognizable. That would be an affront to the Gwendolyn who knew better than most people and was contemptuous of weakness. Changing herself completely was not within her grasp, nor would she want to. She was also wise enough to know that no one would believe the artificial transformation.

'Get a grip. It would be weird if you stopped criticizing me altogether,' Charlotte had informed her when Gwendolyn, trying to be nice, told her how 'lovely' she looked when she invited her family and the theatrical principals out for tea as a celebration. 'I don't look lovely. I look presentable which is a stretch considering I don't like to get dressed up. I am who I am. And sparring with one another keeps us on our toes. You know that.'

Given that Gwendolyn had booked a table at Claridge's for afternoon tea, Charlotte, as a bow to convention, had worn black trousers and a sky blue sweater (purchased by Ariel) and her hair had been washed and brushed. She had still behaved atrociously when they were seated, and asked a million questions, principally about the food but also the décor, Thierry Despont's art-deco foyer. The maître d' had been immediately informed that the foyer in Charlotte's house back in Toronto boasted the exact same black and white tiles, and while there were no gold columns abutting the walls there was a papier mâché bust, a self-portrait, sitting on a black column by the inglenook which she said lent a lot of class to her premises, and usually garnered a remark or two from a client who had stopped by for a cup of tea.

She had been in good spirits and said, more than once, that the scones were almost as good as the ones made by her grandfather, and even managed to get a tour of the kitchen, when she said she had been making her own bread for centuries. Gwendolyn, who had paid an outrageous sum of money for this special treat, was forced, once again, to take second chair to Charlotte's capacity to charm by never shutting up. But Gwendolyn had spent her time listening to her family and arguing with Meggie and Byron, and not felt threatened in the slightest.

While recollecting this event, Gwendolyn noticed her finger had moved on its own accord and the letter was now open and sitting on her lap. She glanced at it, glanced away, and was not surprised to find her heart racing. She took a steadying breath and then began to read, carefully and slowly, savouring each word with a longing she thought she had long discarded.

July 15, 1940

Gwen,

With any luck you will never read this letter. But if you do, it's because I am no longer. I'm dead. Or somewhere else altogether. Whatever you choose to believe. When I finish, I will give the letter Sarah to pass on to you. In the event... you know. I don't have to repeat myself.

I hope we will see one another again and have time to share a meal and talk and walk and tell jokes (do you ever tell a joke?) and laugh. Really laugh. But if not, don't mourn me. I am now doing what I think is important and essential. Does it scare me? You better believe it. The Vickers Wellingtons are huge fire breathing machines, night bombers with specific missions, the coordinates of death and destruction. I can't think about what I am doing, or I wouldn't be able to do it. None of us could and that is the truth.

I've written a few letters to Dad, and I hope he shared them with you. Mostly technical information about the Vickers Wellington and the squadron. But knowing the old man I suspect he kept them to himself. He knows the cost of war and wouldn't want to scare you.

Dad and I had this secret, my flying lessons, my hunger to soar through the clouds. Why did we keep it from you? I don't really know. And yet, sitting here in the dark of the night, I suspect you always knew, and you were mad at me because I never invited you to come along, to sit beside me, to put your hand on the controls and fly us safely through to tomorrow. You know it wouldn't have been allowed, and I needed to have one thing just for myself. The thrill of the take-off, the speed, the lift, the view, the miracle of me, Charlie, nobody special, being held up high in the sky by a machine. A machine that I learned to control, to dip and dive and soar.

I was more than ready when Canada declared. But then again, I decided more than a year ago to leave with Sarah. An adventure. I wanted an adventure. And I got one. A licensed pilot, a British citizen, I was accepted into the RAF almost immediately. And facing facts, they need as many pilots as they can get. Even though I am special. Right?

Bully for Charlie!

Crack a smile, Gwen. If nothing else, it's good for your facial muscles. Keeps them toned. Ha. Ha.

We'll have lots of time to catch up when the war is over, but just in case, there's a few things I forgot to tell you before I left. Want to get it off my chest and try to be up front, say a few things I believe. What the hell?

I've been a piss poor brother. I know that. I tried to be nice to you, but, damn, didn't you always make it difficult. I'm not blaming you. You are so serious. Disciplined, I guess. I didn't understand it. Maybe I made fun of you, but it was never malicious. I wish I could rewrite the past but can't do it. Never been one to dwell on mistakes, but I feel this crazy urgency to make things right. Anything could happen. The nightly raids over London – we are all about the size of an ant and could be obliterated just like that! Whether in a plane or on the ground, I feel the world closing in and I need to protect myself and the ones I love. By the way, there is a surprise coming soon but I'm going to wait to broadcast that.

Here's the most important thing. What I always meant to say but forgot when I would catch you spying on me or taking the Tree of Life brooch and hiding it or turning your nose up at the dinners Mrs. Smith made for us or a million other things that I let get under my skin. You know me. I am always standing with one foot out the door, eager to escape, drive fast, dance, play the piano, fly higher and higher and never look back.

The strangest thing of all? I never really cared about the brooch. Yeah, I know. It was given to Mom by my father, but Ian is my true father, the one who looked after me – and you, too. You could have kept the damn thing, and I wouldn't have noticed. It was all just a game, wasn't it? You'd hide it, I'd find it, and on it would go. But then things got weird. You remember Charlotte and Henry who spent a week with us last summer? She was something else, a great kid, and so was Henry in a quieter way. I always thought that you and Charlotte would make a good team, but you were dead set against her. So be it. Charlotte's the one who found your hiding place for the brooch and returned it to me with a note that I kept. She said I had to keep the brooch safe. Couldn't tell me why but it was that important. I did what she asked and if I made a mistake, I'm sorry. I gave it to Sarah. If you want it, talk to her.

So here it is. A Charlie MacFarlane special. My personal philosophy and not a bad one if I do say so myself. Live your life, Gwen. And I mean really live it. It's the only one you are going to get, and it goes by faster than sugar is spun into candy floss. Take chances. Make mistakes. Stretch yourself. Have fun. It's in those moments that you will feel most alive. Believe me, I know.

Listen. Can you hear it? Look. Can you see it happening? This is the dream —

I imagine us walking along the Thames, me telling you all this, me holding your arm so you don't slip or trip on a rock or maybe just because I need to hold onto your arm. For me. Not for you. And then I see us stop, look at one another. We stand there for the longest time, maybe with the sun setting or rising or somewhere in between and maybe we're embarrassed and maybe not, but we hug one another. And we are, finally, not just brother and sister but friends.

I have to say I get a kick out of this dream. I hope you do, too.

Love from your brother,

Charlie

Epilogue

It was early October.

Gwendolyn MacFarlane sat in a chair in front of an endless bank of windows in Pearson International Airport, back where she had started only a month ago. But everything had changed. She was no longer travelling, soon to be a guest in a foreign country with people she barely knew. She had no luggage, no compulsively organized purse, only a medium size leather satchel that carried, in some disorder, the tools of her trade: scripts, pencils, magnifiers, tape, glasses, an offer she had to finalize on a crumbling old mansion on Admiral Road, and a list of jobs she barely had time to start before more tasks were added.

Her newest project, calculating how much it would cost to gut and renovate a house she was currently negotiating to buy, demanded her complete attention.

The house, a tired and dilapidated mansion on Admiral Road, a stone's throw from her penthouse, was the former Philosophical Club of Greater Toronto – a club that had fallen into hard times due to a dwindling membership and crippling mortgage payments. Gwendolyn did not yet own the house, but that hardly mattered. In an uncharacteristic spurt of generosity, tempered by a keen business sense, she promised to rent to the Philosophical Club the lower level, which was not completely underground, with a private entrance and tiny garden fenced off from the main garden that Gwendolyn was keeping to herself. The rent would pay the property taxes and when Gwendolyn sold her penthouse, she would make back what she spent on the purchase with enough left over to cover the costs of the extensive renovation she stated firmly to her lawyer, her accountant and financial advisor. She might have changed but she hadn't lost her financial acumen.

"Am I right in saying you do not yet own this property?" her lawyer had asked, hoping that she would say no so he could dissuade her.

"Not yet. But I will."

"This is quite a monumental task to take on when someone is moving into their..." he'd paused when he caught the glint of steel in his client's eyes.

"Into their *what*?"

"Prime," he had said, cautiously and was awarded a smile, perhaps the first genuine smile he had ever received from his client of twenty plus years.

"Exactly," she'd said. "I couldn't have said it better myself."

"How many years do I have left?" she'd asked herself after touring the building on Admiral Road. "If it's a disaster, I'll sell it." The main problem, as far as she could tell, was that the Philosophical Club was a mere half block away from The Learning Academy, and Charlotte would be dropping in daily. But along with Charlotte would come the students she needed to make her enterprise a success.

"A theatre school," Charlotte had mused when Gwendolyn revealed her plans. "I'll be your assistant, of course."

Gwendolyn had remained silent.

"First off, we should tour the Tarragon Theatre, and Factory, and Soulpepper too, so if you give me your Visa Card number, I will order tickets for us posthaste and arrange for private tours."

"I can do that myself," Gwendolyn had replied. It would be a cold day in hell before she let Charlotte use her charge card.

"Okay by me. But make sure you get tickets for Henry and for Leo, too. Maybe Dragos and Celeste because we'll all be working together from now on."

That Gwendolyn was, in an oblique way, following Sarah's footsteps did not bother her. Sometimes a person needed a guide before they could truly live their life. Charlie's letter said as much, and she had referred to it many times for guidance.

"The plane has landed," Henry informed Gwendolyn, appearing at her side silently. "It will probably be twenty minutes or so since they have to pass through customs and immigration."

"Where's Leo?" Gwendolyn asked, noting that the seat beside her was empty. She put her papers back in her satchel and patted the seat beside her. Henry balanced on the edge, his feet tapping, ready to escape at a moment's notice.

"He's gone to buy Charlotte a muffin. She's hungry."

"When is that child not hungry?" Gwendolyn asked.

Henry grinned. "Never."

He made a note in the Moleskin he now carried. "I am to record everything that happens today, and Charlotte will review it tonight."

"I find it disorienting to see you with a notebook, Henry," Gwendolyn said.

"Charlotte needs a break." He shrugged his shoulders.

"I am pleased to see you don't record conversations."

"Who said I don't?" Henry asked, snapping the Moleskin shut.

The clapping sound of the pages closing upon one another echoed in the vast open space, a confirming, repeating reverberation from an unseen audience. These distant echoes were followed by a booming laugh as Charlotte, far across the waiting lounge, spun in circles, the wicked fluorescent lighting illuminating the streaks of red in her blue-black hair.

"Besides which, my notes are just practise, getting me ready for our next great adventure." He lifted his hand and flashed a five-pointed star in Charlotte's direction. Patting the bulge at his waist he concluded: "Maybe you'll be coming along, too."

He grinned, a most un-Henry like expression, and vanished.

"Maybe you'll be coming along…" These words were an echo of what Charlotte had said to her five days ago.

"I'm not supposed to do this," she said in a loud theatrical whisper, snatching Gwendolyn's wrist as she walked towards the door at Charlotte's house. "But you got to see this. Don't tell Leo," she added, hurrying Gwendolyn up the curving staircase to the third floor.

Gwendolyn tried to free herself from Charlotte's grip, but the child would not let go until she led her to a black and white photograph on the western wall of the Tower Room and stood back, a smug expression on her face.

Gwendolyn gasped.

For there the long-ago Gwendolyn stood, a lost fairy tale child, in a forest glen, her arms around Charlie, her face buried in his chest.

Surrounding her were friends from the distant past: Helen, Lukas, Sarah, the entire cast from Chekov's "The Sea Gull", Billy from the soda shoppe, Jones who designed and built her bicycle with side car and the vanquished anti-Semite bullies who tried to hurt her and Sarah. But it was the two children on the outer edge of the picture, both part of the scene and not, that caught her attention. Charlotte and Henry. As they were then and as they were now, looking up towards an unseen photographer and smiling in a conspiratorial way.

"Now do you believe me?"

Gwendolyn nodded without speaking.

"Henry and me are going to continue our travels," she said, pulling Gwendolyn towards the door. "Maybe I can arrange it so you will come along, too."

Gwendolyn was drawn from her reverie when Leo returned, settling into the seat beside her.

"Dragos's limousine has arrived. We will split the group into two, and you will ride with Sarah and Ariel to your house. After they rest and freshen up, we will reconvene at my house."

"I know this, Leo," Gwendolyn said, all business. "We've been over it before. But where is Celeste?"

"Resting at home."

Celeste was getting through the last month of her pregnancy with her feet up most of the time, alternating between Leo and Charlotte's house and her own. She had wanted to come to the airport but at the last minute, declined. Her ankles were swollen to twice their size and it hurt to walk. "You'll have to take Charlotte and Henry and Jeremy as the other will have Meggie, Byron, and Oliver. And me, of course," he added. "Dragos will join us presently."

He expected Gwendolyn to argue, but she didn't really do that anymore. What she did do was glance at Charlotte from time to time and shake her head as if the rotation might resolve an unsolvable problem. Leo – having seen that look on countless faces after his visitors to the Tower Room had emerged, refreshed and rejuvenated – remained silent.

A job well done, Charlotte, he thought with a smile.

"I appreciate your offer to house Meggie and Byron. I imagine they might not be the easiest of guests," Gwendolyn stated. Much to her surprise, her wallet had been opened wide enough to buy tickets for the two troublesome souls whose obstinacy during the theatrical preparations and production had matched her own. And yet, when she arrived home in Toronto, she found she missed them. More to her surprise, she missed her entire family.

"All the better," Leo said. He folded his hands across his stomach and grinned. "Easy is boring. That's what Charlotte says, and perhaps she is right."

Gwendolyn wanted Byron's advice and expertise on a mural she had in mind for her new living quarters. Although the deal had not closed, Gwendolyn was confident it would be hers. Who would dare to outbid her?

What surprised her the most, and what she did not share with Leo, was her hope that everyone who was arriving today would stay permanently in Toronto and she would never have to be separated from her friends and family again.

Charlotte and Henry stood side by side, as close to the arrival doors as they could, but there were only shadowy forms, clouded by the opaque glass.

"You never told me what was in the letter," Henry said.

"What letter?"

"Don't give me that. The letter Gwendolyn carries around in her satchel. The letter from Charlie."

"Oh, yeah. That letter." She stared straight ahead.

"So? What did it say? Shouldn't we transcribe it into the Moleskin?"

"I didn't read it," she admitted, turning to face her friend.

"I don't believe you. When have you ever not invaded someone's privacy?"

"I only invade when there is a reason, Henry. When the target ignores my influence. There wasn't a reason anymore. Sure, I'm curious, but I figure one day Gwendolyn will share it with us. It's not like we won't be dogging her footsteps." She grinned, bit her lower lip, and then became serious. "Besides, I get this feeling that Charlie would not like me snooping."

"Really?" Henry was sceptical.

"Really."

"He was my friend," Henry reflected, his voice softening. "I close my eyes, and I can see Charlie, the way he walked, how he spoke."

"Yeah, I know," Charlotte replied. "His eyes took in everything. Do you remember the way his pupils would expand and contract when he got excited?"

Henry nodded. "I always felt this tingling when he entered the room, like something wild was about to happen. He let me and Lukas drive his motor car. No seat belts. No restraints. He laughed when I stalled. I can still feel the gear shift in my hand. And the smell of hay and exhaust and the way the clouds seemed so far away but close enough to touch."

"Got it. Sort of like lying on the banks of the Don River with a best friend close by."

"Charlie talked about how to listen," Henry said in recollection. "To really listen to everybody and every sound, to focus and experience all of it. *'You got to do it, kid, if you want to play jazz piano. Hell, you got to do it if you want to be a genuine person. If you listen you can improvise, gather ideas, let one impression expand to include all impressions. Let the piano speak. If you don't listen, you merely became a parrot. But what the hell,'*" Henry concluded. "Charlie pressed my shoulder and said: *'What the hell, Henry? What do I really know?'*"

"We were lucky to know him," Charlotte told Henry. "Even if it was just for a moment."

Both children peered at the arrival doors, willing them to open by the force of their gaze. The shadows had gathered. It would be any second now.

"Did you feel that?" Charlotte suddenly asked.

Henry nodded wordlessly.

"Like a ghost come to visit," she confirmed, showing him her arm where the hairs had risen above a covering of goosebumps.

"Exactly," he confirmed. "What does it mean?"

"Another visit to the Tower Room," she stated matter-of-factly. "But who? Who will it be this time?"

The doors peeled open, revealing another world filled with weary travellers. These visitors walked in measured steps towards the exit, their tired faces smiling, eager to be free of the confinement and get out of the terminal where they could breathe fresh air. Jeremy held Sarah's arm and didn't let go even though he waved excitedly the moment he saw Charlotte and Henry. Oliver came next, wearing a beautifully cut tweed jacket, with a grey fedora rimmed in black ribbon. He held a cane with a carved lion's head and there was a swing to his step.

"No uniform I see," Dragos sniffed, crowding in beside Henry and Charlotte. He had outdone himself sartorially and was decked out in a great navy coat that hit mid-thigh, polished black knee-high boots and gloves, all purchased with Charlotte's help at the local Army Navy surplus store. His hair crackled with Brilliantine, and he held his chauffeur cap in his hand. "You say he wear uniform," he complained. "But he be gentleman. No talk to likes of me."

"It's just another costume," Henry assured Dragos. "And he will love you. How could he not?"

Ariel, reaching out an arm to Byron, signalled when she saw Charlotte and Henry, and blew a kiss. Byron was not wearing his painter's smock but looked as dishevelled as ever, his khaki shirt wrinkled and stained. Meggie fussed, peering into her carpet bag until she unearthed a cloth and began to blot a red stain on Byron's collar, a stain resembling blood but more likely ketchup.

"Do you want to guess?" Charlotte asked Henry.

"I could try," he replied. And then he realized, without any help from his eidetic memory, that his experiences over the past five months had taught him one essential truth. Everyone suffered loss in their lives, and how they dealt with it was as unique as each of the friends he saw walking towards him. Would it be Ariel, the self-contained enigma, now helping Byron by taking his suitcase so he could slip away from Meggie's hand and straighten the collar on his shirt without assistance. Or would it be Sarah, who had been alive for almost a century, holding so many memories that Henry fancied he saw them twirling in the fathomless depths of her eyes? Or would it be Oliver, deeply scarred and hiding behind a series of costumes and personalities so he could be whomever Jeremy needed him to be? Or Byron? Meggie? Even Jeremy?

It could be any of them, but which one would say, after studying all the black and white portraits lining the walls of the Tower Room, and sniffing the air, fragrant with Leo's special blend of tea: *"It's the strangest thing, but I feel this pull deep inside me whenever I remember…"*

"It's better we are surprised," he told Charlotte. "Don't you think? Or do you already know?" he asked, still uncertain as to what Charlotte knew or what Charlotte would tell. Leading him on had always been her best game but now, instead of resisting, he wanted to play.

"I think I know," she said, her eyes settling on one person, a stranger who conversed with Sarah, and then skittering away so Henry could not calculate the trajectory. "But where will we travel this time?" She shook her head. "How far back in time will be go? What will we have to do?" She paused for a moment and reached for Henry's hand. "Are you scared?"

"Yes," he admitted, squeezing her fingers. "But you aren't leaving me behind."

Printed in the USA
CPSIA information can be obtained
at www.ICGtesting.com
LVHW091231011123
762288LV00002B/10

9 781039 192126